Mad

Mad

CHLOÉ ESPOSITO

MICHAEL JOSEPH
an imprint of
PENGUIN BOOKS

MICHAEL JOSEPH

UK | USA | Canada | Ireland | Australia
India | New Zealand | South Africa

Michael Joseph is part of the Penguin Random House group of companies
whose addresses can be found at global.penguinrandomhouse.com.

First published in Great Britain by Michael Joseph 2017

001

Set in 12/14.75 pt Bembo Book MT Std
Typeset by Jouve (UK), Milton Keynes
Printed in Great Britain by Clays Ltd, St Ives plc

A CIP catalogue record for this book is available from the British Library

HARDBACK ISBN: 978–0–718–18569–5
EXPORT ISBN: 978–0–718–18570–1

www.greenpenguin.co.uk

MIX
Paper from
responsible sources
FSC® C018179

Penguin Random House is committed to a
sustainable future for our business, our readers
and our planet. This book is made from Forest
Stewardship Council® certified paper.

For Paolo

Thou shalt not covet . . .
Exodus 20:17

You have two lives. The second one begins when you
realize you only have one.
Confucius

Much Madness is divinest Sense –
To a discerning Eye –
Much Sense – the starkest Madness –
'Tis the Majority
In this, as all, prevail –
Assent – and you are sane –
Demur – you're straightway dangerous –
And handled with a Chain –
Emily Dickinson

Contents

Disclaimer

There's something you should know before we go any further: my heart is in the wrong place. So is my stomach, my liver and my spleen. All my internal organs are on the opposite side, in exactly the place where they shouldn't be. I'm back to front: a freak of nature. Seven billion people on this planet have their hearts on the left. Mine's on the right. You don't think that's a sign?

My sister's heart is in the right place. Elizabeth is perfect, through and through. I am a mirror image of my twin, her dark side, her shadow. She is right and I am wrong. She's right-handed; I am left. In Italian, the word for 'left' is *'sinistra'*. I am the sinister sister. Beth is an angel and so what am I? Hold that thought . . .

The funny thing is that to look at us, you can't tell the difference. On the surface, we're identical twins, but peel back the skin and you'll get the shock of your life; watch in awe as my guts spill out all mixed up and topsy-turvy. Don't say I didn't warn you. It's not a pretty sight.

We're monozygotic, if you want to know; Beth's zygote split in two and I materialized. It happened at the very earliest stage of development, when her zygote was no more than a cluster of cells. Mum had been pregnant for just a few days and then – poof – out of nowhere, I show up, cuckoo-like. Beth had to share her nice, cosy amniotic bath and Mum's home-cooked placenta.

It was pretty crowded in that uterus; there wasn't a lot of room for the two of us and our umbilical cords. Beth's got tangled around her neck and then knotted pretty badly. It was touch and go for a while. I don't know how that happened. It had nothing to do with me.

Scientists think identical twins are completely random. We're still a mystery; no one knows how or why I occurred. Some call it luck, coincidence or chance. But nature doesn't like random. God doesn't just *play dice*. I came here for a reason; I know I did. I just don't know what that reason is yet. The two most important days of your life are the day you are born and the day you find out why.

DAY ONE:
Sloth

My problem's always been failure to give a fuck.
@AlvinaKnightly69

Chapter One

From: Elizabeth Caruso
ElizabethKnightlyCaruso@gmail.com
To: Alvina Knightly
AlvinaKnightly69@hotmail.com
Date: 24 Aug 2015 at 08.01
Subject: VISIT

Alvie, darling,

Please stop ignoring me. I know you received my last two emails because I put that recipient-tracker thing on, so you can stop pretending. Despite being at risk of repeating myself, I would like to invite you, yet again, to come and stay with us at our villa in Taormina. You would LOVE it here: 16th-century original features, the smell of frangipani in the air. The sun shines every single day. There's a pool to die for. We're around the corner from the ancient Greek amphitheatre, which frames Mount Etna to the west and the shimmering Mediterranean to the east. Even if you can only manage a week – I know you're a slave to that ghastly job – it would be wonderful to see you. I can't believe you haven't met Ernie yet; he's getting bigger each day and is the spit of his Auntie Alvina.

But seriously, I need you. I'm begging you. Come. IT'S BEEN TWO YEARS.

*There's something I need to ask you and I can't do it by email.
Beth x*

*PS I know what you're thinking and no, it isn't still awkward.
Ambrogio and I have forgotten all about it, even if you
haven't. So stop being a mule and come to Sicily.*

*PPS How much do you weigh at the moment? Are you still
9 stone 5? A size 10? I can't lose the baby weight and it's
driving me insane.*

Fucking hell; she is intolerable.

The smell of frangipani in the air blah, blah, blah, *the ancient Greek
amphitheatre* blah, blah, blah, *the shimmering Mediterranean* blah,
blah, fucking blah. She sounds like that presenter on *A Place in
the Sun*: 'Alvina Knightly seeks a pied-à-terre in the stunning
coastal region of Eastern Sicily.' Not that I would ever watch
that kind of thing.

I am *definitely not* going. It sounds boring, old-fashioned.
I don't trust volcanoes. I cannot stand that kind of heat. It's
sticky. Sweaty. My English skin would burn in two seconds; I'm
as pale as an Eskimo. *Don't say 'Eskimo'!* I can just hear her
now . . . *They don't like that name. It's not politically correct. Say
'Inuit' instead.*

I scan my bedroom: empty vodka bottles, a Channing Tatum
poster, photos on a pinboard of 'friends' I never see. Clothes on
the floor. Cold mugs of tea. A vibe that would make Tracey
Emin's cleaner freak. Three emails in a week. What's going on?
I wonder what she wants to ask me. I suppose I should reply or
she'll continue to break my balls.

From: Alvina Knightly
AlvinaKnightly69@hotmail.com
To: Elizabeth Caruso
ElizabethKnightlyCaruso@gmail.com
Date: 24 Aug 2015 at 08.08

Subject: Re: VISIT

Elizabeth, darling,

Thank you for the invitation. Your villa certainly sounds stunning. Aren't you and Ambrogio and, of course, little Ernie lucky to have such a splendid home in what sounds like the perfect location? Do you remember how as children, I was the one who loved the water? And now you have the swimming pool . . .

(and I have the bath with the blocked-up drain.)

Isn't life funny? I would, of course, love to see it and meet your gorgeous little cherub, my nephew, but it really is flat out at work at the moment. August is always our busiest month, that's why I've been so tardy in responding. Apologies.

Let me know when you're next visiting London; it would be good to catch up.

Albino

No matter how many times I type my name, *Alvina*, predictive text always changes it to fucking *Albino*. (Perhaps it knows how pale I am and it's taking the piss?) I'm just going to change it by deed poll.

Alvina

PS Do send my regards to your husband and give Ernesto a kiss from his auntie.

Send.

Elvis Presley's twin brother was stillborn. Some people have all the luck.

I drag myself up and out of bed and step in a pizza I left on the floor. I only ate half of it late last night before passing out

7

around 4 a.m. Tomato sauce all over my foot. A piece of salami between my toes. I peel off the meat and shove it in my mouth, wipe the sauce off with a sock. I get dressed in the clothes that I find on the floor: a nylon skirt that doesn't need ironing, a cotton T-shirt that does. I look in the mirror and frown. Urgh. I rub the mascara away from my eyes, apply a slick of purple lipstick, run my fingers through greasy hair. That'll do; I'm late. Again.

I go to work.

I grab the mail on my way out of the house and rip it open as I trudge down the street sucking on a Marlboro. Bills, bills, bills, bills, a business card for a minicab company, an advert for takeaway pizza. 'FINAL DEMAND', 'BAILIFF'S NOTICE', 'URGENT ACTION REQUIRED'. Yawn, yawn, more of the same. Does Taylor Swift have to deal with this shit? I shove the letters into the hands of a homeless man sitting outside the Tube: no longer my problem.

I push through the crowds in the line for the turnstile, slam my Oyster card down on the reader. We shuffle through the station at 0.0000001 mph. I try to write a haiku in my head, but the words won't come. Something deep about existential struggle? Something poetic and nihilistic? But nothing. My brain's still asleep. I glare at the adverts for clothes and jewellery that cover every spare inch of wall. The same smug, airbrushed model with the same smug, airbrushed face stares down at me just as she does every single morning. She is feeding a toddler in an advert for follow-on milk. I don't have a toddler and I don't need reminding. I definitely don't need to buy follow-on milk.

I stomp down the escalator, push past a man taking up too much space.

'Hey, watch it!' he yells.

'Stand on the right! Dickhead.'

I am a great artist trapped inside the body of a classified

advertising sales representative, a reincarnation of Byron or Van Gogh, Virginia Woolf or Sylvia Plath. I wait on the platform and contemplate my fate. There must be more to life than this? Stale air kisses my face and tells me that a train is approaching. I could jump now and it would all disappear. Within the hour, paramedics would have scraped me off the track and the Northern line would have resumed service.

A mouse runs over the metal rails. It only has three paws, but it lives a life of freedom and adventure. Lucky bastard. Perhaps that train will crush its little skull? It darts out of the way in the nick of time. Damn.

I perch on the shelf at the end of the carriage. A man with a cold sore invades my personal space; his shirt is translucent with sweat. He holds the yellow rail above my head, his armpit an inch from my nose; I can smell his Lynx Africa mixed with despair. I read his *Metro* upside down: murder, drugs, war, a story about somebody's cat. He presses his crotch against my thigh, so I stamp on his foot. He moves away. Next time, I'll knee him in the balls. We stop for a few minutes somewhere in London's lower intestines and then start again. I change trains at Tottenham Court Road. The carriage empties its bowels and we disembark as amorphous excrement. I am defecated at Oxford Circus.

Mayfair, London

Outside, the air is as thick as lard. Traffic noise and police sirens. I inhale a lungful of nitrogen dioxide and start to walk. *Big Issue* sellers, charity muggers and hordes of bored-looking students. Five Guys, Costa, Bella Italia. Starbucks, Nando's, Gregg's. I do the three and a half minutes to the office on autopilot. Perhaps I'm sleepwalking? Or maybe I'm dead? Perhaps I did jump and this is Limbo? I keep on walking and turn left down Regent Street, thinking about Beth. I am not bloody going.

A pigeon craps on my shoulder: grey-green goo. Great. Why me? What did I do wrong? I look around, but nobody's noticed. Isn't that supposed to be lucky? Perhaps it's a good omen for my day? I pull off my jumper and fling it into a bin; it had moth holes anyway.

I push through revolving doors and grimace at the man behind the desk. We've both worked here for years. We don't know each other's names. He looks up, frowns, then goes back to his crossword. I don't think he likes me. The feeling is mutual. I trudge downstairs with leaden feet. I am wasted here, wasted. I don't sell the big glossy fold-out ads at the front of magazines for sexy brands like Gucci or Lanvin or Tom Ford. That would be heaven. That's the big bucks. Then I'd get to sit upstairs. No, I work in *classified*. I sell the crappy little blink-and-you'd-miss-them ads that nobody reads at the back of magazines: hair-regrowth supplements, Viagra for women or obscure gardening paraphernalia that even your gran wouldn't buy. It's sixty-one quid for an eighth of a page. I don't know how I got here and I don't know why I've stayed.

Perhaps I'll run away and join the circus? I've always wanted to be the guy who throws daggers at the woman on the spinning wheel. (Why is it always the *guy* who throws the daggers?) I can picture the big top with its rainbow colours, the clowns, the jugglers, the horses, the lions. I can hear the crowds roll up, roll up, cheering, applauding, screaming in terror as knives fly through the air. The prickly sting of perspiration. The high of my adrenaline rush. I can see her now, spinning, spinning: blades slice through the wheel and just miss his face. Come on, Alvina, that's never going to happen. You're living in cloud cuckoo land. And you can't make any money writing haikus. My sister always said I'd make a great traffic warden. It would be fun to work in an abattoir.

I push through the doors to the basement. Angela (the 'g' is hard) Merkel (not her real name) looks up as I enter the room and raises a well-plucked eyebrow. She has an air that promises today will be torture: like a root canal or kidney stones.

'Good morning, Angela.' *Go to hell, Angela.*

I sit at a wood-effect desk in a room filled with cookie-cutter cubicles and no windows. Despite being 'adjustable', my swivel chair always seems to be the wrong height or shape or angle; I've long since given up fiddling. There's a peace lily that needs watering. The air is stale and dry.

A strawberry Hubba Bubba stuck beneath my computer monitor looks like a pink-grey rat brain. I pop it in my mouth and start to chew. It doesn't taste of strawberries, but then it didn't last week either.

I am exactly twelve minutes late. I think I'm supposed to be on a conference call with Kim (Jong-il, not his real name) but I can't be bothered to dial in. Kim is as pleasant as an ingrowing toenail. I contemplate picking up the phone and harassing people; my job entails cold-calling strangers over and over until they take out some kind of restraining order or finally purchase advertising space. They pay up to make me shut up and go away. Instead, I turn on my PC. Bad idea. My inbox floods with 'Urgent' emails: 'WHERE ARE YOU?', 'REPORT TO HR', 'EXPENSE POLICY VIOLATION'. Urgh, God, not again. I activate my out-of-office so I don't have to deal with anyone's bullshit.

Twitter's still up from Friday from when I didn't log off. I glance over at Angela; she is waterboarding one of my colleagues in the far corner of the room. Fuck it. I take a peek at what's trending, but it all looks boring. Taylor Swift hasn't replied to any of my tweets complimenting her on her recent outfits. Not even a favourite. Perhaps she's busy? She's probably on tour.

'So bored at work I'm gonna watch porn #Ilovemyjob.' Tweet.

I meant it as a joke, but now I'm curious. I call up YouPorn on my phone and scroll through genitalia: 'Threesomes', 'Fetish', 'Fantasy', 'Sex toys', 'Big boobs'. *Oooh, 'Female-friendly'.* Then my phone rings: 'Beth Mobile'. Bloody hell, she's persistent. Why is she calling me at work? I am busy and important. I scan the office, but nobody's noticed. I try to send it to voicemail, but my fingertip slips and I answer it instead.

'Alvie? Alvie? Is that you? Are you there?'

I hear her voice calling my name; it's small and far away. I screw up my eyes and try to ignore her. I want to hang up.

'Alvie? Can you hear me?' she says.

I grab the phone and slam it against my ear.

'Hi, Beth! Great to hear from you.' Seriously, she's made my fucking day.

'At last. Finally, I –'

I grit my teeth.

'Listen, Beth. I can't talk now. I've got to run to a meeting. My boss is waiting. I think I'm getting a promotion! I'll call you back later, OK?'

'No, wait, I –'

I cut her off and get back to the porn: cocks, tits and asses. Someone with both tits *and* a cock. Cool.

'Good morning, Alvina! How are you today?'

I look up and see Ed (Balls: face like a testicle) peering over his cubicle. Oh God, what now? What does he want? Apart from a personality transplant.

'Hello, Ed. I'm fine. What do you want?'

'Just checking how my favourite co-worker is doing on this fine Monday morning.'

'Fuck off, Ed.'

'Right, yes, of course. I was just, er . . .'

'Yes?'

'Er . . . I was just wondering when you might be able to . . .'

'Pay you back that fifty quid I owe you?'

'Yes!'

'Well, not today, obviously.'

'No. Obviously not today.'

'So fuck off.'

'Right. OK then. Bye-bye.'

His head pops back down again. Finally. God. I'll need to avoid him this week at the water cooler. I almost wish I hadn't borrowed it now. I only needed the money to get a vajazzle; in hindsight it wasn't that urgent. I had a super-hot date with a crazy-hot guy I'd met in the Holloway Poundland. I thought a bit of glitter would add some sparkle to our first night of passion. But the sequins went *everywhere,* all over the bed, all over his face, all in his hair. He got one stuck behind his eyeball and had to see a doctor. I kept finding sequins for weeks and weeks after, in my shoes, in my wallet, on a pack of chicken nuggets in the bottom of the freezer (I have *no* idea). The worst thing was that he didn't even appreciate all the effort I'd gone to: his name spelled out in pink diamanté all the way across my crotch: 'AARON'. Apparently it should've been 'ARRAN', like some stupid island in Scotland. So what if I spelled it wrong? It's the thought that counts. By the end of the night, it just said 'RUN'.

I get back to the porn. I lower the volume to mute the moans, but it's still very loud. Moaning and groaning and grunting and swearing. '*I like that ass, baby.*' Someone shouts, '*Whore!*' A 'MILF' is just getting fisted by a man in a mask when I notice a figure in my peripheral vision; Angela is looming over my cubicle. Shit.

'You're tweeting about *porn* from the company account?'

'That was the *company's* account? Oops. My bad,' I say.

'You're fired,' says Angela.

'YOU ARE SOOO FUCKED, BITCH,' says YouPorn.

I grab my handbag, the peace lily, a stapler and the copies of *Heat* and *Closer* from under my desk. I go home again.

Chapter Two

Archway, London

Seagulls the size of illegal dogs squawk overhead. Gang-raped foxes scream. Drunkards with lexicons limited to 'fuck' and 'cunt' shout at passers-by. It's a lovely area, the kind of place estate agents describe as 'up and coming' because it couldn't possibly be any more 'down and gone'. Everything is a dirty grey: sky, walls, streets. Diseased trees grow plastic bags and empty cans of Pepsi. They've been digging up the road for the past eight years. It doesn't *actually* smell of dead rat, but you wouldn't be surprised to catch a whiff. Even the squirrels look rabid.

I'm not sure why I took the stapler. It isn't mine. I don't really want it. It's not like I have people or things to staple. I throw it on someone's front lawn.

The homeless guy runs after me with my 'FINAL NOTICE' letters.

'Hey, you! You! You!' he shouts, stumbling, breathless.

I ignore him and stomp down the street.

People often mistake our doorstep for a rubbish tip: I regularly discover empty lager cans, kebab wrappers, used condoms and broken toys in the mornings. Once there was a fully nude, decapitated Barbie doll. The body lay, pink and prostrate, on the pavement, like some kind of *Toy Story* crime scene. There was no head to be found. We do, at least, have a killer view of the Archway Tower, unofficially the ugliest building in the UK. Ace.

I push through the front door; it always sticks, so you have to shove it. The hinges creak. Someone's spray-painted 'TWAT' in messy graffiti. I don't think it was me.

Living in a flat-share is cheaper than renting a studio, but slightly more expensive than a cardboard box under a subway. The latter, however, has become an increasingly attractive option, especially when queuing for the bathroom at some god-forsaken time in the morning, only to discover that one of the slobs has neglected to flush:

> *You look up at me*
> *With one eye; you want to stay.*
> *I flush you away.*

The first haiku of my day! You've still got it, Alvina. You poetic genius, you. The Nobel Prize is within reach. Never give up on your dreams.

The flat is on the top floor of a botched Victorian house con-version and falling apart. A piece of the roof fell through the ceiling into my bedroom last week. I emailed the landlord, con-cerned about the rain. He offered to buy me a bucket. The wallpaper is peeling off at the seams, the carpets are beige and threadbare. At least I have a roof over my head (partially) and a bed to sleep in (a futon from IKEA), so I try not to complain, especially not to Beth; she'd never understand.

I climb endless stairs. Somebody's bicycle is blocking the hall. There's the unmistakable stench of weed. I climb some more stairs and then some more. I live with a couple of slobs called Gary and Patty, or Jerry and Patsy, or Geoff and Pinkie, or something. They stay in a lot and hot-box the lounge, listening to bands I've never heard of. They both wear the same black drainpipes, black T-shirts with skull motifs and big black hood-ies with ironic dayglo accessories. I don't really wear black.

The slobs are snogging on the sofa when I get in. Gross. They wipe their soggy mouths and look up. Red eyes. Stoned already. Some inane shit blares on the television: home sweet home.

'Hi,' I say, hanging my keys up on the hook.

'All right,' say the slobs.

Empty Wotsits and Skittles packets litter the carpet. There's a half-empty bottle of Dr Pepper. I skulk past them into my room and shut the door. Bolt the lock. They're a chatty pair.

The bed's still unmade from this morning. I kick off my shoes and crawl under the duvet, yawn as wide as a cat; I think I'll take a nap. There's nothing else to do. I'll just lie here and wait for the zombie apocalypse: something to cheer us all up.

The walls are paper thin; I can hear what the slobs are saying next door:

'Oh my God, I just found her Facebook profile. This is freaking hilarious.'

I think they're talking about me.

'Wait, that's not even her,' says Gary.

'It is! Just like insanely Photoshopped and about five years ago,' says Patty. 'How many people do you think there are called *Alvina Knightly*?'

They're definitely talking about me.

'Ha ha! Look at this. She lives in *Highgate*?' says Gerry.

'She works as a *poet* at *The Times Literary Supplement*?' says Patsy.

'She's in a *relationship* with *Channing Tatum*?' says Geoff.

'She's so freaking weird!' say both of the slobs unanimously.

I sharpen my imaginary knife . . .

'Send her a friendship request,' suggests Pinkie. 'Just for jokes.'

'Done,' says Geoff.

I die a little bit inside. It's cruel of them to laugh at my lies. Name me one person who doesn't embellish on social media? Stretch the truth? Exaggerate? It's just little white lies, my Instagram life. So what if I'm not a famous poet? Who cares if I don't have a job? At least I have a goal, some aspiration. What do they have, apart from chlamydia? Crabs?

They are momentarily distracted by *Geordie Shore*: one of the housemates is screaming at one of the other housemates about something. Another housemate enters and starts screaming at them both. Eavesdropping has made me cross. I give up trying to sleep. My phone is in my bag; I grab it and stare at the screen. It's a Samsung Galaxy S5; the hottest phone on the market. I got it on sale at the Carphone Warehouse. I know everyone else has an iPhone, but I like to be different. Anyway, it looks like an iPhone, plus it's cheaper.

Poker? Solitaire? Pinterest? *Minecraft*? One of those games where you have to kill everyone? *Grand Theft Auto: Vice City*? *Dead Trigger 2*?

Tinder.

Time to judge some losers on a dating app. (No one judges me. I use Beth's photo. Clever, huh? I'm not just a pretty face.)

Left.

Left.

Left.

Left.

Left.

Left.

Left.

Left.

God, no!

Left.

Left.

Left.

Gag reflex.

NHS specs.

Too thin.

Creepy grin.

Looks like a frog.

I've seen fitter dogs.

Ears like a jug.

Teeth like a pug.

What's with that hat?
Nude with cravat.
Hitler 'tache.
Contagious rash.
Crossed eyes.
Ate all the pies.
Tattoo on face.
Human race?
Toilet selfie.
Looks too elf-y.
Left.
Left.
Left.
Left.
Left.
Left.
Left.
Left.

RIGHT! Holy fuck! RIGHT, RIGHT! RIGHT! Hello, Harry, 27, from 3 miles away. How are you, sir? Oh sweet Mary mother of Christ, yes! He's a right. That's Mr Right, right there. Come on, baby, I'm gonna swipe you. Oh yes, I could eat you up, Harry, 27, from 3 miles away. You'd better fucking swipe me back.

Fifteen minutes later: nothing.

Half an hour later: still nothing.

One hour later: still nothing. I hate Tinder.

Two hours later: it's a MATCH! Oh my God. Oh. My. God. Breathe, Alvina, breathe. My inner goddess does a triple cart-wheel followed by an arabesque like a fucking thirteen-year-old Belarusian gymnast. Breathe, Alvina, breathe. What happens now? Is he going to message me? Have I got to message him? What are the rules? What do I do? I can't believe I got a match.

Ping.

What's that? What the fuck is that?! It's a message! What's he say? What's he say? Come on, come on, what's he –

'Hello sexy.'

Holy crap. He's a true romantic . . . a master of seduction! He thinks I'm sexy. We're going to have sex. Oh wow. Hyperventilating now. My lady bits clench like my grandmother's gums around a Turkish delight. What do I say? 'Hello sexy' back? OK, OK, here goes:

'Help stay.'

Send.

What? No! *Help stay*? No, that's *not* what I meant! Fucking predictive text. *Help stay*? Oh God, please say I didn't just send that. My inner goddess has me curled up in a ball in the dirt on the floor and is kicking the shit out of me with steel-capped Dr Martens. I am vomiting and bleeding from my spleen. Help *stay*? He's going to think I'm desperate. He probably has commitment phobia and I've already scared him off. That's it! It's over! My life is over. He's going to dump me. My one chance of happiness, gone, for ever. Fuck, fuck, fuck! What do I do now?

My inner goddess offers a, frankly feeble, suggestion to save my ass: write 'Hello sexy' again, followed by a smiley face. Or an ironic winky face? Is that subversive? Or the mark of a retard? Whatever, just do it, Alvina. Here goes . . .

'Hello sexy ;)'

Send.

Pause.

Anticipation hangs over my head like a tropical rain cloud that's about to burst, leaving me drenched to the skin in a see-through top, mascara streaming down my cheeks like a bedraggled Alice Cooper.

Why hasn't he replied? It was the wink, wasn't it? He thinks I'm an imbecile.

Ping.

He replied! Amazeballs.

'I like ur tits.'

Oh. OK. That's sweet, isn't it? Paying me a nice compliment. Such a gentleman. Right, now reply, Alvina.

'Thank you.'

Send.

A kiss? Shall I send a kiss?

'X'

Send.

Pause.

Why hasn't he replied? He's not going to reply. Was the kiss way too forward? Oh, great job, Alvina, well done. Now he thinks you're easy. Why not just write *'Fancy a fuck?'* and be done with it? *'Here's a picture of my vagina . . .'*?

Ping.

'Wanna meet? Do you swallow?'

Ha ha! What's that? Do I . . . Do I . . . Do . . .

My inner goddess takes a fistful of aspirin, then slits her wrists in a warm bath. The blood drains from her veins till the water turns magenta.

Unlucky for him, I'm still sober.

'No, I bite.'

Send.

Log off.

Log on again.

'Wanker.'

Send.

Delete app.

Should have said I was a vegan (that's so hot right now, just look at Beyoncé and Jay Z). I always think of the comeback when it's way too late. Oh well, at least my inner goddess is dead; she was really starting to piss me off.

Facebook.

I log in and scroll through the posts; it's a tic rather than an interest. No one has said anything witty since 8.21 a.m. when I last had a look. There's one new friendship request, from one of the slobs. Reject. Someone I don't know has invited me to play *Candy Crush Saga*. Fuck off. I 'Like' someone's picture of a wet Persian kitten in a bathtub: 'Fugly', then update my status: '*Finally quit my job!*' I add the '*feeling blissful*' emoticon. Post.

Harry, 27, has made me think about sex, not that there's anyone to do it with. My favourite sex toys in descending order are: 1st: Real Feel Mr Dick vibrating 11-inch dildo; equal 2nd: Rampant Rabbit, the Mighty Pink One, and Rampant Rabbit, the Throbbing One; 3rd: Silicon Pink Plus Phallic Vibrator; 4th: Vibrating Jiggle Balls; 5th: Rampant Rabbit, the Little Shaking One. (I didn't really see the point in that last one, I had to fake it.)

I bet Beth doesn't have any sex toys; she's way too square for that. Plus she's got an actual real live husband with a penis, so . . . I guess he does the job. But he isn't ever-ready like Mr Dick. I open my bedside drawer and pull out my No. 1; he is my lover and my best friend. I consider sticking him on the wall (he has a super-strong sucker at the end of the shaft for easy application to shower tiles and doors), but I don't think I've got the energy.

'Sorry, Dickie boy, I'm just not in the mood.'

I give him a peck then shove him back in the drawer.

I smoke cigarette after cigarette and then another one and another one; I don't want them or like them, I'm just bored out of my brain. I play with my lighter, watch the flame rise and flicker, red then yellow, in the stale, still air. It's mesmerizing. I've always admired fire: an elusive enigma, a grande dame of destruction. I'm not a pyromaniac; I just like watching shit burn. It's amazing to think that this one little Zippo could turn this whole city to ash; that's *power*. Nero knew it when he set fire to ancient Rome. He watched from his palace on Palatine Hill, singing and playing the lyre, as the people ran screaming away from the blaze, flames licking their robes and singeing their hair. Nero waited until the flames died down, then he built his new palace in the heart of the city, where the fire had cleared the old houses away. You've got to admire Nero for that; the guy had chutzpah.

Prometheus was a dude too. He knew the rules were there to be broken. He really pissed off Zeus when he lit a torch from the sun and brought fire to man. Turned out Zeus didn't want mankind burning shit down, just like my mother. She didn't want me to burn Beth's teddies or the neighbour's cat or the shed with the dog locked inside. (The dog was *fine*. Mum heard him barking before the roof caved in. He just needed a bath to wash off the soot . . .) Some people don't know how to have fun. My old headmaster was a killjoy too. What did he have to expel me for, just because I set fire to his car?

Who needs school anyway? Kids don't need educating now that we all have the web. The Internet knows everything. It's amazing what you can learn online without having to tolerate head lice and uniforms and soggy school dinners. This week alone I learnt that we are living inside a computer-generated hologram, that Matthew Perry was the actor who played Chandler in *Friends* (I couldn't remember so I had to google it) and that when the male and female anglerfish mate they melt into each other and share bodies for ever. (Apparently the sea is so vast and deep that when a male finds a female he latches on tight, then loses his eyes and internal organs until the fish share one body and a single bloodstream. It's kind of beautiful.) Good to know.

I've read way more than Beth has, with all her fancy degrees (not that it's a competition). My brain is full. I graduated from the University of Life *cum laude*. It's called being an 'autodidact' if you want to be a smart-arse, but there's no need to be sesquipedalian.

I get up and make my way to the kitchen/bomb site. Tea, builder's – none of that fancy stuff my sister orders: Darjeeling or Earl Grey or organic Rainforest Alliance fucking Arabica. I don't care about getting fired; I'm still thinking about Beth, going over it and over it again in my head: *I would like to invite you, yet again, to come and stay with us at our villa in Taormina. I need you. I'm begging you. Come.*

Fuck off!

I wonder what she wants though. Probably some bone marrow or one of my kidneys. She's not getting it from me, she'll have to ask Mum.

'Tea?' I ask. The slobs look up at me funny and shake their heads. I fill the kettle, then flick the switch. Urgh, why is it sticky? Eventually, I find my mug – 'I have nothing to declare except my genius' – under the bacteria-breeding facility and wash it. It looks just as stained when I've finished as it did when I started. There's one teabag left. I plop it into the bottom of my cup and glance at the slobs. They're staring up at me, but snap their heads back towards *Jeremy Kyle* as soon as they catch my eye. Freaks. The bottle of semi-skimmed has less than a centimetre left. I pour in the water, then finish the milk.

'Erm,' says Gary as I head back to my room. 'Can we have a word?'

'Sure. What's up?' I ask, sinking down opposite. This had better be quick. Is that the guy or the girl?

'We've been thinking,' says Gary.

'And we don't think it's working out,' says Patty. Or Pam.

They wait with expressionless faces for me to respond. I don't.

'We think you should move out,' suggests Geoff. Or is it Graham?

That's it. There's no further explanation. Either they've found another emo slob who wants to move in or they just don't like me. Why don't they like me? Perhaps it's because I haven't paid the rent. Unbelievable. I should be kicking *them* out, although I suppose they were here first.

'*Tomorrow*,' says Patty, with a practised scowl.

I wish I had a Samurai sword; it's at times like these that they come in useful. 'Of course,' I say, 'no problem. Actually, I was going to leave soon. I've got to go on holiday to Sicily so . . .' Time to find that cardboard box. I knew today was my lucky day.

I scuttle back into my room and hurl myself on the bed. An old photograph eyeballs me. It's a picture of me and my twin. Beth looks like a supermodel. I look like a tramp having a bad hair day. That photo was taken on Beth's last day at school. She was all blow-dried and lip-glossed and Cheshire-cat smug. I had a hangover from drinking a whole bottle of Malibu on my own in a tree by our house. I honestly can't see any resemblance; as far as I can tell, we don't look alike.

I glare at the photo.

What do you want?

I can hear what she's thinking from the other side of Europe: *Come to Sicily, Alvina, come, come, come!* We're like two quantum particles forever entangled. She is a gluon and I am a quark. I am dark matter and she is . . . well, just *matter,* I guess. It's spooky action at a distance. She hits her head and I get a headache. I break my leg and her knee hurts. She marries a hot, rich Italian guy and moves to Taormina, I get dumped on Tinder and move in with some slobs. I suppose it doesn't always work.

My twin is ever-present in my head like an amputated limb – not a nice one you've lost in a road accident, a gangrenous one that has started to smell and you're glad to chop off. Alvie 'n' Beth, Beth 'n' Alvie, it used to be, but not any more, not since Oxford, not since Ambrogio. Although Beth and I are identical, Beth has always been the attractive one. Beth was the pretty one. Beth was the skinny one. Beth was the first to walk and talk and potty-train and fuck. I force my face into the pillow.

'Raaaagh!'

Facebook.

I have one new 'Like' for my status update from Elizabeth Caruso: that's my sister.

Of course.

I reread the email I sent to Beth: 'Let me know when you're

next visiting London', 'It would be good to catch up' – the kind of thing you'd say to an annoying business associate, not to someone with whom you'd once shared a womb. Looking back over her email again now, it sounds like she genuinely wants to see me: '*I need you. I'm begging you. Come.*' OK, Beth, bra-fucking-vo, you win. I suppose I could buy some factor-50. Hopefully Mount Etna is dormant. I start to type.

From: Alvina Knightly
AlvinaKnightly69@hotmail.com
To: Elizabeth Caruso
ElizabethKnightlyCaruso@gmail.com
Date: 24 Aug 2015 at 11.31
Subject: Re: VISIT

Hi Beth,

Sorry about before. I was having a really bollocks time at work. Now that I'm not working, I have time to come and visit you. You're right, two years is far too long. I am, of course, dying to meet Ernie and your villa sounds gorgeous. I am free indefinitely (and could do with a holiday), so let me know when it might be convenient and I'll check online for some cheap flights.

Alvie

Send.

I'll stick it on one of my credit cards. It's not real money, just numbers. I'll worry about it later. It's only a molehill in comparison to my mountain of debt, a fraction; I'll barely notice it. (I did try writing to the bank manager to let him know they'd made a mistake with my statement but he didn't believe me. Apparently they hadn't mis-sold me any PPI or overcharged me on any service fees either. Bloody typical. Banker wankers. Bash the lot of them, that's what I say.)

Chapter Three

Unidentifiable meat – cat? rat? fox? pigeon? – gyrates in the kebab-shop window. Something yellow drip, drip, drips on to a metal grill below. It sizzles and spits, hisses and singes: pink, then brown, then grey. The air inside is heavy with fat. An attractive man in a smeared white apron and a cardboard hat approaches the counter. He has floppy hair and designer stubble. I imagine what he might look like under his clothes: all thirteen glorious inches of Mark Wahlberg's penis in the final scene of *Boogie Nights*?

'The usual?'

I nod.

'Actually, I'm hungry. Make that two.'

He takes a long, silver knife and flicks a switch. It glints in the neon light. The serrated blade buzzes, vibrates, whirs, rotates. He saws off pieces – thick slices of meat – and catches them all in a bap. Lettuce, tomatoes, hold the onions, extra sauce.

'Eight pounds, ninety-eight.'

How much? That's daylight robbery. I pay him anyway, leave the two-pence piece as a generous tip. I grab my doners and a can of fat Coke and devour both kebabs on the way to the flat, picking out the onions (*Bastard . . .*) and flicking them on to the floor and licking the ketchup that's dripping down my fingers: a splodge on my shirt, a splodge on my shoe, a splodge on the pavement, splat, splat, splat.

There's a second-hand bookshop with a copy of Beth's novel for sale in the window: 50p. I stop dead in my tracks. That's cheaper than toilet paper. I'm still not going to buy it; I wouldn't read it if you paid me. Well, maybe if you *paid me a lot*. I look over my shoulder; it's almost like Beth's following me. I can't believe her book's in that shop. A glance at my phone tells me she has replied:

From: Elizabeth Caruso
ElizabethKnightlyCaruso@gmail.com
To: Alvina Knightly
AlvinaKnightly69@hotmail.com
Date: 24 Aug 2015 at 13.10
Subject: Re: re: VISIT

Darling Alvie,

Of course you are forgiven and of course you must come! I have booked you on to tomorrow morning's British Airways flight to Catania (see attached itinerary). It's club class, darling, so make sure you take advantage of the complimentary champagne. If you aren't gazeboed by the time you get here, I shall be disappointed. I hope that's not too soon, but you did say you weren't doing anything and, well, I simply couldn't wait to see you! Ambrogio will collect you. Be warned: he drives like Lewis Hamilton, but you'll do the 40-minute journey in 15 in the Lambo.

Make sure you bring your bikini and a sunhat; it's murder out here. Actually, don't worry if you haven't got any of that, you can buy Gucci and Prada in Taormina up the road.

See you tomorrow!
Love,
Beth xxx

PS Great news about quitting. You hated that job, didn't you?

PPS How much did you say you weighed again?

I keep my eyes open for a long time without blinking. When

I do finally blink, the email from Beth is still up on the screen. She's efficient: tomorrow morning? She bought me tickets? What a control freak.

And what is her obsession with my weight all of a sudden?

I can't wait to see Ambrogio, eye candy extraordinaire. He's like Brad Pitt times Ashton Kutcher to the power of David Gandy. Maybe Beth isn't such a cow after all?

I fling the empty kebab wrappers on the doorstep with the others and sprint up the stairs two at a time.

I have the flat all to myself, just how I like it. If only it were like this all the time. I've already chain-smoked six cigarettes and drunk most of a bottle of Pinot Grigio I found in the fridge. It's not mine, but I'm leaving tomorrow so I couldn't give a toss.

I empty out my wardrobe and drawers and yank my suitcase from under my bed, blow off the dust and the fag butts and socks. I can't believe I'm going to see Beth again. From birth until college we were practically inseparable (not out of choice: think tapeworm or guinea worm or blood-sucking parasite). That's twenty-six years, ten months and twelve days ago now. Elbowing each other in that salty, amniotic sea, we couldn't wait to get out and become separate beings; nine months is a long time to spend with your face up inside someone's arsehole. Beth escaped first, whooshing down the birth canal like a Canadian bobsleigh star going for gold at the Winter Olympics. I got stuck heading out feet first. The midwife had to yank me, up to her elbows like a farmer birthing a calf; I was doing the splits with one foot behind each ear. Needless to say, Mum had had quite enough of pushing after the first one came out. What did she need me for? She already had Beth. I was surplus to requirements, like a 'buy one, get one free' offer that you didn't really want. The unopened Cheddar that festers in the bottom of the fridge. The second pack of Jaffa

Cakes that you really shouldn't eat. Easy to forget about. Easy to ignore.

Mum was always 'forgetting' about me, like she 'forgot' to mention she was emigrating to Australia. She 'forgot' to get my vaccinations and I caught the measles. She 'forgot' to bring me home from the supermarket or get me off the train to Penzance. She 'forgot' to invite me to our grandmother's funeral. (It wasn't *my* fault she died; I just happened to be visiting when she finally croaked.) You get the picture.

Because I got stuck, I had to go in a fish tank, aka an incubator. Something to do with being starved of oxygen. The first time anyone saw me, I was a violent blue. Because I was in the fish tank, I had to stay in the hospital. I didn't get breastfed, unlike Beth. The nurse gave me bottles. I only ever got formula. Mum left with Beth, her precious firstborn, and the pair of them had a grand old time. When they finally let me out, a few weeks later, they had to leave three voicemails asking Mum to come and get me. Of course by then, she'd really bonded with Beth. And everyone knows three's a crowd. It was a pattern that's lasted for twenty-six years. Mum was lazy, Beth was easy to love: obedient, well behaved, immaculately presented. She never embarrassed us in front of the neighbours, ran away or got into trouble with the police. She didn't set fire to things or swear. She was never a disappointment.

I was named after our father, Alvin (*what an imagination*), and Elizabeth was named for Her Majesty the Queen (a story that Mum never tires of telling . . .). Mum wasn't that keen on our dad, as it happened. They divorced soon after we were born and he went to live in San Francisco. I never saw him again. No great loss – he was probably a twat. Mum would never have lived in America or Greenland or Afghanistan, or anywhere like that; she loved the Queen too much. Devoted, like a bee. The only reason she agreed to move to Australia with her second husband was because in Sydney the Queen is still sovereign. A devoted subject, a true patriot, Mum always preferred Elizabeth to me. If only there had been a 'Queen Alvina'! I check Wikipedia, but no, there wasn't. Just some dumb lost girl in a novel by D. H. Lawrence that I haven't read.

My earliest memory? Sticking pins in Beth's doll. Don't ask me why. I have no idea. I was only about three or four at the time. I didn't know shit about voodoo back then. I just found her doll one day and decided it would be fun to stick pins in it. And it was. I can still see it now, lying there on that dressing table: long blonde hair and big blue eyes, eyelids that opened and shut on their own when you moved its head back and forth. Sit up: they open. Lie down: they shut. Open. Shut. Open. Shut. Hours of fun.

I found Mum's sewing pins tucked away in a drawer. They were the long, thin, silver kind with different-coloured balls all stuck on the ends. There must have been about fifty of them in a little square case. I pulled them out, one by one, and stuck them in. Easy as pie. I expected the doll to cry, but she didn't make a sound, just lay there and took it. I started with the feet, four in each foot between each little pink toe, then another one and another one in two long lines up her legs. They slid into the plastic nice and deep. Stuck good and firm like the spines on a hedgehog.

I kept on going, pin after pin, all the way up her body. When I finished her front, I flipped her right over, stuck pins in her back. Her buttocks. The back of her head. It was all going well until the very last pin, a red one, I think. I don't know what happened. I pulled it out of the packet and then – I pricked my thumb. The shock was colossal. At that age? An earthquake. A bead of blood sprung up on my finger: perfect, round, red to match the pin. I was just like Sleeping Beauty, spinning her wheel. Without even thinking, I licked it. Animal. Instinctive. That was my very first taste of blood. It was like nothing else I'd ever tasted, before or since: salty, metallic. Illicit, like wine. I was speechless. Changed.

But that was then and this is now. I haven't seen my sister for two whole years, not since her wedding in Milan, in the fucking cathedral. And what a disaster that was. I do not want to think about it. I light another cigarette and suck up a lung-ful of cancer, sit on my windowsill and stare at the pigeons. They stare back. Menacing. Murderous. Little black eyeballs glinting with malice. Did one of you jokers crap on my shoul-der? They've been watching Alfred Hitchcock: any minute, they'll attack.

Scenes of Beth's wedding flood my mind, uninvited . . .

I glug some more wine.

For months before Beth's 'big day' my mother used to call me and ask, 'Who's your plus one, Alvina? I need to know for the seating plan/invitations/just to get on your tits.'

'But why do I need to bring *anyone*, Mum? Why do I even need a boyfriend?'

'I'm not getting into this now, Alvina. The sprouts will over-cook and your father won't eat them.'

'He's not my father.'

Silence.

'Why can't you find a nice young man like Ambrosia?' she said.

Oh God, please help me. Here we go again.

'Ambro*gio*, Mum. He's not a rice pudding.' Although, it's true, I would like to eat him.

'Your sister's settling down and you're not getting any younger.'

'No. I know.' I was *twenty-four*.

'Or any more attractive.'

Oh, for fuck's sake. She really knew how to get under my skin. I blinked back tears and sniffed too loudly. It's not like I *wanted* to die alone.

'I'm perfectly happy without a boyfriend, and the last guy I shagged turned out to be a mollusc.'

'What was your last boyfriend called again? Michael or Simon or Richard or something?'

'How on earth should I know?' It might have been *Ahmed*?

'I always lose track, dear, there seem to be so many.'

I grit my teeth.

Despite all this, there was no way in hell I was going to Beth's big white wedding on my own: a loner, a singleton, a social pariah. And one day, when Mum called me, I finally cracked. I said the first name that came into my head.

'Alex, Mum. His name is Alex.'

'Ah! Alexander?'

'What?'

'Is he Greek?'

'No!'

'Is he rich? Is he a shipping magnate? What is his family name?'

'No, no and I don't know.'

'Fine. Well. I'll send you both an invitation. And I'll finalize the seating arrangements. You can sit at the 'Honeysuckle' table between Great-Aunt Vera and Uncle Bartholomew. I'm sure they'll both be thrilled to meet him. They once went on a cruise to Corfu.'

I didn't know anyone called Alex, of course, and as I sat on the easyJet plane waiting for the flight to Milan to take off, I began to freak out. I guess I could say he'd been called away on urgent business – one of his ships had crashed into an iceberg? – but they wouldn't believe me. Single at my sister's fabulous wedding. A reject. A gooseberry. I was starting to get (even more) desperate.

I decided I'd take whoever sat next to me on the plane; random, I know, but strangely arousing. I watched the passengers boarding one by one . . . Ooh, he looks nice: designer jeans, clean-shaven, expensive-looking manbag. Is that Prada? He turns left and sits down with his lingerie-model wife and Gap-ad kid. Great. Ooh, what about him? This one's *gorgeous*. A Tyson Beckford lookalike. Diamond earrings. Ralph Lauren sweater. Sexy smile. He sits in the row just behind me with his even fitter boyfriend. Somebody kill me. Now.

'Hello,' said a long-haired, beardy-faced, excessively tattooed Harley-Davidson type as he sat down next to me in the aisle seat. 'I'm Adam.'

Adam? Almost. That'll do.

Adam smelled of hydroponic marijuana and had an accent that could have been Geordie or he could have been deaf. He had a tattoo saying 'MUM' and a tattoo saying 'CHAR-DONNAY' inked along his pockmarked neck. Old motor oil under his fingernails, scabs on his face from when he fell off his bike. Adam had a mind even filthier than mine. Over the next two and a half hours, it was all we could do not to consummate our lust by joining the Mile High Club right there on the plane, but there always seemed to be a queue for the toilet and, anyway, I knew I had to make him wait or he'd never come with me. We snogged for a bit (much to the annoyance of the little old lady knitting in the window seat) and he fingered me under the drop-down plastic tray. That's when I asked him.

'Fancy coming to a wedding in Milan? I'll make it worth your while,' I said with a wink and a hand placed too far up his black-leather-clad thigh.

'All right,' said Adam, with a wonky smile. This was going to be *perfect*.

I think it's fair to say that he wasn't 'my type', but a bird in the hand and all that; especially when that 'bird' has two fingers in your 'bush'.

It wasn't my fault we were the first in the church and it wasn't my fault that we couldn't keep our hands off each other. He must have liked my crotch-length, strapless spandex dress and silver fishnet hold-ups . . . (I'd made a real effort to dress up for Beth's wedding; I was channelling Pippa Middleton's bum.) We snogged on a pew for a bit, at the back in the corner, but we got some funny looks as the congregation came in. Whispering. Pointing. Tut-tut-tutting. We needed a room. There were convenient little booths (thank God for confession boxes) lined up against a wall inside the church. They were just the right size and had red velvet curtains you could pull across the doorways for intimate privacy. So I grabbed Adam's hand and we snuck in there as the church filled up.

At first, we were quiet (what with being *in a church*), but I think we must have got carried away as he rammed me up against the mahogany walls and I sat on his cock on the bench. I remember getting high on the incongruity: we are shagging in a *church*! Adam tasted of Cornish pasties and did a weird shaking, trembling thing as he came. The mahogany banged against the wall. I seem to remember he yelped. I shouted something like 'Jesus H. Christ!' or 'Fuck me till Sunday!' and Adam shouted, 'Mum!' We fell out through the curtains just as we climaxed and as Beth and her bridesmaids walked down the aisle. Beth went bright red – I can still see her face. Everyone stared. A small boy asked Adam if he was Jesus (I guess it must have been the beard). My mother put her camcorder down. They all looked at Beth, then looked at me and then looked at Beth again. Spectators at an X-rated tennis match.

It never would have happened if Beth had asked *me* to be her bridesmaid.

After that, and once the priest had asked Adam to leave, the wedding was boring. It was a big white affair with hundreds of people I didn't know, mostly Italians. It was all very Roman Catholic. Mum changed the seating plan so I was stuck in the kitchen with the staff. I was sandwiched between a fat pastry chef called Giuseppe and Toto, the pot-wash boy.

Not in a good way. There were thirteen courses at their reception dinner: antipasti, pasta, lobster, venison, veal . . . The wedding cake was six feet tall. Magnum after magnum of vintage Prosecco, shot after shot of bittersweet limoncello. We danced the tarantella all night: a hundred people holding hands, racing around and around as the music sped up, then reversing direction again and again, before collapsing in a dizzy heap on the floor. People kept pinning banknotes to Beth's pouffy dress and I kept pulling them off again. I made €3,000 that night.

Beth had looked so beautiful; she was like a different person. Standing side by side for endless wedding photographs, I'd thought of *before and after* pictures: like that American TV series, *The Swan*. Beth was a fairy-tale princess and I was a frog. Beth had seemed older somehow, more grown up. I know, she is officially twenty minutes older, but older even than that: taller, more worldly, self-assured. Perhaps that's what marrying money does to you? I wouldn't know. Their Alfa Romeo was decorated with flowers to pave the road to *la dolce vita* and as they drove away, I couldn't help it, I cried. Ambrogio was perfect and he should have been mine. It was all so unfair. It was tragic.

Anyway, Beth hasn't really spoken to me since then. Until these emails. Come to think of it, she wasn't really speaking to me before that either, not since the autumn of 2007, to be precise.

I stub out my smoke and flick the butt through the window at a pigeon; I miss. Watching her walk down the aisle that day, it had dawned on me that our divergence was complete. Yes, the doctor had cut our umbilical cords twenty-five years before, but we'd lived side by side until our sixteenth birthdays. Alvie 'n' Beth. Beth 'n' Alvie. We'd shared a bedroom, bunk beds, books. She had defined me. She was the closest thing I've ever had to a friend, even if I had hated her most of the time. And then she was gone.

When we'd moved to different cities, we'd forged different lives. Beth had gone to Oxford, to the university. I'd moved to London two years before. I can't remember why. I guess I'd thought the streets were paved with gold, but it turned out to be dog shit and chewing gum.

I'm like a less successful female Dick Whittington. Did you know, in Archway, there's a statue of his cat? That's what happens if you become the mayor of London; people make limestone effigies of your pets. If/when I become mayor, someone will carve a to-scale replica of Mr Dick for all posterity to behold. They'll erect it on a plinth up in Whitehall. I know Ken Livingstone kept pet newts. Does Boris Johnson have a pet? Is it just me, or do Donald Trump and Boris Johnson look like twins separated at birth? I wish someone had separated me and Beth. Adopted me or Beth. Beth or me. Beth. Beth. Definitely Beth.

I glug some more wine.

Now we have nothing more in common, apart from DNA.

People always assume that twins are best buddies, have a psychic connection, an undying bond. What the hell do they know? Give me a break. How would you like it if your whole damn life you'd been overshadowed by a doppelgänger who outshone you at everything? Whom all the boys had fancied at school? *Ask your sister if she'll go out with me. Get your sister to meet me by the bike sheds after class.* Wouldn't you *hate* them? Just a teeny little bit? Even as you loved them half to death? I guess you could call it a love/hate relationship: Beth does the love bit and I do the hate. At least, I think she used to love me. Tolerate, perhaps. No one's ever really loved me, not loved me properly, like in books. I light a cigarette.

Beth wrote a novel while she was still at uni, like Zadie Smith but devoid of talent. Of course I haven't read it, but I'm pretty sure it's wank. Reading Beth's novel would be like listening to Beth go on and on for ten hours straight; she loves the sound of her own voice. (Living with Beth made me want to tattoo 'Shut the fuck up' on my face.) I don't really like talking, especially not to other people. I prefer poetry.

I wrote another haiku today:

> *Summer emptiness:*
> *The city is deserted,*
> *Save for swarms of wasps.*

I didn't say it was any good. Even haikus are too long for me: three whole lines. I like the poetry of Ezra Pound: 'In a Station of the Metro' is only two lines long. Ideally, it would be one. Or zero. Just silence.

I rifle through a pile of old clothes in a torn plastic bag and find a dress I haven't worn since October 2007: body-con fuchsia à la Katy Perry. Beth got us matching ones for our birthday, so we looked like the Kray twins or those creepy little girls in *The Shining*. Will it still fit? I strip naked and stand in front of my reflection in the floor-length mirror. I am mozzarella di bufala. I shiver at the thought of nudity in the presence of Ambrogio. Yanking the dress over my head, I force the zip. It snags my skin. It doesn't fit. I fling it on the floor and jump up and down on it in bare feet. Must have shrunk in the wash. Not that I've washed it.

I look at the books that line my shelves. There's no way I can take them all with me; they're far too heavy. There's a copy of *The Second Sex* by Simone de Beauvoir that's too fat to read. Some Toni Morrison, Jeanette Winterson, Susie Orbach . . . Perhaps I'll take just one or two. I really need to steal a Kindle.

I throw a few other essentials into my suitcase: knickers, fags, Swiss army knife, passport? Shit! My passport! Where is it? I haven't used it since my trip to Milan. I've moved flats five times since then. It could be anywhere. Did I leave it in Oddbins when they asked for ID? Did my flatmates swap it for crystal meth? Considering only hours ago I didn't want to see my sister, I am now psycho-desperate to visit. (Well, where else am I supposed to go? Beth's place is better than getting bum-raped in an alley by a homeless Cockney. Just.) And now I'm drunk, which isn't helping. I empty my underwear on to the floor: bras and pants that have seen better days. I squat on all fours and squint under furniture, scooping out crap. The room looks like the aftermath of a typhoon. There's no sign of the passport, just the mess I call my life.

I have no identity. I am nobody. Like an unborn child or an unkissed frog. How am I going to tell Beth I can't make it? She's going to kill me. She'll never forgive me. This was my only chance to make up! We have to make up, she's driving me crazy! Skulking about in my subconscious like a Hogwarts dementor. Sucking my soul. Making me mad. Bringing me down, down, down. My bottom lip begins to quiver. Hot, wet teardrops prickle my eyes. I lie on the ground curled up like a foetus and cry myself to sleep using the suitcase as a pillow.

DAY TWO:
Envy

I wish I had an ass like that.
@AlvinaKnightly69

Chapter Four

It was Beth's fault we never had any birthday parties.

Well, not since our first and last one, when we were five.

We were so excited, I remember that much. It was our first proper party. We were running around the house, shrieking and laughing, jumping up and down and waiting for the guests to arrive. Beth had on her new frilly dress with fairy wings and a tutu skirt and I was wearing one of Beth's old pinafores that she'd grown out of. We'd done our hair up in lopsided bunches with our favourite scrunchies and butterfly clips. Mum had made party bags, blown up balloons. She'd even baked a cake with nine candles: five for Beth and four for me because one of them broke in the packet on the way back from the shop. The house was warm with the sweet smell of baking. It was a My Little Pony cake: vanilla buttercream, strawberry jam, hundreds of thousands of sprinkles. I didn't like vanilla. Or buttercream. Or strawberry jam, to be honest. Beth was the one who was mad keen on horses. I preferred trolls. But I thought the cake looked pretty cool: the pink flying pony with sparkly wings and a blue mane that glistened and flowed in the wind. Horses could fly in those days; there was magic in the air. At least, that's what I thought until the guests started to arrive. Then it all went downhill.

'Happy birthday!' The kids all burst in squealing. And then the party games began. Beth won Pin the Tail on the Donkey. Beth won Musical Statues and Musical Chairs. Mum always stopped the music when Beth had the present when we were playing Pass the Parcel. Beth was the one Mum let cut the cake and make a wish (and it was such a beautiful knife!).

That was it. I couldn't take any more. I turned on my heel and sprinted upstairs, my head exploding with thundering rage, my eyes overflowing with tears. I spent the afternoon crying in a locked bathroom surrounded by tissues soggy with snot. I could hear the party in full swing below me, the ghetto blaster thumping Beth's favourite song: 'I Should Be So Lucky' by Kylie Minogue. Mum said I could stay in there '*Until you learn how to behave!*' Beth had a great time. I never tasted that cake. My sister kept trying to make me to come out. Banging on the door. Begging me. Pleading. She twisted the doorknob so hard it came off. She offered me her presents, her cards and cake (she only did it to make herself feel better). But it wasn't the same. Second-hand toys just don't have that sparkle. I didn't want to *share*. Sharing is bullshit. Whoever said 'sharing is caring' did *not* have a twin.

That was the year that the horses stopped flying.

We never had another party after that.

Tuesday, 25 August 2015, 7 a.m.
Archway, London

'Where's my wine, Alvina?'

Someone is shouting at me in Scouse. Who looks for wine at this time in the morning? There's a bang on the door and the handle waggles. Thank fuck I locked it. I'm lying naked on the floor with a crick in my neck; I'll spend the whole day looking left.

'I want my wine,' whines the slob. I try to get up.

'Sorry. I drank it. I'll give you a tenner?' Unlikely.

'Make sure you do.' The waggling stops. Footsteps pad along the hallway. Silence.

I haul myself up; the ground shifts and spins beneath my feet. My mouth tastes like an ashtray that someone's spilt a pint in. I wish I'd bothered to brush my teeth; they feel kind of furry. I notice a pocket on the front of my suitcase that, in hindsight, looks like a sensible place to keep a passport. I unzip it. It's there. I can't believe it!

I read the name on the passport, just to make sure: Alvina Knightly. Yup, that was still me last time I checked. I study the picture. It's an old photograph. I remember when I took it, in a photo booth at Paddington Station in 2007, just before I met Ambrogio. I study the face in the picture, my smile, my eyes. What is that? Hope? Innocence? Youth? I look different, some-how; I look *nice*. I close my eyes and hold my breath, suck in the pain and store it away, lock it somewhere deep in a basement and throw away the key. That was before everything happened. I was eighteen then, so young, still a virgin. I still had a chance . . . I flick past the photo and leaf through the pages: empty, pristine. No stamps, no memories. I haven't been anywhere. Haven't done anything. Haven't grown up. Haven't moved on.

What time is it? Shit. Why didn't I set an alarm? It's 7.48 a.m. I have just over an hour to get to Heathrow. I don't know if I'll make it. I grab the dress that doesn't fit and pull it on over my head, throw on a denim jacket with toothpaste down the front and my beaten-up Reeboks. I search through my drawers for something smooth and pink, grab Mr Dick and throw him in my handbag. I scan the room. There's nothing here that I care about losing. The slobs will probably burn it all when they see I haven't left that tenner. Or the last two months' rent. I resist the urge to set fire to the flat on my way out. I skid down the stairs and out of the house. I'm at the station in under a minute.

The Tube to the airport takes *for ever*. The carriage has no air con; it's a sauna, not a train. A Turkish bath. Fucking Piccadilly line. It's even worse than the Northern. I sit on synthetic orange fuzz and try not to throw up. A hooded youth sitting next to me plays *Angry Birds* at full volume, while stuffing his face with endless chips. Where did he get chips from at 8 a.m.? I glare at his distorted reflection in the opposite window. He's lucky I'm in a good mood.

I wish I had a book to read. I wish I had some sunglasses. The strip light's glare is brighter than the sun. I cover my face with my hands and wait for eternity in a dark world of greasy vinegar smells and hyperactive computer jingles. The bile in my throat rises and falls like the sea's in my stomach. Blood vessels in my brain go THROB, THROB, THROB. Why did I drink all that wine? I haven't been there, yet, but I imagine this experience is exactly like hell. I half expect the fat, black fly crawling up the inside of that steamed-up window to turn into Beelzebub himself and welcome me to perdition.

'Hey there, Alvina!' he would say, in a Disneyland drawl. 'Welcome to the Inferno! We've got torture without end coming up right here in our horrible dungeon, but first, why don't you get to know some of the guys? Osama, Ayatollah, Idi, Pol, Adolf and Saddam, this is Alvina!' What a cockfest. I'd always assumed Maggie Thatcher would be here. But no: all guys. It's like the Bullingdon Club down here, but with no pig heads to fuck and nothing to drink.

Heathrow Airport, London

When I do *finally* get to the airport, security is a nightmare: endless queues for the X-ray machine; I have to take my shoes, belt *and* jacket off. I throw my handbag into the plastic tray and it shuffles away down the conveyor belt. I step through the metal detector and of course, it goes off. BLEEP! BLEEP! BLEEP! BLEEP! Oh great. That's just what I need . . . A sour-faced woman frisks me up and down. I can smell the tropical-fruit fabric conditioner she's used on her blouse. Then things go from bad to worse.

'Is this your bag, madam?' asks a man in a uniform.

'Uh-huh,' I say.

'Please, come this way.'

I'd rather not, but he's got my bag so I don't have much choice.

I start to sweat, racking my brains for incriminating objects that could be inside. The slobs' drugs? But why would they be in my bag? Are they using me as a mule to traffic speed to Sicily? Is there a bottle of water over 100 ml? Are there nail scissors in my purse? Have I accidentally packed a machete? The Swiss army knife is safe in my suitcase. I can't think of anything.

'Your bag appears to be buzzing, madam. Could you please tell me why?'

He looks at me with a face like a funeral. A high-pitched buzz rises from the tray. I think of the fly. He thinks it's a bomb.

'I have no idea,' I say. 'It's definitely *not* a bomb.'

Don't say the 'B' word at airport security or people get tetchy. Everyone stops talking and turns to stare. The sour-faced woman and another couple of uniformed men crowd around me. They scowl. One of them puts on plastic gloves and unzips my bag. The buzzing gets louder. I wish I was dead: I've just realized what's inside.

'Oh, you don't want to look in there,' I say as a latex-covered hand approaches Mr Dick. One of the men in uniform pulls out my Real Feel 11-inch vibrating dildo and holds it up for all to see. Strangers whip out their phones and start to film.

'What's this?' he asks.

It's a bright-pink replica of a man's erect penis. He knows what it is. They all know what it is. The woman tries to hide a smile. I don't reply.

'*What is this?*' he asks again, a little louder this time. Families with small children in the queue behind me crane their necks to get a better view. At least it's not anyone I know . . . at least it's not Ambrogio . . . at least it's not Beth.

'Let me introduce you to Mr Dick,' I say at last, clearing my throat. 'He's a top-of-the-range, eleven-inch vibrating dildo. Variable speed settings. Detachable butt-tickler. Guaranteed orgasm every time. Do you want me to turn him off? You just flick this switch over –'

I reach for the on/off button at the bottom of the shaft, but he yanks it away.

'I'm afraid I'm going to have to confiscate this, madam. You won't be allowed to take it on the plane.'

My mouth gapes open, goldfish-like. 'What? Why not? It's not on your list of banned items.' I gesture to a poster stuck up on the wall with pictures of lighters and razor blades. Notable in its absence is a picture of a vibrating rubber cock.

'It could be used as a weapon, madam.'

'A weapon? How so?'

He doesn't elaborate. The woman laughs, then pretends it's a cough. The man in the uniform tries to take Mr Dick away, but I reach out and grab him. No! Hands off, you bastard! He's mine! Three security professionals and thirty-plus members of the general public gawp en masse as the man releases the dildo and it smacks me hard in the face. WHACK!

I squeeze out a tear and it rolls down my cheek. (It's useful being able to cry on demand.)

'I promise not to attack anyone,' I sniff. 'Look, I'll even take out the batteries.'

I remove two double-A batteries and slam them down on the metal table. 'OK?'

There's a pause. The woman (clearly the one wearing the trousers) nods. I shove Mr Dick in my bag and sprint out the exit. Half of the crowd are still filming on their phones.

I collapse on to the sofa in the British Airways lounge and catch my breath. What is this place? Space age and orchids. Cream leather sofas. Designer lamps and polished wooden floors. There's a place over there where you can get a free massage. It's like some kind of luxury spa hotel. People are staring, the kind I wouldn't usually hang with: businessmen, escorts, well-dressed WAGs. I consider getting naked to give them something to look at, but they might not let me board the plane.

I grab my phone and check YouTube. Yup. Of course. It's

already there. Some loser has uploaded me as 'Sex Toy Tourist'. You can see the back of my head and Mr Dick. Fame at last. Unbelievable. It already has over sixty 'Likes'. I stop the video and throw my phone back in my bag. I'm not going to 'Like' it. They can fuck off.

To my left, a blonde woman sits smelling strongly of jasmine. She's wearing head-to-heel Louis Vuitton logos and matches her hand luggage perfectly: Louis Vuitton skirt, Louis Vuitton jacket, Louis Vuitton scarf. It's as though she were on some covert camouflage operation in a designer store. Perhaps she is? I have shoe envy and bag envy. She looks me up and down with pursed-up lips like a cat's arsehole; I flip her the bird.

My neck is still aching. I rub it a bit and wiggle my head.

The inside of my mouth has turned into the Sahara. At first I think it's a mirage, the product of a dehydrated brain, but there really is a free bar.

'Water?' I say. It's all I can do not to lie on the floor.

An impeccably groomed lady hands me a bottle of ice-cold Evian and flashes me a million-dollar smile. They don't do that in the Costcutter in Archway. She doesn't ask for any money. 'Actually, champagne?' Hair of the dog; much better. I'm following Beth's orders: the more bubbly the better. I can't believe it's free.

'Will Laurent-Perrier Grand Siècle be to your taste, *madame*?' she asks in a Marilyn Monroe voice. I think she's speaking French. She hands me a flute and I take a sip: liquid sunshine. I could get used to this! I take a selfie with the champers and post it on Instagram. 'Getting gazeboed!' Twelve exclamation marks. I upload it on Twitter: '@ChanningTatum Wish you were here!'

Four glasses later, I skip out of the departure lounge to search for a gift. What do you get the girl who has everything? I only have five minutes before boarding and my brain's not working. Vodka. If it's going to be painful, then we might as well get pissed. I grab a bottle of Absolut and push to the front of the queue.

'Sorry, got a plane to catch,' I say to whomever.

'Don't we all?' complains a mouthy Russian in a mink coat. What's 'fuck you' in Russian?

I race past shop windows: Burberry, Prada, Chanel, Ralph Lauren . . . trying to ignore the duty-free wares that call like sirens to a sex-starved sailor. 'Buy me,' whispers a pair of boots in snakeskin leather. 'Love me,' shouts a dress in lace and PVC. There's a pair of glittering sandals with gold ankle straps in the window of Prada. I press my face against the pane, clouding it up with my hot, wet breath, streaking the glass with my sweaty little palms. There's a bottle of 'Poison' by Christian Dior for only £43.50. Tom Ford's lipstick, 'Violet Fatale', is only £36. Think of all the money I could save if I bought these sunglasses here: these Raybans are only £159; that's twenty per cent cheaper than on the high street. If I buy them now, I'll be forty quid richer. It's a no-brainer, but I don't have the time. Or money.

'This is a customer announcement: could Elvira Kingly please make her way to gate fourteen? Boarding for the British Airways flight BA 4062 will close in two minutes' time. That's Elvira Kingly. Gate fourteen. Thank you.'

Elvira? That's a new one. Who am I? Elvira: Mistress of the Dark? Do I look like an '80s horror hostess on American TV? The Hallowe'en Queen? *Elvira?* Give me a break. At least it's not *Albino*.

I run to the gate and stride past the queue. Club class, darling. I'm not waiting around. I want to get out of here. No money, no house, no boyfriend, no job. Are you fucking kidding me? I never, ever want to come back. This was never the plan, all this chaos and squalor. I had high hopes when I ran away from home. I remember it now like it was yesterday; it was a Sunday, the middle of the night. We'd just turned sweet sixteen. I thought I was on some fantastic adventure: *Treasure Island* or *Huckleberry Finn*. I crept out of the house with my world in my rucksack, hitch-hiked my way through the night into town. I woke up in the middle of Piccadilly Circus. That was as good a place as any: the bright lights flashing, the neon billboards, the kaleidoscope of colours that sparkled and swirled. I got a job in a Japanese restaurant, chopping up tuna and squid for sashimi. Found a room in a hostel that I could afford. In my spare time, I'd sit for long hours on park benches, scribbling away in my spiral-bound pad: haikus mostly, sonnets and lyrics, quatrains, epigrams, a couple of ballads. Teenage woe and melancholy. I had angst to rival any of the bards'. I thought by now I'd be a world-famous poet, married to a gorgeous model-slash-actor (Channing Tatum?) or (even better) Ambrogio. I thought I'd have a baby girl as pretty as an Anne Geddes flower fairy, a Range Rover, a dachshund and a mansion in Chelsea. Where did it all go so wrong?

I look out of my little oval window: darkening thunderclouds over the tarmac, big, fat raindrops smashing into the ground. Isn't it supposed to be summer? I check the calendar on my phone: apparently it's still August.

On the plane, an air hostess gives everyone warm, wet towels in case they haven't washed. I scrub my arms, face, hands, feet and knees. I have more legroom than I know what to do with. I start doing quad exercises as though I were swimming the breaststroke, practising for Beth's pool like an adolescent tadpole. It's only about a three-hour flight, but you don't want to risk DVT. A man sitting next to me peers over rimless glasses, as though I were a rare specimen of pond life he'd never seen before. I stop.

He looks the other way, out of the window, so I start again. Whatever.

The plane takes off with a wobble and a high-pitched whine. I don't like flying. It just isn't natural. There's no way that this long lump of metal will float. I grip the arms of my chair and my knuckles turn white. I consider grabbing on to one of the man's hands, but he doesn't look like the hand-holding type. I neck a fistful of Valium instead. At least I'll be high when we burst into flames in a tangle of kerosene and flesh on the runway. It might even be fun?

The seat-belt sign pings off. We're safe! I study my rarefied section of aluminium tube; it's nice to be up here at the front instead of back there in cattle class. I feel like a V I P, a celebrity. This is what it's like being Taylor or Miley. But I'd rather be *infamous* than famous. Britney was better when she fell off the wagon. Winona and Whitney are by far the best. I don't know why people are so mean to Lindsay. She looks like she's having a ball.

The Louis Vuitton-lover is here; I can smell her perfume. Across the walkway is another fashion victim/stick insect with Kate Moss cheekbones. (How I wish I looked *that* anorexic; I mean, really, she looks only hours from death.) An octogenarian man with a Berlusconi tan has fallen asleep with an unlit cigar dangling between his lips. One too many Bunga Bunga parties? (He might be dead, but I'll leave that to the cabin crew.) There are absolutely no kids and no one is kicking the back of my seat or head.

'More champagne,' I call, pinging the hostess button. I wonder what happens if you mix champagne and Valium. 'Have you got any food?'

This is absolutely fucking awesome.

Chapter Five

Catania-Fontanarossa Airport, Sicily

The heat slams into you like a Mafia getaway car. I shield my eyes from the dazzling glare, squinting and blinking like a naked mole rat that has never seen the sun. I stagger out of the plane, dive rather than walk down the last few stairs to the runway. Fuck, that hurts: skin scrapes concrete, metal dents bone. I think I might have fractured my elbow; I'm bleeding profusely from my right arm, but I'll worry about that later. People are staring (again; what's their problem?). Beth will be pleased: I'm completely 'gazeboed'. I dust myself off and get on to a bus. I guess that's the end of club class.

We're at the terminal waiting to collect baggage when a thought hits me with a comic-book *POW*: Ambrogio! He's here. I look a mess and have toothpaste down my front. I'm bleeding from my elbow from when I fell out of the plane; my Katy Perry dress is splattered with blood. I still haven't managed to brush my teeth. I tie up the laces on my weather-worn sneakers (I can't let Ambrogio see me in these trainers), then I get an idea. I'd noticed the Louis Vuitton-lover arguing with someone at passport control. She was having a problem with her visa and hasn't made it this far. She'd looked about my size when I was checking out her booty in the departure lounge earlier. That's her suitcase on the conveyor belt; I could take it! Shall I do it? Mr Dick's still in my hand luggage, otherwise I'm guessing she's packed better than I have and, let's face it, I could do with a makeover.

I grab both our cases and sprint for the exit, my heartbeat pounding in my throat. I duck into the disabled toilet and look in the mirror. It's worse than I thought. I look shit and my hair looks shit, so I find a beanie in the bottom of my bag; it covers my hair, but not my face. I could do with a burka. Perhaps a balaclava? I wipe the blood off my arm with a piece of wet toilet paper. Surprisingly, it's only a graze. I lift up the Louis Vuitton suitcase. There's a miniature padlock on the zip. How am I going to get that off? I try to pick it with one of my hair clips. That stuff works in movies, but never for me. I jiggle it around and wait for the click, but nothing clicks. I jiggle and jiggle and swear under my breath. I have no plan B. This has to work. I jiggle some more, but the padlock stays shut. A bead of sweat slides down my neck. It's not going to work, is it? Time to think outside the box. Come on, Alvie, where's your genius when you need it? I glare at myself in the mirror. The girl in the mirror glares back. Nice. I could find something to smash off the padlock? I scan the toilet. What can I use? The tap on the sink? That looks heavy. I unscrew the tap and twist it off: clunky metal. This could work. A jet of water shoots up from the pipe: the shock of cold spray in my face. The sink overflows and water cascades down on to the floor. I'll have to be quick or I'll get everything wct! I pull out the padlock so it rests on the ground, lift up the tap and smash it down hard.

WHACK! WHACK! WHACK!

CRACK!

I can't believe it, it worked!

I open the case with trembling fingers. There's a little black dress by – surprise – Louis Vuitton; the cool satin fabric feels soft on my skin, smooth as silky double cream. I slip it on. It looks amazing. The cut is incredible. I suddenly have curves in all the right places. I actually have a waist. There are some stilettos in my size, which seem to go. I step into the heels and I'm six inches taller. My shoulders pull back. My chest lifts higher. I'm as poised as a dancer, a prima ballerina. I spin around and check out my bum: it's a bona fide miracle!

This woman's make-up bag is bigger than my suitcase. I find some pretty pink blusher by Yves Saint Laurent and apply a slick of Dior Show mascara. I add my own signature bright-purple lipstick. Right. I guess that'll have to do. I look in the mirror, unsteady on my heels. I look like somebody else, someone much more attractive. Someone with money. With taste. With class. I shove my blood-covered clothes into my battered old suitcase and now I'm ready. I can do this. I can finally face my sister's hot husband, the sex god, the stallion: Ambrogio Caruso. Hic.

I close the door on the flood.

A tsunami of faces crashes into me. Where is he? I scan the crowd for a Davidoff model, but it's a sea of strangers waving pieces of cardboard with other people's names: 'Alessia', 'Antonio', 'Ermenegildo'. I don't think any of those are supposed to be me. But perhaps they've sent a driver? A driver with dyslexia? Could I be 'Elena'? 'Aldo'? 'Alessandro'? I bet I'm 'Adrian'. I'm sick of this shit.

There's a group of nuns in black-and-white wimples, cruci-fixes around their necks. They have a tranquil aura about them: calm, enlightened, happy, serene. I should have been a nun, but it's probably too late now. I could have done something with my life. Could have written more haikus. Won the Pulitzer. The Nobel Prize. I let myself get distracted too easily. Too many men. Too much drama. I should have focused on poetry, not on boyfriends. Apart from Ambrogio, Ambrogio is different. Ambrogio and Channing Tatum. Sigh.

Come on. Come on. Hurry up. I'm standing here like a lemon.

There he is. Oh my God! How could I have missed him? The world stops spinning. The scene seems to freeze. I focus in on his beautiful face. He's so cool. So handsome. The shades *inside*. The A-list tan. His shirt as crisp and white as hotel bed sheets. A dis-tracting bulge in his too-tight jeans.

Beth is *such* a bitch.

'Alvina!' Ambrogio waves, whipping off Wayfarers. 'Wow! *I didn't recognize you.* Over here!'

I wave back and smile. I know what he means; I usually look a bit crap.

'How are you?' he says.

His skin is bronzed, there's a hint of stubble. He has a lovely chin. A lovely smile. Actually, he's got a lovely everything. He's perfect. I want him. He should have been *mine.* I totter over in my heels, swerve, skid and nearly fall over. I collapse into his arms. Mmm, now I remember his aftershave: Armani 'Code Black', sensual, exotic. He was wearing that when we first met.

'You look great! Have you lost weight?'

I mumble something incomprehensible, like *bleurgh.*

'You're drunk,' he laughs.

'Beth told me . . . champagne . . .'

I'd forgotten about his Italian accent; it's impossibly cute. I look into his brown eyes and I'm sinking, drowning, falling in deep: Nutella or Nesquik or molten hot chocolate. And suddenly I'm back all those years ago in Oxford. My first time . . . our only time . . .

Shit. What's that? Louis Vuitton logos? Is she here? Is she following me? I take a sharp breath. My frantic eyes dart around the crowd. But it isn't her. It's somebody else. I need to get out of here. It could get awkward. Not that I couldn't floor her if it came to a fight. I definitely could. Definitely. Possibly. Probably not.

He puts an arm around my waist and with the other picks up one of my bags; he is warm. Skin tingles all over my body. I lean on his shoulder and breathe in his scent: an oriental fragrance, tobacco, leather. I already want him. This is going to be hard. I concentrate on walking in a straight line to the car. It's more difficult than it sounds.

The crowds part to let us through. Everyone's staring, *yet again.* Who are they looking at? Me or Ambrogio? It must be

Ambrogio. I understand. I can't take my eyes off him either. We take the lift to the ground floor. I've always wanted to have sex in a lift. Has he got better-looking? How is it possible? It's been *two years*. But men are like that; they get better with age, like foreign cheese, good wine and George Clooney. It's so unfair. I look shit. I bet Beth's already had lipo and a tummy tuck, lip fillers, a boob job and everything lasered. I probably won't recognize her. She'll be the spitting image of Megan Fox and ninety per cent plastic, at least.

The Lamborghini is parked on the pavement by the entrance to the airport. Strange. It is very, very shiny and very, very red. It has fuck-me curves like you wouldn't believe. I study the logo on its gleaming bonnet: a golden bull on a slick, black shield. It's the kind of bonnet on which bikini-clad glamour models pose. I wonder if the girl comes free with the car? Perhaps the model's in the boot, clawing to get out? We'll discover her later with scuffed-up nails, her French manicure ruined, her gel tips scraped off. I've never been so close to a car this expensive and I hesitate before touching it. Ambrogio notices, laughs and tries to explain.

'She's a 1972 Miura. Come on in, Alvie, she won't bite.'

No, the car won't bite, but I might . . . Oh God! I study his Marlon Brando lips: luscious, pouting, fleshy, fat. I could kiss them or bite them or rip them off. I would kill for a snog, just a taste of his tongue as his soft, warm lips press into my own. He would taste like the cocoa on tiramisu. He would feel like the breeze on a gondola.

He throws the cases into the boot (no glamour model). He holds the passenger door wide open and I slide on to leather. It smells exclusive. It is foreplay on wheels. I've decided that I like Lamborghinis; they're now my favourite kind of car (the Batmobile is a very close second, followed by the DeLorean time machine). There's a parking ticket stuck on the windscreen and a fat policeman approaching our ride. He hurries over, huffing and puffing, his shirt buttons straining, his comb-over flapping. He rips off the ticket and tears it up, then opens the door for Ambrogio to get in. Weird.

'Signor Caruso!' says the policeman with a deep, low bow. '*Mi dispiace! Mi dispiace!*' Ambrogio ignores him.

Very weird.

'Beth sends her apologies,' says Ambrogio. 'She did want to come and meet you at the airport, but as you can see, it's a two-seater.'

'Oh no, don't worry. It's fine,' I say, looking away as he holds my gaze. Don't blush, Alvina. Don't say anything fucking stupid. This isn't *awkward*. This is fucking excruciating, but at the same time, I suppose, I love it. I need to calm down. I need to chill out. I close my eyes and breathe in deep, count backwards in my head from three hundred: 300, 299, 298 . . .

It's not working.

The engine starts and my whole body trembles. This engine is *powerful*. My seat vibrates – it's rather nice: a thoughtful design feature? There's a high-pitched shriek as the wheels skid. We swerve out of the airport and before I know it we're halfway up the autostrada. Ambrogio's playing 'Nessun Dorma' at full volume.

'Pavarotti,' he shouts with a wink. 'It's great you could come. Beth was delighted you could make it at such short notice. Have you visited Sicily before?'

That's it, Alvie: small talk. You can do it. Just play nice . . .

'Erm. No. I've been to Milan, obviously, for your wedding . . .' A pause. I blush. Probably best not to mention that. 'And Beth and I went on a school trip to Pompeii . . .' I am twelve years old. Our eyes meet. He reaches over and squeezes my hand. *What?*

'Nice nail polish,' he says with a grin.

I look down at my luminous lime-green nail varnish. I'm not sure if he likes it or if he's taking the piss.

'I travel a lot. All the time,' I say quickly. 'I was in LA last weekend, New York the weekend before that, Sydney the weekend before that . . .'

'You flew to Australia for a weekend?'

'Er . . . yes?' I say. What's wrong with that? I hear Beth in my head *tut-tut* about carbon.

'Cool.' He laughs. 'Anyway, we're both delighted you could come.'

I lose the power of speech.

I lean back in the leather, sink down in my seat. Seeing him again . . . it's all too much. Seeing him *alone* . . .

The Sicilian landscape reclines before us, curves to rival Sophia Loren's. We power through her at 180 kph. He floors the accelerator. The engine purrs. I get the feeling Ambrogio's showing off for me, and I like it. The corners of my mouth twitch into a smile. I grip the edges of my seat with my claws like a cat. Vineyard after vineyard blur through the windscreen. Olive grove after olive grove merge into one. Faster, faster, faster, baby. Let's drive to the horizon and never look back. I want to get lost in this glorious landscape, just me and Ambrogio. I want this island to swallow us whole.

We turn off the motorway where a sign says 'Taormina'.

'Nearly there.' Ambrogio grins, running his fingers through shampoo-ad hair.

We climb a steep path; he doesn't slow down. Faster, faster, never stop. I want him to keep on driving and driving. I never want this moment to end.

'The villa's at the top of this hill.'

We're surrounded by acres of Technicolor citrus orchards; it's like being in an oil painting: yellow, orange and green. Their zest is overwhelming: sharp, delicious. The lemons are the size of melons. We drive through the trees to the top of the hill. I imagine Ambrogio pulling into an alcove (I've always wanted to have sex in a car), only this time it would mean something. This time it would matter. This time he wouldn't leave me for my twin.

But he doesn't pull over.

He turns into the driveway – electric gates open as if by magic – and kills the engine.

'We're here!'

Chapter Six

Taormina, Sicily

Holy fuck; my sister lives *here*?

Dollar signs flash in my eyes. The villa is ridiculous. This place must cost a bomb.

'Do you *own* this?'

'I inherited it from my parents.'

Oh yes. I remember Beth said. They died. Poor Ambrogio. He was only thirteen. Thirteen and a millionaire. Actually, that's *awesome*. He probably didn't mind. And lucky for him, he's an only child, no snotty big sister to split it with.

'*Benvenuto!*' he says.

Ambrogio opens my door and takes my hand. The seats are so low I need it, especially in these heels. How do people walk in these things? He pulls me up and I steady myself on the top of the car, shield my eyes and blink into the sun.

'Wow.'

It looks like the set of a luxurious fashion shoot: *Vogue* or *Elle* or *Vanity Fair*. I expect to see Gisele Bündchen reclining on a sunlounger: gold lamé bikini, daiquiri, tan. Where are the cameras? The lightbulbs flashing? The photographers clicking? I'm reminded of the faraway fantasy worlds of *Condé Nast Traveller* and *The Sunday Times Travel*, of all those dream properties in *A Place in the Sun*; except, clearly, I am here, so this must be real.

Ancient pink buildings with terracotta roofs sprawl across acres of garden: manicured lawns, manicured flower beds. The flowers are so beautiful they're singing: red geraniums, purple fuchsias, every shade of blue, frangipani, bougainvillea, jasmine.

It's paradise, Eden: roses and cactus flowers, violets and camellias. Towering palm trees wave in the breeze, their green leaves exploding like fireworks.

Then I see the pool: cool, deep, seductive. Lava-stone tiles frame opal blue. Inky water sparkles in the stark Sicilian sun; flecks of light blind me as I stare. Palm trees and roses reflect in its mirror: a Hockney painting, an oasis. Cream linen deckchairs and parasols surround it, quiet and neat on the crazy paving. The water looks calm and far too inviting – it's all I can do to stop myself jumping in. I want to splash around like a hot girl in a pop video, pretend I'm a teenager on spring break.

I turn around and gawk at the house. The villa itself doesn't even look real, like a still from a golden-age Hollywood movie, something romantic by Federico Fellini or the set from *Roman Holiday*. I look around for Audrey Hepburn and Gregory Peck. Crumbling walls are covered with ivy, emerald leaves shining almost too green. The sign by the door says: '*La Perla Nera*'. I catch a glimpse of marble through an open window, curtains billow in the breeze like tethered clouds.

I don't know how long I stand here staring.

I think I'm dreaming.

Someone calls my name.

'Alvina?'

I see myself (myself on a good day) running towards me, arms outstretched; my stomach flips. It must be Beth. It's strange, two years is a really long time. I've forgotten what it's like to be half of a whole . . . a double . . . a carbon copy . . . an extra in my own fucking life.

'Alvie! You made it! Oh my goodness! You're here!' My twin leaps on me, a violent embrace. 'I can't believe it! You came!'

'Thanks for the flights. You shouldn't have,' I say, struggling to inhale through her arms and exuberance. Beth smells sweet, like breathing in candy floss. She kisses me on both my cheeks and then releases me. At last.

'What? Don't be silly. I can't believe you're actually here. Come on, let me show you around.'

Beth takes my hand and I follow after her. She leads me into the cool of a beautiful lemon tree, chattering merrily like a songbird all the way.

'You look amazing. Make yourself at home. I can't wait for you to meet Ernesto; he's asleep right now, but he's all yours when he wakes up. How was your trip?'

Why is she so happy to see me? Over-bright. Jumpy. Almost *nervous*. I'm about to reply when a single cloud floats to cover the sun. The garden is suddenly cooler and darker. A lone man dressed in head-to-toe black with blackout sunglasses and a black-and-grey hat glides like a bat from the villa to a car parked up on the gravel. He opens the door of a shiny black people carrier and steps inside. A light breeze flows across my neck and down my spine. I shiver.

'Who is *that*?'

'No one.'

Yeah, right.

I watch the car crunch over gravel and crawl soberly off down the long, snaking drive. The electric gates slide silently open. The people carrier drives around the corner and disappears.

'Come inside,' says Beth, then keeps on talking.

Is she talking even more than usual? Or am I just not used to her incessant chatter? Ambrogio hauls the suitcases from the boot and follows just behind. I'm not really listening; I can only stare. There's too much to look at; all my other senses fade. Elizabeth's body. Elizabeth's face. Elizabeth's hair. My eyes rest on my twin's tanned shoulder. Her skin is glowing, iridescent. I look into her eyes: viridescent, alive. Her sun-kissed hair is highlighted blonde. *She* looks amazing. I don't even think she's had any work done. It all looks so real. Perhaps it's good genes? No, it can't be. It must be the money. The money definitely helps. She looks literally half my age.

I am Narcissus, looking at Beth. Falling in love. Sick with envy.

I follow her through a pergola with pink climbing roses, over mosaic tiles, Moroccan rugs. Inside the villa it's bright and spacious: a majestic atrium, the scent of magnolia. I've never been to the Ritz, but I think it must look exactly like this. Everything seems to be made of white marble; specks of silver shimmer like diamond dust in shafts of light. Chaise longues and armchairs are all upholstered in cream and gold. Beautiful tapestries and portraits of ladies hang up on the walls: Renaissance noblewomen in sumptuous silk robes, beads in their hair and sparkling jewels, emeralds, diamonds and shimmering pearls. I follow Beth past gilded mirrors; our faces reflect to infinity.

16th-century original features . . .

Beth was right, I already love it here. I mean, who wouldn't? I never, ever want to leave.

We climb a flight of marble stairs; I stop to admire a picture hanging on the wall. It's a portrait of a boy, his skin white and luminous against a shadowy background. Black on white. White on black. He is sleeping, peaceful, sweet, angelic. It's the most beautiful thing I've ever seen in my life. Beth sees me looking.

'Oh, do you like it?' she says with a smile.

I'm about to answer, but she's already turned and sprinted upstairs.

I watch her feet disappear up the staircase: glitter platform sandals with gold ankle straps. They're the same ones I saw in the window of Prada. They're the second most beautiful things I've ever seen in my life. I think I'll throw away those old Reeboks. It's not like I need any trainers. It's not like I do any sport.

'Your room,' she says, beaming.

Beth flings open the double doors and leads me into a sun-filled guest bedroom; it's on the first floor with a poolside view. It is vast, palatial: the ceiling's twice as high as in my old room in Archway. The bed is enormous; there's room for at least three people in here (I should be so lucky . . .). On the wall is a painting of the crucifixion, all primary colours and sunny blue sky. Christ looks radiant – in Taormina everyone is happy. There's a Juliet balcony with wrought-iron railings and an antique screen in the corner of the room. I trace my fingers over Japanese brushstrokes: a stylized image of a bird in flight. A bouquet of flowers stands on the dressing table; their sugary scent fills the room.

I hold my breath; it's all too much. This can't be real: it's a beautiful dream. In a minute, she'll pinch me and I'll wake up. I'll be back in Archway surrounded by slobs, searching for a passport I'll never find. I rub my eyes and I blink.

'I bought you some things in case you need them,' says Beth. 'I thought you might be travelling light.' She flutters voluminous Benefit eyelashes, bites her glossy bottom lip. 'I hope you don't mind . . .'

I salivate. Six or seven oversized bags line up against a wall. They're shining white with 'PRADA' written along each side, tied up with ribbons in pretty black bows. Beth has hit the shops. Is this all for *me*? So that's why she wanted my dress size. Wow.

'Oh, you shouldn't have,' I say. Is that the right way to respond?

'Just a few essentials really . . . swimming costumes, sarongs, sunhats, skirts. Let me know if there's anything else you need.'

I empty the bags out on to the bed: dresses and camisoles still with their tags. A summer skirt in floral print. A little crochet cardigan. The bikini alone cost €600. I usually shop at TK Maxx! I run my fingers over luxurious fabrics, stroking, caressing . . .

'It's so wonderful to see you,' she says.

I stop and look up. I'm not sure I buy it. No one's ever been this happy to see me, except for maybe my grandma's old dog, but that was because he liked humping my leg: 'Fenton! Fenton! Get off Alvina!'

'So you don't mind about –'

63

'The wedding?' she asks.

I look away. I was going to say Oxford. 'About the wedding?'

She hugs me, *again*. 'You know, I've forgotten all about it.'

'OK,' I say. Her hair smells amazing, like a meadow full of flowers. Perhaps she really has forgiven me. Perhaps she does love me after all?

A cuckoo's call floats in on a breeze through an open window.

I think I will make myself at home here, Beth. I think I will.

'What kind of tea would you like? Earl Grey? Ceylon? Rooibos? Darjeeling? I've got some lovely oolong in at the moment, loose leaf, from Tibet?'

'Erm,' I say. I can't ask for builders' or P G Tips.

'I'll make us some of the oolong.'

'Great.'

I watch Beth's back disappear into the kitchen. Her hair swishes behind her, a glossy blonde mane. She looks like a Barbie doll. Brigitte Bardot. She looks like the new and improved version of me: Alvina Knightly 2.0. It's not a nice feeling. I sit on the edge of a creamy-white armchair and try not to touch anything in case I get it dirty, keep my distance from the glass-topped coffee table, in case it breaks. There's a tight feeling in my chest, like someone's wrapped me up in duct tape; I can't move my ribcage in or out. I dig my fingernails into the fleshy bits in the palms of my hands and wait for Beth to come back. Sweating. I wonder what she wants to ask me. I wonder why I am here . . .

A cream carpet fills the room, with flowers embroidered along its edges, a swirling pattern of green and white. They're lilies, I think. I remember our ancient carpet in Archway with *things* living in it. I don't recall anyone ever vacuuming. I don't think we even had a Hoover. I wriggle my toes in the deep, soft pile. It's all so spotless. Beth probably has staff.

There's a photo on the coffee table of Beth and Ambrogio; its silver frame sparkles like it's just been polished. They look like Brangelina or another golden Hollywood couple. Peroxide teeth, too-big smiles: they don't look real. There's a blue-and-yellow china vase hand-painted with lemons and frangipani. There's a fireplace so clean I doubt it's ever been used.

'Here we are,' says Beth, gliding through the door and making me jump. She's carrying a silver tray, which she sets down on the table. She takes two little teapots, two delicate china teacups and two matching floral saucers and positions them symmetrically on the table before me. She pours the tea from the individual teapots into the individual teacups, as gracefully as a geisha. The tea trickles and tinkles prettily as it fills the cups. It's positively ceremonial.

'Is that colour OK for you, Alvie?' she asks. 'Not too weak?'

'No, it's fine,' I say.

'Not too strong?'

'No.'

She sets down the teapot. This is it. Whatever it is she needs, here it comes . . .

'Would you like some sugar? I have white or brown. Don't worry, it's fair trade.'

Did I look worried? 'No, thank you,' I say.

'Or I can get you some sweetener? There's some stevia in the kitchen.'

What the fuck is stevia? It sounds like an STD. 'No, thanks,' I say.

'It's no trouble.'

'I don't want any.'

I look around for the milk.

'Can I have some milk?'

'Oh, you don't have milk with oolong.'

'Oh.'

Of course not. Silly me.

'So,' I begin, 'you had something to ask me?' But then I get distracted. Sidetracked, more like. Beth takes the cover off a cake stand, lifts the shiny silver dome to reveal the amazing confection beneath. It's a cake with pastel-yellow cream and a pretty pattern in swirling pine nuts. The pine nuts look toasted, golden, delicious . . . the cream looks fluffy and light.

Beth sees me drooling. '*Torta della Nonna*. It's my favourite. You're going to love it.'

She cuts a generous slice of cake and hands it to me on a dainty plate with a folded napkin and a tiny silver fork: the scent of lemons and sugar. The plate is painted with blossoms and rosebuds. The fork looks like an antique.

'Aren't you going to have any?' I ask, incredulous, when I see that it's just me.

'Oh no,' she says. 'I'm on a diet: gluten-free, dairy-free and sugar-free.'

What the hell does she eat then? Air? I take my fork and stab at the cake.

'Mmm,' I say.

Beth smiles.

'Told you.'

She watches as I chew.

I take another forkful, then another and another. Oh my God. I can't get enough. Is it possible to have a taste-bud orgasm? I think I just did.

'Can I have another slice?' I ask, wiping my mouth with the back of my hand and licking my lips. That was good. Really good.

Beth's expression changes. Her face falls slack. Her lower lip begins to curl . . .

I stop chewing, my mouth full of cake. Oh no, what have I done?

'Alvie, you're getting crumbs on the carpet.'

Chapter Seven

'Alvie? Alvie? Are you OK?'

I must have drifted off or glazed over. We're sitting in the nursery, all sailing boats and tank engines, surrounded by toys and baby paraphernalia: a changing table, a cot, a shoe rack with matching pairs of blue booties, tiny and new. There's a row of miniature cardboard books, *Baby's First A to Z*. I feel like a giant in a Victorian doll's house: I don't belong.

'Are you all right?' Beth asks, touching my arm. I pull away.

'Yes.' No. I'm not all right. What does she want? What's going on? She didn't invite me here to play mummies and babies. I didn't come here for a tea party.

Ernie beams a big, stupid grin, blows a little bubble of saliva out of the corner of his mouth.

'Ga, ga, ga,' he says, looking up. I study my nephew's face.

'I'm fine. It's just . . .' Just what, Alvina? *That he looks like you?* I pick out the features on his tiny face: those are my eyes. That's my nose, my mouth and my chin. I'd recognize them anywhere. He looks like me when I was a baby. He could be my son.

The pain floods from my gut like a freshly opened cut and I remember: the sting of the clinic's disinfectant, the stench of bleach, the blank stare of the ceiling, suffocating curtains, too-white walls, an empty vase on the bedside table, the sounds of other people's cries, shining needles, cardboard sick bowls and the driving pain that drove me insane with nothing to show but the bite marks on my hands and the

blood,

blood,

blood.

It's been eight years.

It's all her fault.

'It's just . . . he's so beautiful,' I say at last, surprising myself. But he is; he's angelic. Beth smiles; she knows.

'Thank you,' she says proudly, running her fingers through his golden curls, planting a kiss on his cherubic head. Ernesto is gorgeous, like one of the baby models in the adverts on the Tube, like the sleeping boy in that painting in the hall. Big, blue eyes like drops of ocean. Ernie smiles up at me with that naive kind of optimism that only children can do. His cheeks are round and pink as marshmallows: he's a life-size jelly baby. Sugary. Sweet. I never told her about the pregnancy. She doesn't know I miscarried. But ignorance is no excuse.

'Do you want to hold him?'

'What? No!' I am filled with panic.

'Ernie, do you want to have a cuddle with your Auntie Alvina?' Beth asks, picking him up and holding him out towards me.

'No, it's OK, I've never really held –'

'Don't be silly, you'll be fine. He likes you. I can tell.' She laughs. 'Do you want to give him his bottle?'

And he's on my lap, so light yet so plump. I grip him tightly, my body rigid, terrified I'll drop him or break him or worse. Ernie looks up at me, gurgling, giggling.

'Ma, ma, ma.'

He seems OK.

I listen to him breathing, in and out, as shallow as a kitten, and smell his bubble-bath-scented hair. I blink back tears. It's so unfair. This should be *my* baby. I never want to let him go.

'Mama,' he says, reaching for Beth.

'Aaah,' Beth says. 'He wants his mummy.'

'You take him,' I say, giving him back. 'He's yours, you take him.'

Beth frowns.

My cheeks are flushed. It's far too hot. Has someone turned the heating on?

'Ma, ma, ma.'

It's all her fault and I'll never forgive her.

'Ma, ma, ma, ma, ma.'

'So what happened with your job?' she says, handing me the scissors to cut off the tags on my new bikini. It's a black-and-red bandeau set from Prada with sparkling gemstones along the front. The scissors are nice and sharp.

'Oh that . . . ?' Snip. 'I was doing so well that a competitor found out about me.' Snip. 'I was headhunted.' Snip. 'Can you believe it?'

'No way!' she says. 'I didn't know they headhunted poets.'

'Loads more money. Company car.' I toss the scissors on to the bed.

'Uh-huh? Who was that then?'

'Who?' I say. I unzip my dress and peel it off: red lines on my flesh from where the seams have dug in.

'The competitor?'

'Erm . . .' I snap off my bra. '*Esquire*? The magazine. They needed a head poet.'

She looks me up and down. I don't think she buys it. 'So you were fired, then?'

'Fired? *No.*' She watches me remove my pants, eyes my bikini line. I turn away.

'And what about your new place in London? How's it going with your flatmates?'

I leave my clothes in a pile on the floor, but Beth looks horrified, her lips pursed into an accusing line, so I fold them up neatly and place them all at the foot of the bed.

'Graham and Pam? Oh . . . you know, they're great,' I say. 'More like family than friends. We really clicked, right from the start.' I step into the bikini bottoms, yank them halfway up my legs. Something crackles. The plastic bit's still stuck in the crotch. I take them back off and rip it out.

'Right . . . so, you hate them, then?' says Beth with a smirk.

How does she do that? It's like she can read my fucking mind. I look at the scissors. Round, black handles. Long silver blades. Glinting. Shining. Sparkling in the dazzling sunlight. Calling my name.

'They're . . . *fine*,' I say. I adjust my bikini, the straps digging into my flesh like a cheese wire. She doesn't need to know they kicked me out.

Beth's in a teeny-weeny G-string bikini in pink-and-beige Missoni stripes. I hide my new bikini under a Louis Vuitton sarong and floppy straw hat. How can Beth and I be the same dress size, but I look fat?

We're lying by the swimming pool soaking up the rays; I'm melting into my lounger like vanilla *gelato*. The sun is brutal: my skin's already starting to singe despite the factor-50 I slathered on inside. My knees have turned an alarming shade of red. I watch my sister grab her iPhone and punch in the PIN: 1996. Well, that's easy to remember; it's the year the Spice Girls released 'Wannabe'. She writes someone a message with lots of 'X's.

A woman comes out on to the patio carrying a tray of vodka and iced limonatas. It's the Absolut vodka I bought for Beth. Thank fuck for that, I'm beyond desperate. Beth hasn't stopped talking for over an hour. I can't take much more of this. The woman has dark eyes, curly black hair and leathery brown skin. She smiles at me.

'*Mamma mia!* But there are two Elisabettas!' she says, clapping her hands together and touching her lips with the tips of her fingers.

Oh, here we go: the free entertainment, the freak show, the double act. The fucking point-and-stare routine. We ought to charge them by the minute. We'd both be millionaires (instead of just Beth).

Beth laughs her signature carefree laugh.

'*Non ci credo*; you both look the same!' says the lady.

I don't think so. She must be simple. Don't they have twins in Italy?

'Alvie, this is Emilia, our amazing nanny and housekeeper. Emilia, this is my sister, Alvina.'

'*Piacere*,' says the woman, looking me up and down. I shift on the lounger. Hide under my hat.

'All right,' I say.

My sister has *slaves*? Of course she does. I'd have three slaves if I could afford it: one to cook my food, one to clean my house and one to fan me in the garden with an enormous leaf – fuck me, it's hot.

'Does she *live* here?' I ask when Emilia has gone.

'Goodness, no. She lives in the little pink cottage around the corner. The one with the hanging baskets by the door. She only works here from seven a.m. till nine p.m., six days a week.'

'Oh. Is that all?' How on earth does Beth cope?

'I thought about having someone move in to help at night, you know, with all the baby stuff, but he's such a good sleeper, I don't really need it.'

'Hmm.'

All the baby stuff . . . God, she's so lazy. She's even outsourced being a mum. I mean, come on. How hard can it be? Octomom has *eight* kids, Beth's only got *one*. It's not like she's got anything else to do, like work. No, working on her tan doesn't count. Please don't tell me she's writing another novel. I can't bring myself to ask.

I slurp my limonata: cool, crisp and citrusy with a stiff vodka kick. I'm already contemplating a second. Emilia makes a mean vodka cocktail, I'll give her that.

'You speak English to her? Emilia?' I ask.

'Yes,' Beth says.

'You didn't learn Italian?'

Beth gives me a look. 'No, what's the point?'

Told you: *lazy*.

'Everyone speaks English. Anyway . . . I don't want to stay here for ever . . .' She stops, as though she's said too much.

'Really? Why not? What's wrong with it?' Seems perfectly all right to me. I watch the sunlight reflect off the surface of the pool, like a thousand shimmering diamonds.

'Oh, nothing. I guess . . . the language never appealed. I prefer German.' She closes her eyes and reclines on the lounger. End of subject. Next thing I hear, they'll be moving to Munich.

It's the first time Beth has stopped talking since I arrived. The alcohol in my bloodstream and the warmth caressing my back are sending me to sleep when a high-pitched buzz blares from somewhere to the left of the garden. I crank open my eyelids. Beth's already sitting up, poised to investigate. She springs from the sunlounger, a gazelle or flying squirrel, and sprints towards the noise. I heave myself up and haul myself after her across the lawn, wrapping the sarong around me as I go.

A man with a chainsaw is cutting down a tree. It's a nice chainsaw.

'Hey, what're you doing?' shouts Beth.

He clearly isn't the gardener. He continues to saw until the tree crashes down. It was a lemon tree. Now it's firewood. The stench of burnt petrol and citrus leaves. The man pulls off his Perspex goggles to reveal icy-blue eyes, glacier-cool like Daniel Craig's. He turns off the chainsaw and takes the cigarette from out of his mouth. He is naked from the waist up, tall, broad and dripping with sweat. From the bulge in his cut-offs, I'd guesstimate eight inches. Certainly girth. He looks like he works out. He reminds me of Channing Tatum. (Damn, I should have brought that poster with me. I knew there was something . . .) He has a 'kiss me' dimple in the middle of his chin, so perfect it looks Photoshopped. His dark-blond hair is more messy than tousled, scraped back from his forehead with a black Alice band – a little girly, perhaps. But like Leonardo DiCaprio and Premier League footballers, he somehow pulls it off.

Who knew Beth kept sexy lumberjacks in her back garden? This was worth waking up for.

'I told your husband it had to go. It was still here. Now it's gone,' he says in a thick Italian accent. He is clearly a local. A local who didn't like that tree.

'Salvatore, you can't just chop down other people's trees,' says Beth.

'I can. I did.'

There's no arguing with that.

'Ambrogio's going to be pissed off.'

Salvatore takes a drag. He doesn't look like he cares.

'I told him, the tree is stealing my light. I need the light for my sculptures. Either he goes, or the tree goes. He should be happy it's the tree.' He smiles; he's cute, with a rock star's laid-back nonchalance. Hair on his chest. Expensive watch. He must be a successful artist if he can afford a Patek Philippe. He wipes sweat from his brow with the back of his hand.

We stand and stare at the tree. Then Salvatore sees me.

'You two related?' He laughs, gesturing at us with his cigarette butt. Our eyes meet. He holds my gaze; it feels vulnerable and invasive at the same time. Beth is about to respond when Ambrogio runs out from the villa. Shouting.

'*Ma che cazzo hai fatto?*' he yells across the garden. He looks a little red. 'My father planted that tree! *Merda*, Salvatore, I'm sick of you and your fucking sculptures!'

The men begin a shouting match in animated Italian. I have no idea what they're saying, but it sounds intense. Beth and I wait for a while in the furnace heat and watch the show. The men compete for the most exaggerated hand gestures and deafening decibels, getting closer and closer until they're practically fucking, screaming into each other's faces, progressively more puce.

'Let's get out of here,' Beth says at last, rolling her eyes. She takes my hand and leads me back towards the villa. 'Come on, let's get dressed; I want to show you something special.'

'Sure,' I say, not that she was *asking*. I bet this is it . . . the *real* reason she's invited me.

I would have preferred to watch the fight.

Chapter Eight

We plough through the heat till we reach the amphitheatre. Posters of prima donnas advertise an opera; Verdi's *Nabucco* has just been on. Ah, Nebuchadnezzar, the mad king of Babylon; wasn't he the guy who exiled the Jews from their homeland in *The Book of Daniel*? I knew being forced to go to Sunday school every week for the best part of ten years would come in useful one day. It's finally paid off.

A crowd of baseball caps and rucksacks pour out of a coach and click-click at the view. They wear ill-fitting T-shirts and socks with sandals. They swarm around the entrance like a plague of locusts. I fucking hate tourists. I know, strictly speaking, I am one, but I still fucking hate them. We didn't get any in Archway; I guess that was a plus.

Beth knows the security guard, tall and blond with a twinkle in his eye. He looks about twenty-five years old, dressed in his uniform of starched white shirt and khaki shorts. Not hot. He ushers us through past the queue, winking at me too, enjoying his double vision. Pervert.

'We're kind of friends,' Beth says. 'I come here a lot . . . I find it inspiring.'

Inspiring? Please. Could she be more pretentious? Inspiring for what? Writing *chick lit*? I'm sure the muse has better things to do than wait around in amphitheatres for my twin to show up. She's not an author, she's a trophy wife. If Beth writes another *romantic comedy* with a love-struck heroine and happy ending, I will kill myself. Or perhaps she just means she's fucking him? But no. Not my twin. That's more my style than Beth's. Not that I'm *easy*.

She leads me up some crumbling stairs to the back of the

auditorium. I pant as we climb endless steps. I really can't be bothered; it's far too hot. I want another vodka and iced limonata. But when I reach the top and turn to face the view, I see the point.

'Holy shit.'

'Do you like it?' Beth says.

This is what people call 'earth porn'. A stage reveals nature at her most dramatic. I can almost hear Michael Palin's voice-over: something about Corinthian columns, Euripides, Sophocles and Aeschylus.

'What's that mountain?' I say, pointing at an enormous black mountain-shaped thing.

'It's not a mountain. It's a volcano. Mount Etna? Remember?'

'Oh yeah.' Of course. How could I forget?

'Is it dormant?' I ask, straining my eyes to study the summit: Etna smoulders against a cloudless sky.

'No, but don't worry.'

I'm still going to worry. I saw what happened to those people in Pompeii.

'The Italians call it Mongibello: "beautiful mountain",' she says.

'Told you it was a mountain.'

It doesn't look very '*bello*'. To me it looks deadly. I shiver and look at the sea. Columns frame the volcano's slopes as she flows from her crater right down to the ocean. And yes, the Mediterranean really does shimmer; I guess Beth was right about that. I take a deep breath, taste salt in the air. *Mamma mia* . . . this is even better than in the magazines. I could take a photo without any colour filters and post it now on Instagram. But thousands of people have already taken thousands of identical photographs, so I'm not going to waste my time.

We sit side by side on hot stone, looking out over ancient Greece. I turn to face Beth and glimpse something blue on her arm for the first time; it's a bruise, a big one, the size of a man's fist. She's tried to hide it with make-up, concealer, but some of it's rubbed off on her dress.

'Shit, Beth! What's that?' I ask, pulling up her sleeve to take a look.

'Nothing,' she says, pulling it back down again. 'Doesn't matter, forget it.'

'It's not *nothing*. How did you do it?' I look into her eyes.

'Fell off the ladder in the garden,' she says.

Well, that's a lie. Beth shakes her head.

'Alvie, listen, I need to ask you something. It's important. OK?'

Changing the subject. I don't think so.

'Fucking hell, Beth. Did Ambrogio do that?' I say, but I don't believe it, not for a second. He's too hot to be a wife beater. I doubt he drinks Stella or owns an old vest.

'Alvina! Please. Just listen,' she says.

Beth didn't deny it, but why won't she tell me? She's getting more and more high-pitched.

'Oh God, what is it?' I ask at last. It's far too hot for this conversation. I fantasize about a bathtub filled up with ice.

A Japanese girl with a Hello Kitty T-shirt and a backpack that's bigger than she is appears out of nowhere and gestures to her iPhone.

'Please?'

I look at Beth, but she doesn't move.

'If I must,' I say, standing up. She holds up two fingers in a victory sign and beams into the lens. She's cute. I position the camera so her head's out of the frame and you can just see her knees and her feet: pink platform sneakers and white crochet socks. I click. The girl skips off and I sit down again.

'Alvie?' says Beth. Oh, OK, here we go then. Let's have it. This is the real reason I'm here. She didn't just *miss* me. I'm not giving her a kidney; she can forget it. She should have looked after her own. Beth's mouth is set in a grim line. I study the freckles that speckle her nose and wonder if mine are exactly the same. They probably are, not that anyone would ever bother to check . . . 'Tomorrow, I need you to be me, just for a few hours. Will you do it?'

'*What?*'

'Tomorrow afternoon, after lunch, I need you to swap places with me. It won't be for long. No one will know. Please, say you'll do it?'

WTF?

So that's why she's invited me here, sounded so desperate, paid for the tickets: *I need you. I'm begging you. Come* . . . She's unbelievable, my sister.

'Like when we were at school, remember? We'd swap classes all the time and no one ever noticed,' says Beth.

'But that was when we were younger, when we looked *the same*. Of course people will notice. Look at you and look at me . . .'

'Alvie, we're identical. *Identical.* Get it? I know *we* don't think we look alike, but everyone else does. It'll be easy. You say you're going out for the afternoon, that you want to take Ernie out for a walk. We'll swap clothes, do our hair up the same, but I'll leave.'

I narrow my eyes. 'Why? Where are you going? What are you doing? Why the big secret?' My sister's got this all planned out . . .

'Please, *please* don't ask questions. I really need this, Alvie, I do. If I could tell you, I would. You'd understand.'

'So tell me and I'll understand!'

How dare she? Spoilt brat. Expecting me to ask 'How high?' when she yells 'Jump!' *Do this, Alvie. Do that, Alvie.* I curl my fingers into fists. I feel my shoulders tensing.

'No!' She leaps up. I think she's going to leave but she looks up to the sky and raises her voice. 'Oh God, Alvie, *please*! I need you.'

Her lower lip begins to wobble. Is she actually going to fucking cry? We're kids again, arguing, fighting over a toy, Beth always getting her own fucking way. I set my jaw.

'Alvie, please, you have to do this.' Her big green eyes fill up with tears. 'For me?'

Oh, for fuck's sake . . . If I do this, perhaps she'll leave me alone? If I do this, she'll owe me. It could come in useful. She knows she'll have to pay me back. I wonder what she's going to do. Rob a bank? A drive-by shooting? Perhaps it's a Prada heist? But no, not Beth. She's too much of a goody-goody. Far too well behaved. She's probably just going to her local library to avoid paying a late fine.

I look down at Beth's feet.

'The shoes,' I say. 'I'll do it, but I want the shoes.' I regret it as soon as I've said it. It's a terrible idea; there's no way Ambrogio will fall for her trick. He'll know it's me in two seconds flat.

'Which shoes, these ones?'

She sticks out her leg and cocks her ankle. We look down at the glittering stiletto sandals, sparkling, golden, at her feet. They look like disco balls on crack. I love them more than life itself.

'Of course!' she says, beaming. She flings her arms around my neck, plants a wet kiss on my cheek.

'But I'm only swapping for the afternoon,' I say.

She owes me. Big time. More than just shoes. Although they are gorgeous.

'And a bit of the evening . . . a few hours, that's all.'

She puts her hand on my shoulder, tears in her eyes.

She smiles a sad smile.

'Thank you, Alvie.'

She loves me again.

We walk back to the villa as the sky turns terracotta. Beth insists upon linking arms; it's almost like we're BFFs. But we're not friends. We haven't been friends since Oxford, since I slept with Ambrogio. I know that and she knows that. She's pretending because she wants something, something only I can give her.

Perhaps if I do this, she'll forgive me? Perhaps if I do this, we're quits?

Chapter Nine

Ilean out of my Juliet balcony fuming and chain-smoking cigarettes. It's evening now, so slightly less oven-like, but I still feel like a lobster being boiled alive. Fucking Beth, what is she playing at? This is insane. *Do this, Alvie. Do that, Alvie* . . . She's not exactly being a team player. She's not exactly playing fair. Beth was the one who liked netball and hockey . . . all those vapid team sports with group hugs and high fives. I was more of a long-distance runner. The further the better. Away from my family. Away from the world. I never liked cooperating unless coerced. 'There's no "I" in "team", but there's a "me" if you look hard enough.' And there are two 'I's in Alvina Knightly.

Beth and Ambrogio are talking on the patio. I can't hear what they're saying. He whispers something in her ear, then leans over and kisses her on the lips. She ruffles the hair on the top of his head, then walks back to the villa. God, they're such a smug married couple. I'm so glad I'm not married. Some husbands last for sixty years. Can you think of anything worse? I've never been able to stand a guy for longer than a night.

Once upon a time . . .
And they both lived happily
Ever after: LIES!!!!!

Beth believes in fairy tales; I bet she watches porn on fast forward to see if they get married at the end. I prefer watching porn on rewind, cocks suck up spunk like vacuum cleaners; it's fucking hilarious.

I watch Ambrogio pace the crazy paving at the edge of the

pool and shout into his mobile. He's gesticulating as though the person on the end of the phone could see. Oh, perhaps he's on FaceTime? I watch him, smoking cigarette after cigarette and blowing white clouds high into the evening sky. The tobacco tastes sweet. He turns, sees me watching, and waves with a smile. I take a sharp breath and wave back. Who am I kidding? I'd love to be his wife. I wish I'd had his baby. Who cares if he's a wife beater? He is *Adonis*.

I have my heart set on an Italian man (ideally Ambrogio, although Salvatore now ranks at a very close second. I'm pretty sure Channing has Italian ancestry. It's that or German . . . or Native American . . . or perhaps it's Welsh?). I think it must be the language. I go weak at the knees for anything Italian-sounding. Just listen: *'figlio di puttana'* – mellifluous, no? It means 'son of a bitch'. *'L'anima de li mortacci tua'* – beautiful! 'You're really starting to piss me off.' *'Vaffanculo'* – surely the poetry of Petrarca himself? It means 'fuck off'. You can listen to an argument about prostitutes and piss and it sounds like a sonnet sequence about courtly love. You don't want to know what *'Ti prego, scopami in culo'* means . . . (I learnt Italian swear words by watching Italian porn.)

I stub my cigarette out on the rail of the balcony. It falls to the floor and I kick it over the edge. I make my way back into the bedroom. I'm feeling pretty sticky; this heat is insane. It's really impossible to cool down. I can feel my blood bubbling and boiling, my brain roasting, my internal organs all simmering and frying. Perhaps I'll take a shower? I choose some of the Louis Vuitton-lover's beauty products and head into the en suite. It's one of those walk-in wet rooms with a rain shower: blue mosaics and sparkling silver. It couldn't be more different from the slob's place in Archway, the hairs in the plughole, the mouldy old shower curtain, the avocado bathtub with the blocked-up drain.

The shower gel is *Chanel No. 5* and I'm loving the scent of roses and jasmine as cooling water washes over me, clearing my mind, caressing my back. Mmm, Ambrogio . . . his piercing eyes, the square of his jaw. I can't resist touching myself; seeing him again has made me think naughty thoughts. Earlier today, in the Lamborghini, I got the feeling he liked me too. I'm pretty sure he was flirting. My fingers brush my pulsing clit, my lips are wet and smooth, warm and slippery to touch. I push two fingers deep inside, rub my clit hard with my thumb. I feel the pressure building, building, feel the warmth spread higher, stronger, but no. It's not enough. I'm not doing Ambrogio justice.

I push through the door and back into the bedroom, dripping wet. I grab Mr Dick from inside my handbag (I've put some new batteries in), then run back to the bathroom. I stick him behind me, hip-height, at ninety degrees on the wall. Usually Channing with no clothes on pops into my mind, but tonight it's Ambrogio, standing behind me, wrapping his arms around my waist, his biceps pressing into my breasts, his strong, broad fingers massaging my clit, firm yet gentle, round and round. He says something sexy in Italian, like 'cappuccino'. I ease back on the dildo, but it's Ambrogio pounding me from behind, making me wet, sending me weak at the knees. I close my eyes and drift away on wave after wave of perfect pleasure. It's pretty intense. The water crashes and splashes around me; I nearly slip and break my neck.

Who is she talking to? I push my ear against Beth's door. The wood feels cool and smooth on my cheek. The paint is glossy and white.

'Please? Please? You have to do it.'

Why's she so whiny? What's going on?

'It has to be tomorrow. Salvo, please? We're running out of time,' Beth says. Her voice is high-pitched, nasal, shrill. It echoes around her bedroom.

I lean against the door, but it's not locked and I trip into the room. Beth looks up when she sees me falling in, shocked, off guard, her eyes ablaze.

'I'll call you back.'

She hangs up the phone.

'Don't you knock, Alvina?' Beth snaps.

'No. Sorry. I, erm, I . . . Have you got any deodorant?'

She rolls her eyes, stomps off to the bathroom. I look around her beautiful room, sit down on the bed. It's really high up, not like my futon. The mattress feels firm yet springy to the touch. The bedspread's embroidered with butterflies.

'Who was that? On the phone?' I call after her. Beth rummages around in her en suite. Her phone's on the bed, I could log in now and take a look. I could check her caller history. I know her PIN: 1996. But I wouldn't have time.

'Nobody. Nothing. Why? Were you listening?' She pokes her head out sideways through the bathroom door.

'No. Just curious.' I pick up her phone and then put it back down again. I wouldn't have time.

'Actually . . . it was Mum. Did you want to say hi?'

'God, no.'

'I can call her back,' she shouts from the bathroom.

'No, don't do that. It's fine.'

It wasn't our mother, it was someone called 'Salvo'. I heard her distinctly. Is that *Salvatore*?

Beth emerges with a bottle of Dove Go Fresh Pomegranate. She throws it at me. Hard.

'Here you are. Go crazy,' she says.

Chapter Ten

Well, this is awkward.

We sit at a table for three in the pimpest restaurant I've ever seen. Is that Kanye West over there with P. Diddy enjoying the seafood platter? That looks like Drake at the bar doing shots with Snoop Dogg. I look from Beth to Ambrogio and then back from Ambrogio to Beth again. I try to smile. I feel like the kid that the parents took out because the babysitter cancelled. It's that or your worst job interview ever. A waiter comes over and interrupts the silence.

'*Buonasera, signori.*' He bows at Ambrogio. '*Signore Caruso, sei troppo fortunato! Che belle donne!*' He grins at me and then grins at Beth. '*Gemelle?*' he says.

'*Sì, gemelle,*' says Ambrogio, with a sexy smile.

The waiter grins even harder. He hands me a menu that I can't read. Ambrogio says something in Italian and the waiter laughs.

'*Un vodka Martini, per favore,*' says Ambrogio.

Beth says, 'A Virgin Mary, please.'

'*Certo, signora,*' says the waiter. He looks at me.

'What's that?' I whisper to Beth.

'It's like a Bloody Mary, but without the vodka.'

'So just, like, *tomato juice*?'

Beth nods.

'I'll have a Bloody Mary,' I say. I can't just ask for vodka. That would be weird.

'*Certo, signora.*'

The waiter goes away.

'Well, aren't I just the luckiest man alive, sitting here with you two *belle donne . . .*' says Ambrogio, winking at me. No one replies.

'You look beautiful tonight, honey,' he whispers to Beth. He brushes an invisible lock of hair away from her cheek and then kisses her softly, cups her chin oh-so-gently in his hand, looks into her eyes. It's as though I'm not here. It's as though they were all alone together on their very first date. Their honeymoon. They could start screwing at any second.

'Ahem!' I cough loudly, then light a cigarette.

They turn and stare. The silence is agonizing, the tension so tangible you could slice it open with a box-cutter and watch it bleed all over the starched white linen.

'I know a new joke. Do you want to hear a joke?' Ambrogio says, leaning back in his chair and smiling at me. He's just remembered I exist.

'No. We're all right,' says Beth, picking up her menu and sinking behind it. Bitch.

I look at the view to avoid making eye contact. We're perched up high on a cliffside terrace. From up here, the water looks still, like mercury or molten silver. A cruise liner in the bay sparkles like a jewellery box against dark velvet. A soft breeze flows from the water, washing over the terrace, caressing my skin.

If Beth weren't here, it would be seriously romantic.

The terrace looks out over a sheer, steep drop. Terracotta rooftops, palm-tree canopies and far, far below, a pebble beach. Scalloped bays like crescent moons twinkle with fairy lights, getting smaller and smaller until they disappear. Then, in the distance, there's Mount Etna. Again. She's omnipresent on this island; there's no getting away from her. I'm relieved to see that she's not yet erupting. The last of the sunset sears her silhouette; jet-black slopes glide down to the sea. She's majestic. Prehistoric. A sense of eternity. Something sublime and yet fucking terrifying.

Really, if it weren't for Beth, the whole thing would be perfect.

Everything is white inside the restaurant: tablecloths, curtains, columns, chairs. Diamanté chandeliers. A gleaming show-off grand piano. I study the table: pristine napkins, cut-crystal glasses. I don't want to touch anything; I'll smudge it or smear it. The cutlery sparkles; I pick up a knife and leave fingerprints. White candles flicker. Elegant vases. Crimson geraniums the only splash of colour.

If only Beth would just fuck off.

I look over to the bar at the end of the restaurant. It's glittering white, like inside a snow globe. White leather sofas. Polished tiles. Shelves lined with bottles reflecting in mirrors: Campari, grappa, sambuca, amaretto. A waiter appears with a polished silver tray, a white tea towel draped over his arm. It could be the same one or somebody else; they all look alike. To be fair, I'd sleep with any of them. It wouldn't make any difference. Smart black trousers, starched white shirts. There's something about a man with a drink on a tray . . . it's super sexy. He sets down two glasses filled with blood-red juice, sticks of celery and long black straws. Ambrogio picks up his vodka Martini and takes a sip; I watch his throat move in and out as he swallows it down. I wish I'd ordered that now.

Cheer up, Alvie. Pull yourself together. You're supposed to be on holiday. You're supposed to have fun. Just look where you are. This is a nice place. At least we aren't Siamese.

'Excuse me, ladies,' says Ambrogio, standing up suddenly. 'I'll just go and powder my nose.'

Does he mean coke? Or is he taking a whizz? If it's cocaine, I want some.

He walks across the restaurant. Everyone turns to stare. It's like he's some kind of megastar celebrity: Cristiano Ronaldo or David Beckham. I watch his back disappear past tables and diners dripping with diamonds, bouffant blow-dries, impeccable Italian suits. Waiters with trays piled high with spaghetti. The swaying leaves of palms. Ambrogio has a lovely back, a lovely bum. Like Channing Tatum.

'Alvie,' says Beth. She has a look like she's going to tell me off. 'Stop thinking about Oxford.'

'I wasn't!' I say. That's really unfair. I literally wasn't.

'OK, fine, well, stop thinking about Ambrogio then.'

I give her a look back. 'I was thinking about Channing Tatum.' Kind of.

'You know what I mean.'

'I will think about whatever or whoever I want. Who are you, the thought police?' I light another cigarette. Beth snorts a laugh. 'Where are we, 1984?'

'No,' she says, flicking her hair. She has fabulous hair. 'We're in the best restaurant in Taormina and I don't want it to be awkward.'

'S'not awkward,' I lie.

'Do you know how difficult it is to get a reservation here?'

'No. Tell me. What do you have to do? Sell your soul? Bring peace to the Middle East? Solve the Theory of Everything?'

'What? No, you just have to know somebody.'

'Right.' So . . . she sucked off the manager.

Beth sighs. 'Just make an effort, OK? You haven't said anything since we left the villa. I want us to enjoy this supper.'

'What do you want me to say? I was admiring the scenery. It's very nice.'

'Good. I'm glad you like it,' she says.

'I do,' I say.

'Good.'

'Fine.'

'Fine.'

I blow smoke at the sea and glare at the seagulls.

'Look,' says Beth, 'just stop thinking about Ambrogio. He's not who you think he is. That night, in Oxford, he thought you were me . . .'

My sister's always had impeccable timing. She chooses this moment to drop that bombshell? It can't be true.

'I don't believe you. He probably just said that to get you off his case.' That or she's lying to my face. 'He said . . . he said . . .'

'What did he say?'

'It doesn't matter.'

Beth raises her eyebrows.

'Well, that's what he told me.' She shrugs.

I feel my heart begin to quicken, my stomach tighten. My palms slick and slippery with sweat. I want to scream. I want to throw her off the fucking cliff. That night was special. It's all I've got. How dare she try to take it from me?

Armani Code Black. We both look up. Ambrogio's approaching the table.

'Everything OK?' he asks, sitting down next to Beth. He drapes his napkin over his lap. 'Shall we order? I'm starving.'

I glare at my sister.

'Make conversation,' she mouths.

What the hell am I supposed to say? Oh, Ambrogio, darling, funny fucking story: my sister just told me some interesting news. That night, eight years ago, in Oxford, you remember? The first time we met? That one-night stand? Well, apparently, according to Elizabeth . . . how shall I put this? You thought I was her? Hilarious, isn't it, because all this time I've been under the impression that you slept with me because you wanted to, because you wanted *me*. Me! Not my sister! Imagine that! But you mistook me for my twin. Easy to do. No bother about that. You got drunk, you fucked me, you got me pregnant and all along . . . you thought I was Beth.

'*Polite* conversation,' she mouths.

I slurp up my cocktail until it's all gone, wipe my mouth with the back of my hand; my purple lipstick stains my skin. It looks a bit like a bruise.

'So,' I say, turning to Ambrogio, 'what is it that you do, exactly? You know, for a living? Something to do with art?'

Beth shakes her head and looks down at the ground. She kicks me under the table, hard.

'Ow!' I say. What's wrong with that?

Ambrogio frowns and forces a smile.

'Yes,' he says, clearing his throat. 'I'm an art dealer. I buy and sell art from all over the world. It's really not that interesting.' He laughs. I watch him fold his napkin into a dove and then unfold it again. The silence is agonizing. He turns to Beth. 'Darling, do you want anything in particular, or shall I just order for the table?'

Ambrogio turns to me and smiles and then turns back to Beth. Beth is still scowling.

'So you're an art dealer?' I say. 'That sounds really interesting.'

'Yes,' he says.

I nod and smile, encouraging him to go on. This is called *polite conversation*.

'Sometimes . . . people . . . well, you know, they die. And sometimes . . . these people . . . they have art. Art that other people want to buy. I'm just the middle man,' he says with a shrug.

End of subject. End of conversation. Beth looks relieved.

Prosciutto e melone is first on the menu. The melon is sliced into miniature gondolas with Parma ham draped languidly across. It looks mouthwatering, juicy, sweet and delicious. The melons are local to the island. Apparently the ham is twelve months old. Then it's tuna *carpaccio*: slices of tuna, finer than rice paper, spread out on a plate, a deep bloody pink. It's drizzled with lemon and virgin olive oil, garnished with parsley and *Pachino* tomatoes. *Carpaccio di polpo* is prettier than flower petals. Octopus tentacles undulate like corals, white with pink edges, the scent of the sea. *Spaghetti alle vongole* smells incredible: white wine, garlic, clams, tomatoes. The aroma is heady, distinctive, addictive. Lobster, langoustine, swordfish, crab. Then for dessert, it's honeycomb *semifreddo*, drizzled with salted caramel sauce, white chocolate hearts and lashings and lashings of real gold leaf.

I can't eat any of it. I've lost my appetite.

It's too cold to sleep. I'm tossing and turning. Wriggling and writhing. Chattering and shivering. My head is a swirling mass of neuroses. My feet are like ice. *That night, in Oxford, he thought you were me.* How could she say that? What if it's true? I throw off the blanket and sit up in bed. Flick on the light. Glare at the air-conditioning unit, a scowl cracking my cold, numb face. Why does it have to be arctic or sweltering? Can't there be some kind of middle ground? I jab at the buttons on the zapper to turn the air conditioning off, but the batteries are dead or I'm too far away. I jump up and march over, punch all the buttons until the little green light flashes off. The fans stop whirring and the cold blast of air dies down in the room. At last. That's better. Perhaps now I can sleep?

That's when I hear it: a blood-curdling scream. A sound like somebody skinning a cat. I stop dead in my tracks. Is that Beth? What the fuck? I rush over to my bedroom door and edge it open, just a crack. I peer out into the hall. It's dark. It's still. Then I hear it again. A scream. And then crying. It sounds like Beth; I'd recognize her whining anywhere. Her sobs build louder and louder in volume, more violent, intense. All the muscles in my body tense. This is seriously uncool. It's gone 1 a.m.

I go back to bed and pull the pillow over my head. Stick my fingers in my ears. Why the hell won't she shut up? I can still hear her shrieking. Piercing through the feathers and flesh and bone. Worming its way into my brain. What if he's beating her? Hitting her, now? People shouting: muffled, distorted. I can't hear what they're saying, but I'm sure it's my sister and Ambrogio. More screaming. More crying. I'm going to have to get up.

I'm about to head out when I realize I'm naked. I like to sleep nude, like Marilyn Monroe. It's inconvenient when there's a fire alarm. I run over to my suitcase and grab a pair of knickers, rifle through my clothes until I find an old T-shirt and pull it on. Inside out. I stick my head out through my door and look both ways down the corridor. Nothing. It's suddenly quiet. Perhaps I imagined it? Perhaps she's dead! But then screaming. Again. Oh my God! He's beating her up right now, isn't he? *I saw the bruises*. I'm going to have to find a weapon. I step back in my bedroom and look around. If he's attacking my twin, then I have to stop him! I'll hit him right back! I'll do it! Just watch! She might be a pain in the arse, but she's *blood*. I don't want him *killing* her. Not tonight.

I search through my bag for my Swiss army knife, but I can't find it. There's an old iron poker by the grate in the chimney. I'll use that. I grab it – it weighs heavy in my hands: long and black and twisted. Perfect. I hesitate, press my ear against the door. Hold my breath so I don't miss a beat. There it is again! That screaming! It sounds like someone's being murdered!

I push through the door and creep down the corridor, the poker raised above my head, my bare feet padding the thick pile carpet, my silhouette monstrous against the wall. There are so many bedroom doors; it's like a hotel. Which one is it? I follow the sound. The screaming gets louder and louder and louder as I tiptoe along. I inch towards the edge of Beth's door. My heart is pounding, my eyes are wide. What is going on in there? The poker's shaking in my hands when the door swings open. Ambrogio steps out. Messy hair. Bare chest. A body like an Olympic swimmer. He's wearing nothing but pyjama trousers. I take a step back and shrink into the shadows. I wish I could vanish. I wish I was in bed.

'Oh, hey there, Alvie, I didn't see you.' He looks me up and down and frowns.

'Hey, Ambrogio,' I say casually.

'Your sister's just fallen asleep with the baby. I hope we didn't wake you up? He can be quite loud.'

'No. No, it's OK. I wasn't sleeping.'

There's a pause and I wonder if he is lying. I study his hands for signs of blood. There aren't any.

'Well, goodnight,' he says at last. 'Sleep well. I'll see you in the morning.' He walks the other way down the hall, but then stops. 'Do you need a hand with that poker?'

I look at the 'weapon' in my hands. It suddenly looks ridiculous. What did I think I was going to do with it? I hide it behind my back.

'Oh no, it's fine. I was going to start a fire in my room, but I turned the air con off instead.'

He stares at me like I make no sense.

'It got a bit chilly,' I say.

When Ambrogio's gone, I wait and listen. I can hear myself breathing. All is quiet inside Beth's room. The thin line of light that had outlined the door has disappeared. I stifle a yawn and rub my eyes. Whatever. I suppose it could have been the baby. I'm going back to bed.

DAY THREE:
Wrath

Sometimes, I get so mad I could punch a hole through the mirror.
@AlvinaKnightly69

Chapter Eleven

It was Beth's fault I never got any Christmas presents.

I grew up thinking Father Christmas hated me. Every year, I would write my wish list and post it to Lapland like all the other little girls and boys. Every year, when Santa didn't come, Mum would say exactly the same thing: 'Perhaps if you weren't so naughty, hadn't tried to kill the dog/set fire to the school/kick the headmaster in the gonads, you'd get some presents? Look at all the lovely gifts Beth's got; she's been as good as gold.' Beth. Beth. Mum's little princess. Always the good one. Always the golden girl. Why did she have to be so perfect? She only did it to make me look bad.

Every year it was exactly the same. Christmas Eve, I wouldn't sleep all night. I'd stare at the ceiling, waiting, hoping, scared to breathe in case I missed the reindeers' hooves tap-tap-tap on the rooftop, the tinkle of sleigh bells, the heavy thump of shiny black boots. At the first light of day, I would run downstairs and see all the gifts piled high beneath the tree. Sumptuous red ribbons cascading and flowing, green and gold paper shining and crisp. A single stocking would hang from the mantelpiece, full to overflowing with festive treats. I'd sit and watch my sister open present after present, for hour after hour, simmering, seething, secretly planning what I'd do to Father Christmas if ever I saw him. While Beth was unwrapping My Little Ponies – Twinkle-Eyed Ponies with rhinestones for eyes, Brush 'n Grow Ponies with long, silky hair – or clutching yet another Care Bear, I was plotting my sweet revenge.

Perhaps I'd gouge his eyes out with an HB pencil? I sharpened mine up, just in case. I could use my compasses to slit his throat? But his bounteous beard might get in the way. There was always the rat poison Mum kept under the sink that we weren't allowed to touch. I could tempt him in with a mug of hot cocoa; he'd take a sip, then pop his clogs. I imagined him writhing around on the rug by the fireplace: fluffy white bobble on his floppy hat bobbing, shiny black boots kicking up in the air. He'd roll around and around in his crimson coat, vomiting, gagging, frothing at the mouth. Even that was too good for him. Knob.

Then, one December, I went shopping in a mall with my mum and my sister. Children were singing Christmas carols: 'Jingle Bells' and 'We Three Kings'. Trees were draped with tinsel and candles. Cinnamon was wafting through the air. Mum and Beth were holding hands and I was trailing just behind. *Now, Alvie, remember, behave yourself! I don't want you causing another scene.* Mum didn't usually take me out, in case I embarrassed her. I didn't know what all the fuss was about.

We turned a corner and there he was: I saw the fat, red bastard and I ran! I sprinted, screaming, mad as a banshee, pushing past crowds to his elf-infested grotto, kicking up polystyrene snowflakes in my wake. I leapt on to Santa, ripping his beard, clawing his bespectacled face. I remember the stench of rancid mince pies and sour-smelling whisky on his breath. Santa shouted, 'Get 'er off me!' With superhuman strength, I kicked at his shins, my limbs flailing wildly, until Mum pulled me off.

It did the trick. The fucker always filled my stocking after that. Mostly with things like self-help books and fitness DVDs, but still, it was better than nothing. In hindsight, I know it was Mum.

Wednesday, 26 August 2015, 11 a.m.
Taormina, Sicily

I push open the door and step inside, close it quietly behind me. Decorated in old rose, cream and gold, Beth's bedroom looks like Coco Chanel's boudoir in 1920s Paris. I cross the room over deep-pile carpet, run my hand across a bedspread: cool, smooth silk. The air is vanilla scented, temperature controlled. A Jo Malone candle flickers on the mantelpiece; wax slips down its sides into a silver dish. Mozart's playing in the background, like in the dressing room of a designer store. I look around for some speakers, but I can't see any.

Beth's popped into Taormina to buy something trivial. Ernie's with Emilia in the playroom downstairs. I don't know where Ambrogio is, out with his mates somewhere, I think. I'm not supposed to be in here, but I couldn't help it. 'I can resist everything, except temptation.' Who said that? I walk over to Beth's dressing table: mahogany, antique. Jewellery boxes are piled high like tiny presents, wrapped in Tiffany turquoise, baby pink, blood red. They say the best things come in small packages. I wouldn't know.

I pick up the largest box on the table; red velvet feels soft against my skin, like the ears of a spaniel. It's a heart-shaped box, heavy in my hands, heavier than I'd expected. I want to look inside. I glance over my shoulder towards the closed door. There's nobody there. I hesitate, make eye contact with myself in the mirror, daring myself to do it. Go on, Alvie, you know you want to. I bite my lip, riding the waves of anticipation, and lift the heart's lid.

Diamonds the size of planets dazzle me. Perhaps that's an exaggeration: meteors, or comets. Either way, they're fucking enormous. And I bet you a fiver they're real. Oh my God, look at this thing! I'd kill for some bling like this. I can't move. I can't breathe. I can only stare. They're mesmerizing. I want them. I need them. I wish they were mine. Eleven diamonds in ascending size are set in white gold in a beautiful necklace. The diamond in the middle is shaped like an egg. My fingertips want me to touch it, want me to stroke it, try it on. They reach into the box and lift it from its satin lining. The necklace feels heavy, loaded like a gun, the stones weighing it down like bullets. I let it dangle, limp yet alive, between my fingers and watch as it glitters in the sparkling light. I think of the Crown Jewels in the Tower of London. When I can drag my eyes away from the diamonds, I glance at the door.

What if someone comes in? I don't care. Fuck it. I'm going to try it on.

I pull my hair away from my neck and drape it over one shoulder. My chest looks bare in my reflection in the mirror. Naked. Too white. I lift the necklace with trembling fingers and hold it up against my skin. It looks surreal. Dreamlike. Unreal. I feel like a fucking princess. I undo the clasp, pull the ends of the necklace back together at the nape of my neck. I try to fasten it, but my fingers feel clumsy. I struggle and strain, but I can't do it up.

'Here, let me,' comes a man's voice from behind me.

Ambrogio! How the hell did he get in here?

'No, it's OK –' I say, trying to take the necklace off, but Ambrogio takes the clasp and fastens it around my neck.

'Let's see,' he says, standing next to me in the mirror. 'They look great on you, Alvie. *Molto bella.*'

The diamonds hang around my neck and I want to be sick. I want to rip them off and throw them across the bedroom floor. He smiles.

I turn to face him, avoid making eye contact by looking at his shoes. He has lovely shoes; they're made of soft Italian leather, expensive-looking designer brogues. He reaches up towards my face and tucks a lock of hair behind my ear, so he can get a better view of the diamonds, I guess. His fingertip feels warm against my cheek. I cover my chest with my hands.

'You look beautiful.'

'Oh!'

I look up into his eyes and then look away. I'm sure he can read my burning embarrassment. Why did he have to walk in at this moment? Why is my heart racing so fast? He's standing a little too close to me now. I can smell his scent, the coffee on his breath. For a crazy moment, I think he's going to kiss me. I don't move a muscle. I hold my breath. I can't believe I'm standing right here in Ambrogio's bedroom. I can't believe what he just said.

'Hey, guys,' says Beth, strolling in. Breezy.

'Oh, I was just leaving,' Ambrogio says.

He gives me a smile and then turns to leave. I watch his back walk away through the doorway. He closes the door. Where the fuck did *she* come from? Sneaking up on us like a stalking cat.

'I thought you were out,' I say, reaching for the necklace. *This better go to me in your will*, I don't say.

'Oh, I was,' Beth says quietly, whispering almost under her breath, 'but I wanted to come back and see you.'

'Really.'

'To make sure you were ready for later.'

'Uh-huh.'

'That you hadn't changed your mind.'

Finally, there's a click as the clasp unfastens. I pull off the necklace and hand it to Beth. I notice her fingers are trembling slightly. There's a quiet desperation in her dark-green eyes.

'It's fine,' I say. 'Whatever. It's fine.'

The sooner this is over and done with the better. Then I'm taking the shoes and going home, wherever that is. I never, ever want to see her again.

Chapter Twelve

'Couldn't you at least tell me where you're going?'

'I just can't, Alvina, I'm sorry,' she says.

'If you don't tell me, then I'm not doing it.'

She gives me a look and then looks at the shoes. I look at the shoes. She knows how much I want them. I sigh. I just want to get her off my back, off my mind, out of my life, this time for ever. Why the hell did I even come out here? I'm taking the shoes and I'm leaving.

We're arguing in Beth's bedroom, getting changed for our swap. I feel like we're back in our old room at Mum's house, Beth demanding she have the top bunk bed, taking the biggest slice of fruit cake, claiming the Hear'Say CD for herself. *If you don't let me have it, I'll tell Mum what you did to that hamster/that squirrel/my doll. Do this, Alvie. Do that, Alvie. Do my homework. Polish my shoes.* Tweedledum and Tweedledee. Jedward.

We stand side by side in the full-length mirror. There's one obvious giveaway.

'You need a tan,' says Beth. 'Come with me.'

Beth pushes me towards her en suite in my underwear. She rummages through her beauty cupboard and pulls out a bottle of St Tropez instant tan. I shiver as she rubs the cool, slimy liquid all over my arms and legs, chest and back. It smells of biscuits. It looks too dark.

'You ever wax your legs?' she asks.

'This is *not* going to work.'

I watch Beth undress and hang up her clothes. Her post-baby belly wobbles slightly like mine, not the Pilates-flat tummy she used to have. We both have an inch or two of muffin top. She'll probably get hers lipo-ed off. I would if I could afford it. But I'll just keep eating cookies and doughnuts and triple-chocolate, salted caramel and bacon brownies until I suffocate in my own stomach flaps and my body fat engulfs me like a glutinous pink alien. Something to look forward to. Still, it's better than Pilates.

Beth pulls on the little black dress I wore yesterday. It looks better on her. She shimmies around so I can help with the zip. It glides past bronzed shoulder blades to the base of her neck; it's white beneath her hair where the sun hasn't reached it. I study the fine white hairs on her skin. She's so vulnerable from this angle.

'It's really unfair. You ask me to *be* you, but you won't tell me why,' I say.

'I won't be gone long.' She spins back around to face me. 'Just stop with the questions, OK?' she says.

There's another bruise on Beth's other arm, in exactly the same place. Greenish-blue and purple all at once. I don't know how I missed it yesterday. Perhaps it's new?

'Does this have anything to do with the bruises?' I ask. Surely it can't have been Ambrogio? He is Prince Charming.

She pretends she hasn't heard me and disappears through a door. I follow her like Alice in Wonderland chasing the White Rabbit. We emerge into a room lined with hundreds of dresses, all perfectly co-ordinated in a textile rainbow. It's my very first walk-in wardrobe, so beautiful I gasp. There are Polaroid pictures of all of her outfits stuck up on the walls and dozens of drawers; my sister is Cher from *Clueless*. I think of my room at the slobs' place in Archway; my clothes lived in hessian sacks from the launderette, overflowing in piles all over the floor.

'Just wear this dress.'

She flings a floral frock in my face: violet chiffon with a tiny waist and full skirt, the kind of thing I wouldn't wear if you paid me. How did I let her talk me into this?

'Really?' I ask, making a face. I can't wear that. It might look nice on Beth but I'd look like a four-year-old going to church.

'Really,' says Beth.

I check the label on the dress.

'What size is this?' I ask, trying to get out of it . . .

'It's a thirty-eight,' she says. 'Don't worry, it's right; we're both a size ten.'

I sigh. I pull on the dress, my arms thrashing through layers of petticoat, waving around like I'm drowning in tulle.

'For fuck's sake, you could at least tell me what this is about. And the bruises. You still haven't told me about the bruises.'

Beth rolls her eyes.

'I did. I told you yesterday, remember? I fell off the ladder in the garden.'

'Twice?'

'What? What do you mean, *twice*?'

'Well, that's a new one.' I prod at her arm. 'That bruise wasn't there yesterday.'

'Ow!' she says, pulling away. 'Don't be stupid. I only fell once.'

She rubs her arm where I prodded her, glaring.

'Well, we both know that's bullshit.' I can tell when she's lying. She's not very good at it. 'I heard you last night. You were crying,' I say.

'Just leave it, OK?'

Beth turns away. She finds some nail-polish remover in the drawer of her dressing table. She hands me the bottle with some cotton wool. I don't think she's going to tell me. Perhaps she really did fall off a ladder? She was picking some organic kumquats or something. She wanted to make some sugar-free kumquat and quinoa jam. Perhaps that bruise was there in the amphitheatre and I'm going mental? Perhaps all that crying *was* Ernie.

'Do you have the . . . er, green?' she asks, looking at my fingertips, a frightened expression on her pretty face. Beth's never worn anything but baby pink. She's going to have a seizure.

'Yup, right here,' I say, reaching for my handbag. I grab the nail varnish and throw it in her lap.

'Will you do it for me, Alvie? I can't do it myself . . .' says Beth.

'No, do it yourself – it's better if it looks a bit crap. Authentic,' I say.

Beth picks up the varnish as though it might bite.

'So why were you crying then?' I persist.

'Crying? When?'

'Last night,' I say.

'Ernie was crying. I think he had colic.'

'Colic?' *Yeah, right.* It sounded like someone being tortured.

I scrub at my nails with the cotton-wool pad until all of the neon green has come off: the acrid stench of moisturizing acetone-free vitamin-E-enriched nail-polish remover flooding my nostrils. Then we sit and watch Beth's nails dry. It's like watching paint dry, but more boring because Beth's here.

'Interesting colour,' she says, wiggling her fingers. 'Now let's do our hair up exactly the same.' She forces a smile.

Beth stands in front of the mirror with a hairdryer and curling brush. I watch as she magics her hair into a Malibu Barbie-style blow-dry. Blonde locks cascade down her back in loose waves. It takes hours of maintenance and days of treatments at top salons to achieve that balance of sexy and dishevelled; it's perfect. I think about my greasy locks and three-inch roots.

'It's not going to work,' I say. 'My hair's a mess.'

Beth stops what she's doing and frowns. I untie my hair and it falls over my shoulders. She examines a mousy strand; it hangs, limp, between her manicured fingertips.

'You've got split ends,' she says, horrified. 'I'll call my stylist. She should be able to pop over and fix it.'

Beth's got an answer for everything.

She grabs her mobile from her handbag and jabs at the touch-pad. I flop down on the bed and study the array of perfumes and potions on Beth's dressing table. This *is* Wonderland: Drink Me. Eat Me. Rub Me All Over Your Naked Body. The bottles look like miniature artworks, tiny sculptures in porcelain and glass. I wonder what age-defying alchemy they contain and think of the half-empty bottle of Clean & Clear I left on the sink at the slobs' place. Great, I'll probably have a breakout now. That's just what I need. I bet Beth never gets spots.

'It's no good,' comes Beth's voice from behind me. 'She's booked up till Thursday. We'll have to think of something else.'

Lucky. Maybe Beth will change her mind? This is never going to work.

Beth pulls out a drawer of a mahogany chest and rifles through lingerie: pink silk, diamanté, intricate lace in dazzling white. There's even a pair of fluffy pink handcuffs still with their tag on. They've obviously *never* been used: an ironic gift from her hen weekend in Puerto Banús? I wonder if they made her wear sparkly L-plates and drink pina coladas through penis-shaped straws. I would have done if I'd been invited. That's probably why I wasn't invited.

'Found it!' she says, pulling out an industrial-strength bra. 'My Wonderbra: wear this and no one will be looking at your hair.'

I can see the logic. I struggle out of the dress and into the bra. It's the first time in my life that I have cleavage. It looks fucking unbelievable. I feel like I could dance onstage for money, rock the Moulin Rouge or the Crazy Horse. My eyeballs pop out of my head and roll around on the floor. I feel sorry for Ambrogio.

'What about Ambrogio?' I ask, staring at my chest in the mirror. 'You don't think he'll notice?'

He'll notice *these*, that's for sure.

'Here's a hairband and a brush.' She hands me the dryer. 'Tie it up like this . . .'

She pulls my hair up into a ponytail, then winds it around into a topknot. She's tugging at my hair, yanking it, pulling it.

'Ow! Get off! I can do it,' I say, moving away. I pull the dryer to my side of the mirror. It would be so easy to strangle her with the cable; I could twist it around her neck and finish her off in two minutes flat. Shall I do it? Beth does her hair up exactly the same. With my hair pulled back like this, you can't see my roots. It really does look just like Beth's.

'Wait,' she says. 'I haven't finished.'

She dabs on a blob of Crème de la Mer and massages it into my face and neck. She applies Diorskin foundation with a minuscule sponge. Next, she finds some finishing powder by Chanel and an enormous brush. Her face is the picture of concentration. It must be a difficult task.

'Put this all over your face and décolletage,' Beth says, handing me the powder. I think that's French for 'tits'. She sweeps on bronze eyeshadow and pulls out a wand of volumizing mascara: Benefit's They're Real! in 'Blackest Black', as though black weren't already black enough. My eyes water as she jabs at my lashes. She takes a Juicy Tube out of her make-up bag and squeezes it on to my parted lips. It smells sickly sweet; it tastes like caramel. Then Beth finds a perfume bottle decorated with a tiny silver bow: Miss Dior Chérie.

'Wear this,' she orders, handing me the perfume. I spritz my neck: patchouli and orange. Damn, now I even smell like Beth.

'And these,' she says, pulling off her watch (a mother-of-pearl Omega *Ladymatic* with tiny diamonds where the numbers should be) and her eye-popping engagement ring. That rock cost more than the GDP of a developing country. I want it. It looks good on me. Fuck me, I want it. 'And these; Ambrogio had them made when I had Ernesto.'

She hands me a pair of diamond earrings: the finishing touch. The earrings, in the form of teardrops, look really expensive. I could buy a flat in Archway if I sold them. I don't want to know what Beth would do to me if I lost one. She watches as I put them on.

I pull the frock back on and we stand, once again, side by side in the mirror. This time, I look like Beth and Beth looks like me. Our transformation is complete. Even I'm confused. I move my hand and wave it a bit, so I can check which one's me. I guess this is happening then; this is actually happening. Oh my God, she's so annoying. At least it's just for a couple of hours . . .

'Your handbag,' she says in an upbeat voice that sounds more strained than chirpy. She gestures to our bags on the bed. Why do I feel like a marionette? Beth is my puppet master. My life plays out before me, like I'm dancing on a stage, my limbs controlled by invisible strings.

'Beth,' I begin, but I know it's futile before I even start. 'I don't think this is a good idea.'

'Alvie,' she snaps, her eyes piercing mine like needles. 'Let me make the decisions, OK? We know who has the better track record . . .'

'What the fuck is that supposed to mean?' I say, although I know precisely. Look at me and then look at you. Look how rich, happy and successful I am and then look how shit your life is in every possible way. BITCH! BITCH! BITCH! My hands are shaking. I could punch her or slap her or throw her out of the window. If I smash that mirror, I could use one of the shards to slit her throat . . . I try to control it. I can usually control it.

'Oh, nothing,' she snaps.

I clench my jaw.

Beth empties her handbag out on to the bed: a Mulberry purse in the softest peach leather, a pair of oversized Gucci sunglasses and another caramel Juicy Tube. I pick up Beth's beautiful Hermès tote and stroke it. I give her my battered Primark wallet, a packet of Marlboros and a cherry ChapStick. She spots my signature purple lipstick in the bottom of my bag. It's the one I was wearing yesterday when Ambrogio picked me up.

'Ooh, can I have some of that?' she asks. 'Please?'

I give her the lipstick. She pulls off the cap and twists up the lipstick, picks a bit of fluff and a crumb off the end.

'You haven't had, like, a cold sore or anything, have you?' she asks, turning the lipstick around to examine it.

'Are you asking if I have facial herpes?'

'I guess . . .'

'Fuck off.'

She sighs and applies the lip colour, looking deep into her eyes as she pouts in the mirror. God damn it, the purple looks better on her.

'We'll need to swap ID. Just in case.'

She gives me her passport, so I give her mine. This all seems a little over the top. Why is she being so thorough?

'And you might need these,' she says without looking up. She tosses me the keys to the villa.

'Keys? I don't think so. I'm not going anywhere. And anyway, you're only –'

'Just in case.'

Once we're finished, she's ready to go.

'Now remember, you're *Beth*,' she whispers in my ear.

'Yes, I get it.' She thinks I'm retarded.

'And remember what I said.' She looks at me now, gripping on to my forearm and fixing me with a fierce stare. 'Tell Ambrogio you're going to sit in the garden and read. My book's on my bedside table. I'm about halfway through . . . Try not to have sex with him.'

'What? He's your husband. I wouldn't . . .'

'And darling, I really, *really* appreciate it.' She squeezes my hand then pulls me into a hug. I pull away.

'OK, fine. You'd do the same for me, so just go.'

'I'll get Ernie ready,' she says, and then pauses. 'I love you, Alvie.'

I stop in my tracks. The last time I heard that was when Ambrogio said it, eight years ago now: *I fucking love you.* I scrunch up my eyes so the tears don't come. Draw a deep breath in through my nose and let it out slowly, through my mouth. Whatever. God, she is *so* manipulative. Just keeping me sweet so I don't jump on her husband or blow her cover. Or blow her husband. I can read you like a book, Elizabeth Caruso. Not the vomit-inducing toilet book you wrote, a good one with an actual plot that's easy to read; hence the simile.

'I really love you,' she says.

I think I hear her voice falter. She smiles, but she's fighting back tears, real tears. I can see them. For a second, I panic – a sick feeling in my stomach – is she leaving me alone with a wife-beating thug? Am I going to end up in A&E? Or, even worse, dead? Where the hell is she going to anyway? But she's promised she'll come home. She hasn't even left yet and I want her to come back.

'The shoes?' I say.

Beth sighs. She hands me her glittering golden stilettos. I give her the Louis Vuitton-lover's heels. I sit on the bed and try them on, feed their delicate straps through the tiny gold buckles, wiggle my toes amongst the jewels. They fit perfectly, look heavenly. I admire my feet, sparkling, dazzling. I have the feet of a Victoria's Secret model. Beth turns and walks out of the room.

'It's not going to work,' I call down the corridor, one last time just to make sure she knows.

I'm not very good at acting. The last time I did it I was the back end of a donkey in a nativity play, and that was unconvincing to say the least. Not that anyone was watching me, Beth really stole the show as the Virgin Mary. Years and years later, when we were eleven or twelve or thirteen, we found the videotape of the play. 'Let's watch it!' Beth said, wiping off dust and sticking it into the machine. One hour and fifteen minutes of close-ups of Beth; the donkey was nowhere to be seen.

Chapter Thirteen

I wait in my room and look out of the window, chewing my nails. Ambrogio's been for a swim in the pool and I can see him sunbathing on the patio: black Speedos, a deep tan and an Action Man six-pack. He might be a wife beater, but he's still fucking hot.

I see Beth, I mean Alvie, I mean Beth, walking out on to the patio with Ernie in his pram. She looks up to the window right at me. I can hear what she's thinking, loud and clear: *Alvie, get your ass down here. Move!* I guess it's time to go. Ambrogio sits up and runs his fingers through wet hair. This is crazy. I don't think I can do it. He's going to notice . . . maybe not right now, but at some point today. There's no way he'll think that I'm his wife. I'll just have to tell him it was all Beth's idea. She can be very persuasive at times.

I want to jump in the shower and scrub off the make-up; I feel like a drag queen. But then I think of Beth, of *I love you, Alvie.* Of the shoes. Fucking hell. I head downstairs. She's going to have to pay me back . . . perhaps a handbag to go with the shoes? And I want that diamond necklace.

The air is still and dry. The sun beams down as though that fiery ball were but a few metres away. All I can smell is fucking frangipani.

'Hello,' I say, way too loudly.

They look up and stare. I freeze, an unnatural grin plastered across my caked-up face. Ambrogio smiles back and then turns to my sister.

'Alvie, that's quite a tan you've got just from yesterday.' Ambrogio laughs. He's looking at Beth. This is going to get confusing.

'I'm kind of cheating.' Beth giggles. 'It's St Tropez. I couldn't stand looking so pale next to her.' She nods at me. I am Beth.

'Well, you both look great,' Ambrogio says, beaming at us both. His eyes rest on my souped-up chest; so this is what it feels like to be Eva Herzigová. I feel like waving, 'Hello, boys,' with a wink and an air kiss, but that might not be appropriate given the context. Damn, I want to take a selfie though. I may never look this good again.

I have no idea what to do or what to say. What would Beth say? I just stand here and grin like an extra in a stupid movie, *Dumb and Dumber* or something.

Beth turns towards me. Wow, she does actually look like me: the lipstick, the dress, the green nail polish. Me on a good day, still a little bit shit.

'Beth,' she says (that's me . . . right?), 'I was just telling Ambrogio that I think I'm going to head out to Taormina, do some sightseeing. I probably won't be back until tonight.'

'Uh-huh.' I nod.

Please don't leave me. Please don't go. Ambrogio's going to bust me as soon as you turn your back.

'I want to check out D. H. Lawrence's villa and that famous old church on the square. It will be nice to explore . . . get lost . . . you know?'

Beth's looking at me.

Ambrogio's looking at me.

'Sure, that sounds . . . that sounds like fun,' I say. Nice and breezy. Was that Beth's voice?

'Is it still OK if I take Ernie out with me? Have some bonding time? I'd love to play Mummy for the afternoon,' she says. Ernesto sticks an arm out of his pram and grasps one of her fingers in a chubby fist.

'Of course,' I say.

I'm starting to sweat. It must be getting hotter; according to Beth's Ladymatic, it's just gone midday.

'So it's just you and me?' Ambrogio says, leaping up from the sunbed. He stands behind me and wraps his arms around my waist. I look down at Ambrogio's strong forearms – bronzed, defined – clasped tightly around me, his large hands trap me in an iron grip. 'Finally! You can spend some quality time with your handsome husband,' he says.

He kisses my skin where I've sprayed the perfume. The hairs on the back of my neck stand on end. My body stiffens. I can't see his face, but I imagine Ambrogio winking at Beth. I stare at my twin, my eyes wide with disbelief. She smiles, but it looks a little forced. Is she jealous? Jealous of me? That would be a first.

'Yes, I should let you two lovebirds spend some time together. Have a great day.'

What is she saying? 'No!' I mouth. He's going to get amorous, I know he is. Babies are cyanide for your sex life; Beth is taking Ernie out and this is his window of opportunity. This man is going to jump on me. Before I know it, Beth has turned on her heel and is walking through the gate. What exactly does she think is going to happen here? What can *possibly* be so important that she'd risk all this? Ambrogio's hand slides over my hips towards my ass, and I start to freak out.

'I'll come with you and help you with Ernie,' I say, freeing myself and running towards her. Well, I say running, it's more of a trot. Six-inch heels are not made for sprinting. Sitting in, maybe. Sitting and sipping a Sex on the Beach. I don't get very far before I give up.

'No, don't worry,' Beth calls over her shoulder. 'We'll be all right, won't we, Ernie?'

'Don't you want a lift into town, Alvina?' Ambrogio calls after her.

'No thanks,' comes her voice. 'It's not that far.' We watch her back disappear around the corner.

'Do you even know where you're going? You'll get lost.' He laughs.

'That's what Google Maps is for!'

He turns to me and whispers under his breath. 'Are you sure Ernie's going to be OK? Your sister is hardly Mary Poppins.'

It's all I can do to stop myself screaming, '*No!*'

'He'll be fine,' I say.

And with that, she's gone. I stare at the space on the patio where Beth used to be. Now I'm really sweating. I imagine fake tan dribbling down my legs in blatant rivulets. I check, but it's not. I cringe and make my way back towards the villa.

'Hey, where are you going?'

'Bathroom,' I say without stopping.

'OK, well, come back when you're done,' he calls. 'I have an idea.'

Seriously, I cannot read this fucking shit. I slam the book down on the table and slouch back in my chair. The novel Beth told me to read is *awful*. Now what am I going to do? I'm avoiding Ambrogio, obviously. The man's a walking ad for Viagra. A serious liability. Ordinarily, I would jump at the chance to jump into bed, but not like this. Not while I'm Beth. It's just not the same.

I look around Beth's library: walls of shelves piled high with books. Half of them are in Italian; they must be Ambrogio's: Machiavelli, Dante, Tomasi di Lampedusa. The other half are in English, but that's not necessarily good news. I discount everything with pink swirly writing down the spine as saccharine chick lit. Romance stories make me queasy; I doubt I'm their target reader. If I'm going to read a novel, I want it twistier than a boa constrictor and with twice the bite. It has to stop my heart and swallow me whole. That ain't *chick lit*, I'm afraid. Or whatever that girly crap Beth wrote is: *Cocksucker and Tampons* or *Hurricane of Love*.

There's a small section of books on a shelf that look promising, but when I pull one down, it turns out to be erotica.

Harlequin bodice-rippers, Mills & Boon. *Heartless, Risky Business, The Outrageous Lady Felsham.* How is this *erotic*? There aren't even any pictures. I don't really get it. What's the matter with her? Beth has the single worst taste in literature of anyone I know. And she calls herself a *writer*? *Puh-lease.* When we were young, we used to read to each other: Enid Blyton, Roald Dahl, Beatrix Potter. That feels like a million years ago now. That feels like a distant dream. I used to want to read Gothic horror. She liked talking animals and midnight feasts.

I'd kill for a copy of any of the classics: *Lolita, Psycho* or *The Silence of the Lambs.* I brush dust off the spines of some old brown books, forgotten in a corner. I love the smell of ancient paper. (It would be so easy to burn this place down.) These haven't been read in a long, long time. Shakespeare: *All's Well That Ends Well, The Merry Wives of Windsor, The Winter's Tale, Macbeth.* I pull out the Scottish play and flip it open at a random page. Lady Macbeth:

> Come, you spirits
> That tend on mortal thoughts, unsex me here,
> And fill me from the crown to the toe top-full
> Of direst cruelty. Make thick my blood.
> Stop up the access and passage to remorse,
> That no compunctious visitings of nature
> Shake my fell purpose, nor keep peace between
> The effect and it! Come to my woman's breasts,
> And take my milk for gall, you murd'ring ministers . . .

Awesome. I like her style. I don't know what she's going on about 'remorse' for though. Lady Macbeth is a brilliant character. She has balls; she's not afraid to go after what she wants, like Hillary Clinton. (I bet she wins the election next year.) That's rare these days. I can't help but admire her.

I close the book and put it back on the shelf. *Othello*'s right next to it: my favourite play. I open the book towards the end:

I have done the state some service, and they know 't.
No more of that. I pray you, in your letters,
When you shall these unlucky deeds relate,
Speak of me as I am. Nothing extenuate,
Nor set down aught in malice. Then must you speak
Of one that loved not wisely, but too well.
Of one not easily jealous, but being wrought,
Perplexed in the extreme.

Oh God, shut up, Othello. Such an idiot. 'Of one that loved not wisely, but too well.' Blah, blah, blah: bullshit. He was just a wife beater, end of story. A moody, jealous thug. He deserved to die . . . Iago's by far the best character in this play. He was the clever one. He was the prankster. Such charisma! He should have had the title role. Why wasn't the play called *Iago*? Shakespeare really missed a trick there.

I toss the book back down on the table. I'm stressed enough already; I don't need a tragedy. I'll order some poetry on Amazon in the morning, something uplifting like Siegfried Sassoon.

'Beth! Beth?'

I hear Ambrogio's voice down the hall.

'Beth?'

Shit. He's getting closer.

'Beth?'

And closer.

I pull out the chair – the legs scrape loudly across the tiles – and hide under the table. I can hear his footsteps just outside. I pull the chair back in towards me, slowly, quietly; it blocks the view. I hold my breath. Ambrogio opens the door.

'Shakespeare?' he says to himself. He must have spotted *Othello* up there. Whoops. I'm going to have to remember to dumb it down if I'm going to pass as Beth . . .

I can see his feet and the bottom of his ankles. The Italian shoes. I can hear him breathing. Can he see me? At last, he turns and leaves the room. I hear his feet pad down the corridor. This is ridiculous. How much longer am I going to have to stay down here? I've already got cramp in my neck. My sister really fucking owes me. Where the hell has she gone?

I crawl out from underneath the table, rubbing my neck. I flop down in the chair. That was close. He almost caught me. And what if he had? We'd be fucking right now over this eighteenth-century walnut table. Oh my God, I just want to shag him. Even his ankles looked sexy. But I can't get Beth's comment out of my head: *That night, in Oxford, he thought you were me.* What if that's true? What if it really was an accident? I don't want to sleep with Ambrogio as *Beth*. I want to seduce him and fuck him as me. I'll win him back. That's the ultimate victory. Perhaps tomorrow, when I'm myself again.

Chapter Fourteen

Where the fuck is she? It's past ten o'clock. Swallows swoop down from the sky and across the garden. They dip into the pool, skim its surface and then fly off again like silent spectres. I wish I had a BB gun or a bazooka. Perhaps a Kalashnikov? I'm sitting on a sunbed on the crazy paving, watching night fall and shivering with rage. I take a swig from the bottle of Absolut I have hidden under the sunbed and pick at the bits of skin at the sides of my thumbnails until they bleed. I'm seething, simmering. Tense as a cobra. Sticky with sweat. It's been *ten hours* – I could fucking kill her. And doesn't that child need to go to bed? It's irresponsible, that's what it is. It's fucking deranged.

A full moon rises. I'm feeling a bit like a lunatic tonight. I wonder if it's true what they say about the moon: 'She comes more nearer earth than she was wont. And makes men mad.' The stars come out slowly, one by one. There are trillions and trillions of them. It's as though they'll never end. I'm sick of waiting. I've managed to avoid Ambrogio so far, but I can't hold him off for ever. Now the French doors creak open and footsteps pat the patio. I've been staring at the gate, so I know it's not Beth. It's either going to be Emilia or him.

'Beth?' comes a man's voice. 'There you are, I was wondering where you'd got to. What are you doing sitting out here in the dark on your own?'

'Oh, hi,' I reply, trying to sound breezy. *I am Elizabeth. I am Beth.* He sits down on a deckchair and scrapes it towards me: the scent of pheromones and Armani Code Black. It's definitely Ambrogio.

'Has your headache gone? Did the aspirin help?' He runs a warm hand along my thigh and lets it rest upon my knee. Oh God, he's even sexy in the dark when I can't see him. I close my eyes and swallow hard.

'Yes, thanks. Much better,' I say. My voice sounds small and far away, as though I were being strangled somewhere off in the distance. Where is she? God damn it. He's going to find out.

'Your sister will be back soon with baby Ernie and I've missed my beautiful wife,' he says, leaning in closer and resting his cheek, rough with stubble, against my cheek. *Ambrogio, Ambrogio, Ambrogio, Ambrogio*: even his name sounds like manna. I breathe in his aftershave. I already want him. Whatever happens, I'm not going to kiss him. Beth could be back any second.

'Yes,' I say, quiet and breathless.

I feel his lips press against my lips and he's kissing me. He pulls my head towards his face and kisses me deeper, his tongue in my mouth and I – I can't help it – I'm kissing him back. He tastes of espresso and sweet tobacco. I run my hand through thick warm hair at the back of his head and I moan – I want him. Fuck, I want him so bad. He's all I've ever wanted. Ever since that last time, my first time, our only time. (Those 300 one-night stands meant nothing.) I feel him hard through the flies of his jeans. My skin prickles, my thighs melt apart. His hand slides up my inner thigh, his fingers brushing my knickers; fuck! It's electric. My pussy is pulsing and wet. He has no idea who I am; I could have him right here, right now. It would be fucking orgasmic. All I want is to tear off his clothes, but then I remember. Not like this, not while I'm Beth. I pull away.

'I can't. I'm sorry,' I say, standing up. 'Alvie will be back any minute. I don't want her to catch us.' Perfect, that's just the kind of thing Beth would say. She's such a boring prude.

He's sits on the sunbed, his head cocked to one side. Even in the dark I can tell he's pissed off.

'Where is your sister anyway?' he says. 'It's late. Shouldn't Ernie be in bed?'

'I'm sure she'll be back soon. I'll give her a call,' I say. Keep it cool. Keep it casual. I am Mount Etna, ready to erupt.

'I have to –' I start. But I don't know how to finish. Have to what? Scream? Yes, I have to scream. She shouldn't be this late. I know it and Ambrogio knows it. What if something has happened to her? I fucking hope not. I can't stand much more of this.

'Sorry, darling,' I say suddenly, remembering who I'm supposed to be. I run my fingers through his hair and massage the top of his skull as though he were a cat. His hair feels silky and soft. 'I'm sure they're on their way back.'

He nods and I kiss him on the forehead, taste salty skin. Good cat.

'I'll see you inside,' he says, standing up. He doesn't smile; he just turns and leaves. I watch his back disappear. Again.

Great, now Ambrogio's in a huff with me . . . but it's not me he's annoyed with, he's annoyed with Beth. I wait for him to go back in the villa and shut the door, then flop down on the sun-lounger, scream silently inside my head.

I've done nothing but call Beth for the past three hours, listening to her voicemail, again and again. 'Hi, you've reached Elizabeth Caruso. I'm sorry, but I can't take your call right now. Please leave a message.' Then hanging up and ringing again, over and over like a crazy stalker. But her phone is off. I have no idea why her phone would be off. She's got a new iPhone, so the battery shouldn't have died. She must have turned it off on purpose. Bitch.

I grab the bottle of vodka and glug some down. It's warm. Alcohol burns the back of my throat. I swallow some more. Then some more. And some more. Until I've finished the rest of the bottle. I slam it back down on the crazy paving: the sound of concrete scraping glass. The garden spins around and around like I'm caught in a vortex being sucked down a drain. That's a better feeling than sober.

If I sit here any longer, I'm going to explode.

A high-pitched whine pierces the silence; a mosquito trills inside my ear, the top note on a violin. I hit myself hard on the side of the head. I'm being eaten alive. Clouds of mosquitoes hover over the pool. Do they have malaria in Sicily? We're practically in Africa. I leap up from the sunbed and head out into abominable darkness. It's proper black out here in Taormina, not like that monochrome orange-grey we get back in London. I miss light pollution. There are so many fucking stars.

I try Beth's number again, but – of course – her phone is still off. What was I thinking? I'm such an idiot. How did I get myself into this mess? I kick off Beth's shoes and leave them under the sunbed; they are already pinching. I was wrong about them fitting. Of course, Beth's feet are smaller than mine. Skinnier. Daintier. I feel like Anastasia or Drizella, the ugly stepsisters in *Cinderella*. I feel like the pumpkin that turns into the coach.

I walk with bare feet through coarse grass. I push past a rose bush; my dress snags on a thorn. I pull it. It rips. I didn't like it anyway. Trees block my path like malevolent corpses, their long, gnarled fingers clawing up at my skin. What is Beth playing at? I should never have agreed to this. I knew it was a mistake from the very start. A spider's web sticks to my face; something fast scurries up my neck. I scream and wriggle and whack at my back. I think it's hiding in my hair.

I reach the road at the bottom of the garden. I don't really know where I'm going from here. I take a deep breath – rotting leaves – and turn back towards the villa. I should have just slept with him when I had the chance. Beth deserves it. That was it, my only shot. I wanted to, hell, I really wanted to, and Ambrogio did too. I could feel it. *He* wanted *me*. We could have been fucking right now: our bodies pressed together on the sunbed, Beth's husband whispering, 'I love you,' in my ear. It would have been great. But no, here I am, being a good girl, doing exactly what she wants, Beth always getting her own fucking way. A marionette. A puppet. Shit! There's a crack. Something hard and sharp, then something slimy squeezes up between my toes. I just trod on a snail. I run across the grass and try to wipe it off. Gross! Gross! Gross!

When I look up, I realize I'm in Salvatore's garden. Security lights flick on and I'm dazzled: a fox caught in headlights. I freeze. I don't breathe. I look around, moving only my eyes, but the lights are automatic; there's nobody here. The driveway is empty; Salvatore has taken his car and gone out. I can move again. I can breathe. I crunch over gravel and follow the driveway towards the house. Slowly. Carefully. His villa isn't as obscene as Beth's, but it's still very impressive. I press the palms of my hands up against a window and look inside. It's Salvatore's entrance hall: modern, arty. Exposed brickwork, palm trees in ceramic vases, paintings on the walls . . .

That's when I see it: a statue of a woman, a woman who looks exactly like me. She's life-size and made out of marble, standing on a plinth in Salvatore's front hall. She has my face, my body, my build. But then I realize: it's not me, it's Beth. Salvatore has made a sculpture of my sister. Either he has a very fertile imagination or he's seen my sister in the nude. The fullness of her breasts, the curve of her hips . . . she's perfect. It's like looking at Beth naked, Beth made of stone. No wonder Ambrogio doesn't like his sculptures. I want to reach my hand through the pane of glass and touch her lips: they'd be cool, smooth. I think she's going to speak, to laugh, to move. It's fucking weird. He must be fucking my sister! I can't believe it. Surely not Beth? That's just not her style. I don't get it.

The growl of an engine makes me jump. Headlights flood the driveway and I freeze. I'm made of stone, just like that statue. Is that Salvatore? Who's in that car? Tyres screech to a halt at the bottom of the driveway. Shit. What do I do? I'm not supposed to be here. I hesitate, then make a run for it, pushing into the bushes between Salvatore's garden and Beth's. Sharp branches dig into my flesh. Thorns scratch my back. Then I hear it — fucking finally — Beth's voice: breathy, husky. She sounds strange; is she *drunk*? Then a man's voice: Salvatore? What are they saying? Shouting? Arguing? They're fighting about something by the car. I catch a few words. Salvatore says, 'Crazy.' Beth says, '. . . my sister.' Someone slams a door. What the hell is going on? 'You promised,' says Beth. I don't hear the rest. They go on fighting for a few minutes longer, until the engine revs and tyres scream. A BMW coming towards me, spitting up gravel, so close now I can smell its hot engine, feel its force as the earth seems to shake. I crouch down low behind some leaves; if I don't move, then he won't see me. But I can see him.

Salvatore opens the door of his car and steps out. He's wearing jeans and a tight black shirt, taut across his broad chest and shoulders: a bear or wild animal, a beast of a man. I hear his footsteps crunch over the gravel. I hold my breath. Please don't see me; don't look up. He pauses, turns and looks towards the road. What is he waiting for? Beth has gone. A key clinks metal and he pushes the door. When I hear it shut, I remember to breathe.

Chapter Fifteen

Beth! She's back. I'm going to find her. I crawl through the bushes and into Beth's garden, yanking leaves from my hair and a twig from my chest. Fabric rips. The dress is ruined. Beth will be cross. That's the least of my worries. I sprint across grass, stumbling under branches, swerving past trees. I pause for a moment to catch my breath and still there's spinning in my head. The lawn undulates and swirls. Why did I drink all that vodka? The whir of wheels and rapid footsteps. I make out a figure pushing a pram: black against black. A glance at Beth's villa tells me everyone's asleep: all of the lights are off.

'Pssst!' I call. 'Over here.'

Beth's silhouette stops, then turns, looks around, but something's not right. She's not walking straight. She's wobbling, tripping, unsteady on her feet. She parks the pram by the sunbeds and then – somehow, slowly – meets me by the edge of the pool in the dark.

'Beth, what the fuck? Where have you been?'

She doesn't answer. Her head hangs low.

'Beth? What's the matter? Are you wasted?' I say.

I'm whispering, but I want to shout, grab her by the shoulders and shake her and shake her. Man, I need a cigarette. Where are my smokes? I'd kill for some nicotine. The stench of chlorine. The sour taste of vodka cloying my throat.

'I'm fine,' she says at last, looking up. Her eyes look funny; she can't really focus. Has she been *crying*? Oh God, not again. Talk about emotionally unbalanced. I haven't cried since 1995.

'Shh. Be quiet. You'll wake Ambrogio.'

My shoulders tense. Something bubbles up inside. How the

hell is it still this hot? It's the middle of the night. The patio's radiating heat. Humid air presses down on my shoulders, presses down on my chest and I'm starting to sweat. A mosquito buzzes: whining, insistent. I feel it bite my neck.

'Fuck Ambrogio. I hate him,' Beth says.

My hands are trembling. My teeth are clenched. How dare she say that about Ambrogio? He is *perfect*. She doesn't deserve him. Beth stole him from me and now I bet she's going to chuck him like an old kebab. She's sleeping with that sculptor; that's what this is about! What a slut! But why take the kid?

Beth starts to sob.

Ernie starts to cry, a high-pitched, desperate, desolate cry, like somebody strangling an unwanted cat. I guess they do sound kind of similar. I still don't know who was crying last night. For fuck's sake, this is the last thing I need: a hysterical child. A hysterical Beth. She's unbelievable, my sister. This swap's the only reason she's invited me here. I knew it was too good to be true.

'Shut up, Beth.' I take a step closer.

'I wish I was a million miles away . . .'

Beth speaks in a strange, slurred voice I've never heard before.

'I wish I was dead,' she says to the floor.

I step a little closer. She nearly falls over. I grip her arms with both my hands and squeeze her tight. She's laughing now, laughing and crying all at the same time.

'Fuck Ambrogio and fuck Salvatore. You can have them both.' I feel her breath hot on my cheek. 'You'd like that, wouldn't you?' she laughs in my face, an awful, hollow, joyless laugh. 'At last, somebody who wants you back.' Her eyes seem to flash in the moonlight.

'You're a bitch!' I say.

'You're crazy!' she says. 'Fuck you too. You think it's easy having a sister like you? I always tried, I really did. The one time I needed you! Everything's fucked!'

She's shouting now, so angry she's shaking. Something's very, *very* wrong – my perfect sister doesn't *swear*.

'What do you mean, *a sister like me*?'

'You're a freak! You're a loser. Everyone knows.'

Volcanic rage bubbles up inside.

'What do you mean, *everyone*?'

'You nearly gave Mum a nervous breakdown. Why do you think she wanted to emigrate?'

'Because she married –'

'Do you think Ambrogio would ever choose you? You're so fucking deluded. You think I stole him? I bet you tricked him. You probably pretended to be me to get laid!'

Where did that come from? *So unfair.* Lashing out because her life isn't *perfect*.

'No, I didn't! What is it, Beth? What's going on?'

'Sure. Whatever.'

'He got me pregnant,' I blurt out. 'Yeah, that's right. I never told you. You stole this life from me, Beth! That should be *my* baby! He should be *my* husband! This should be *my* fucking house!' I gesture to the villa, to the gardens around us, galvanized silver in the light from the full moon.

'I don't believe it! You weren't pregnant. Same old Alvie Knightly bullshit. Same old stupid made-up lies.'

'I was! I was! I lost the baby. You stole Ambrogio! And I . . . and I . . .'

I shake her and shake her and shake her and shake and she's slipping, slipping, slipping through my fingers. She falls – silent – backwards towards the swimming pool. There's a stomach-churning *crack*. Everything happens in super-slow motion, time stretching out like a stringy piece of gum. Her head smashes against the edge. Her body crashes into the water. Splash! I'm soaked through. Cold water shocks my body and I scream. She sinks down, down, down into the water and I stand – frozen – watching her disappear.

Shit. Now what?

I watch Beth's life flash before my eyes: the money, the husband, the baby, the car. *She* stole Ambrogio from me. She stole *everything*, right from the start. And I let her! No wonder my sister called me a loser. Well, I'll show her. Two can play at that game. I'll steal him right back. I'll steal her life. This is everything I deserve. This is poetic justice.

I crouch down low behind a sunbed, pray that nobody will see. I suddenly feel wide awake. Every nerve ending's alive. I'm buzzing, rushing. Out of my mind. I'll wait four minutes by Beth's Ladymatic. If your heart stops for four minutes, you're officially dead. I read that somewhere recently. Or perhaps it was on the Discovery Channel? I watch that sometimes if I can't sleep.

The four minutes pass like decades; every second drags. I look around for security cameras, but there are none; that's strange. I scan the garden: every shadow is Ambrogio. I glance next door, study the villas: will Salvatore run out? But it's safe. It's still. Ernie's stopped crying. The cicadas continue to sing.

I watch the second hand crawl.

One minute. Bubbles rise to the surface. Will Beth come up for air? If she swims up, do I hold her down? Or pull her back up? I hear my heart beat in my chest: BU-BUMP! BU-BUMP! I watch the pool for signs of life. The bubbles stop.

Two minutes. Shit. Where are the bubbles? I've got to get her out. She's fucking drowning in there! BU-BUMP! BU-BUMP! What am I doing? If I don't go now, it'll be too late.

Three minutes. This is it. This is it. Keep calm, Alvina. Just keep calm and carry on. Hold your nerve, you can do it. BU-BUMP! BU-BUMP! BU-BUMP! BU-BUMP! I bite the inside of my lip and watch the water like a hawk. Just a little while longer. I've waited my whole life for this moment.

Three minutes, thirty seconds. Oh my God. What have I done? I run to the pool and jump in. The water's a scalpel cutting into my skin. Fuck, it's cold. I can't breathe. I can't move. My arms feel heavy. My legs are like lead. I try to swim, but my dress weighs me down. BU-BUMP! BU-BUMP! BU-BUMP!

'Help me!' I shout through gulps of water. 'Somebody help! Help! Help!'

I've forgotten how to swim. My limbs flail and flap; I'm going to drown. Water closes over my head. Darkness. Silence. I grab on to the edge, a mouth full of water. I'm panting, shaking, cursing. Fucking hell. Her body has sunk to the bottom of the pool; I'm not strong enough to bring her back up. I dive down again, again and again, grab Beth's hand, but it's slippery, floppy; I can hardly hold on. I'm high on adrenaline, tripping on panic. I can't . . . I can't . . . I can't pull her up. At last, the lights in the villa flick on and a figure runs out: Ambrogio.

'Help!'

The baby starts screaming. Again.

'What happened?'

'She's drowning . . .'

Ambrogio dive-bombs into the water and swims right down to the bottom of the pool. I grip on to the edge like I'll never let go.

He comes up with a splash and with Beth in his arms.

'Help me,' he says.

I push myself up and out of the water. The world swirls; I'm going to be sick. I grab Beth's arm with shaking hands. It's a dead weight. I can't hold on. Ambrogio lifts her body higher; it rolls on to the patio, heavy and limp. Her head lolls horribly from side to side. Has she broken her neck?

'Breathe,' I cry, shaking Beth's shoulders, pounding her chest. 'Breathe, breathe, please, breathe!' She's a rag doll with no bones. I lean over her on the crazy paving, put my mouth to her mouth – something I learnt in first aid years ago: you blow, you blow, you blow and you blow. Ambrogio jumps out of the pool.

I'm waiting for the cough, for the splutter of water. But nothing comes. I roll her over and whack at her back. 'Breathe, please. Please, breathe!'

'Let me try,' Ambrogio says, pushing me away. He sits her up and leans her forwards, whacks at her back. Whack! Whack! Blood trickles down from a wound on her head at the top on the right, her cheek is red, her neck is red. Blood curls across her chest and down her shoulders. Her head flops down to one side.

'Alvie, Alvie, can you hear me?' he shouts, 'Breathe, Alvie! Fucking breathe!'

He whacks and whacks and whacks at her back. Beth's eyes are blank and wide as a mannequin's. They stare at nothing, dumb and dull. Unblinking. Unseeing. Unknowing. Dead. Bile rises in my throat and I retch, throw up. I vomit all over my feet, all over the ground, again and again until there's nothing left. I shouldn't have drunk all that vodka.

'Fuck, Beth,' Ambrogio says into the darkness. He turns towards me. 'This wasn't the plan.'

The earth stops spinning on its axis. The planets stop orbiting the sun.

'The *plan*?' I say. What is he on about?

'You weren't supposed to kill her *here*. *You* weren't supposed to do it at all.'

I open my mouth but no words come out.

'Why couldn't you just stick to the plan?'

We stand side by side by my sister's body; stunned silence. There was *a plan*? What the fuck does that mean? The baby has finally stopped screaming; he's cried himself to sleep, poor thing. It's quiet. Even the cicadas seem to cease their incessant serenade. Something dark and liquid spreads from underneath my sister's head, forms a pool on the crazy paving. I lie down next to her and try to cry. I'm watching a low-budget horror, a gory B-movie or one of the *Scream*s. This isn't real life. This is a nightmare, a terrible dream. A plan? A *plan*? What kind of *plan*?

Were Beth and Ambrogio plotting to kill me? Surely not Beth? I don't understand. Am I paranoid? Or completely wasted? I must be hallucinating.

I reach for Beth's hand. It's wet, ice-cold. Her silhouette curves against the light from the villa. Her head. Her hips. Her calves. I expect her to get up and walk away. I expect her to call my name or say something annoying. But she's as still as that statue in Salvatore's villa. Cold and still.

Eventually, it's Ambrogio who calls me.

'Beth, come on. Let's go inside. There's nothing we can do.'

Beth, Beth, Beth. He keeps calling me Beth. He finds my hand at the end of my arm at the side of my body. His fingers are wet from the pool. I snatch my hand away, afraid. I don't want to go anywhere with this man. He wants me dead. He wants to kill Alvie! But he reaches back down and grabs on to my hand with an iron grip that I can't resist. He yanks me back up to standing. I look into his eyes. A strong jaw. A handsome face. He's as beautiful as Channing Tatum. But I won't be deceived; I know I can't trust him. What the hell was this plan?

Ambrogio pushes the pram with one hand and holds my shoulder with the other. My handbag is hanging on the handle of the pram. I pick up Beth's shoes from under the lounger. I'm acting on auto, my mind racing. I feel like I've survived a tsunami: destruction around me, disorientation, persistent ringing in my ears. I stagger forwards towards the villa, one step at a time: a lost child stumbling home. We don't speak as he leads me to his bedroom, the bedroom he used to share with Beth. I stand in the middle of the room and look around. Beth and I got changed here only hours ago. It feels like a different room, another life.

Ambrogio finds two towels in the en-suite bathroom; he offers one to me. I don't move. He drapes it over my hunched-up shoulders, then dries himself. He takes off his shirt, his trousers, his boxer shorts, and rubs himself all over with the towel. He is completely naked. His penis looks smaller than I remember, but that was a long time ago and I guess it isn't erect now . . . I watch him dry his muscular body, his back, his thighs, the tan lines on his bum. I am completely numb. I look down at my hands and play with Beth's ring, spinning it around and around on my finger. Her engagement ring looks good on me.

He thinks I'm Beth. He thinks I'm dead.

Ambrogio rolls his wet, bloody clothes into a ball and throws them in the bin. He changes quickly into a brand-new set: a white shirt, cream chinos, blue-and-white striped socks. How does he do that? It took him two minutes and he looks as polished as a catalogue model, too cool to be true. He walks over towards me.

'Beth,' he says, taking my hand. It's as limp as an eel. I let him hold it. 'Beth, please, get dressed. Come on. You'll catch a cold.'

A cold is the last thing I care about. 'Don't we need to call an ambulance?' I say.

'I'm afraid it's far too late for that.'

I look up at Ambrogio, at the worry written all over his face. He has no idea. He doesn't have a clue who I am. I lean my cheek against his chest and try not to cry; mascara streaks across his shirt. He'll have to get changed again.

'We need an ambulance to take the body away.'

'Shh, Beth,' he says, stroking my hair. 'Let's get you dry.'

He takes my hand and leads me to the bathroom on shaking legs. I feel as though I were a hundred years old. I lean on the sink and Ambrogio unzips the back of my dress.

'No,' I say. He can't see me naked. 'Let me do it . . . on my own.'

I take the towel, push him out of the en suite and close the door. I lock it. I stand with my back pressed up against the door and take a deep breath. Holy fuck. What just happened? I peel off wet clothes: Beth's dress, the Wonderbra, my soaking knickers, and throw them on the floor in a heap. There's blood on my hands, my arms, my face. I look like a fucking axe murderer. I look like an extra from *Saw*. I run the shower over my feet, washing off vomit, over my hands, washing off blood caked under my fingernails, the red streaked across my forearms, my neck, my cheeks.

'I'll put Ernie to bed,' Ambrogio calls through the door.

'OK,' I say. Baby Ernie . . . oh my God, *now I'm his mum*.

I turn off the tap and step out of the shower. I still don't feel clean, but I've been under the water for what seems like an hour. I pull on Beth's dressing gown – warm and fluffy – and a pair of Beth's slippers, the complimentary kind from some fancy hotel. I stand in front of my reflection in the mirror and study my face. Do I really look like Beth? I'm squinting, swaying, light-headed from the shower. I steady myself on the sink. I can't see any resemblance.

I still have mascara streaked down my cheeks like fake, black clown tears. Beth's cleansing cream is on the side; I wipe off the make-up over my eyelids and under my eyes, scrubbing and scrubbing until my skin's red raw and all of the blackness has gone.

Chapter Sixteen

'It was an accident. She slipped,' I say.

'It's OK, Beth, you don't have to explain.'

Ambrogio sits on the edge of the bed, his head in his hands. He looks up when I enter the room. I creep into the bedroom slowly, slowly, millimetre by millimetre, inch by inch, as though approaching a sleeping tiger, as though avoiding a roadside bomb. Ambrogio's face looks pale and drawn; it's almost like he has suddenly aged. There are wrinkles on his forehead I hadn't noticed before. Is that a grey hair on his head?

'It was an accident,' I repeat, sinking down next to him. If I keep on saying it, perhaps I'll believe it?

'What do you mean? Of course it wasn't an accident. We were going to kill her. Just not in our own backyard. *Merda.*'

They were going to kill me. He can't mean it, surely? Beth would never agree to something like that. And anyway, why would they want me dead? That's ridiculous. I've done nothing wrong. I know my sister said she hated me, but that was in the heat of the moment. She didn't mean it. Not Beth.

'I didn't mean to,' I say at last. My voice is phoney and weak.

'What are you saying? It's just a coincidence?'

'We were arguing by the pool and she fell.'

Ambrogio looks up in disbelief. He studies my face with searching eyes. He thinks I'm lying.

'It was. It was an accident,' I say. 'Synchronicity? Serendipity?'

Ambrogio sighs.

'OK. Fine. It was an accident. But it might not look that way to the authorities. If we call the ambulance, the police will get involved. A British tourist dying out here? Their press would be all over us: a media circus. You could get done for manslaughter. I can't have a scandal. I can't be investigated by the fucking police.'

He speaks quickly, urgently; there's a desperate tone to his voice like an infant whining. *He* can't be investigated? What's *his* problem? Keep your mouth shut, Alvina; if you were Beth, you'd know.

'It's not a risk I'm willing to take. Not *now*, in the middle of this deal . . .' His voice is raised. He leaps up from the bed and punches the door – BANG! The wood cracks. He stands with his back to me, shoulders heaving. What the fuck is he talking about? Is he angry with *me*? Will he punch *me* too? I shrink back against the headboard and curl into a ball, brace myself for the hit.

Nothing.

Ambrogio turns; his face is hard. He paces the room, pacing, pacing, an angry gorilla in a cage at the zoo.

'So, what do we do?' I say at last, when I see he isn't going to jump me. 'We can't just leave her lying there.'

'Let me think,' Ambrogio snaps.

He paces some more.

All he cares about is getting busted. He doesn't give a shit about Alvie. About me!

'Listen,' he says, coming towards me. 'Who knew Alvie was coming to Sicily? You, me and British Airways. Anyone else?' I shake my head. 'Any of her friends?'

'She didn't have any friends.'

'No friends? Are you sure?'

I nod.

'Everyone has friends, Beth. What about at work?'

'I doubt it. Honestly. I think she just got fired.'

I look down at my hands, play with Beth's ring. Diamond and onyx, black and white.

Ambrogio sighs. 'It's all happened too quickly. The plan was to wait. The plan was to fucking stay in control.'

'I'm sorry,' I say, because I feel like I should. 'I'm sorry about everything.'

Ambrogio sits down on the end of the bed.

'If anyone checked her flights, it would show that she landed in Catania. Who knows she arrived here at this villa?'

'You, me, Emilia, Salvatore,' I say. I think of Ernesto and the guard at the amphitheatre, but I don't know his name. Beth knew his name, but now I can't ask her.

'Is that it?'

I hesitate. 'Yeah . . . yeah, that's everyone.'

'OK, now listen to me, this is what we're going to do. Under ordinary circumstances, of course we'd call an ambulance. But given the nature of my business, *our* business, we can't have the authorities snooping around.'

He's lost his cool. An angry vein has appeared on his forehead, purple, throbbing, jagged.

'Now, this bit's important,' he says, moving towards me up the bed and leaning in close. He takes hold of my hand and squeezes it hard. There's a fleck of white spit on his lower lip. He lowers his voice. 'We tell Emilia and Salvo that Alvie went home. It's tragic about your sister. I'm very sad. But you have to understand: we're going to have to deal with her body ourselves.'

I leap up from the bed.

'*Deal with her body?*' I repeat. 'She's only just died and you're talking about *what?*'

'Beth, listen to me: we only have a few hours left before it gets light. Emilia will come. The neighbours, the postman . . . We can't just leave her bleeding all over the fucking patio. Even if it was an accident –'

'What do you mean, *if?*'

'Even though it was an accident . . . the police will be all over us. There's too much at stake.'

133

Why, what's at stake?

'They could even suspect you of murder.'

There's that 'M' word. I don't like it. I hold his gaze. I think he's trying to protect me.

'So what're you going to do? Bury her in the garden?' I say at last.

'And then the gardener finds a woman buried under my lawn? Are you out of your mind?'

I don't think I meant it, but I have no idea. I've never done this before. I don't know the protocol.

'What, then?' I say.

Ambrogio lowers his voice. 'I'll call my guys. They owe me a favour; they'll sort us out. But it has to be now. Right now. Tonight.'

'Where will they take her? What about a funeral?'

'Shit, Beth, you're not exactly a devout fucking Catholic. Don't go all religious on me now and pretend you care about a church fucking burial. That was only part of the plan to give us time to get away. Don't pretend you're worried about her soul. *Cristo! Dio!*'

He punches some buttons into his phone then shouts into the mouthpiece in angry Italian. It's supposed to be a beautiful language, mellifluous, romantic, but tonight it echoes like gunfire. I glance at the clock on the bedside table. The numbers are jumping, flashing red on black. I can only just read it: 1.13 a.m. After a while, he hangs up the phone. His voice is softer now, gentle.

'Beth, do you want to go outside and say goodbye?'

Oh shit. I *do not* want to see her. I suddenly feel sick. I can still taste the vomit at the back of my throat. 'Where will they take her?' I ask again.

'That's not our problem. We don't need to know. In Sicily a lot of people *disappear*. Right now, I need to make another phone call.' He gestures to the door.

Would Beth be cool with this? Disposing of my body in the

middle of the night? Calling some guys up to make me 'disappear'? I shake my head in disbelief. Beth would definitely not be cool with this; there's no way in hell, it's fucking insane. But me? You know what? I don't want the police showing up here either. That's one thing that's going my way . . .

Chapter Seventeen

I look at the hand as though it were a stranger's; I don't seem to recognize it. I can't remember who it belongs to. I don't know the back of my own fucking hand. It's shaking, shaking so hard I can't steady it. I try to reach the handle and open the door that leads out to the patio, leads out to my sister, but I can't quite grasp it. My fingers tremble, my palm slips away and I can't – can't even open the fucking door.

Ambrogio's on the phone again, speaking to his 'friends'. Who are these guys who owe him a favour? Who dispose of dead bodies in the middle of the night? I don't care as long as they get rid of her. I never want to see her again. I don't know how long I stand here trembling with my hands flap-flap-flapping like a bird's broken wings, but – eventually – the handle snaps down and I step through the door.

It's dark. It's quiet. I expect to see a policeman leap out from the shadows: 'You're under arrest!' – or hear Salvo sprinting up the driveway: '*Ma che cazzo hai fatto?*' But it's silent; there's no one. The cold night air is making me shiver. The temperature seems to have dropped by twenty degrees. Beyond the pool, the garden stretches out into nothing, nothing but blackness. The light from the villa illuminates the pool and the long, monstrous figure of my sister's corpse, lying along the edge of the water.

The stars look down at me, judging me, blaming me, like trillions of tiny eyeballs, the eyes of God. The moon is beginning to set behind Etna. Soon, the sun will rise and reveal the bloodshed. The postman will come. Salvatore. Emilia. I need to hurry up.

I concentrate on moving my legs. And I'm walking, one silent foot after the other, soft slippers padding. Dreamlike, I'm floating, walking on air. I look down to steady myself, focus on the ground to stop myself drifting up, up and away. I'm weightless, lunar, walking on the moon. I stop a few inches from my sister's head. A pool of blood spreads out from her skull: a slick black lake. And now that I'm here, I don't know what to do. I just stare. Once again, I am staring at Elizabeth, silent and speechless. Elizabeth's body. Elizabeth's face. Elizabeth's hair. A shiver runs down my spine. She's dead and I killed her. So effortless. So quick. It's like nothing has happened. The stars are still shining. I'm in the same garden. The volcano's still there. It doesn't seem real.

I can't believe it.

I need more proof.

I reach my hand towards the blood, extend a finger, dip it in. The blood feels warm in the cool night air. It feels slippery, thick and wet. I study my fingertip: shiny, red-black. It's something instinctive, primitive, primal. I have to do it. To check that it's real. I lick my finger: warm, wet iron. Unmistakable. Blood.

Ambrogio stands as I burst into the room. He's finished on the phone. There's a strange look on his face I can't read. He raises a hand towards my head – oh fuck! – I wince and turn away – but he wipes a strand of hair from my cheek.

'What's the matter? You flinched.'

'Nothing,' I say. I'm hyper-vigilant, jumpy as a cat.

'You did, you flinched. *Amore*, come here. You know I'd never hit you! What is this?' he says. He pulls me in close and squeezes me tight. I think I believe him. Just about. Perhaps he's not a wife beater after all? He wouldn't hit Beth, but would he hit Alvie? The scary thing is, I don't know.

'Did you say goodbye?' he asks, at last.

'Uh-huh.' I nod.

'*Bene.*'

He puts his arm around my waist and leads me over to the bed. 'Nino will be here in fifteen minutes. I'm going to start cleaning up. I think you should sleep, try to get some rest.'

'OK,' I say. Who is Nino? I down a glass of water and the nausea passes.

'I'm so sorry, Beth,' he says again, planting a kiss on to my forehead. 'It sounds awful, but . . . I'm just so glad it wasn't you.'

My stomach sinks; the earth falls away from beneath my feet. What the *fuck*?

I give him a look like I want him to die. I must look cross because he says straight away, 'I'm sorry, that was out of order. It's just – I love you so much.' He tries to kiss me, but I turn my head. I can still taste vomit. He hugs me instead. 'The whole point of this is to keep you safe, don't forget that. This is for you! You, me and Ernie. When I saw her lying there – the spitting image of you – I just . . . We're doing the right thing. For our family.'

'Thank you,' I say, because I can't think of anything else. My brain isn't working; I've forgotten how to talk.

I pull back the sheets and sit down on the bed. Beth's bed. My bed. I'm about to lie down when Ambrogio says, 'Don't you want to wear your nightie?'

I don't know where Beth kept her pyjamas. I look up at him, lost. I have no idea. I can't let him see that I'm struggling here. I'm aware of my heart: BU-BUMP, BU-BUMP. All the muscles in my shoulders tense. Eventually, after what feels like hours, he turns to the mahogany chest and pulls out the second drawer down. Oh. So that's where. He hands me a tiny silk nightdress by Giorgio Armani. It's lighter than air. I hold it and look at it, at the little pink roses embroidered along the hem, at the beautiful lace, the delicate straps. It smells of Beth: Miss Dior Chérie. I lie down on the bed and close my eyes.

There's a rap on the door and Ambrogio jumps.

'Ah, Nino,' he says.

DAY FOUR:
Lust

My lady-bits clench like my grandmother's
gums around a Turkish delight.
@AlvinaKnightly69

Chapter Eighteen

It was Beth's fault my heart got broken.

It was the last night of Freshers' Week and our nineteenth birthday. It was lust at first sight.

Five pints of snakebite, three drinking games and one bottle of Malibu into an evening in the Corpus Christi College bar and I was seeing double. All I'd eaten during the day was a packet of dry roasted peanuts. I was smoking my way through a twenty-pack of menthols that I'd found in the loo, wearing the dress my sister gave me: body-con fuchsia, so tight I couldn't breathe. Beth was wearing one just like it. I was concentrating hard on not falling off my stool when Beth stopped talking and looked at the door. A man walked in.

'Who's *that*?' I asked.

At first he was a blur, but as he approached, a Mediterranean demigod emerged, as if through dry ice at the back of the stage at a Backstreet Boys concert. He was Hollywood handsome, blue jeans, white shirt – I remember the top two buttons were open – tuxedo jacket. Dark hair fell in waves to his shoulders. His teeth were shiny and Colgate-white. What was *he* doing in Oxford? All the other guys looked like Gollum from *The Lord of the Rings*. And why was he so tanned? Beth reached out her hand and pulled him in for a hug. I watched in disbelief. My sister *knew* him?

'Alvie, this is Ambrogio. Ambrogio, this is my twin sister, Alvina,' Beth said.

'Twin sister? No way; that's crazy. You're identical, right?'

We looked at each other and shrugged.

'Beth never mentioned she had a twin,' Ambrogio said.

Beth made a face. She hadn't told me about *Ambrogio* either: not something I'd forget.

'Unbelievable!' he said. 'You two look exactly the same . . .' I shook the hand he offered me. His skin was warm and smooth. 'Pleased to meet you. Which college are you at?'

He spoke with an accent I couldn't understand. I thought he might be Spanish.

'Oh, she doesn't go here,' Beth said. 'She's just visiting for the weekend.'

I forced a smile and nodded. 'That's right.'

'Oh. You're at another university? What are you reading?'

'Erm, no, I'm not,' I said to the floor. 'I work at Yo! Sushi.' I couldn't go to college because I didn't get any qualifications. I didn't get any qualifications because I got expelled. It wasn't going well. And what an odd question. I'd recently finished reading *The Satanic Verses*, but he didn't need to know that. 'What are *you* reading?'

'I'm doing a master's in history of art.'

We left the bar. Ambrogio and Beth linked arms as they walked and I trailed a few feet behind, listening to Beth flirting and giggling and staring at Ambrogio's Diet Coke-ad bum. We walked through wind and sideways rain to a subterranean sweatbox called the Orange Dolphin or Turquoise Goldfish or Golden Aardvark or something. It smelled of BO. The ceilings dripped. There was a little puddle of vomit in the middle of the dance floor. I think the DJ must have been deaf/dead/shitfaced because he played 'The Power of Love' by Celine Dion thirteen times in a row. Nobody else seemed to notice. In Oxford, this was what people called a nightclub.

I drank some WKD and some shots of tequila. The music was so loud I couldn't hear what anyone was saying. Neither could anyone else. We stood in a circle sipping luminous alco-pops through straws. Beth went to the bar to buy another round of Bacardi Breezers and I smiled at Ambrogio. He smiled back. We swayed out of time to the music for a bit, then he put his arms around my waist and pulled me towards him. It was clear from the start that Beth fancied the pants off him. Well, guess what? So did I. And she'd known the guy for less than a week. So fuck it. He was a free man and all mine for the taking. I held him tight.

'You're beautiful,' he whispered, and I melted.

No one had ever said that to me before. They always said it to Beth. His breath felt hot against my ear. His aftershave was dreamy. I rested my cheek on Ambrogio's chest and we danced. It was probably only for twenty seconds, but it felt like for ever. Time does funny things like that. 'The Power of Love' blasted around us. The dance floor seemed to disappear. All too soon they turned the lights on and suddenly the music stopped. Beth said it was time to go home. A group of us staggered down the street and into some kind of fast-food establishment. I ordered cheesy chips with beans and Ambrogio ordered a burger.

'I don't want anything,' said Beth. 'I'm going back to halls. Are you coming?'

I looked at my cheesy chips and then looked at Ambrogio. 'I'll see you up there in a bit.'

Beth scowled. Ambrogio swayed; I think he might have been drunk. Drunker than me, or I wouldn't have noticed. We sat down at a table for two to eat our food. I reached for the ketchup.

'*Ciao*,' said Ambrogio with a wave. 'See you later.'

Beth rolled her eyes and stormed off.

I don't remember eating a thing, I was staring at Ambrogio, his Disney-prince eyes, his kiss-me lips. He didn't look real. He looked like an advert for some kind of supplements that make you younger and better-looking. He looked like an extra from *Zoolander*.

'Let's go,' he said, standing up and taking my hand. I couldn't believe what was happening to me. Why had he picked me, not Beth?

Next thing I knew, I was in Ambrogio's room, listening to 'Umbrella' by Rihanna and thinking it was fate, like in *Romeo and Juliet*. It was obvious we were meant to be together. It was clear this was our destiny. I just hoped that we weren't star-crossed lovers like in that play. That had ended badly.

There was a lava lamp on Ambrogio's desk by his unmade single bed. Something red bubbled and blobbed in a column of silver and glass. I watched it morph like magma or lava . . . (Oh, *lava* lamp; I guess that's the point) boiling, simmering, hot. I was hypnotized. Mesmerized. When I looked up again, Ambrogio was taking off his top.

'I know I've just met you,' he said to his navel as he struggled to unbutton the buttons on his shirt. 'But I really fucking love you.' He gave up on the buttons and pulled off his shirt up over his head. He unzipped his flies and pulled down his pants. I stared in shock. I don't know why. I guess I'd never seen a man naked before. Of course, I'd seen pictures and photographs. I knew what to expect. What they looked like. But not in real life. Not close up. Not like this. It was crazy. Electric. I suddenly felt wide awake. I sobered up. Kind of.

'What did you say?'

'I love you,' he said, reaching for the skirt of my dress and pulling it up.

His words hit like bullets and lodged in my chest. No one had ever said that before. 'You *love* me? Really? Are you sure?'

'I swear to God. Will you marry me?' he asked. He yanked off the boxers that were caught on his foot and tripped over his feet and on to the bed.

'Stop it,' I said, turning away. He was slurring his words. 'You're drunk, you don't mean it.' He was taking the piss.

'Yes, I do. I really do.' He reached for my bra and tried to undo it, but the clasp was too difficult so he gave up.

'You prefer my sister, just admit it. Guys never like me. They think I'm *weird*; the *weird sister*. The loser. The freak.' I got up off the bed and looked around for my shoes. There was only one, like Cinderella. He stood up too and grabbed my waist, pulled me towards him and held me tight. I could smell the Jägermeister on his breath. He was so close I could taste him.

'I like *weird*.'

I looked into his eyes and we kissed.

It all goes a bit hazy after that, but in the morning, when I woke up, I could tell I wasn't a virgin any more because there was blood on the sheets and Beth seemed pissed off.

I left Oxford in a hurry. I had a shift at twelve at Yo! Sushi in London and couldn't afford to be late. Again. I was already on my final warning. And I needed the money. So I wrote my number on the back of an envelope and stuck it next to him on the pillow: '07755 878 4557: ALVIE. CALL ME X'. He'd looked so peaceful I hadn't wanted to wake him. I just snuck out quietly and pulled the door to. I tiptoed down the corridor, beaming, a wide smile across my face. I don't know why they call it 'the walk of shame'. If anyone had spotted me early that morning, sneaking out of his room at 8 a.m., they would have thought I was a 'dirty stop-out', or judged me for my messy attire. No shoes on (because I had lost one, and surely no shoes are better than one?), wrinkled dress and tangled hair, make-up smeared across my face, love bites, cum stains, morning breath. But I didn't feel dirty, or shameful, or embarrassed. I'd met the man I wanted to marry. I felt elated, ecstatic, fucking euphoric. Happy for the first time in my life. You know what I felt? I felt whole.

Later that week when he hadn't called me, I phoned my twin just to check what was up. Beth said Ambrogio had asked her out and that they were a couple. An item. Officially together. She said she was head-over-heels in love. She'd forgiven *him* for his one-night stand. She was practically planning the wedding.

Thursday, 27 August 2015, 10 a.m.
Taormina, Sicily

If recreational drugs were tools, then alcohol would be a sledgehammer – no, scrap that, a steam hammer (Newton's second law: more force). I don't recall drinking, but that BANG! BANG! BANG! inside my head is a sure-fire sign of a hangover. The vodka fairy must have visited and kicked my ass; I don't remember much of last night. I don't know where I am. A soft cotton bathrobe feels warm against my skin; there's a pink silk pillow I don't recognize. I yawn, stretch, rub my eyes with my fists. I slept well (passed out, more likely; stop doing that, Alvina, it's not good for your liver). My retinas shrink and writhe in their eye sockets. My eyes open to blinding light; I shut them again. Where the hell am I? This isn't my bedroom. This isn't my bed.

I sit bolt upright and scan the room: this is Beth's bedroom. This is Beth's bed. I look across the mattress, but there's nobody there. I feel the sheets, but they're cold. Where's Ambrogio? Doesn't he sleep here? Did I sleep with my sister's husband? (Again.) I shake my head; I'd remember *that*. The room looks exactly the same as it did yesterday, when Beth and I were getting changed. There's a nightie on the pillow with little pink roses embroidered on the hem.

Beth!

Realization seeps in like blood trickling through wet hair on to crazy paving. Beth. I killed her. Did I push her, or did she slip? I can't remember. Am I a murderer? Holy shit, what have I done? I leap out of bed and run to the window, look out through

148

the slats in the blind. The garden at the front of the villa is empty. I can't see the pool from in here.

Where is she? What am I going to do? And where the fuck is Ambrogio? Wasn't there something about a plan? Keep calm, Alvina, I say to myself. Keep calm and carry on. Play it cool. Act normal. You can do this. You're a rock star. Just think: what would Beyoncé do? I breathe in deep.

OH MY GOD: I did it!!!!

Euphoria bubbles up inside.

I feel so high I could fly to the sky and I'm soaring up now, floating, drifting, looking down on her body, looking down on the Earth. I could dance, I could sing, I could fucking explode. I'm free! At last! I want to laugh. I want to cry tears of joy. That rush. That high. An involuntary smile spreads across my face; I cover my mouth with my hands.

Elizabeth is dead! Long live Elizabeth!

That was Alvie lying there with blood in her hair, a wet, black dress with one strap ripped and skin shining white in the dying moonlight. She looked serene. She looked beautiful. Alvina. No one will miss her. There's no husband concerned about her whereabouts. No baby crying to be held. No friends back in England expecting her to write, to call, begging her to come home. It's better this way. It's good that Alvina has died.

I always tried, I really did. What the hell was my sister on about? Her voice is still in my head.

No, I'm here and I'm staying. I'm up for the fight. I've got nothing to lose and everything to play for. Ambrogio's the one who should be frightened. Well, guess what, mister? Now *I* have the plan. I plan to live my sister's life and enjoy every single fucking second. Just as long as he thinks I'm Beth, I am golden. Everything's rosy. Nothing to fear. But the very second he suspects, it's goodbye, dream boy. *Arrivederci*, Ambrogio. If I've killed once, then I can kill twice. He's the one who should be freaking out. I'm not going to be afraid. (Wow, I'm even more badass than I thought. I'm Lisbeth Salander. Joan of Arc.)

My handbag sits on a chair by the dressing table. Beth's handbag. My handbag. Ambrogio brought it in last night. Now I remember – it was on the pram. I pick it up and look inside: my Primark wallet, my cherry ChapStick and something else, loose in the bottom of the bag . . . Beth's diamond necklace! What's that doing there? Why did she take that out for a walk? I could stand here for ever trying to figure it out, but I really need to pee.

I stand at the sink and study myself in the mirror.

'Hello, Elizabeth,' I say.

I turn on the shower and step inside. I still feel dirty from last night. I scrub at my body with a loofah, use a whole bottle of Molton Brown. I might as well shave my legs and do my bikini line while I'm in here. Beth was naked from the eyebrows down. I find Beth's razor on a little shelf and lather on some shaving foam. I step out of the shower in a cloud of hot steam and wrap myself up in a towel.

My mouth feels rancid. Two electric toothbrushes are charging on a shelf; I pick one at random. I've never wanted to brush my teeth so much in my life. The high-pitched buzz makes me jump, like a chainsaw in a garden, like a drill to the brain. I look in the mirror and scrub at my teeth. I am Elizabeth. I am Beth, I tell myself over and over.

Then I stop. Shit, if I am Beth, then I'm right-handed. I switch hands. Try again. Brushing your teeth with the wrong hand is next to impossible. I feel as clumsy as a toddler, but I keep on going. I need to practise. I've got to get this right. Then a figure in the mirror makes me jump; it's Ambrogio.

'Good morning, darling,' he says behind me.

Ambrogio's voice is croaky, throaty. I stop the whirring, a mouth full of paste.

'How are you feeling?' he asks.

I spit the toothpaste into the bowl and turn on the tap. I study his face: bags under his eyes, stubble on his chin. He doesn't look like he's slept at all.

'Emilia's with Ernesto; they've had some breakfast and they're playing in the nursery. She wants to take him to the park, if that's OK with you.'

What about the body? What about my fucking sister?

'That's fine,' I say. I want to see Ernie . . . to kiss him, to hold him. Baby Ernie! He's all mine!

'Listen, Beth,' he says. 'Um . . . well . . .'

I stoop down to the tap and rinse my mouth with lukewarm water, spit it out in the sink.

'There's a problem.'

'A problem?'

'Yes.'

I find a towel and wipe my mouth. 'Your mother,' he says.

'My mother's in Australia.'

'I know, *amore*, but she's a loose end. At some point, she's going to wonder what's happened to your sister.' He pauses and frowns at me in the mirror. 'The last place Alvie will appear on any records is at Catania Airport, visiting you.'

Shit. He's right. My mother's a loose fucking end.

'So what are we going to do? Where's the body?' I say. I dry my face with a towel.

'The body's with my guys, right here in Taormina.'

'And?'

'I think it's best if we act as if nothing has happened. Just like before she arrived,' he says.

'And my mother?'

'You need to call her and tell her that Alvie has died. Invite her to the funeral.'

What the fuck?

'The funeral? What funeral? I thought we couldn't have one?'

'Say the funeral's *today*. She's on the other side of the world;

she's not going to come. But if she does, it's OK. Nino has the body over at his place, just in case. This is Sicily; we can organize a funeral off the record. It's a pain in the ass, but we can do it. It happens all the time.'

I run water into the sink and rinse away the toothpaste. It swirls around and around in the bowl and spirals down, down, down into the drain: glugging, belching, disappearing. He's probably right. My mother would come if it were Beth who'd died, but that's one hell of a long way to travel to watch some strangers fill a hole in the ground with somebody you didn't like. I dig my nails into the plastic grip on the handle of the toothbrush.

'I'll call her,' I say. I've got no choice. But if she comes, I'm screwed. She's the only one who could ever tell us apart. 'I'll call her today . . . but I want to see it.'

'Want to see what?' Ambrogio puts his hands on my shoulders, massages my neck. It hurts. I'm tense.

'Where they put her. Where they bury her.' I want to make sure she goes in the ground.

'You don't want to see it; it won't be nice.'

'I *need* to see it.' I need to know that she's not coming back.

We make eye contact in the mirror; he is standing just behind me.

'*I'm coming,*' I say.

He sighs, shakes his head. 'OK. You can come. I'll call Nino and tell him.' He wraps his arms around my waist and holds me close. 'It's going to be all right, Beth.' He is warm, he feels good, and suddenly I believe him. Everything's going to be A-OK. I still have the toothbrush in my hand; I put it back on the shelf.

'Hey, why are you using my toothbrush? Use your own,' he says.

Chapter Nineteen

I stand in the middle of the walk-in wardrobe and look around: a kid in a sweet shop. Just look at all these gorgeous clothes! They're all couture, expensive, designer. How could Beth afford all this? She can't have made that much cash from her novel. Did Ambrogio buy them with his parents' inheritance? Or does he make a killing dealing art? What shall I wear? Something black, surely? But no. Go on as if nothing has happened, just like before. That's what Ambrogio said. All right, darling: whatever you say . . .

I pick a bright-yellow dress by Roberto Cavalli with golden trim at the collar and sleeves. There are some yellow wedges in patent leather that match to perfection. Bright and beautiful sunshine yellow matches my mood. As long as everyone thinks I'm Beth, I've got nothing to worry about. There's no law that says you have to save people's lives. Four little minutes: what's that? Nothing. In a court of law, I think I'd get off.

If I can just stall my mother, I've hit the jackpot. No more fucking Alvina Knightly. I've got it sorted; I'm a millionairess. I twirl in the mirror and admire the dress. I look like a reality T V star, someone glam off *Geordie Shore*. I'm married to the hottest guy on the island, the guy I deserve. Who cares if he was going to kill Alvie? I'm not Alvie. I am Beth. I am safe. *I'm* the one who's in control here. I'm the one who's still alive. As long as Ambrogio still thinks I'm Beth, then I'll be all right. I'll be the best goddamn Beth that I can be. I'll be even more Beth than *Beth*. There's no way I'm going back to Archway, not when I can have all this!

And at last, I am a mother! I just gained a son without going through labour. But then again, so did Beth; she had a caesarean (too posh to push).

All my Christmases have come at once!

I take my time to apply Beth's make-up, humming to myself under my breath: Kylie's classic: 'I Should Be So Lucky'. Chanel foundation, Juicy Tube lip gloss, Benefit mascara . . . a generous spritz of Miss Dior Chérie. I find Beth's brush on her dressing table and scrape my hair back into a bun, just like yesterday. It looks pretty good, but I must remember to call that stylist. I'll find Beth's iPhone later on. Perhaps I'll get a manicure too? A facial, a massage and one of those wraps where they cover you in silver foil like an oven-ready turkey. I wonder how long this fake tan will last. I must make sure I sunbathe today. I check the mirror: no sign of Alvina. I'm good to go.

I stumble down the corridor, unsteady on the wedges. This is the hardest thing about being Beth: the six-inch heels. She always dressed like she was fresh off the catwalk: London Fashion Week, Paris, Milan. I hold on to the walls to steady myself. I find a window that looks down to the pool. I take a sharp breath and peer out: there on the patio is the space where Beth's body had been. It's empty. It's clean. The pool looks tranquil, as if nothing has happened. The blue water sparkles in the morning sun. Perhaps I'll have a swim later on? I can do whatever I like.

I get a sudden rush through the whole of my body, a tingling from my head to my toes. A thrill. An explosion. All of my wildest dreams have come true. I lean out of the window and take a deep breath. I can already feel that it's going to be hot, seriously fucking scorching hot. I guess Beth had warned me in her email: 'Bring your bikini and a sunhat; it's murder out here.' Today, you know, I don't mind the heat; it's perfect weather for working on my tan. Beth was as bronzed as Tom Hanks in Cast Away. I won't get caught. I will not lose! This is my game and I'm going to win: knock it outta the park!

I wander around the villa until I find the kitchen. This place is a labyrinth. I look around for David Bowie. The gym. The cinema. The living room. The music room. The library. Eventually I locate it; the kitchen's enormous. It's traditional Sicilian: yellow-and-white tiles and a wood-panelled ceiling, shining copper pans hanging down from a rail. The scent of fresh lemons and something baking. Hand-painted ceramics arranged on a dresser. It looks like a Cath Kidston advert. It all looks squeaky clean.

There's a woman standing with her back towards me. Is it Beth? I freeze. My whole body tenses. But she's got the wrong hair: curly and black. She turns and sees me staring.

'*Ciao, signora*,' she says with a smile.

Now I remember. It must be Emilia. Emilia and Ernesto have been to the park. My face cracks. I can't speak Italian (just the swear words . . . and '*pizza*' and '*cappuccino*') so I just say, 'All right.' Lucky Beth never bothered to learn Italian. That could have been awkward.

'How are you?' she says.

'Good,' I say. Never been better. I am Elizabeth. Everything's great.

'How are you? How is Ernie?' I walk over to the pram and take a look inside. He is sleeping like a baby. His mouth hangs open and a little bit of dribble runs down his chin. I can't believe how beautiful he is. He's perfect. He's gorgeous and he's all mine. I reach over and stroke his soft cheek with my finger. His eyelids flicker, but he doesn't wake up.

'Ah! He sleeps!' Emilia says, reaching over to embrace me the Italian way: a peck on each cheek and a bone-crunching hug. Emilia smells lovely: lavender soap? I'm glad I remembered Beth's perfume.

'That's good.' I smile, letting my eyes crinkle with warmth, the way I'd seen Beth smile when talking to the nanny.

'Where's your sister, Alana?'

Oh God. Really? Why does she care?

'Alvie had to go home, back to London,' I say. 'Some crisis at work. She has a terribly important job. She's the head poet at *The Times Literary Supplement*.' Emilia looks back at me blankly. 'Cappuccino?' I say.

'I'll make it, *signora*,' she says with a smile.

I don't really need any caffeine; I'm already buzzing, wide awake. I've forgotten I have a hangover. That *never* happens. Sometimes hangovers last for two or three days. Sometimes four. Once I spent a whole week in hospital. Emilia busies herself with a silver pot and a bag full of coffee beans. I don't take my eyes off her. She may not always be available and I need to know how to make a coffee in my own damn kitchen. There's no Nescafé granules and no kettle; I wouldn't have a clue where to start.

Emilia locates a small silver contraption up on a shelf and then dismantles it. She fills the base with water from a filter. Into another machine, she pours chocolate-brown beans and then flicks a switch. There is a deafening whir and the crack-cocaine scent of freshly ground coffee. My mouth waters. She scoops out a spoonful of finely ground beans and places it into the silver thing. Next, she turns on the gas and lights the hob with a long thin match. I watch where Emila keeps the matches, just in case I ever need one: they're in a little ceramic dish to the left of the stove.

'*Due minuti*,' she says.

I think that's '*two minutes*'.

'You want milk?' she asks.

I nod. The contraption bubbles. Emilia pours out a centi-metre of coffee into a minuscule cup and then adds a teaspoon of steamed milk. *Is that all?* That's not going to cut it. I'm used to Starbucks' ventis: two litres of froth in a bucket with a caramel swirl. That cup's the size of a thimble.

'Thanks,' I say. Great.

I take a sip. *Holy shit*. It's like drinking acid.

'Ugh! I need some sugar,' I say.

She looks at me like I've just landed on this planet. 'But *signora, mi dispiace*! Always you say, "*sugar is evil*"?'

'Yeah, well, I've changed my mind.'

I shovel in a couple of spoonfuls and stir away the bitterness. She looks at me strangely, her head cocked to one side. Hmm, Emilia; I'll have to watch out for that one. If this were a novel, she'd be the one to bust me. It's always the staff in mystery stories who know exactly what's going on: the butlers, the maids, the nannies or housekeepers. Twitching the curtains. Listening at the door. They're the eyes and ears of the establishment. No scandal escapes them. No secrets get past them. Yes, I'll need to keep an eye on her.

'Where's Ambrogio?' I ask.

'Swimming,' she says. I look out of the window at the pool. Still as a millpond. 'In the sea.'

Ah, yes. I'd forgotten about the sea. Now what shall I do? I need to release some nervous tension; I'm a slinky spring at the top of some stairs. Perhaps I'll go for a walk and explore my new neighbourhood? I can practise wearing my new shoes.

'I think I'll take a walk . . . to the amphitheatre!' I say. Beth used to go there. She found it 'inspiring'. And perhaps that security guard will be there; he could shed some light on what was going on with Beth.

'I'll see you later.'

I lean over the pram and give Ernie a kiss; his tiny cheek is warm and soft. I walk out of the kitchen and into the hall. I'm doing pretty well with the high heels. But then I remember: I need to make that long-distance phone call. Oh God. This is going to be painful. I'm going to have to wake her up; it's the middle of the night in Sydney. The last thing I want to do is talk to my mum.

Chapter Twenty

'What do you mean, *she's gone*?'

'Gone as in *dead*, Mum. Sorry.'

There's an awkward silence. I squeeze the handset closer to my head and twiddle the curly wire around my fingers. 'Hello?'

'Beth? Beth? You're breaking up, honey. I didn't hear a word you just said.'

I take a deep breath. This is going to be torture. I haven't spoken to my mother for months and months. Or maybe a year. I mostly avoid her telephone calls, not that she ever picks up the phone. She doesn't know how to use email. She doesn't know Facebook or Twitter exist. I once got a postcard from Ayers Rock, but that was December 2009. I wince at the Australian twang in her voice. Everything she says sounds like a question; there's an upward inflection at the end of each line. It's like having a relation from the cast of *Neighbours*: Madge Ramsay or someone. Is she still in it?

'It's Alvie, Mum,' I spell it out for her slowly, like I'm talking to a difficult child. 'There's been an accident. She's *dead*.' As in *dodo*.

The line goes quiet for about a minute. I think she's been cut off.

'Hellooooooooo?' I say. 'Mum?'

'Oh my goodness . . . Who is it that's dead?'

Fucking hell. '*Al-vi-na*.' I sigh.

'Oh, I see,' she says at last.

I can sense the relief in her voice from the other side of the world. Oh my God. I knew it! It's true. She's always hated poor old Alvie. What did I ever do to deserve it? It's so unfair. She's not even sad. Hardly upset. I blink back tears.

'The funeral's today, so you probably won't make it. *Definitely* won't make it.'

'How did it happen?' my mother asks, talking over me. She sounds a bit sadder now, I'm pleased to hear, though I still wouldn't call her *distraught*.

'There was an accident in the swimming pool. She was drunk,' I say. That sounds about right. Alvie always liked a drink. Or two. Or three. She liked to drink until she was numb and the world was a better place. And then drink some more. And some more. And some more. And not remember how she got home. And sometimes (often) not make it home at all. (Places I have slept that weren't a bed: corridors, ditches, bushes, stairwells, elevators, buses, ponds.)

'Drunk,' Mum repeats. 'The swimming pool. I see.' She sounds far away, more distant now, further than the southern hemisphere, or Jupiter or Mars. 'Typical Alvina. I can't say I'm surprised. She was always –'

'Like I said,' I interrupt her, 'the funeral's today . . .' I stretch the telephone wire between my fingers until it's taut and straight as a hangman's rope. She's not surprised. She half expected it. She's probably even *glad*.

'I'll book some flights.'

Shit.

'No! Mum, you don't need to come.' My voice is raised; I try to control it. 'You won't make it in time and, anyway, really there's nothing you can do.'

There's a pause as my mother considers this. I hold my breath. I hear her brain cells whirring like the cogs are churning. *It's a long way. It's a lot of money. It's only Alvina that's died, not Beth.* Please don't come, Mum, I'm willing her silently. Do not fucking come.

'Can't you hold off the funeral, dear? I don't understand.'

'It's just the way they do things over here. It has to be today. It's a Catholic thing. You'll definitely miss it. I'm sorry,' I say, letting my voice break with just the right amount of 'sad'. I wish this phone call would end already. If it were Beth who'd died, then she would come, no question. If it were Beth who'd died, she'd be on the next fucking plane. I should just hang up now. Shall I cut her off?

'Well . . .' she says, thinking it through. 'If you say so, dear. I really should be there. But I am *very* busy with the parish cake sale and . . . well, it's just a shame I'll miss my own daughter's funeral.'

'Hmm.' Like she cares. Unbelievable. She's practically dancing – no, *twerking* – on my grave.

'I'm just sorry I can't be there for *you* . . . are you OK?'

'I'm fine,' I say. 'I mean, well, obviously . . . we're all in shock.'

'Of course,' she says. 'It all sounds awful, but, Beth, I'm just so glad it wasn't you.'

Oh my God, not *again*. I can't take any more. First Ambrogio and now my own mother. I shove my fist in my mouth and bite hard. The pain distracts my eyes from crying, but not for long. At least my mum wasn't plotting to kill me. Unless she was in on that plan with Ambrogio? I can't trust Ambrogio. I can't trust my mum. I grit my teeth and hold my breath. Hold it together, Alvina. Come on!

We hang up the phone and it's just what I wanted. My mother's not coming, I'm not totally screwed. But part of me is completely livid. She didn't take much persuading. How dare she not come to my funeral? The parish cake sale? Who gives a shit? This confirms my lifelong suspicion: my mother never did like Alvina. Right from the start, it was all about Beth. She always thought we were Jekyll and Hyde. I absolutely refuse to cry. My mother is dead to me now.

There's an antique vase on a polished wooden table in the corner of the room. It's hand-painted blue with pretty white flowers and a delicate pattern around the rim. I pick it up carefully, both hands around its base and hurl it on to the mosaic-tiled floor.

It shatters into a thousand pieces.

It's only two minutes' walk to the amphitheatre but I wish I'd got a cab. The air is still and furnace-like. It's far too hot to move. I kick up dust on bone-dry ground and try to walk like Beth: chin up, shoulders back, calm and confident. As opposed to Tuesday's badly dressed crowds, there's hardly anyone here. It's eerie, forlorn, practically deserted. I join the other two tourists in the queue and try to blend in. It doesn't work; they turn and stare. I'm too well dressed. Or perhaps it's the lollipop-lady yellow? I'm about to scowl and give them an evil, but then I remember, I'm supposed to be Beth. I try my sweetest 'Hey there!' smile. They look a little bit frightened. They turn their backs and whisper.

The sea is an ugly greenish-blue; clumps of seaweed crowd the seabed like bruises. Sunlight reflects off the water and burns my retinas. The sky is unbearably blue.

'Elisabetta! Elisabetta!'

A man runs over and joins me at the back of the queue, out of breath. He has pale-blue eyes and messy blond hair, unusual for a Sicilian. It must be that security guard, the one we saw yesterday. He's wearing a uniform. It's definitely him.

'Elisabetta? Is that you? Or . . . are you the other one?' We make eye contact. I pause. Look away.

'It's me, *Elizabeth*,' I say.

'Of course it is. Is everything OK?'

'Sure,' I say. 'How are you doing?' What's his name? Beth never told me. I can't exactly ask him now. I wish he was wearing a name badge.

'*Bene, bene.* Where is your sister?' he asks with a grin. He looks over his shoulder to search for my twin, missing his free entertainment.

'Oh, Alvina went home,' I say, feigning casual. I'm suddenly too hot. My palms feel clammy; I wipe them up and down Beth's bright-yellow dress. I wish I could have a drink.

He frowns. 'Already? But she only just got here.'

'Yeah, I know. Crisis at work . . .'

He studies my face. I look at my shoes. I pretend to yawn and cross my arms, look distracted by a poster of *Nabucco*.

'So . . . are you . . . are you really OK?' he asks, *again*. 'Why are you still here? I thought the plan was to get away? I thought you were leaving last night?'

I look down to where he's touching my arm: bitten-down nails, a digital watch. I don't want him to touch me; I don't know where he's been.

'I'm fine,' I say, pulling away. Get out of my space. Why does he care? What does he know about this *plan*?

'You are *Elisabetta*, aren't you?' he says.

His voice trails off. His eyes trail my body, right down to my toes. Breathe, Alvie. Breathe. It's *fine*. This is a very 'Beth' outfit. I couldn't possibly look any more like my twin. So why am I shaking? Why is there a bead of sweat sliding down my chest? Why is my heart pounding so loud in my ears? Shit, I hope he can't hear it.

'Yes, it's me. I already told you. Alvie had to go home.' Oh my God, what's his problem? I shouldn't have come here. It was a mistake.

He sighs and shakes his golden head; he suddenly looks worried. He reaches his arms around my neck and pulls me in for a big bear hug. I can smell the styling gel he's used in his hair – that means he styled it? It must be the just-got-out-of-bed look. I stand, stiff as a corpse; I don't like being hugged by total strangers. But then I remember: he isn't a stranger; I'm supposed to be Beth, we're supposed to be friends. Apparently, I've told him *everything*. Apparently, he knows all about this plan. So I hug him back. I need to find out what this guy knows. I decide to take a gamble.

'I was going to leave late last night,' I say, pulling away.

'I know, so why are you still here? It's *dangerous*, Betta.'

'Oh, I thought I might just stay here, actually.' I gesture around to the view and the theatre. 'I guess it must be growing on me.'

He looks at me strangely for half a second, a puzzled look on his youthful face.

'But Elisabetta, you told me you had no choice.' His eyes dart from left to right, searching the empty amphitheatre. 'You stay here, you die. You and the kid.'

I wait for him to burst into laughter, for him to say it was just a joke, but he shifts on his feet in the uncomfortable silence and waits for me to reply. I don't. I look at my watch like I've got a meeting and don't want to be late.

'Shit. I'm sorry. I've got to go.'

I turn on my heel and head for the exit.

'Elisabetta? Where are you going?'

'I'll see you later,' I shout over my shoulder.

'Don't go home! It isn't safe!'

I run from the theatre as fast as I can in these fucking ridiculous yellow shoes. I run down the road and down the hill gasping for breath, swerving, swaying, sprinting through alleyways, then over a fence and into a garden. Another garden. An alley. A road. Then I'm lost in the citrus orchards with trees spinning around me, caught in the branches, tripping over their roots. I run and run until my lungs are burning and I'm gasping for breath in the stifling air. Bees and wasps buzz in my face. I flap and slap at myself with my hands. I'm already covered in mosquito bites. This country is trying to eat me.

I collapse at the bottom of a gnarled old tree, lean my back against its trunk, my chest heaving, my hands shaking. I look down at my body slumped down in the dirt. It doesn't look a bit like me. I don't feel myself. Oranges and lemons are strewn across the orchard. 'Oranges and lemons, say the bells of St Clement's.' Beth and I used to sing that at school.

You had no choice, the security guard had said. *You stay here, you die.*

I don't know what I'm going to do. Part of me wants to run and run and never stop. It's an island. I'd soon reach the sea. Then I'd swim and swim until I could swim no more. Part of me wants to go back to the villa, grab my passport and race to the airport. I have nowhere to go. No family. No friends. Even my mother thinks I'm dead. 'Oranges and lemons, say the bells of St Clement's. You owe me five farthings, say the bells of St Martin's. When will you pay me? say the bells of Old Bailey. When I grow rich, say the bells of Shoreditch.' I fight the urge to blubber.

Pull yourself together, Alvie. For fuck's sake, fucking sort yourself out.

I wipe my cheeks with a finger and sniff. I'm going to stay. It's what Beth would have wanted. Ambrogio needs a wife. Ernesto needs a mum. It's the selfless thing to do.

But why was that security guard so worried about me? Why did Beth make me swap places with her? What was wrong with her last night? Why was she crying? So upset? And why the fuck was she covered in bruises?

I have no idea what's going on.

The only way I'll ever find out is if I am Beth. So I've got to keep going. That's the only way out. I'll be Beth for ever if I have to. I'll keep being Beth until the day I die. I haul myself up and dust myself down. I've got dirt all over Beth's nice dress. She'd kill me if she saw it like this. I check the label. Urgh: dry clean only. Great. Of course it is.

Chapter Twenty-one

Parco dell'Etna, Sicily

Nino looks like he's stepped straight off the set of *The Godfather*. I guess that's just the fashion in this part of Sicily. He looks cool, in the same way that Al Pacino as Michael Corleone looked cool. Horseshoe moustache. Black jacket, black tie, grey fedora with a ribbed black band. Now I remember: he's the guy I saw sneaking out of the villa when I first arrived.

'Nice hat,' I say.

He doesn't reply. Nino doesn't say anything as we climb into his shiny black people carrier and speed out into the Sicilian countryside. He's playing Metallica at eardrum-mutilating decibels ('Master of Puppets', I like that song) and nodding his fedora to the sick, phat bass.

'*Dov'è il cadavere?*' shouts Ambrogio.

'*Bagagliaio,*' says Nino.

'Huh?' I say, turning to Ambrogio. I'm sitting in the back on my own eating cheese-and-onion Pringles (emergency food smuggled over from Blighty).

'You want one?' I offer. Ambrogio gives me a funny look and shakes his head.

Nino and Ambrogio sit at the front. A bubblegum-scented air freshener dangles down from the rear-view mirror. There's a picture of Jesus sellotaped to the dashboard. A wooden-bead rosary with a silver crucifix.

'Your sister's in the boot.'

I shiver and turn towards the back of the car, put the uneaten

Pringle back into the tube and close the lid. There's a thick, black cover pulled over the boot, so I can't see inside.

'Really?' I shout. 'She's in there?'

'Yes,' shouts Ambrogio.

'Are you sure?'

'What?' shouts Ambrogio, looking over his shoulder. 'Do you want to get out and have a look? Do you think Nino forgot her? We're going to bury a corpse, but we forgot the corpse? This guy's a professional, aren't you, Nino?'

'Professional,' says Nino.

I suppose I believe him; it just seems very unlikely that my sister's dead body should be in the boot of the car. We're driving through the streets in broad daylight, after all. Nino's driving is worse than Ambrogio's. It's like he's got a death wish. I guess everyone drives like this over here, so we shouldn't get stopped by the police. It would look suspicious if we stuck to the speed limit. But what if they do a random stop and search? Just a routine check? Then we're screwed. I strain my eyes and scan the road for a panda car, but I can't see any. I slide from side to side across the back seat, slamming into a door at every street corner. Perhaps this is how Beth got all those bruises? There aren't any seat belts. It's not very safe.

I look out of the window at the tall cypress trees, tapering up towards the sky like long, green candles, at the exposed, grey rock faces staring down from the hills. The motorway to Catania snakes along the coastline and we're never very far away from the sea. Perhaps they'll dump her body somewhere out in the ocean? Buried at sea like Osama bin Laden. I hope she won't float like a witch.

'Where are we going?' I ask, at last.

'Nino's friend is building himself a country house.' Ambrogio raises his voice over the music. 'Isn't that right, Nino?' The lead singer screams, 'Master! Master!' The bassline goes DOOF! DOOF! DOOF!

'Country house,' says Nino.

'Right . . .' I say. 'So what?'

'You'll see.'

We drive to a remote part of the countryside, somewhere not too far from Catania. Nino turns down a dirt track and we drive for a few minutes into a wood. The road is full of tree roots and potholes. I bounce up and down on the hard back seat. The trees are packed really tightly together so they block out the sunlight. It's gloomy, getting darker and darker. When we come to a clearing, Nino stops the car. At first I think there's nothing here, just a clearing in amongst the trees, earth on the floor and a small patch of sky peering down through the canopy. Then I notice a pile of breeze blocks, a hole in the ground and a pick-up truck, parked some way back behind the branches. There's a cement mixer on the truck. It's basically a building site.

'You want to get out? You can stay in the car if it's all too much.' Ambrogio forces a smile then jumps out of the people carrier. I flinch as he slams the door shut.

Urgh. Why did I even want to come? And now Ambrogio's in a mood, because I caused all this trouble and didn't follow his stupid plan. I watch the men through the tinted window: Ambrogio, Nino and somebody else. Nino stands by the hole in the ground: silent, still. His back towards me. He doesn't seem to be moving at all. Not even breathing. I've never seen anyone looking so calm. There's something about him. I can't put my finger on it. It suddenly feels far too hot in the car. Suffocating. Clammy. The air con's turned off. The bubblegum air freshener's making me gag. I need to get out; I feel sick. I can't breathe. I open the door and step out of the car.

'Domenico, *è pronto il cemento?*'

'*Sì, sì, è pronto. È pronto.*'

A large man in dirty blue overalls sits on the back of the pick-up truck smoking a Cuban cigar. I guess that must be

Domenico. He looks up when he sees me – acne scars, a broken nose, hair-shaved real short like they wear it in prison. He leaves his cigar burning on the metal ledge and jumps down to the ground.

'Professore,' says Domenico, nodding at Ambrogio.

Why did he call him 'Professore'? Domenico turns to me.

'Your sister died?'

I don't say anything. It's fucking obvious. That's why we're all here. I don't feel like doing chit-chat with a total stranger, especially not someone who looks like he just dug his way out of jail: muddy black fingernails, dirt on his face, ripped-up trousers, convict hair: he's like the ugly love child of Steve McQueen and a mole, but less attractive.

'Yeah, my brother died last week,' says Domenico. 'Disembowelled.'

Fuck, that's gross.

Ambrogio shakes his head. 'What the hell are you saying that for in front of a *lady*?' I think he means me. He squares up to Domenico.

'Yeah,' says Nino. 'Who gives a fuck about your brother? He was a fucking idiot.'

'Don't say that about family, man,' Domenico says, turning to Nino. His voice is sandpaper.

'He wasn't *my* family,' Nino says. 'My mother didn't have sex with her brother. Fucking idiot. Should have killed him myself.'

'*Figghiu ri butana.*'

'*Minchia.*'

'*Stronzo.*'

'*Che palle,*' says Ambrogio, stepping between them. They separate, growling, like dogs. '*E basta. Calma! Calma!*' he says.

'What happened?' I say, turning to Nino. 'To his brother?'

'Ate too much pussy and went *pazzo*,' he says, lighting himself a Marlboro Red and flicking the match in Domenico's face.

Oh, well. I guess that explains it.

Now I want a fag.

Nino and Domenico walk around to the back of the people carrier and open the boot. I shrink back next to Ambrogio. He lights himself a cigarette. Now I *really* want one.

'Erm, can I have one?' I ask. I know, I know, Beth didn't smoke, but I feel like these are exceptional circumstances. Plus if I don't get some nicotine, things could get ugly. I mean, even uglier. If that's possible.

He gives me a look, but then nods. He places the cigarette between my lips, then lights one for himself. I take a deep drag. I feel a bit better. He puts his arm around my shoulder and squeezes me tight.

That's when I see her and I gasp.

Beth's not in a coffin or anything. She's not even in a bag. She's half naked and pure, milky white. She's still wearing that Louis Vuitton dress I stole, just about. The strap's ripped. There's dried blood on her face and her hair's a mess. I don't know why that's so surprising. I guess it's just that her hair's always perfect. She's always so well groomed.

'Oh my God,' I say. I cover my face with my hands.

Nino and Domenico carry Beth's body by the shoulders and ankles and bring her over to the hole in the ground. Her neck is stiff and her arms seem stuck to the sides of her torso. I guess that's rigor mortis. She looks just like that Barbie I found in the trash, but her head's still attached.

'*Uno, due, tre,*' they say, and then heave her into the ditch.

Thud.

'The foundation for the building,' Ambrogio says.

Ambrogio walks over to the men and stands at the edge of the ditch. I follow him. The four of us stand by the hole in the ground and stare at Beth's body. She's lying face down in the dirt. The dress has risen up and you can see her ass. She might be wearing a G-string, but if she is, it's so small you can't tell from this angle. To me, it's obvious that it's *Beth's* ass. Mine feels much bigger. Stretch marks. Cellulite. I glance over at Ambrogio, but he doesn't seem to have noticed. Weird.

Beth's skin is so white, it's as though all her tan has washed off in the pool. I've never seen her looking so pale. I look down at my forearms. I think the fake tan has washed off in the shower, so we're both the same colour. Lucky.

Domenico walks back over to the pick-up truck, gets in and starts the engine. It coughs and chokes and splutters to life. The truck makes a high-pitched bleeping sound and a light on the top of the cab flashes blue as it reverses towards the ditch. It crawls slowly, painfully fucking slowly, backwards and then comes to a stop. Domenico jumps out of the cab and does something to the cement mixer. It grunts and groans and spins and tilts and thick, wet concrete slides down towards the hole in the ground. It makes a fat slap-slapping sound as it hits the freshly cut earth and covers the corpse. Her feet, her calves, her knees, her thighs. Slap, slap, slap. Her ass, her back, her shoulder blades, her head. I smell burning oil. Black smoke wafts from the cement mixer. Within a few minutes, there's no more Beth, just a rectangular hole full of pale, grey porridge.

What would Beth do if she were here at my burial? Would she be this stoic? Reserved? Relaxed? Sobbing and blubbering hysterically? I have no idea. I've got no benchmark for this shit. All I know is that if it wasn't my sister down there in that hole, then it would be me. I'll never know how close I came. Did Beth just ask me here to kill me? I shake my head. No. Not Beth. No fucking way. But maybe Ambrogio? I glance over at him, but he's distracted by his phone. I'll need to keep an eye on him. I guess I should be happy that I'm still here.

I breathe a long, deep sigh of relief, stub my smoke out and crush it into the ground. Ambrogio, Nino and Domenico simultaneously make the sign of the cross across their chests. It's as though it were choreographed and rehearsed, like backing dancers at a T Swiz concert. I copy them.

We get back in the car.

I take a look at Beth's Ladymatic: 1.42 p.m. I hope the drive home doesn't take too long; I've booked an appointment with Beth's beautician and I don't want to be late.

Chapter Twenty-two

Taormina, Sicily

'*M*amma mia, your hair grows so quickly. We put those highlights in two weeks ago and now look at your roots! *Non ci credo . . .*'

The beautician, whose name is 'Cristina Hair and Beauty' according to Beth's iPhone, is standing behind me, running her fingers through my hair. Her kohl-lined eyes are wide with surprise. She shakes her glossy head.

'Hmm,' I say, flicking through Italian *Vogue*. Ooh, I love that dress by Valentino: beautiful, flowing ruffles and a plunging neckline. It's very red carpet. Perhaps I'll get it for dates with Ambrogio? Beth has some gorgeous Jimmy Choos that would go really well. Shall I go shopping in Taormina or fly to the mainland for a trip to Milan? What's that famous fashion street called? Via Monte Napoleone? I bet all the celebs go there . . .

'Have you been taking supplements? Or eating oysters?' asks Cristina.

I look up from the magazine that's open on my lap. We make eye contact in the mirror. 'What? No, I haven't,' I say.

'Oysters are full of zinc. Zinc makes your hair grow.'

Well, who would have thought it? There's a lot of zinc in semen too. Funny she didn't ask if I've been giving loads of head.

'And what happen to your eyelash extensions? They fall off?'

'Yeah, they fall off. In the pool,' I say.

'Already? No problem. We do them again . . .'

I take a sip of the chilled Prosecco that's sitting on the dressing table: light and fruity. I pop a strawberry in my mouth and start to chew. Beth's iPhone is lying on the table; I pick it up and stare at the screen. I miss Twitter. I can't believe Beth doesn't have an account. What did she do all day if she wasn't tweeting? I'm going to set one up for her. For me. For her. You're welcome.

'@TaylorSwift Hey there, Taylor! My name is Elizabeth Caruso. I think you know my sister, Alvina. Anyway, I just wanted to say hey!' Tweet. I bet she'll reply to Elizabeth. She never replied to me.

Cristina runs her fingers through my hair, massaging my scalp. Her gel tips scrape against my skull. She pulls my hair back into foils and paints my roots with peroxide dye. It smells like bleach or Toilet Duck. It takes her an hour to cover my hair with shiny little silver packets. Cristina tells me *at great length* about Gina's break-up with Matteo, her son's trials with the local under-eleven football team and Stefania's wedding that she attended last weekend. She goes into minute detail about the trouble she's been having with her new fridge-freezer, her husband's bloated stomach (perhaps he's allergic to eggs?) and what happened last night on the show *Inspector Montalbano*. I nod like I give a shit. I think I'm supposed to know these people, fictional or otherwise.

I study the classified ads at the back of the magazine. I can't read them, but I can look at the pictures. They're as crappy in Italy as they are back in England. I can't say that I miss that job. I don't really miss that basement. I certainly don't miss Angela Merkel and I doubt she misses me.

'We have to wax your eyebrows,' says Cristina. If she could wrinkle her forehead through the Botox, she'd frown. 'And you need a manicure and a pedicure. We could be here all day . . .'

Cristina pulls an electric heater over my head to speed up the peroxide lightening my hair. Then she takes her file and works on my fingers and toes. She paints my nails the 'usual' baby pink with little white tips in French manicure style (I fancy the

Chanel 'Rouge Noir' but it's not very *Beth*). It really is so much more convenient when the stylist comes to you, don't you think? She lifts a corner to check the colour, then pulls the foils off one by one. She rinses the bleach out with the shower head over the bathtub. The water feels lovely and warm. She blow dries my hair into big, loose waves then turns her attention to my face.

She takes several dozen tiny eyelashes and sticks them on to my lashes with glue. It takes *forever*. I hope Cristina knows what she's doing. I want to be able to open my eyes. I need to be able to see. She layers a little melted wax on to the skin below my eyebrows. With a quick yank, she pulls off one strip and then another and another. I scream! It's hot! And it fucking hurts!

When she's finished, we look in the mirror.

'You like?'

'I love.'

Tweet. Tweet. Tweet.

It's a message from Taylor Swift, responding to Elizabeth Caruso: 'Hey there, honey! So great to meet you! Hugs xoxox'

'Emilia? Emilia!'

'*Sì, signora?*' A voice from the far side of the villa.

'I'm taking Ernesto out to the shops.'

Ambrogio's out somewhere with his mates. It's time for a little retail therapy.

'*Sì, signora,*' says Emilia.

'I'll be back by three.'

'*Sì, signora. Ciao, signora.*'

'*Ciao,*' I say.

I like saying '*ciao*'. It makes me feel cool. It's just the way they talk over here, so it isn't pretentious. Chow, chow, chow.

I lay Ernie in his pram: a Silver Cross 'Balmoral'. Beth said the Duchess of Cambridge has one just like it for Princess Charlotte.

'Let's go shopping!' I say.

Ernie smiles up at me, pleased; his big, blue eyes are wide with delight. I ruffle the soft, gold curls on his fat, round head. He giggles, dribbles, flaps his chubby little arms up and down like a newly hatched chick.

'Ma, ma, ma.'

I stroke his pink cheek.

'Cutie-pie.'

I feel a surge of motherly love. I still can't believe that he's all mine. I always wanted Ambrogio's baby. I've dreamed of this moment for eight whole years, and now here he is! My very own child. I can't help feeling it's meant to be. I lean over the pram and take a selfie of me and Ernie all snuggled up. I post it on Elizabeth's Facebook: 'Me and my gorgeous boy!!!!' I push the pram down the drive and on to the road.

It's a beautiful day. I pull on Beth's shades to shield my eyes from the dazzling sun, then pull the cover over the pram to shelter Ernesto. See, I am a good mother. I don't want him to get sunburnt. I even brought some tap water in a baby bottle (for if he gets thirsty) and some Belgian chocolates I found in the kitchen for an afternoon treat (I'll eat those if he doesn't want them). Shit, I forgot the sunscreen! And the nappies! And the baby wipes! And a spare change of clothes! And his teddy bear! But it's OK. We won't be gone long. I'm sure he'll survive. I'll take good care of my baby. Take him to Disney World, enroll him at Eton. Violin lessons, cricket. A butler. A horse. All the things that I never had. He'll be spoilt rotten and then some more. He'll be glad I'm his mum.

The wheels of the pram make a whirring sound as we roll down the hill. I feel like skipping. Ernie's singing something incomprehensible; it could be an attempt at 'Baa Baa Black Sheep', but I wouldn't put money on it. I'll get him singing lessons when he's a bit older. Perhaps he'll be a famous opera singer? The lead in *Nabucco* one day? The new, younger, slimmer Pavarotti? He's half Italian, after all. And his father's a looker.

I take a deep breath. Ahhh, crisp, clean air, the scent of lemons. No, I never, ever want to go back to London: car fumes and rubbish bins, dog shit, grease. Why would I leave when I've got all this? I could be the luckiest girl in the world. Beth's Mulberry wallet (soft as peaches) is in my handbag (Beth's handbag) and it's bursting at the seams: €713.50 (I counted it) and three shiny bank cards. I'm a little bit worried about not knowing her PIN. But I'll cross that bridge when I come to it.

We turn a corner and walk along a narrow winding street: ancient buildings with crumbling walls in pastel pink. Trees filled with blossoms in deep, shocking violet. A marble church with sculptures of cherubs. The view is picture-postcard perfect. Etna's in the distance, framed by some palm trees. Beyond the volcano, a turquoise sea. The scent of frangipani. The sound of birdsong. This place is fucking paradise.

We turn another corner on to Via Umberto. No, *this* is paradise: shopping heaven. Shops stretch out as far as the eye can see: designer stores, little boutiques, art galleries, restaurants, bars. Beautiful people sit out on parasol-pretty terraces, watching other beautiful people pass by hand in hand. This is the perfect place for a honeymoon. I hear them chit-chat in sing-song Italian, blow cigarette smoke into the well-dressed crowds. I taste their second-hand nicotine and smile. Ah, this is the life.

There's an ATM beyond the café. I try the first of Beth's shiny cards. Push it into the narrow slot and jab at the touchpad. I'm going to try the same PIN code that unlocks her iPhone. If I knew Beth, she wouldn't want to remember more than one. What was it? 'Wannabe': 1-9-9-6. *SCORRETTO* flashes red on black. An angry bleep. It spits out the card and I chuck it into the bottom of Beth's bag, pull out the next one: 1-9-9-6. *SCORRETTO*. Nope. Another angry bleep. It spits out the card. Shit, this last one better work. I pull out the remaining card with trembling fingers. It's a gorgeous, glossy black with glitzy silver lettering: '*Signora Elizabeth Caruso*'. Platinum.

Premium. If this one doesn't work, I'm totally screwed . . . 1-9-9-6. YIPPEE! I knew it! I check Beth's balance and nearly pass out. She has €220,000 just in this current account. I withdraw €500, just because I can. The notes shuffle out and I grab a thick handful, smooth and crisp. They look delicious. They smell brand new. It's all I can do not to rub them against my cheek or my face. It's all I can do not to lick them. I open the wallet and shove them in; now it's so fat that it won't close. I take out Beth's credit card and kiss it.

I'm suddenly torn: do I want to sit out at a starched linen table and order Prosecco and a dish of green olives, or do I want to go shopping? Decisions, decisions . . . What do you think, baby Ernie? A street artist sits with his wares on display, pictures of actors, singers, politicians. They're actually quite good; he's very talented. They have a real likeness, almost photographic. You can tell who they are meant to be. There's Nicole Kidman and Gwyneth Paltrow, Channing Tatum and Tom Cruise. Whoa! Wait a minute. Channing Tatum? Shopping it is!

'*Ciao*.'

'*Ciao*.' The man looks up.

'How much for the picture of Channing Tatum?'

'*Venti euros*.'

'What's that? Twenty?'

'*Sì*. Twenty.'

'I'm not paying that. That's way too much. I'll give you ten.'

'No, is twenty.'

'Fine. Eleven. That's my final offer.'

'Is twenty. Is twenty.'

'OK then. Twelve. Take it or leave it.'

'No.'

'Thirteen?'

'No.'

'Fourteen?'

'No. *Mamma mia!*'

'Fifteen then? That's my final offer.'

'*Venti euros!* Twenty! Twenty!'

'Fine. I'll give you sixteen euros. Not a single cent more. And I want it gift-wrapped.' Even though it's just for me.

'No. Is not possible.'

'Seventeen?'

'No.'

'Eighteen?'

'No.'

Motherfucker.

I should just snatch the thing and run, but the pram might slow me down.

'Right! That's it! I don't want it anyway. Look, just watch. I'm going away!'

I turn on my heel and march down the street, pushing the pram at a breakneck speed. The vendor doesn't even flinch. He takes a swig of his Nastro Azzurro and looks the other way.

'R A A A A A A A A G H!' I fly back down the street and sprint towards him. 'N I N E T E E N E U R O S! O K? Are we done here?'

The man looks up at me and frowns. 'Twenty euros for the picture.' Tough cookie. He isn't going to back down.

I look at the portrait of Channing Tatum: his beautiful face, his puppy-dog eyes. I really miss my poster of him. If I'm going to replace him, I guess this is it.

'O K. All right. Nineteen euros, fifty cents. How about that? It's a great deal.'

The man stands up and shakes my hand. Y E S! I knew he'd crack eventually. Alvie: one. Street-art guy: nil.

'*Bene, bene. Finalmente.*'

He reaches up and takes the picture. I find a twenty in Beth's purse.

'Oh, do you have any change for a twenty?'

'No change. I'm sorry. *Mi dispiace.*'

He shrugs and gestures to a wad of banknotes folded up inside a tin. There's no silver to be seen. He doesn't have any coins.

I thrust the twenty in his face and snatch the picture. It rips a bit. 'OK, fine. Whatever. Fuck it. Here, just take it. Take it all!'

'*Arrivederci, signorina,*' he calls after me.

I shove Channing in the pram with the baby.

A crocodile-leather handbag sits pride of place in a clothes-shop window. A matching belt and clutch bag lie beside it on a replica of a Corinthian plinth. Emporio Armani. It's unbelievably sexy. I already want it. I'm going to check it out. The store is called Marianna. I push the pram towards the front door. I want to buy myself something special, God knows I deserve it. After everything I've been through. After everything I've done. I don't just want to wear Beth's old clothes for ever and ever. I want my own wardrobe. Something new. Unique. I'll need something hot for dates with Ambrogio: his new hotter, better, sexier wife. Perhaps he'll take me to that restaurant again? Or he might know somewhere else, a nightclub, perhaps, or a cute little bar right down by the sea. I can see myself gliding in a floor-length dress: luminous green or sunset orange. Something eye-catching. Something expensive. I want heads to turn and crowds to part, people to murmur, point and stare: 'Who's that girl?' (But in a good way.) I want my share of the limelight.

And then, of course, there are the accessories . . . I'll need some new diamonds, obviously. Some earrings, a bracelet and a few more rings. I've seen some beauties at Van Cleef & Arpels. I want a Valentino clutch bag. And thigh-high boots by Miu Miu.

The shiny glass doors swish wide open and I step into the cool of the store.

'*Ciao, Betta!*' squeals a shop assistant, tottering towards me on towering heels. Oh shit, she knows me. '*Ciao, Ernie!*' she says.

'*Ciao!*' I say in my best 'Beth' voice: breathy, husky. I force a smile.

The size-zero shop assistant with shiny black hair and almost non-existant bum comes over to greet us. Air kisses. Hugs. She bends down to the pram and coos at Ernesto.

'*Come stai, bimbo Ernesto? Mamma mia, che bello,*' she says, tickling him under his double chin. He gurgles with delight like they're long-lost friends. Does *he* know the shop assistant?

She looks up at me and smiles: invisible braces, fuchsia-pink lips. She smells sickly sweet, like undiluted Ribena. Cheap perfume. I much prefer Beth's. 'Betta, I have the amazing new shoes! Come on! Look! You're going to love them!'

She doesn't actually grab my hand and drag me across the floor of the shop, but it feels like that. I follow her across marble tiles, past walls piled high with shoes on glass shelves. Sparkling. Shimmering. Shining. Spotlights, like tiny suns, illuminate row upon row of priceless handbags: Dolce & Gabbana, Gucci, Hogan, Roberto Cavalli, Tod's. She stops and spins around towards me, an expectant smile on her youthful face. She gestures towards a new pair of shoes.

'Look!'

They're made of red Perspex with black-and-white stiletto heels. They're fucking hideous.

'Oh. Right,' I say.

I bought them. Of course I did. I had no choice. I bought the shoes, even though I hated them, and the matching Perspex belt and the matching Perspex handbag: €4,498. I bought them because Beth would have bought them. If I hadn't fucking bought them, she'd have guessed I wasn't Beth. I stomp down the paving slabs of Via Umberto grinding my teeth. The shopping bag handles cut into my palms. This stuff is fucking heavy.

A dress. I'll buy myself a dress. That'll cheer me up nicely. An ancient fountain blocks my path. Water pours from the mouths of stone fish. Splashing me, wetting me, soaking my clothes. Water's supposed to be relaxing, isn't it? Fountains are supposed to sound tranquil, soothing, like in Japanese gardens – all lily pads and Buddhas – but this one is pissing me off. I storm past the fountain and off down the road. I've got to find another clothes shop. I need to find myself a dress.

I come to a store with two tiers of windows. The glass panes glint in the dazzling sun: they must have used litres of Mr Muscle to make them all shine bright like that. Glossy white mannequins wear shining silver, luminous yellow, dazzling white. Prada, Fendi, Pucci, Missoni. It all looks so perfect. I step inside. They're playing some kind of electronic music: ethereal, magical, strange. A long, bright corridor leads towards the shining lights of the interior. The hall is lined with yet more mannequins, posing, watching with perfect faces. Polished mirrors. Sacred space. The mannequins inhabit square glass boxes: lifelike, immobile. I study their plastic heads. Their dead, blank eyes look just like Beth's. They stare back at me. Move. They're coming to get me, I'm sure of it. I catch a glimpse of Beth in a mirror.

I jump.

I panic.

I run!

And I'm back in the street, gasping for breath, gulping down air. Suddenly faint, I hang my head between my legs. The ground is spinning. What the fuck? That was Beth! I swear it. I saw her! I look around, but she's not here. Sweating. Hyperventilating. People staring. Where's the pram? I suddenly realize I don't have it. Ernie's gone! My stomach drops. Where the fuck has the baby gone? I look all around, search back in the shop. Run back down the Via Umberto, pushing past tourists, tripping over my feet. That fucking fountain in my way. My blood pumping. My brain throbbing. My mouth dry. I need a drink. Oh my God, Beth would kill me . . . Which shop was it? There are so many. Have I left him inside there? Did somebody take him? I race from window to window to window, searching for that stupid handbag: crocodile leather? Or was it snake? Emporio

Armani? Or D&G? Come on, Alvie, he's got to be here! Some-where. Somewhere. If I weren't so fucking dehydrated, I think I would cry. Bottega Veneta. John Galliano. Emilio Pucci. Moncler . . .

Eventually I see it across the street: Marianna, Emporio Armani, crocodile leather. Thank fuck for that. I fall through the door, crashing, tripping, panting, sweating, everyone stares. The pram is still there, parked by the doorway. I thought I'd lost him, I really did. Baby Ernie's fast asleep. The shop assistant opens her mouth and then closes it again. I grab the pram and head back to the villa. I can't believe that I almost lost Chan-ning. I'll buy a dress another day.

Chapter Twenty-three

'But why do I need to come?' I ask, running down the road after Ambrogio.

We're heading back into Taormina, past a little bar called Mocambo with chairs on a terrace. Chequered table-cloths. The scent of *caffè*. I was hoping Ambrogio would stay out with his mates a little while longer, so I could get my head straight. Make a plan of my own. But no, here he is. He showed up at the villa and, apparently, he needs my help.

'Because he likes you,' says Ambrogio.

'Who does?'

'The priest.'

This makes no sense, but if it's important to Ambrogio, then I guess I should go. The dutiful wife. The adoring spouse. I'm going to be the perfect partner. I didn't think Ambrogio was religious, but apparently today we're going to church. I hope I've picked the right kind of outfit. What would Beth have worn to church? Is Prada appropriate for a priest?

We cross a square called Piazza IX Aprile, over black-and-white tiles, past a riot of flowers. There are wrought-iron lamp posts with old-fashioned lanterns. The church is the Chiesa di San Giuseppe. It looks like a wedding cake melting in the sun. Little old ladies pour on to the square after Mass. A boy kicks a football too close to my head. Little fucker. That almost hit me. If I wasn't Beth, then I'd kick it back hard, right in his face. Another boy, wearing a 'Totti' T-shirt, kicks the ball against the church wall. 'Goal! Goal!' They run about laughing and cheering and shouting. I try not to scowl. Or swear.

We leave the sun and the sea view to the crowds of tourists all praying to the vista and step inside the cool of a seventeenth-century baroque church. Pastel-coloured paintings. Flying cherubs. I always feel funny when I go into a church, like I'm trespassing or something. A subtle but persistent feeling of being out of place. (The last time I was in a church was that cathedral in Milan, but I think I'll keep that to myself.)

Ambrogio leads me by the hand through the dimly lit nave. Incense. Dust. My eyes adjust. This is what Limbo looks like: this chiaroscuro. I can smell several centuries' worth of sins all stacked up.

The priest is saying the liturgy at the front of the church. He's tall, unusually tall for an Italian, thin and stooping, with a long, hooked nose. He sounds bored out of his brain. He's said it a million times before. I guess the words have lost their meaning. There's no emotion in his voice. I'd sound like that if I had to speak Latin every day for – by the looks of him – a hundred years.

I follow Ambrogio down the aisle and we join the line of worshippers still waiting to take communion. I have no idea what I'll do when it's my turn. The priest says, '*Corpus Christi*,' and they each say, 'Amen'. They open their mouths one by one, and the priest places a wafer on to each of their tongues. OK, it looks pretty easy. I let Ambrogio go first. The priest looks pissed off when he sees Ambrogio. He purses his lips and frowns. Odd. Then it's time for my wafer. The body of Christ is dry, like eating a Pringle. I could do with some wine to wash it all down. Or the blood of Christ, I should say. Ambrogio and I sit down on a pew at the front on the left and wait in silence for the priest to come.

Rustling vestments.

'*Salve*,' says the priest. 'Elisabetta! Good to see you! As always!'

He kisses my hand. I can smell the espresso he downed and the cigarette he smoked before starting his shift. 'Good to see you, father. How are you?' I know how to speak to priests. I used to watch *Ballykissangel*.

'Much better now I've seen you,' he smiles, looking deep into my eyes and clasping my hand a little too tightly. Creepy. Flirty. Inappropriate. I wish he'd let go of my hand. What is he doing? Is he searching for my soul (and failing to find one)? Is he reading my mind? Does he know I'm not Beth? Did Jesus just tell him?

A shiver runs down the length of my spine. The church is cold. The priest turns away.

'Ambrogio,' he says, shaking his hand and embracing him like a long-lost son. '*Come stai?*'

'*Bene, bene, grazie, padre.*'

Ambrogio turns towards me and puts his hand on my shoulder.

'*Amore*, why don't you wait for me here?' He gestures to the pew. 'I'm going to confession. I shouldn't be long.'

I watch Ambrogio and the priest walk arm in arm towards a dark wooden box at the side of the church. The confession box looks like a giant wardrobe. Is heaven like Narnia? Does God look like Aslan or Mr Tumnus? What are they going to talk about in there? I hope it's not me. They pull a scarlet velvet curtain across the little door. There's the scream of a metal grille. I think about Adam. That guy never called me.

I imagine them kneeling as I've seen people do in films. Bless me, father, for I have sinned. I wonder how many Hail Marys I'd get? I hope this isn't going to take too long; I'm already bored. What am I even doing here? I stare up at Jesus, nailed to the cross, and I know exactly how he feels. Hurry up . . .

I sit and study the statues and paintings. It's a little unnerving, to tell you the truth. There are lots of pictures of people on fire. Everywhere you look there are women in flames. Screaming silently, writhing in pain. I think that's supposed to be a picture of Purgatory. There's a Renaissance painting of Jesus and Mary: a stunning Tuscan landscape extends behind them, rolling hills, lush green trees and a pale-blue lake. It doesn't look much like first-century Judea. For some reason, Mary always reminds me of Beth. I wonder if Mary had a sister. I hear a noise coming from the confession box. Someone says something that sounds like 'Caravaggio'. Ambrogio and the priest are shouting in Italian, or at least Ambrogio seems to be. I have no idea what they're saying. I'm going to need to learn Italian if I'm staying in Sicily. Although I guess Beth never bothered. If you say things loudly and slowly enough in English, then people tend to get it.

Ambrogio pulls the curtain aside and storms out of the confession box.

'Elizabeth! We're leaving,' he says.

His voice reverberates and booms, echoes around the walls of the church. Even the floor seems to shake.

'Come on. Let's go,' Ambrogio says, grabbing my hand and yanking me up. Oh shit, he seems cross. Did the priest just tell him that I'm the wrong twin? Is he angry with me or with the priest?

'Hey!' I say, falling over my heels. He doesn't let go. He drags me along towards the front door and pushes me out into the blinding sun.

'Fucking priest,' says Ambrogio, when we are outside. He slams the church door shut behind us. Well, that answers that. I hope.

'What happened?' I ask.

We walk around the corner to Bar Mocambo and sit out at a table overlooking the square. Ambrogio orders two shots of grappa. He's shaking with rage. I'm shaking with fear.

My hand trembles as I reach over to Ambrogio's packet of cigarettes lying on the table. I take out two smokes. Then I remember: I am Beth, so I'm right-handed. I struggle to light them with the wrong stupid hand and mess up the lighter. Ambrogio looks up.

'What? Still smoking?'

'Yeah. I'm stressed out.'

Somehow, I manage to light one for Ambrogio and place it in

between his lips. I light one for me and take a drag. Ahh, formaldehyde and tar: that's better.

'Since when did you start smoking?' he frowns.

'Since now,' I say, trying to sound cool. I don't think he knows. I think it's OK. 'So, what was all that shouting about?'

He gives me a look: *not here*, he scowls. The waiter arrives with two shots of grappa balanced on a little tray. I check out his ass. Not bad at all, but not a patch on Ambrogio's. We down our shots. It's not very nice. I think I prefer Malibu.

'Let's go for a sail, take our minds off this shit,' says Ambrogio, slamming his glass back down on the table. 'Come on. We can talk properly out there.'

Oh no. Not a boat. Not a yacht on the water. Not me and Ambrogio alone at sea. I watch that scene play out in my head and it doesn't end well at all for me. Perhaps he's bluffing? Perhaps he knows? He's just playing me along until he gets me alone. I don't want to go. I know I can't trust him. He was going to kill me. That was the plan! He'll knock me out and throw me into the water, the second he gets a chance.

'Can't we just stay here?' I say. It's safer in public with all of these people. Surely he can't touch me in the middle of town? In the middle of the day?

'We're going,' he says, standing up.

Chapter Twenty-four

Ionian Sea

'More champagne, darling?' Ambrogio asks.

He tops up my glass with a bottle of something old and expensive-looking.

'Mmm, Krug 1983,' I say, reading the label. Is that 'Kr*u*g' as in 'pug' or 'Kr*u*g' as in 'Hoover'? He gives me a look. I switch the glass from my left hand to my right. Knock back the champagne in one go. He crunches the bottle back into the ice bucket. That ice won't last long out here in this heat; it feels like the sea is about to catch fire. It's as though we're sailing on smouldering coals. I'm definitely getting a tan.

'I think this one's better than the '86, don't you?'

I have absolutely no idea. 'Oh yes. Definitely,' I say.

'It's the Grande Cuvée; it's got a lower dosage and more refined texture. The Pinot noir tastes like apples, don't you think?'

It tastes like Lambrini. 'Yes, apples, definitely apples,' I say.

Ambrogio smiles; he seems pleased I agree. I'm glad he's calmed down a bit now, at least. I don't think he's plotting to lose me at sea. I wonder why he was so cross with that priest. I need to find out what's going on. I want some more champagne.

Our towels are spread out on the deck. The dark wood scalds the soles of my feet. I'm wearing one of Beth's tiny bikinis; it's by Agent Provocateur. It's basically dental floss (lucky I did my bikini line). With these sunglasses on, I look pretty convincing, but I'll keep my sarong on, just in case. Ambrogio lies next to me in his vacuum-pack Speedos; our bodies are pressed close together. Ambrogio's as hot as a Bondi Beach lifeguard (not that I'd ever watch *Bondi Rescue* or daytime TV). His skin feels hot. He's practically naked. Man, oh man, I want him so bad. All this danger is turning me on. (I know, I know, it's pretty messed up, but that's an actual *thing*, it's not *just me*. Like during the Blitz in 1941, Londoners spent all the air raids shagging. Fear is a natural aphrodisiac. I'm getting off on the menace.)

A light wind has picked up, I'm pleased to say; there's just enough breeze to keep us cool as the yacht bobs along the languid Ionian. It's a perfect evening. The azure sky is empty, endless. The sea stretches out, infinitely blue. The water sparkles and twinkles around us as the sun sinks towards the distant horizon. This is heaven. Paradise. Bliss. Better than all those travel brochures. Better than *A Place in the Sun*. (OK, so maybe I watched it just once or twice.) I look out at the water, clear as diamonds, and begin to relax. I can figure out all of this craziness later, but for now I just want to chill out.

'Would you like some more oysters?' Ambrogio says.

'Oh yes. They're lovely,' I say.

You know, I never thought I'd like them (they're ugly little critters with their wrinkled grey shells and slimy brown organs) but they were my sister's favourite food and, surprisingly, quite nice. Plus there's the zinc! Apparently.

'The Languedoc oysters are so skinny these days; these Italian ones really taste of the sea.'

'Mmm, yeah.' Whatever you say.

He brings over a heavy, ice-filled platter and squeezes some lemon juice over the oysters. He adds some shallots and a dash of Tabasco. A little chopped parsley and ground black pepper.

'Open wide.'

I open my mouth and swallow it whole. I feel like a seal at a Sea World show.

'Yum,' I say, giggling just like my twin: carefree, girly. Ambrogio's right. They do taste of the sea. But in a good way.

We lie side by side on the deck. Ambrogio strokes my hair and I snuggle into him. I rest my head on his pillow-like chest. I feel safe, protected, like a chick in a nest. He has no idea that I am Alvie. I like being Beth. It's growing on me. I can see us growing old together, Ambrogio and me. Alvie and Ambrogio. Ambrogio and Alvie: A A, like the Automobile Association or Alcoholics Anonymous. I picture countless hours spent sailing his yacht, his million-fucking-dollar yacht. Afternoons turning to evenings. Evenings turning to night. We would lie, side by side, right here on this deck, watching suns set and bleed into the ocean, watching moons rise and stars burn out. It's perfect, dreamlike. Almost too perfect; it doesn't feel real. But it is real and I've earned it. Just like L'Oréal: *because I'm worth it*. I worked hard for this shit. It's all I've ever dreamed of. I deserve it. I do.

'Do you fancy sailing to Lampedusa?' Ambrogio asks, running a warm hand along my shoulder to the base of my neck.

What the hell is Lampedusa? 'Erm,' I say, looking around. Is it some kind of lighthouse?

'You can see it starboard.'

I look towards the left.

'No, that's port. *Starboard*,' he says. 'What's with you today? Did you bang your head?'

Damn. I know. Beth would have known that. I smile sweetly and look off into the distance, towards the right. I shake my head. I can't see anything.

'No, you're right. Let's just stay around here. One island looks very much like another. After a while all the beaches look the same. It's boring.'

We lie back and watch the graceful seabirds dance high in the sky, waltzing and swirling in twos and threes, their bright-white feathers as pale as ghosts. Perhaps we'll have a baby, Ambrogio and me? A little girl, to go with the boy. She'll look like me, but be half Italian. Darker hair. A better tan. And what about the name? Something Italian-sounding: Sophia? Angelina? Monica

Bellucci? Yes, that would be perfect. Our perfect family. Our perfect home. I'll take thousands of pictures and post them on Instagram. Facebook. Twitter. Tweet about my gorgeous family. My beautiful life. Look how sexy my husband is. Look how cute all my kids are. I'll have more followers than Kim Kardashian; I'll get hundreds of thousands of 'Likes'.

And with all this money, I won't need to work. I'll eat and drink and shop and eat. Emilia can help me with the children. Perhaps we'll hire some more staff too? I'll finally have time to work on my poetry. A collection of haikus. An award-winning book. Perhaps I'll buy a handbag dog? A little chihuahua to replace Mr Dick? Or perhaps a pet bear, like Lord Byron. That would be cool.

'Beth?' he says.

'Yes, my darling?'

I turn to look at my handsome husband. My wonderful, beautiful, gorgeous man. I still don't know where Beth got those bruises. Why was my twin so cross with Ambrogio? Why was she running away from him? The diamonds in the handbag? That row with her neighbour? What is Ambrogio going to say? He suddenly looks serious. Is he going to kill me? He's going to wrestle me, strangle me now and throw my body out into the sea!

'I'm so sorry about your sister, about the way things turned out.'

Oh *that*. I see.

I sit up on my elbows and squint into the sun. I find Elizabeth's Gucci shades and pull them back on.

'Oh. Yes. Me too,' I say, turning to face him. I pull my lips down into a pout. Crinkle my nose up like Beth used to do.

'I mean, the way that it happened, not being able to bury her properly . . . I know we were going to have a proper funeral, no expense spared. I feel terrible about it.'

I reach across and take his hand. It feels good.

'I understand,' I say, stroking his fingers. Can we change the fucking subject? I was starting to have fun.

'It's just — it couldn't have happened at a worse time, you know, with this deal? With the Caravaggio? I don't know what we're going to do now. We need to make another plan.'

I literally could not have less of a clue. 'I know,' I say, 'the whole thing's just . . . messed up.'

'We'll have to think of something else. We're running out of time. This is our one shot. Our only way out. We can't afford to make a mistake. You know what could happen . . . what they might do . . .'

'Mmm, yeah. Sure,' I say.

Ambrogio sighs and sits up on his elbows. He takes a sip of his champagne.

'I mean, in a way, it's better that she's dead, you know, like euthanasia?'

My skin bristles; my shoulders tense. 'No, darling, I don't know what you mean.'

'Well, you know you were always saying what a freak she was . . . how sad her life was. At least this way her suffering has ended. Perhaps it's for the best.'

She said *what*? How could Beth say those things about me? I want to slap her, but she isn't here. I want to drag her down to the bottom of the sea and kick her and punch her! Two-faced cow! How could she? How dare she? Slagging me off behind my back to the man of my dreams! Lying about me! Bitch!

He gives me a reassuring smile, so I smile back and pretend to agree. 'Yes, it's for the best.'

I stare at the seabirds. I think that's an albatross.

'Beth?' he says *again*.

Oh my God, what is it now?

He stands up suddenly and gives me a twirl. 'You didn't say anything. Don't you like my new Speedos?'

I gawk at Ambrogio's swimming trunks. His tight butt

cheeks are an inch from my nose. They're just plain blue Speedos. 'Oh, are they new?'

He turns around and shows off his bum.

'Yes. You really don't remember? I couldn't decide between the red and the blue . . .'

'So you bought the blue.'

'So I bought them both! These are the blue. Don't you like them?'

He runs his hands over his *Men's Health* abs and smooths the fabric of his shorts.

'They're nice,' I say. 'I mean, they're *perfect*.'

'You prefer the red ones, don't you?' he says.

'No. I don't. I like them both.'

He leans in and kisses me full on the mouth: a soft, warm, lingering kiss. He tastes of apples – oh, the champagne.

'Can you ever forgive me?' he asks under his breath, kissing my jaw, my throat, my collarbone. 'About your sister?'

Oh, Ambrogio . . .

'I already have.'

I run the palms of my hands along his hot, bronzed, muscular back and breathe in deep. His scent is pure sex: Armani Code Black, pheromones, tobacco. It's driving me nuts. Whatever happens, I'm not going to sleep with him . . . not here. Not yet. I don't feel ready. I need more time to get into character. I need a chance to 'transform'. If I sleep with him now, I'm totally screwed. There's no way I fuck at all like my sister; Beth was a doormat in bed. Guaranteed.

Ambrogio feels under the straps of my bikini, reaches down and cups my breasts in his hands. My nipples harden. I bite my lip. He leans in towards me, kissing my neck, pulling me closer. I pull away.

'*Merda!*' says Ambrogio, jumping up suddenly.

He runs over to the helm of the yacht. Cliffs loom mere metres away. What the fuck?

'Help me,' he says, grabbing hold of the wheel and steering it frantically.

I get up and run over. How did we miss that? Oh my God, we're going to crash. It's the *Costa Concordia* all over again. We stand side by side and tug at the steering wheel. Then I realize: my sarong; it's gone. It's still on the deck over there where I left it. I look down at my body, suddenly self-conscious. I'm freaking out. I need to distract him. I jump on the steering wheel and pull it down hard. Ambrogio grabs it and pulls it back up.

But it's too late.

CRASH! BANG! BOOM!

The yacht lurches, shudders and shakes. Are we going to capsize? There's a crack as the rudder smashes into some rocks.

'*Merda!*' he says again. 'I hope we're not stuck!'

But we are. Stuck fast.

'I'm so sorry. I fell.'

Ambrogio looks out across the sea, but there aren't any boats.

'Come on,' he says eventually. 'Let's jump in. We can swim to the shore. It isn't far.' He takes my hand and leads me to the edge of the yacht. I peer down into the dark-green water; it looks very deep. It looks really scary. 'We'll have to go back and get help.'

He disappears and I hear a SPLASH! Before I know it, he's swimming away. He looks just like a dolphin, slick and shiny in the water. He looks like a far better swimmer than me.

Ambrogio turns around in the sea and shouts, 'Come on, Beth! Jump in! Let's go.'

I stand at the edge of the yacht and look down. I don't have much choice. I can't exactly stay here on the fucking *Titanic* all by myself. Scenes from *Jaws* flash through my head. Row upon row of razor-sharp teeth. Floating limbs. Bits of gristle. The salt water crimson with gallons of blood. I scan the horizon for fins. Nothing there. OK, here goes. I close my eyes and pinch my nose. One, two, three – jump! I cannonball into the water. It looked so warm from up there on the boat, but it's not! It's freezing, glacier ice. My arms and legs are thrashing, crashing, flailing about like I'm an electrocuted frog. Come on, Alvie, *you're a mermaid*. Ambrogio's watching. Swim like Beth.

I do my best impression of Ariel and front crawl slowly towards the shore. I look about for shadows in the water. If you see a shark, you've got to punch it in the nose. Ambrogio takes my hand – at last! – and pulls me up to the rocks by the shore. I look back at the boat sinking slowly behind me. A gash in the hull is filling up with water. The yacht is completely destroyed.

Chapter Twenty-five

Taormina, Sicily

We fall into bed, our limbs entwined, our bodies pressed together.

'Sorry about the yacht. I'll make it up to you,' I say.

Ambrogio doesn't reply, he just kisses me deeper; his mouth is greedy for my mouth. He can just buy another boat, surely? I pull away and he rips off his polo. I watch his stomach muscles ripple and stroke his abs with my finger. His skin is hot and smooth and tanned a deep, dark, golden brown. He's so delicious, he's practically edible. His stomach looks like a bar of milk chocolate. I reach across to the lamp on the bedside table and flick the switch, pull a corner of the sheet to cover my breasts. I don't want him to see me, just in case. But I can't wait any longer; I want to fuck.

'Don't turn it off,' Ambrogio says. 'You know I don't like to do it in the dark.'

'I've got a bit of a headache,' I say.

We're doing it! Right now! We're actually doing it! I reach for his boxers and yank them down, feel for his penis.

'Oh,' I say.

'What's wrong?'

'Nothing.'

'Why have you stopped?'

More cocktail sausage than bratwurst.

I'm sure it was bigger than that in Oxford. Actually, come to think of it, I can't remember . . . I was really, really drunk and it was a long time ago. It's not like I had a benchmark in those days. I had no experience with men.

Ambrogio pulls me in towards him, licks my neck and bites my earlobe. He squeezes my tits like a stress ball. I reach down his belly towards his penis. Maybe if I touch it, give it a stroke, it might get bigger? Our legs twine together. I feel the inside of his foot with my toe. Oh.

'Aren't you going to take off your socks?'

'What? Why should I? It never bothered you before.'

'It doesn't matter.' I roll my eyes in the semi-dark.

He moves down my body between my legs. Something soggy: his chin in my bum hole, his nose on my clit. His tongue hangs out somewhere south of my vulva. It's not really working.

'Are you done yet?' I ask.

He wipes his mouth, then clambers on top. My whole body tenses. What if I feel different to Beth? What if she wasn't a doormat after all, did some mind-blowing tricks I don't know? Did she know tantra? Could she suck like a Hoover? Could she hook her heels behind her neck?

Is it in yet?

I needn't have worried.

Ambrogio pounds me for four or five minutes, sweating, groaning, panting, straining. It's not very nice. I think he might actually chew off my ear. I'm just going to fake it. I remember that scene in *When Harry Met Sally*. I recall my experience with sex toy No. 5.

'Ohhhhhhhhhhhhhhhhhhhhhhhhhhhhhhhhhhhhhhhhhhhhh-hhhhhhhhhhhhhh!'

Ambrogio comes in three short bursts and then flops down hard on his side of the bed.

Well, that sucked. Seriously? Is that it? I must have been *wasted* in Oxford. He seemed to enjoy it, I suppose, but I think I prefer Mr Dick. I can't believe it. After all these years. It's so unfair! I'm gutted.

'*Merda!*' says Ambrogio, jumping out of the bed and shrinking back from me, his back to the wall. 'What the fuck? *Alvina?*' he says.

He's looking me right in the eye like a shark, trying to read me like Larry David, like an operative from the C I A. A shadow falls across his face.

'*Alvina?*' I say. 'Why – why would you call me that?'

Not a single hair on my body moves. Not that I have any. I shaved them all off when I became Beth. I'm petrified, stone-still, immobile, like one of those people in the museum in Pompeii, like that marble statue of Beth.

'You're not Beth. You come different,' he says.

Do we? Oh shit. Of course, I see: he means we *fake* different.

'What the hell's going on? You'd better fucking explain!' he shouts, punching a fist into the headboard. 'What the fuck did you do to my wife?'

I *could* explain, but it wouldn't make any difference. By the look in his eyes, he wants to rip me apart.

'I don't know what you're talking about,' I say at last, my voice shaking. I'm going to *die*. This is it.

'Oh really?' he shouts. His voice is thunder.

'Really,' I say.

He stands up tall on the other side of the bed, flexing his fists. He looks really cross.

'What did you do? You killed her, didn't you? You fucking bitch, you killed my wife!'

'No! I didn't! Please . . . just listen!'

'You killed your sister! I should have known! You've been acting off all fucking day. Beth would never eat a whole pack of Pringles! And all that business with the yacht – Beth knew her way around a boat. She . . . she . . . she . . . she . . . we were supposed to kill *you*!' Ambrogio is tugging at his hair, practically pulling it out at the roots.

'I'm Beth! I'm Beth! I promise I'm not Alvie!'

I shrink back into the headboard, choking back tears. He grabs my ankles and pulls me back down the bed. Climbs on top and pins me down.

'What did I get you for Christmas last year?'

'I-I-I don't remember.'

'Where did we have our first date?'

'I-I-I don't recall.'

His face is less than an inch above mine; I can feel his saliva spray into my eyes. If I wasn't so scared, I'd be so grossed out. His immense weight presses down.

'Which football team do I support?'

I'm going to just guess . . . 'Is it Italy?'

Behind Ambrogio, there's a doll on the mantelpiece, the one that Elizabeth had as a kid. It flops over the fireplace staring right at me, something flashes in its shiny glass eyes. One solitary pin sticks out from its toes. It's like Beth is here. It's like she is watching me, right now, this very minute. I can feel her presence. I can feel her wrath.

'Is there something you want to tell me, *Alvina*,' Ambrogio says, leaning in closer. He's shaking now, his eyes are wide. I hadn't noticed how strong he was, bulging shoulder muscles, biceps, pecs. He could snap my neck like a twig.

'How . . . how do you know we come different?' I say. *It's worth a shot . . .*

'I fucked you in Oxford. Or were you too drunk to recall?'

'Shit,' I whisper, covering my mouth. 'So you did know it was me? It was Alvie?'

'Of course I did. What, do you think I'm an idiot?'

I shake my head. 'No, of course not.'

Ambrogio loosens his grip a little. Rubs his temples, closes his eyes.

'I just . . . I just . . . I don't understand. Why the fuck were you dressed up as Beth?'

I seize the moment. He looks confused; this is my chance! I

wriggle out and leap up off the bed. I grab my dress and sprint for the door – lucky it's on my side of the room. Ambrogio's naked and, from the corner of my eye, I see him scrambling around for his pants. I fly out the door, don't look back.

I run down the hall, down the stairs, through the villa, pulling my dress on over my head. My palms are sweaty; perspiration prickles all over my body, my back, my neck. The cool night air makes me shiver. I push through the door and sprint across the terrace, bare feet smashing the patio tiles. I run down the driveway and on to the road. I don't turn around but I can hear him running close behind me, his feet crunching gravel, his voice raised.

'ALVINA! COME HERE!'

He's going to kill me.

It's quiet. It's dark. I won't be able to outrun him, but I think I might be able to hide. I race down the road towards the amphitheatre. It's only about a two-minute walk, so it shouldn't take long. There's got to be somewhere to hide around here: a bush, a rock. I look around, searching, searching. I run down the hill with my limbs flailing wildly. Sweat streams down my face. My dress clings tightly to my skin. I wish I was wearing some pants. Sharp stones pierce the soles of my feet. I kick something hard – Fuck! That hurt – I think I've broken a toe! The adrenaline's pumping, I'm stumbling, falling, but it's better than the alternative: Ambrogio, pissed off.

I see a rock against a fence in the semi-darkness and leap up on to it. I scramble over the top and catch my thigh on a rusty nail – Ow! Shit! – skin rips. Now I've got tetanus. Something warm trickles down my leg. What is it? Blood, sweat, semen? But I don't have time. I'm over the top. I jump down now and sprint for the theatre. Ambrogio's coming, a few metres behind.

'Alvie! Stop! Come here and tell me. Why the fuck were you dressed up as Beth? What was she up to?'

The fence crashes down as he scrambles up over it.

'I want to know what the fuck's going on.'

The only light comes from the moon; I can just about see the auditorium below me. I run down the steps towards the stage. I trip in the darkness and smash my knee. My face smacks the earth: grit and iron. There's dirt in my eyes and they're watering, stinging. I blink and blink and breathe in dust. Footsteps pounding close behind me; Ambrogio's closing in. Oh fuck! I heave myself up and off the ground, my knee throbbing, my toe aching. I'm coughing, spluttering, struggling to breathe.

I run for the stage and climb on to the platform. There are columns at the back and I head towards them. I hide behind a column, squat down, hold my breath. I see him running towards the stage. I scramble across to the next column along.

'You can't run for ever,' says Ambrogio. 'Come here, Alvina! Everyone's going to know what you did. Do you hear?'

No! No! No! No! I shake my head to block out the shouting. Sing to myself in my head: 'I Should Be So Lucky', 'Shake It off' . . . He jumps up on the stage. I see him stop and look both ways. A glint of silver. Something in his hand! What the hell is that? A knife? A gun?

He's going to fucking make me pay.

He doesn't know which way I've gone. He turns his back and creeps towards the opposite side of the empty stage. I tiptoe away to the next column along. I crouch down low in a shady corner, panting, cursing, my heart exploding, my forehead pressing against cool marble. My skin's burning up. My throat is dry. There are at least three columns between Ambrogio and me. I need a vodka. I want to cry.

He turns around and walks towards me.

It's a motherfucking gun!

I make myself small and catch my breath, breathing as softly as I can. Don't make a sound. Keep quiet, Alvina. Do not fuck up. I wish I had my Swiss army knife, or a corkscrew like that girl on the train. I wish I had a gun. I feel a rock on the ground by my feet and grasp it tightly with trembling fingers. It's the size of a Sicilian blood orange, heavy and round with a pointed end. He's getting closer. Closer. Closer. He knows I'm here . . . somewhere . . . somewhere. I see his figure moving, stealthy, creeping on tiptoes, a black silhouette. He's trying to be quiet, trying to hide. He inches towards me, peering into the shadows. It's quiet, save for Ambrogio's breathing. Animal. Dangerous. It's almost a growl. I hold my breath, though I want to scream. If I can hear him, then he can hear me. He's only a couple of metres away. Two metres. One metre.

'Why were you dressed as Elizabeth, Alvie?' Ambrogio says into the darkness. 'That wasn't the plan. What's going on?'

I leap up high and smash the rock down hard on his head. I pound him again with all my strength. He falls to the ground and drops the gun. Collapses, face down on the stage. I stand over him now, the pointed rock still clutched in my fingers, my whole body shaking, poised to attack. His arms thrash around at both his sides and he reaches out for my ankle. Grabs it.

'Shit!' I scream.

His grip is firm. He's far from dead. I need to finish him off, but I'm falling! He's got both my ankles and he's pulling me towards him. I stagger and fall down on to his chest. I raise the rock above my head, bring it down on top of his skull, smashing his head again and again and again and again and again.

CRACK!

CRACK!

CRACK!

CRACK!

I'm screaming and crying and shaking all at once. He's stopped moving now, fucking finally, but his fingers still curl around my ankles, gripping as tight as iron shackles. I kick my feet free. I drop the rock, my fingers unable to grip any longer. There's something slimy all over my hands, all up my arms and down my dress. A fleck of blood clings on to my lip: the taste of steak cooked rare. Drops of blood splatter my face, my neck. My whole body's burning, radiating heat. I'm panting and sweating and sweltering hot. The cool night air wraps its tentacles around me like a squid or an octopus or a corpse's fingers. I look down at the body and shiver.

I jump up and stagger back, see the gun where Ambrogio dropped it, only a few feet away. Why did Ambrogio own a gun? That was close. He could have shot me! Who the hell are these people? I thought I knew them. Thought they were family. I don't know anything at all. I run over and grab it. I've never seen a real gun before, only toy ones and water pistols. I've never been paintballing or to Laser Quest. I weigh the gun in both hands: cold and heavy, surprisingly heavy. Alien. Strange. A rush of excitement surges all through my body. Ambrogio's gun! I'm going to keep it. Now it's mine!

I look down at Ambrogio's sprawling figure. He's naked apart from a pair of black boxers. The back of his head is matted with blood. I stand, doubled over, my hands on my knees, catching my breath. My whole body's shaking, uncontrollable. My arms ache. My thighs throb. He isn't moving. Surely he's dead? I clutch the gun in my left hand, aim it, vaguely, in the direction of his head. I inch slowly forwards towards the body, reach down low to find his jugular. I feel with my fingers; I'll count for ten seconds. One, two, three, four . . . Thank God: no pulse. I snatch my hand away from his neck, expecting him to turn and bite me, jump up and grab me or scream in my face. I'll shoot him down if he does. But he's still. He's dead. I can't believe it. He's gone! I'm safe!

Now what the hell am I going to do?

Chapter Twenty-six

I bang on the door as hard as I can.

'Salvatore! Salvatore!'

I bang and bang until footsteps thud inside the villa. Shit, the gun! He'll freak out. I throw the gun under a bush by the front door and kick some leaves over the top. I'll come back and get it later.

'*Che cosa? Che cosa?*' I hear a voice say.

A man swings the door open. He's tall and broad, larger and taller than Ambrogio; it's Salvatore. He reminds me of a celebrity wrestler, someone hot from W W E. He rubs his eyes. Poor thing; he's been sleeping. I've woken him up. He must think this is his worst ever nightmare, his mistress at his door dripping with blood.

'*Oh minchia!* Are you O K?'

He thinks it's my blood.

'Salvatore,' I say. I fall into his arms, burst into tears and sob on his chest. He pushes me off and steps back, in shock.

'Beth? What's happened? What time is it?' He looks at his wrist, at the place where his Patek Philippe would be if it were day, but it's not. It's the middle of the fucking night.

'Please, please, you have to help me,' I say, gripping on to his forearms, my nails digging in, my eyes wide as graves. 'He was going to kill me, I had no choice!' He's *dead*.

I watch his face begin to change as Salvatore registers what I've just said. 'What? Who? *Kill* you?' he says.

'Ambrogio.' I bite my lip. I can still taste the blood. I run my tongue along the front of my teeth and swallow hard.

'Ambrogio? Kill you?' says Salvatore. 'I don't believe it!

Ambrogio would never lay a finger on you. He's a fucking *cornuto*. A pussy.'

'He had a gun,' I say. 'He did!'

He takes my hand and pulls me inside, leans outside and scans the garden. Nothing. No one. He slams the door shut. Salvatore leads me into the kitchen and turns on the lights: unbearably bright, they hurt my eyes. I've been hanging out in the dark too long, like some kind of owl.

'Sit,' he orders.

Salvatore's wearing a tight white T-shirt and blue-and-green striped boxers by Calvin Klein. I've already seen him half naked in the garden. I know he looks better with his top off. He towers above me, tall and muscular. He must work out, like, every day. I can see what my sister saw in him. I'm sure I'd probably have an affair. How are Italian men so impossibly attractive? I'd go crazy on Tinder if I lived over here! But it's just not like Beth to be unfaithful. It's so out of character. Why was she cheating? Running away? Ambrogio was perfect. Although, I suppose, he was crap in bed. But still, there must have been something else. She would never have wanted to leave her husband. It's just not in her nature. I don't understand.

Salvatore pours me a glass of tap water. My hand is shaking; some of it spills. I gulp it down and look up at a clock hanging up on the wall: 1.13 a.m. Funny, that's exactly the same time that Beth died. Salvatore stands over me, looking at me strangely. He must be about six foot six. If it wasn't for the blood splattered all up my arms and all over my dress, I'm not sure he'd believe me.

'So, you think you've killed *Ambrogio*?' he says.

I can tell he still doesn't believe me.

'Yes.' I nod.

'And you're sure he's *dead*?'

A wave of doubt rises. The earth shifts suddenly beneath my feet. What if Ambrogio wasn't dead after all? What if he got up and followed me here? My eyes dart to the front door at the end of the hall, but it's closed; it's dark. There's nobody there. Salvatore checked. He looked in the garden. The automatic lights would detect any movement. I take a deep breath.

'I'm sure,' I say.

'How did you kill him?'

'With a rock.'

Even to me that sounds absurd. There's a pause while he considers this fact.

'*Minchia!*' says Salvatore. 'A rock.'

It's just sunk in. He glares at me now, his blue eyes angry and accusing. What have I done? Is he going to help me? Or is he cross? Will he turn me in to the police? Salvatore paces the kitchen, his muscular arms twitching and flexing, his bare feet pounding the flagstones: six foot six of pure meat and muscle. No wonder Beth wanted *him* onside. An angry gorilla. A grizzly bear. Oh my God. I suddenly get it; the bruises on Beth's arms. They weren't from Ambrogio. *He's a pussy.* They were from *him*!

'Why the hell was he trying to kill you? Is it because he found out about us?'

'Yes,' I say, suddenly dizzy. I think I am about to faint. He's going to hit me. Beat me up. Oh, why did I chuck that gun?

'How did Ambrogio find out?'

'My sister told him.' Does that sound plausible?

Salvatore pauses. 'Now why would she do that?'

'I think she wanted him all for herself. She is a bit of a cow like that.' Good: present tense. Like she's still alive. Well done, Alvie. Thinking on your feet.

Salvatore sighs. I think he believes me. Why does he believe me? What has Beth told him about Alvina? He thinks she's a bitch.

'So . . . where is it? The body?' he says.

'On the stage in the amphitheatre.'

'In the *amphitheatre*? What the hell is he doing up there?'

I wish I knew.

'I don't know. He chased me,' I say, and my voice breaks. My head is spinning. My vision is blurry with tears. I'm about to wipe my cheek with my hand when I see that it's covered in blood.

Salvatore is shaking with rage. I've woken him up and brought him a problem. He looks pissed off.

'Why should I help you? After what you said?'

What the hell did I say?

'I-I-I . . .'

'I didn't think you were speaking to me. You never wanted to see me again. If I wouldn't help you, you didn't want to know.'

What? Oh. The row with my sister. I remember them arguing by his car.

'I do want to see you. I'm sorry,' I say. Do I sound convincing? Is that the right amount of remorse? The tears are falling freely now; they flood my eyes and slide down my face. Real tears; I'd forgotten what they felt like. Oh my God, am I actually *crying*? I must be turning into Beth. He's not going to help me. Why did I come here? He'll beat me up or call the police.

'So, in fact, you don't wish I was dead?'

'No.' Really? Is *that* what she said? I wonder what he did. It must have been bad.

'But that's what you said . . .'

Shit. Nice one, Beth.

'I didn't mean it . . . not really. Please?' What would Beth do? I flutter my eyelashes. Flirting probably works best when one's not covered in blood. 'Please. Please.' I sob into my hands now. Who cares about the blood? I'm already messy. If he doesn't help me, I'm totally screwed.

'Wait here. I'll get dressed,' he says at last. I look up at him – *really?* – blinking through tears.

'Oh! Thank you! Thank you! Thank you!' I say. Salvatore, my saviour!

He disappears through the door down the hall. Climbs the stairs with heavy feet. I hear him moving around upstairs. Floorboards creak. The lampshade wobbles. He's a big guy. Two hundred kilos? As heavy as a prize-winning bull.

I finish the water and put the glass down in the sink. His kitchen is sleek and super modern, bespoke, designer. Bosch. Smeg. Nespresso. Alessi. It all looks brand new, like it's never been used. Glossy white surfaces glisten. Minimalist appliances. Italian design. There's a trace of blood from where I just leant my arm on the white plastic table. I take a piece of kitchen paper, run it under the tap and wipe it off. It's one of those kitchens where the bin is hidden; I have no idea where to look. If I touch anything else, I'll stain it with blood. I stand in the middle of the room with the wet paper dripping pink on the white tiled floor.

Salvatore runs back down the stairs. THUD. THUD. THUD. He's changed into dark-blue jeans and a smart black shirt. The shirt fits perfectly; it must be tailor-made. He stops and stares at me for a second, sees the kitchen paper in my hand. He grabs it and throws it into a bin. The bin is hidden in a cupboard under the sink. Ah, so that's where it was. I'll remember for next time. If there is a next time.

'We'll need some water to clean up the mess. Some buckets and a sponge?'

'Let's go,' he says.

'Where is he?' says Salvatore.

I wish we'd brought a torch. It seems to have got even darker. A big, black cloud has swallowed the moon. I scan what I can see of the stage. Columns. Rocks. Sea. Holy shit! Oh my God, is Mount Etna erupting? I knew I couldn't trust it. Isn't that dangerous? The volcano's crater sparks and flickers. Red-hot lava leaps up high: orange, yellow, gold, magenta. A cloud of smoke spews up from the summit. Lightning flashes fill the ash cloud. There's the faint scent of sulphur. The taste of heat. I glance at

Salvatore, but he doesn't seem bothered. Perhaps it does that all the time? I stare at the summit. It looks incredible. I guess it would be cool to survive an eruption. If we survive. Something neat to tell the grandkids?

At first I can't see him. I think he's gone; he's hauled himself up and staggered away. It seems so unreal, like I made it all up: a figment of a fucked-up imagination. I look over my shoulder, perhaps he's still here? Sneaking up on us right now with a rock or a gun? I picture a zombie from *Dawn of the Dead*. But at last I spot him, lying there on the stage in the place where I left him. A long black figure against grey flagstones. Silent. Still. Dead.

'There, on the stage. Look!' I say. I bite the inside of my lip so hard it bleeds.

Salvatore looks in the direction that I'm pointing; I feel him tense. He hadn't believed it. Not till he'd seen it. Neither had I. We run downstairs to the front of the stage. We've brought two buckets, overflowing with water, to clean up the mess: the water in the bucket is slopping and slapping. My feet are wet, my legs all splashed. My knees are weak as I take the steps two or three at a time. The steps seem to stretch to infinity.

What the hell am I doing? It feels like I'm watching myself from afar, a spectator at an ancient Greek tragedy: the more blood and guts spilled the better. Everyone's dead by the end. From out here in the auditorium, the murders seem real, but it's just a play, a three-hour thrill, exciting, entertaining, cathartic. I know the blood is just food colouring. The intestines are those of a pig.

We reach the edge of the stage and jump up. Salvatore first, then he gives me his hand, but I just stand here and stare. I really don't want to get any closer. I think I might throw up. He grabs my hand and hauls me up too, as though I were as light as a feather (*I wish*). I follow him towards the columns that form a line at the back of the stage, towards the body. I stop dead in my tracks. Ambrogio's eyes are still wide open, shining white in the light from the moon. He's looking back up at me. Big stupid eyes like a fish on ice at a fishmonger's; his mouth gaping open, his tongue lolling out. Do fish have tongues? His head is cracked; the blood trickles out. His hair is wet and black. I catch a glimpse of something pale: what is that? His skull?

Beyond the corpse: a heart-stopping view. Etna's still erupting. I'm starting to like it. Flashes of red spark in the night. It's stunning, awesome, epic, sublime. Now that I've figured out it's not death by lava, I can't take my eyes off the fire.

'Beth? BETH? BETH!'

'What?'

'We gotta clean this shit up,' he says.

I turn back to the body, step in a bit closer. The stench of fresh blood makes me gag: blood mixed with sulphur and sea-salt air. It fills my nostrils, lines my throat: a punch in the mouth, a missing tooth, a bleeding tongue. I'm gargling blood; blood floods my mouth, my stomach, my lungs. I'm choking, drowning, sinking in blood.

The flagstones are dark, slippery, wet. I wring the sponge in the bucket and squeeze. Cold water splashes my shins, my feet, feels cool against my broken toe. I scrub at the stones with the sponge. It's not coming off. Even in the dark, I can see it's still there: slick, black blood. I scrub harder and faster, my knuckles scraping, bleeding, raw. My arms are beginning to ache. Shit, it's not working. It's just getting worse. Blood is a bitch to get up.

'Beth?'

'Yeah?' Oh God. What now?

'I thought you said Ambrogio had a gun?'

'He did. He did! He had a gun.'

'So where is it?' he says. 'It isn't here.'

'It must . . . he must . . . he must have dropped it.'

'It's not on the stage. I can't see it.'

Shit.

'It's got to be somewhere in the theatre.'

He gives me a frown and then looks all around him. The theatre is dark and filled with shadows. The auditorium is huge.

'He had one. I promise. I saw it,' I say.

Salvatore sighs.

'OK. Whatever. Help me move him,' he says at last.

I shove the sponge back into the bucket. Salvatore stands at Ambrogio's head, his hands clasped under his armpits, ready. I wipe my forehead with the back of my hand: slimy, wet. I don't want to touch him. I know his skin will be cold.

'The feet,' he says.

I stand up, wincing: my knee! My toe! I bend to grab Ambrogio's feet, hold on to his ankles, but then . . .

Footsteps.

A flashlight.

A silhouette.

'*Che cazzo fai?*' comes a man's voice.

A torch shines bright into my eyes. I'm blinded. I gasp. I drop the feet and stand up.

'Shit,' I say.

'*Merda*,' says Salvatore.

The figure approaches. The footsteps get louder. He runs down the stairs and in two seconds flat he's standing below us by the stage.

Messy blond hair. A uniform. The security guard. Of course. Who else?

'Betta?' he says.

Now would be a good time to cry. I sink down on my knees and sob.

'*Che cazzo?*'

He jumps up on the stage. I feel an arm around my shoulders.

'Oh my God! Betta? What have you done?'

'I-I-I . . .' I say.

'What happened? Betta? Are you OK?'

'She's fine,' says Salvatore, his voice loud and booming on the dead-quiet stage. 'Her husband attacked her, so she knocked him out. He'll be OK.'

The security guard stands up. He shines the torch on Ambrogio's body. It looks even worse like this in the light. A spotlight illuminates the corpse, like some kind of theatrical prop. The bile rises in my throat. I look the other way.

'*Ma è morto?*' says the security guard.

'*Forse è morto,*' Salvatore says.

'Please,' I say, at last, standing up. 'Please, please don't tell anyone about this. I had to do it. I had to,' I say.

The security guard looks into my eyes; in the light from the torch, I can read his terror. Fucking hell, he's going to freak out. This must be his very first body.

'*Madonna mia,*' he says under his breath. 'Betta, *you* killed him? Not this guy?' He shines his torch at Salvatore. Salvatore flinches, turns away. He shields his eyes with his hands.

'I did it. I did it. Please don't say anything.' I grasp hold of his shirt. The security guard shines his torch back at me. I close my eyes. 'Please. Please.'

'*Madonna mia.* Are you crazy?' he says. 'Are you out of your mind? Do you know what you've done? That's *Ambrogio Caruso*! And you're still *here*? You gotta get out of here! They're going to kill you. You gotta fucking disappear!'

I look at the security guard. His eyeballs are bulging out of their sockets, like one of those goldfish with telescope eyes. He looks genuinely scared. Who's going to kill me? Nino? Domenico? Emilia? Salvatore? I'm the only one that's killing around here. Is *that* what he's worried about?

'Shit,' he says, as though this were an afterthought. 'What do I say to my boss?'

I stand up slowly, shaky, unsteady, put my arms around his neck. I wish I knew his fucking name. I pull him into a tight embrace, my hot breath wet against his ear. 'Don't worry. We . . . we'll clear it all up. He was going to kill me, so I-I-I . . .' My chest heaves – heavy – as I sob. I push my breasts up into his body, rest my cheek against his cheek. My fingers run through tousled hair. If I knew his name, I'd whisper it, softly. What the hell is this guy's name?

The security guard steps back, pulls away. He looks into my eyes; I'm begging him, pleading. I wish I was a hypnotherapist. I wish I practised mind control.

'Clean this up. Right now,' he says. 'My boss will be back in an hour.'

Chapter Twenty-seven

A-18 Autostrada: Messina—Catania

Salvatore helped me load Ambrogio's corpse into the boot of his BMW. We're driving to a scenic cliff he knows a few miles away. It has a direct drop to the sea. I wonder if that's where we crashed the yacht. That would be a coincidence. Salvatore's in the Beamer and I'm in the Lambo, following just behind. We're going to leave Ambrogio's car on the edge of the cliff, so it looks like he drove there. I wish I could keep it. Perhaps I can get it back later when this is all over; it's such a beautiful car. It really does suit me. With the soft top down and the wind in my hair, I'm a poster girl for *la dolce vita*.

The gearstick jams and grinds and stutters. I'm not sure what all the different buttons do, don't know what all the dials mean. It's not an automatic car. I only just managed to start it. We're racing around hairpin bends as the sun slips up over the sleepy horizon. It must be about 5 a.m. There's nobody else on the roads. I floor the accelerator, the adrenaline pumping. Salvatore's driving fast and it's dangerous. I fucking love it. I've almost forgotten about the corpse in the boot. I've never felt more alive. Now that I know that Salvo is helping, I'm feeling a bit more chilled out. If we weren't being secretive, undercover, I'd crank up the volume on a Taylor Swift record. Find a Miley track on the radio and scream.

The wind is blowing through my hair, whipping my face and stinging my eyes. I pull a strand out from my mouth and lick chapped lips; they're dry from the dust in the amphitheatre, hurt a bit from when I bit them. I can still taste blood. I feel like a vampire, but now that I'm Beth, I'm a hot one at least: Rosalie Hale Stewart as Bella Swan.

We turn a corner and wheels screech to a stop. I look over at Salvatore's Beamer; he's pulled over and is getting out of the car. We must have arrived at wherever we're going. I pull over too, then jump out of the Lambo and follow Salvatore towards the edge of a massive cliff. We stand side by side and look out at the view. The breeze is warm and cashmere-soft. A crescent of coastline stretches before us, bright lights sparkling into the distance, the long black curve of the sea. In a few minutes, Ambrogio will be down there in that abominable darkness, plunging through cold water, out of sight, out of mind. He'll be sleeping with the fishes, is that what they say? In just a few minutes, the fish will come nibbling. In just a few months, there won't be anything left. At least, that's the plan. Do they have piranhas in the Mediterranean? Do they have great white sharks?

'Beth,' Salvatore says, throwing open the boot of the car.

He grabs hold of Ambrogio's legs and gestures with his head for me to come over. I walk over to the Beamer. OK, here goes . . . I take hold of Ambrogio's arms, cold, heavy, unreal, and together we heave him out and on to the ground. THUD. Oh my God, he's got even heavier. How is that possible? Shouldn't he be lighter? They say the soul weighs 21 grams. I glance down the road in both directions. This would be the wrong time for a car to pass by, for a coachload of tourists or the police to show up. I picture that Japanese schoolgirl waving and smiling out of the window, iPhone camera at the ready: CLICK, CLICK, CLICK. Straight on to Pinterest: 'My European Holiday'. Another X-rated film on fucking YouTube. Really, I could have a career; I could be Zoella's evil twin. I swallow hard and glance at Salvatore.

'We gotta make it look like suicide,' he says into his hands; he's lighting a cigarette. It dangles out of the corner of his mouth, like a Wyoming cowboy *circa* 1954. He looks really sexy.

'Good idea,' I agree. If anyone asks, Ambrogio was depressed. Manically fucking depressed. On the verge. On the edge. He cried himself to sleep every night. I'm not surprised he topped himself. It was only a matter of time.

'If you're gonna jump off a cliff, you don't do it naked,' I say, touching Ambrogio's torso with the tip of an unbroken toe. 'Even if you did, somebody's got to find your clothes.'

It's an excellent point. Ambrogio's nude apart from a pair of black boxers. It wouldn't look right. I think I'm getting the hang of all this now. I'm catching on . . .

'True,' he says.

See? I'm an asset to this operation. I'm learning on the job. Being helpful. Being proactive. That's a first.

I watch as Salvatore whips off his shirt and tight blue jeans, then bends down low to dress Ambrogio. I check out his bum. I take a sharp breath; even in this darkness, I can tell he looks hot. His broad chest, his muscular back. He has the build of a star rugby player, one of the All Blacks: he's as tall as a lock. He must work out at least twice a day. I picture Salvatore naked, fantasize about windswept cliffside sex. It's very distracting; we're supposed to be disposing of a corpse.

'Help me,' he says. 'Pick up his legs.'

We pull on the jeans and then the shirt. The clothes are a little too big for Ambrogio; Salvatore's probably the next size up, a large not a medium (or an X X L?), but they'll have to do. We don't exactly have much choice.

'What about shoes?' I ask, looking at Salvatore's trainers. I think they're Air Jordans. They look really cool. He probably wants to keep them. I know I would.

'Shoes can fall off,' he says. That's true. 'And we're different sizes . . .'

If the cops find a corpse wearing the wrong-sized shoes, then I guess that would look pretty odd. I look down at Salvatore's feet: they're huge, like flippers. I bet he's a good swimmer. I wonder if it's true what they say about big feet? I hope I get to find out.

Salvatore reaches down and grabs hold of Ambrogio's ankles. I bend over and feel for his wrists. I find his shoulders and grab him under the armpits.

'Ready?' he says.

'One, two, three . . .' We heave him up and stagger over towards the cliff. Shit, now that I'm here, standing right at the edge, I can see it's a fucking long way down. I can just about make out the white spray of the waves as they crash against the rocks far below us. That's good, there are rocks. If anyone finds him, it will look like he hit his head as he fell. *When* somebody finds him. I guess it's inevitable, just a waiting game . . . anything else is just wishful thinking. This is Europe, Alvina, not la-la land.

I don't want to stand any closer to the edge; I'm scared of heights and I don't want to fall. I'm already dizzy. Slightly queasy. Am I swaying or is it the sea? We have to stand right here on the verge to throw him off or he'll never go over. We shuffle towards the edge of the cliff, inch by inch. I daren't look over. The body hangs like a hammock between us. I feel my palms begin to slip; we need to chuck him; I'm going to drop him! I wish we could just hurry up.

'Wait a second,' says Salvatore.

Wait? What now?

'Why? What's the matter?'

We drop the body down on the ground. I'm panting, sweating. I want to get this over with. We need to get rid of this corpse.

'Beth, I need to ask you something.'

Now? Are you serious? We're kind of in the middle of something. What if a car comes? The fucking police?

'Sure,' I say. 'What is it?' *Let's chat.* Let's play that party game: *Have you ever . . . ?*

I look into his eyes, but it's dark; I can't read them. What's going on? He looks away. Oh my God, is he still cross? Is he going to throw *me* off the cliff too? What the fuck does he know?

'Beth, after this, will you stop acting crazy? This whole past week . . . it's just been too much. First all that stuff about your sister and now all this? I just . . . don't feel like I know you any more. You're not acting yourself.'

'I promise. I promise. No more crazy. No more mad. I'll just be me.' Whatever you want. Whatever you say. I try a reassuring smile.

What does he mean about my sister? I don't understand. It must be something to do with their fight. I need to know what she was up to. Perhaps Salvatore can fill me in?

Salvo doesn't move a muscle. He doesn't say another word. I hope he's convinced. I hope he believes me. I look down at Ambrogio's body on the ground in the dirt. He looks pretty harmless lying down there like that, not the terrifying monster I'd seen earlier, not the bloodthirsty man I'd been running from.

We pick up the body and hurl it over the edge of the cliff.

Riserva Naturale Orientata Fiumedinisi e Monte Scuderi, Messina Province, Sicily

Back in the Beamer, we don't speak. I want to light one of Salvo's smokes; there's a pack of MS down here by the gearstick, but I'm still being Beth and I don't want to explain. Plus I guess it's too windy. I look over at Salvatore, his profile silhouetted against the road. Fuck, he's sexy: Roman nose, heavy jaw, a body like an action hero. He could be a stunt double for Jason Bourne. Or maybe Thor? My sister had good taste in men, I'll give her that.

Salvatore's hair, thick and black in this light, rather than its usual dirty blond, streams behind him in the wind. I study the stubble on his face; it doesn't look like he's shaved for a week. He has a look that screams *I am an artist! I don't give a fuck*. It's incredibly sexy.

Salvatore is taking a different route back from the cliffs and I don't know why.

'Where are we?'

'In a park.'

'This isn't the way we came.'

'I know.'

We drive through dense woodland. He pulls on to a path that's more dirt track than road and suddenly stops the car. The forest smells of rotting leaves and damp earth. It's deadly silent. *The hour is darkest just before dawn* – I heard that somewhere, but it's only now that I realize it's true. It never really got dark in central London. It never got this quiet. The only sound comes from the birds chirruping in the trees that surround us. The wood is starting to wake up. Why have we stopped here? I'm beginning to freak out. In my experience, Sicilian woodland is a place for burying dead women. Women who look exactly like me. There's a strange expression on Salvatore's face . . . He'll either kiss me or kill me. Fuck.

We're both dirty and sweaty and splattered with blood. I'm wearing a torn summer dress and no shoes or underwear. He's wearing nothing but trainers and Calvin Klein pants. If anyone sees us, we'll look more than suspicious. It wouldn't take a genius to link us to that body washing up on the rocks by the cliff. I'm still bleeding from my knee and that cut on my thigh. My broken toe is starting to throb. I can hear myself breathing, short and shallow. If he tries to attack me, I'd have no chance out here, not on my own, not with his muscles. I've got no weapon. No Swiss army knife. Not even a rock. Why didn't I hang on to that gun? It's dark, but I can just about see the thick curve of his biceps; he's as strong as an ox.

'Salvatore?' I whisper.

I can't get Beth's bruises out of my head. Black and purple and blue and green. On both of Beth's arms. First one, and then two. She'd tried to deny it. She'd tried to cover them up with concealer. I scrunch up my eyes and hold my breath. Every muscle in my body tenses. My heart pounds in my chest like it's trying to escape. What am I doing here in the dead of the night? In the middle of the woods? I want to go home.

Salvatore turns and kisses me hard on the mouth – of course he does, he thinks I'm Beth – and before I know it, I'm kissing him back. He grabs the hair at the back of my head, his fingers digging into my skull, and pulls me in for a desperate kiss.

'I'm sorry,' he whispers, into my mouth, 'I couldn't wait any longer. I want you so bad.'

And I go along with it. Of course I do. I guess Beth really was having an affair! I don't know why. It's just not like my sister. Even if Salvo is hotter than hot. Perhaps she was using him to help her get away. Using him like she used me. That's the only thing that makes sense! I play my part and, do you know what, I really want him. I mean, who wouldn't? He's fucking sexy: Channing hot. Suddenly all my fear has gone. My skin feels alive, almost too sensitive. My heart is racing far too fast. He reaches for my dress and rips it off, the straps digging into my arms and my neck. His strong hands pull me closer, squeezing me into him. And I'm kissing him back. His hot, smooth skin, his sculpted shoulders. I'm already wet; I'm aching for him. It's the most turned on I've ever been. He's kissing my neck, biting me, licking me. I can feel him stiff through the front of his boxers: throbbing, erect. I slide my fingers down his shorts and grasp his hard cock in my hand; it's smooth and sleek like Mr Dick. It's absolutely enormous.

He throws me down on the passenger seat and thrusts my chair back all the way. He pulls a lever at the side of my seat and I lie back. He's done *that* before . . . with my sister? He climbs on top. I'm lying here, dirty, naked, covered in blood. I'm sure I look a total mess. But I'm hot for him and he's hot for me too. I want him inside me, I'm begging him, silently. I just want to come.

I rip down his boxers and they get caught on his leg; there isn't much room. Fuck, he's huge; it's true about the feet. I take him, strong and throbbing, in my hands, then in my mouth: sweet, delicious, a perfect dick. I love the taste of him; I want to eat him up. I suck him, deep and strong, moving my head up and down the shaft, he's smooth against the tip of my tongue. Salvatore groans.

He grabs my arms and pulls away, spins me around so I'm bent over the seat. It's lucky this car's a convertible, or there wouldn't be space. I hear the rustle of foil from the condom. He pushes my face down into the seat and I taste leather. Oh God, I want him; I can feel him behind me; I want him to enter me all at once. He grabs my shoulders. It hurts a bit, but I don't care. I know I'm going to come as soon as he touches me. I'm going to fucking explode. He pushes inside me; his hands grab my breasts. The seams on the seats give me friction burns.

'Oh, baby, oh yeah . . .'

I'm lighter than air.

A cuckoo calls somewhere out in the forest.

Taormina, Sicily

I look down at the water washing all over my swollen feet; it's grey with dirt. I run it over my thigh and wash away blood; the water turns pink. The cut stings. I rinse my knee. Bits of gravel are stuck to the edge of the cut where it's started to scab. I pick them off. The cut opens up and starts to bleed; the water turns red. I pick up a shower puff and scrub at my skin. I'm thinking about Salvatore, about how good it was. I can still taste him now: his hard, sweet dick, his salty skin. I close my eyes and listen to the water crashing and splashing around me. I smile.

Then I'm thinking about the body.

That was close. Ambrogio could have killed me! It's lucky I got in there first. What the hell was Ambrogio planning? It couldn't have been my perfect sister; I'm sure the plan was all just *him*. It's driving me nuts. But my sister has gone. And so has Ambrogio. Suicide. I've got nothing to fear. In the morning, once I've had a little lie-in, I'll get up and ask where Ambrogio's gone. I won't be too concerned. I'll just get on with my day. Maybe have a relaxing massage. Get my nails done. A facial. But then, after a couple of days, when he doesn't show up or answer his phone, when his friends have no idea where he's gone, I'll call the police, out of my mind with worry. 'Ambrogio? Yes . . . now I come to think of it, he *was* depressed. He seemed upset about something. Now I remember! He did threaten suicide. I never really listened to him. I thought it was just a figure of speech: "If your mother calls me again, I will kill myself", "If Italy don't win Eurovision, I will kill myself", that kind of thing.'

Should I kill that security guard too? Just in case? It might be safer. But I guess he helped us . . . and he might come in handy somehow down the road. I'll have a little think about it . . . I think he likes me. He liked Beth.

I dry myself with a fluffy towel and pull on Beth's Armani nightdress, the one with the little pink roses embroidered along the hem. It's super cute. I crawl into Beth and Ambrogio's bed. It's a superking, so there's plenty of room to stretch out and yawn, roll around and get comfy. I sink down into plump and snuggly pillows, wrap myself up in soft satin sheets and fall asleep. It's been a tiring day.

DAY FIVE:
Gluttony

How many Pringles can you fit in your mouth?
My record's nineteen.
@AlvinaKnightly69

Chapter Twenty-eight

It was Beth's fault I got arrested for shoplifting Woolworths' pick 'n' mix in 1999. It was Beth's fault I started stealing.

Beth had an imaginary friend called Tallulah when we were growing up; she used to annoy the hell out of me. Only Beth could see her and only Beth could hear what she said. 'Oh, Tallulah, you're so funny,' Beth would say with a giggle. I knew they were talking about me, taking the piss. They would role-play for hours, all Beth's favourite games: princesses, fairy princesses, mummies and babies. I don't know what she wanted an imaginary friend for, she already had me. I don't know where she got her from either; I could never find one, not that I wanted one or tried. Perhaps that was why I was lonely?

Our mother encouraged it, setting a place for the imaginary friend at the dinner table every night, buying Tallulah treats from the shops, writing Tallulah her own birthday card, inviting Tallulah on holiday. 'Beth, darling, will Tallulah be joining us for our trip to the theatre? We'll have to buy her a ticket!' It was fucking insane. Tallulah got more attention than I did. Tallulah was far more important than me.

Then, on our eighth birthday, I decided enough was enough; it was *my* special day, not Tallulah's. Cow. I stole a Mars bar from the tuck shop at school. I snuck it up the sleeve of my too-big blazer when the dinner lady wasn't looking, my mouth watering, my heartbeat pounding in my ears like a drum. The rush was insane. I kept it all day in the bottom of my school bag: a dark-blue Jansport backpack. It was all I could think of for the rest of the day, all through English, history and art. Just knowing it was in there got me high. Then that afternoon, when I got home, I tucked the Mars bar under my pillow out of sight. Later that night, when I could hear Beth snoring on the bunk bed up top, I tried to bribe her 'friend' to come out.

'Hello? Tallulah?' I said sweetly, 'I've got a chocolate bar right here. If you come out, you can have it . . .'

I waited and waited, the pillow at the ready, not because I wanted to make friends, but because I wanted to smother her to death. I waited and waited, for what seemed like hours, but she never showed up.

Eventually, I ate the Mars bar myself.

The chocolate tasted sweet, illicit, delicious. It was the first in a spree of clandestine confectionery that ended in Woolies in 1999. A security guard caught me, my hand in a jar full of Sherbet Dip Dabs, my pockets bulging with multicoloured gobstoppers and a mouth full of pink chocolate mice. He called the police and the police called my mum. I was too young to go to prison. I expected my mum to go batshit crazy, scream the house down, have a fit. But she didn't even bother to punish me. It was like I didn't exist.

I wasn't usually allowed chocolate. Mum never gave me any pocket money, said I was too naughty, I didn't deserve it, I was fat enough already, morbidly obese . . . Mum said I was built like a brick shithouse, that I looked like the back end of a double-decker bus. I couldn't buy sweets like my sister and every-body else. I know, I know, Beth used to share hers, tried to sneak me a treat when our mum wasn't looking, smuggle me half a packet of Nerds. But I wanted them *all*, all to myself. I wanted our mother to buy them for *me*.

It had been so easy to steal that Mars bar, so quick, so effort-less. Mum never noticed. She had no idea. I didn't need her stupid pocket money now that I could steal. I didn't need any-one else.

So, that was my first time and, like I said, it was all Beth's fault. So don't blame me, blame her.

Friday, 28 August 2015, 9.52 a.m.
Taormina, Sicily

'Mamma! Mamma!'

It's little Ernesto. I'm awoken by Emilia with the baby in her arms.

'Good morning, *signora*,' she says. 'How are you?'

'Mamma,' cries Ernie, his hands reaching out towards me. A fat, round tear rolls down his face. Poor baby.

'Oh, good morning, Emilia,' I say, sitting up and stretching. My bones crack. My joints creak. Something's malfunctioned. I don't feel right. I rearrange the pillows and take the baby. Please stop crying. Please shut up. 'Shh, shh, shh, shh.' I cuddle Ernesto up close to my chest, give his back a nice rub.

'He wanted his mother,' Emilia says with a shrug. 'Shall I bring some *caffè*? It's nearly ten o'clock.'

'Yes, thank you,' I say.

He doesn't stop sobbing; hot tears against my skin, soggy wet snot all over my breasts. I hold him tight and stroke the hair on his tiny head. 'Shh . . . shh . . . don't cry.'

Emilia smiles, then turns her back and walks away.

'Emilia?'

'Yes?' She's halfway through the door.

'Have you seen Ambrogio?'

'No, *signora*, I haven't. Not today.'

'Do you know where he is?'

'No, I don't know.'

'Perhaps he's gone swimming again, in the sea?'

'Perhaps, *signora*. No car in the drive.'

'OK. I'll call him. Thank you,' I say.

I turn my attention to the infant hollering in my arms. Emilia leaves. Oh God! Now what? What am I supposed to do with this baby? He didn't come with an instruction manual. I don't recall any lessons on child-rearing at school; that would have been more helpful than fucking PE. Name me one context where lacrosse is useful? This learning curve is going to be steep.

I get out of bed, cradling Ernie in my arms, and nearly fall over. Shit, my toe! I can barely stand. Ernie's cries hit a new high pitch and I worry that the windows around us will shatter. I shush him and rock him to and fro. To and fro. Please stop crying. Please shut up. I look into his eyes and see pure panic. Can he tell I'm not his mum? Babies have an amazing sense of smell, like pigs or Alsatians. I must remember to apply some of Beth's perfume: Miss Dior Chérie. That ought to do the trick.

The baby cries.

And the baby cries.

The cries get louder and more persistent.

They get shriller and shriller and more high-pitched, until only bats can hear them.

The baby howls; big monster sobs shake his tiny frame.

A choking sound.

A muffled whimper.

A gulp for air.

Oh help. Where's the 'off' button? Where is the 'pause'?

Emilia comes back in with my coffee on a tray. She sets it down on the bedside table and looks up. Her face is pale.

'Oh, *signora*!' she says over the sobbing, gawping and pointing and staring at my arms. 'Are you OK?'

I look down and see bruises all over my arms and across my shoulders; they're nasty-looking, blue. Where did they come from? I hadn't even noticed. Emilia hasn't spotted my toe or my knee (swollen and red and far uglier than the bruises). I've pulled all the muscles in my arms and legs. The soles of my feet are raw.

'And you've cut your knee!' she says, pointing at my leg.

'I'm fine,' I say. 'Really.' I look a *state*.

I wish I was wearing more than this skimpy little nightie. 'I got up in the night to go to the loo and tripped over the rug. Do you want to take Ernie while I get dressed?'

She narrows her eyes and shakes her head. I don't think she believes me. '*Signora*, you want I call the police?'

'God no, I'm *fine*.' I laugh, unconvincingly.

Emilia pauses, as though she's going to say something else, but then changes her mind. I pass the baby to her; he's screaming and flailing his arms and legs. He looks like an angry octopus. Emilia hugs him and kisses his forehead.

'Ma, ma, ma,' he says.

Ernie stops crying almost immediately. Emilia must have some kind of knack that I lack; she's telepathic, like a horse whisperer. She has some special seventh sense. She gives me another look, up and down, her expression concerned, her face disapproving. But eventually she goes out to the hall and closes the door. Thank fuck for that. Screams ring in my ears, echoing, deafening. My head spins, aches. I can still hear that crying, like the sea in a seashell. I wipe the snot from off my chest. It's *really*, *really* hard work being a mother. What on earth would I do without help?

I walk into the bathroom and look in the mirror. The bruises on my arms look exactly like Beth's. They're in the same place, the same size, the same shape, although hers were more purple, I think, almost black. I shake my head and frown in the mirror. Ambrogio never touched me. I don't understand. That must have been where Salvatore was holding me when we fucked in the car. I remember the pressure, I guess it was hard; it was definitely rough, but at the time I barely noticed. It must be genetic. Beth and I both bruise easily. Well, that explains that.

But it doesn't make sense. If Ambrogio's not a wife beater, then what was Beth's problem? She'd seemed so miserable: swearing, crying. I've never seen her that wound up. She seemed to have snapped. Lost the plot. Those diamonds in her bag suggest she was running away. I rub my palm over the bruises; they hurt a bit, but

229

they look worse than they feel. OK, fine. So he wasn't a thug, but something was up. Ambrogio thought they were working together. According to him, they had a plan. A plan! And they were *both* on board. At least, that's what Ambrogio thought. That's what he said. But I know Beth planned our swap in secret . . .

Perhaps she wanted to save my life!

Yes, that's it. It has to be. *He* was the one with the murderous mindset. *She* was trying to keep me safe. She was plotting to leave without him. That's why Ambrogio had seemed so shocked! *Why were you dressed as Elizabeth, Alvie?* She double-crossed him. Sneaky bitch.

I still need to get to the bottom of this, but this is really an excellent start. I must say, I'm impressed by my powers of deduction. I'm a veritable Miss Marple. I'm Sherlock Holmes. Perhaps I should join Scotland Yard?

I grab a toothbrush – it doesn't matter which one – and brush my teeth.

I'm swimming lengths in the pool. Breaststroke, so I don't get my hair wet. Up and down. Up and down. Up and down again. It's fucking hot and it's cooling me off. That and it's good for my bum. Beth had a bum like an under-ripe peach. I need to tone up. It's key to my look. I saw some drop-dead-gorgeous (but tiny) little hot pants by Balenciaga in Beth's walk-in wardrobe, but right now it would be a crime to wear them. Hot pants don't work well with cellulite, that's a true fact. I want a bum like a Kardashian, perfectly pert, better than Beth's.

It's going to have to be swimming. I hate all other forms of exercise (other than sex). I used to run a bit when I was younger, but now I don't really like it. I don't like sweating (other than sex). When you swim, you can sweat in the water, so you don't really notice. It's perfect for me. Shit. If I'm Beth, I'm going to have to do Pilates. I bet she has a personal trainer. They're going to wonder why I'm so crap.

I concentrate on counting my lengths: nine, ten, eleven, twelve. I'm going to try to get to twenty before passing out and lighting a fag. I'm trying to clear my head. To relax, to meditate. I've been all wound up and I need to chill out. It's all been quite stressful. I wasn't expecting such a hectic trip. It's supposed to be a holiday, for crying out loud! I want to unwind. But Ambrogio's tanned and handsome face keeps popping up inside my head. I can't seem to get him off my mind.

I'm disappointed, to tell you the truth. For eight long years, I've fantasized about this guy. Ever since that fateful night when he walked into that college bar, when he changed both our lives for ever. I truly believed that he was *the one*. Eight years wasted, when I could have been obsessing about somebody else. I could have had a chance with Channing Tatum. I know, I know, he's a Hollywood megastar . . . but I could have moved to LA. Found out where he lived. Followed him home one night from a shoot . . . thirteen, fourteen, fifteen, sixteen.

But I digress.

I had high hopes for Ambrogio. We could have been perfect together. Could have lived here for ever, right here in this villa, in this perfect fucking villa, with our perfect little baby. With his sexy-ass car. But no, Ambrogio had to mess it all up. Ruin everything. Shove it all back in my face. Couldn't he see I was trying to help, to make the best of a bad situation? Why couldn't he just have played along? Who gives a fuck if I'm Alvie or Beth? I mean, really, tell me, what's the difference? I was playing the part. I was doing my bit. He could have made a *little* more effort. He needed a wife. Ernie needed a mum.

Ambrogio . . . Ambrogio . . . Ambrogio . . . fuck you. You know, it's lucky that I'm on the pill or I could be pregnant with that man's child (yet again)? Why do I always have to think of everything? Typical guy. Seventeen, eighteen, nineteen, twenty. There's a streak of dried blood on the edge of the pool; it's where Beth cracked her head when she fell in. At the top on the right.

I can still hear the CRACK! I do not want to think about it. I splash some water up on to the stain and scrub it off with my fingers. Gone. I look back at the villa and there is Emilia, standing in the kitchen window, watching, staring. She turns away, gets on with the dusting. She can't have seen the blood from back there. I've got nothing to fear. There's no way that she'll have worked it all out. Play it cool, Alvina. Don't sweat it, kid. I climb the three little silver steps, glinting in the bright white sunlight, and rub myself dry with Beth's beach towel. No more obsessing about Ambrogio. He was regrettable. A disappointment. He was a fucking liability, far too lethal to have around. He pulled a gun on me, for Christ's sake! I light a cigarette and lie back on the sunbed. Close my eyes and breathe out smoke. I'll obsess about Salvatore instead.

'*Signora*, Nino's here to see you. Shall I let him in?'

Emilia's voice startles me. I hadn't noticed the doorbell ring. Nino? What the hell is *he* doing here? Oh, he's probably looking for Ambrogio.

'Sure,' I say, fixing my hair and sitting up straight on the sunbed. 'Tell him to come through.'

'*Sì, signora. Un momento.*'

Emilia looks at my Marlboro Light and frowns, then turns away and walks back to the villa.

I wipe the beads of sweat from my brow. I'm already baking. The midday sun is brutal here. I pull my sarong up over my shoulders to cover the bruises, slip on Beth's enormous shades. I stub out my fag. My disguise is complete. Nino bursts through the French doors with a deafening crash. I hear his feet smash the crazy paving. He scans the garden as he marches towards me. Ha! He isn't going to see Ambrogio, however hard he looks. He's getting closer. He looks right at me. My stomach sinks. I hug my knees. I wonder how well Nino knew my sister. A chill spreads along the length of my spine, making me shiver.

'Where the fuck's Il Professore? He was supposed to meet me!'

Shit

I pull the sarong around my body so it covers me up like a cocoon. Nino looms over me and my sunbed like some kind of ominous monolith. Waiting. He whips off his shades. Eyes like black holes. A long, thin scar along his left cheek, as pink as an earthworm.

'Il Professore?' I say. I wonder why they call him that; is it because he's got a degree?

He smiles a half smile and reveals a gold tooth. 'Your fucking husband. Where are you hiding him?'

Hmm, the antagonistic type.

'I don't know. I haven't seen him since last night. I slept in this morning and when I woke up, he was gone.'

Nino frowns: a deep, dark crevice at the centre of his forehead. He doesn't believe me. I study his face, his substantial moustache, his slender figure: taut, lithe, mean. If Nino were an animal, he'd be one of those birds that they use in cockfights in Thailand: an angry cockerel. Peck out your eyes. Scratch out your throat. But Nino's got something magnetic about him. You just can't take your eyes off this man. He's mesmerizing, hypnotizing, like that snake in *The Jungle Book*, Kaa. He's not handsome so much as charismatic, one of those people with natural charm, unshakeable confidence. It's strangely alluring. He's not old, maybe thirty-five? Forty tops. But his skin is creased from too much sun: lines on his forehead, lines by his mouth. He doesn't look the type to mess around with sunscreen. And I doubt he uses night cream.

'He's not answering his phone.'

'I know,' I say, biting my lip. 'I just tried calling; I assumed he was busy. He didn't pick up.' I shrug. 'I called several times.'

Nino takes a packet of Marlboro Reds from his jacket pocket; it's a black leather jacket, with big silver studs. He must be boiling in that. He offers me a cigarette, but I shake my head. He takes a match and lights a flame, blows the smoke into my face.

I watch the match fall to the ground; the fire flickers; it's still alight. I watch as it burns itself out.

'What happened to your foot?' Nino asks. He points to my feet. 'Your toe looks fucked.'

'Oh, nothing. I fell over.'

I tuck my legs beneath me on the lounger, look away towards the pool; there's a very slight breeze, so feathery light you can hardly feel it, but the surface ripples like corrugated iron. Nino sits down next to me on the sunbed, his arm against mine. He smells of leather. His jacket is scorching hot from the sun. Nino stares into my face, searching, assessing. His bullshit-radar must be finely tuned. My whole body tenses. I'm rigid.

'Betta, I am gonna ask you again. Where is your husband?' More force in his voice. 'I think you know.' I can taste the tobacco on his breath. I can see the rage in his eyes.

I look up at him, pleading. 'No, I don't know. I'm sure he'll be home soon. He's only been gone for a couple of hours . . .' My voice trails off. The handle of a gun sticks out from the belt of Nino's trousers: black, metallic, big enough to do serious damage. The initials G. M. B. spelled out in mother-of-pearl. Shit. Note to self: don't mess with Nino. And go and get Ambrogio's gun. I left it in that herbaceous border. I hope it's still there . . .

Nino holds my gaze, as though reading my mind. Staring me out. Watching me squirm. He looks down at his watch, a fat, gold Rolex, glinting like fire.

'It's nearly three. We were supposed to meet at ten o'clock. It was an important fucking meeting. Did you speak to Domenico?'

'Domenico? No, why?' I say.

I shrug. The sarong slips off. Nino sees my arms, my shoulders, the bruises. Shit.

'What the fuck? Who beat you up?'

'No one. It's nothing.' I reach for the sarong.

He grabs my wrists with rough, dry palms and hauls me to my feet.

'*Ow!*' I cry out in pain: my broken toe! The sarong falls away and he slowly examines me, studying my black-and-blue body – I'm regretting the choice of Beth's G-string bikini. He bends down low to get a better view, fingers the gash in my thigh, the cut on my knee.

'*Ow!*' I say again.

The bruises on my arms are turning purple. Out here in broad daylight, I look pretty messed up.

'Who did this?' he says.

'No one. I fell.'

'*Vaffanculo.*' He spits on the ground. 'Who was it? Tell me.' I'm getting a feeling of déjà vu. 'Il Professore would never . . .'

'No, no, of course not,' I say.

He releases his grip. I flop down on the lounger. I wrap the sarong around my shoulders, although it's far too late to hide. I curl up small into a ball. I should have worn a ski-suit or one of those onesies with teddy-bear ears.

'Betta, Betta, Betta,' he breathes. 'There's something you're not telling me. If your husband isn't home by this evening, I'm coming back.'

I nod.

Not good.

He bends down towards me on the sunbed, leans in close so that his eyes are just two inches away. Hot flecks of spit land on my face. 'This is the wrong fucking time to disappear.'

Nino flicks his cigarette down to the ground, crushes it with the silver toecap of a black leather boot. It glints and sparkles in the sun. They're the kind of boots designed for kicking the shit out of people. I watch his back, lithe and black, disappear across the crazy paving and through the French doors. I take a deep breath and then slowly exhale. My whole body's trembling; that was intense. He seems like a real bad boy. That's my kind of guy. Nino is seriously fucking hot.

Chapter Twenty-nine

Nino's turned me on so much I get dressed and pop next door to see Salvatore.

'Ah, Elizabeth. Good. I was going to come and get you,' he says. 'I want you to pose for me.'

Pose for him? What? Oh yeah, he's an *artist*.

'Um, OK,' I say. Not that he was asking.

Salvatore leads me through his villa and upstairs to his studio. The space is vast, light-filled, spacious: sculptures, sketches, folding ladders, long wooden tables, paintings, clay.

'Get naked,' he says.

I don't move. 'Um, are you sure? I'm pretty messed up.'

He gives me a dark look. He doesn't like repeating himself. 'Get naked. Now.'

Salvatore turns and walks towards the back of the studio, then brings an easel to the centre of the room. The easel is taller than him by a couple of feet, with enormous sheets of creamy white paper. He takes a piece of charcoal from a box on a table and looks up.

He gestures to a chair. 'Put your clothes on there.'

I undo the buttons on my dress with trembling fingers. Sure, Salvatore, whatever you say. Just so long as you fuck me again like you did last night. That blew my mind.

'You want a drink?' he asks. 'Vodka?' He doesn't wait for an answer.

'Sure,' I say, smiling. That's just what I need. It's been one of those days . . . How did he know?

He walks over to a drinks cabinet at the back of the studio. The creak of a hinge. The clatter of glass.

'Ice?'

'No, thanks.'

I take off my bra and hang it over the back of a carved wooden chair. I wonder if *he* carved it. My hands are shaking. Salvatore walks towards me carrying two little glasses and a bottle of Grey Goose. It looks like nice vodka. I usually buy Tesco's own brand when it's on offer.

Salvatore walks like John Wayne. Now he's standing so close I could reach out and touch him. I look down at my body, battered and blue. Salvatore doesn't even seem to notice.

'And your pants,' he says, gesturing to my knickers.

I pull them off and drape them over the chair. They're Beth's red lace French knickers, my favourite of hers. I'm even wearing the matching bra (that *never* happened when I was Alvina). He sets down the glasses on the table, fills them to overflowing with crystal-clear vodka, then hands one to me. He looks into my eyes, his pupils dilated. Is this turning him on? We down the generous shots. The vodka burns the back of my throat. The rush is instant. Now what?

He takes my hand in his.

'Sit like this,' he says, moving me into position. He places a wooden stool behind me, then lowers me on to it. He crosses one of my legs over the other, then spins me around so that I'm facing the wall. 'Turn around like this. Look over your shoulder.' He takes my arm and moves it around my waist, then cups my chin and positions it too. He takes a step back, looks me up and down.

'*Perfetta*,' he says.

I smile. He's so sexy: the cut-off jeans and paint-splattered shirt. His top has a rip all the way up one side; I can see his stomach through the tear: Channing Tatum abs and a heatwave tan. There's a dimple on his chin that I really want to kiss. He reaches over and pours out two more shots. He looks into my eyes and I look back.

'Don't move,' he says, bringing a glass up to my lips and pouring the vodka straight down my throat.

This man really saved my ass last night. Now we have this shared secret, this history between us, it's like he knows me inside out. It's like we're partners in our crime; we'll keep our secret till we die. I've never felt this close to anyone. I feel like he can read my soul. But of course he still thinks I'm Beth . . .

He downs his shot, then walks over to the easel. He runs his fingers through dark-blond hair, strands of white where the sun has bleached it. If I didn't know he was Sicilian, I'd have guessed that he was Swedish. Swedish or Dutch; the Dutch are tall. I brush a lock of hair from my face; it's tickling my nose.

'I mean it, don't move. Not even a millimetre.' His voice is hard.

I giggle. That vodka's gone straight to my head. Is he trying to get me drunk? I hope so.

'OK, Salvo, whatever you say. I won't move a muscle.'

'Stop laughing. You're moving,' he says. Now he's cross.

I force my face out of a smile.

Salvatore takes a piece of charcoal and stands behind the easel, a few feet away. I suck in my stomach, sit up a little taller. I am Beth. I am *gorgeous*. I suddenly feel sexy, sexier than ever. I feel my hair draped over one shoulder. I am sensual. Powerful. I hold my breath. His blue eyes trace the curves of my body, linger on my neck, my shoulders, my breasts. I've never felt a gaze so intense. It's fucking hot. He looks down at my hips, a frown on his face, and then starts to draw, sketching with long, wild, frantic gestures. His hands move across the length and breadth of the page, shaping, shading, sculpting. He looks up at me, then back down at the page, over and over and over again. Charcoal scrapes across the paper. My breathing is shallow. There's the faint scent of burnt coal.

I scan the room: the sculptures and sketches all look just like Beth. They look down at me now, glancing over their shoulders with Beth's wide eyes, Beth's beautiful face. It's strange. It's like she is still here, watching us. Watching me. The studio walls are filled with paintings and drawings of women all sketched from behind; their buttocks are round and pert and perfect. Beth. She must have been his muse.

I watch his forearms moving, working; they are muscular, tanned, defined. I want to touch him, reach out and kiss him. But I stay still. My pussy's aching; I really, really want to fuck. I already feel myself dripping wet. He slams the charcoal down on the table. I catch my breath.

'OK, we're done,' Salvatore says.

'What? Already? Can I see?'

'No,' he says.

There's no explanation; it seems a little unfair.

'Oh. OK. Well, I guess if you're finished . . . then I'll get dressed.' I rise and reach for my clothes.

'No need,' says Salvatore. 'It's just you and me now, kid.'

He pushes me back against the wall, the surface is cold and hard against my skin. He wraps his arms around my waist and he's already kissing me, his tongue deep and hard inside my mouth. His hands run through my hair, grabbing it in fistfuls. His body is pressed against my skin.

'Hey!' I say, into his mouth. He's pulling my hair and it hurts; I love it.

He tears off his shirt and throws it down on the floor. His torso is perfect, a work of art. His abs are sculpted: Michelangelo's *David*. He's a fucking masterpiece. He pushes me back down on the stool and firmly, roughly, spreads open my legs. He kneels down before me and gives me a look – a hungry predator – then shoves his face between my thighs. The bridge of his nose, cheekbones, eyebrows, tousled hair slicked back from his forehead. His tongue, thick and wet, slicks up and down, left and right across my clit, forwards and backwards and round and round. His fingers inside me. His soft lips kiss and his hard, hungry mouth eats me out with a mad, bad rage and a crazy, burning desire to make me come, to tip me over the edge of the here and now, up into eyes-rolled-back-in-their-sockets ecstasy.

'Oh yeah . . .'

I grip the edges of the stool with scrunched-up fingers, claw at the wood. I push my cunt towards his mouth. Eat me. Eat me. I want him to swallow me whole. I want him to suck me into his hot, sweet, sexy body.

'Oh . . .'

He is *so* much better than Ambrogio.

His shoulders heave and glow in the sunlight streaming in through the studio windows. His skin is creamy, glistening, smooth, like a Henry Moore. He's polished and now he's polishing me with his tongue and the cool, circular motion of an oyster swishing and swirling a pearl around inside till it glows. And I'm glowing and groaning and growing warmer and warmer until I think I'm going to come. His hands reach up over my belly, his fingers smoothing my hot skin. Every nerve is alive. I'm dizzy, weightless. I'm going to come, I have to come, but he stops –

I open my eyes and see Salvatore, in all his spectacular half-naked glory, staring at my stomach, at the bit of skin just down from my navel, like it's the most interesting thing he's ever seen in his life. There's a strange, faraway look on his face.

'Salvatore?'

I grab his shoulders and pull him up my naked, panting body. I kiss his hot, wet, cunt-covered mouth, feel his chin stubble wet and his hot breath warm on my cheek. The smell of sex.

'Fuck me,' I breathe, into his hair.

He flips me around so I'm bent over the table with my back pressed up against his chest. His fingers trace the lines of my shoulders, my back, my ass. His hands feel rough, a sculptor's hands: dry and calloused, strong and broad. They glide up the inside of my thighs and reach for my clit; I groan. He's massaging my clit with his thumb and I sink into him deeper – he pushes me forwards over the table, my face slams flat against wood: the taste of beeswax, the cold, hard oak. He unzips his flies, the rustle of denim; pulls off his cut-offs, kicks them down to the floor. He reaches around and grabs my breasts, pulling me into his sexy body so hard I can't breathe.

'Oh God. Do it,' I say.

He pulls on a condom and pushes inside me all in one go, strong and deep, so hard I gasp. He's pounding me now, over the table, its legs scraping across the floor. The wooden edge digs into my thighs. He's so big and hard and I want him, I need him. He's rough and I'm moaning; I'm going to come. It's building, building, that faraway feeling. He grabs my neck with both his hands; his fingers close around my throat. And he's squeezing, squeezing! Harder. Tighter. I'm choking, gagging, panic filling my mind.

'What have you done with your sister, huh?' he pants in my ear. 'Where the fuck is she? You're not Beth.'

And I come so hard on his dick that I think I'll never come down. And I don't know where I am or what he's saying, but I hear him groan and I feel him coming in waves inside me, squeezing me, pulling my hips against him, throbbing and pulsing and filling me up.

Fuck.

Fuck.

Fuck.

Chapter Thirty

We're panting and sweating, collapsed on the table. He pulls out and I flop down, breathing hard. What the hell? He knows? But how? I think of my stomach. What the hell was he looking at? Of course! Beth had a caesarean scar. That's it! The only physical difference between us, the only way you could tell us apart.

'This is fucked up,' he says at last. 'I should have known. Your sister has a spectacular ass.'

I clench my jaw, dig my nails into the wood.

'I can explain,' I say into the table. My voice falters. *Can I explain?*

'So where is she?' he asks. He takes a cigarette from a pack on the table and slams the pack back down on the wood.

'She – she asked me to swap places with her. She went away,' I say at last.

He lights the cigarette, sees me watching and offers it to me. I inhale. It tastes good. I think it helps; at least it's something to do with my hands. He lights himself another.

'Now why wouldn't you tell me that? You don't think I would want to know?'

'She said to keep it secret between us. Are you cross?' I hold my breath. My hands are shaking. My heart is pounding. He shakes his head.

'No. Whatever. You're both good to fuck.' I try to smile, but I'm not sure if it's funny. 'You want another drink?' Salvatore says. He bends down and pulls up his boxers.

'Vodka.' I need it. I grab my pants from the back of the chair and pull them back on.

'So, what was your name again? Olivia or something?'

'Alvina,' I say. This is embarrassing.

'Nice name. I like it.' He pours out two more shots. 'Alvina. Well, it's nice to meet you. *Piacere*,' he says.

'Thanks,' I say, taking my glass, avoiding his gaze. My hand is trembling; I don't want to spill it. I don't want Salvatore to see that I'm scared. I down it in one and then blurt it out: 'But aren't you in love with my sister?'

He smiles a half smile. 'What? No way. She thought I was. She wanted to run away with me. Can you believe it? She wanted to hide out in London.'

'Oh?'

So that's where she was going, why she took Ernesto, why she was 'stealing' those diamonds. Was Beth really going to elope? With this guy? No, I don't believe it. Ambrogio was plotting something against me, but clearly my sister had other ideas. I knew she would never have wanted to *kill* me. That was insane.

'But you didn't want to run away?' I ask him quietly. This is my chance. I need to find out what the hell's going on. I inhale smoke. I like his cigs; they're stronger than mine. My head feels light with my nicotine high.

'Me? No way. And leave all this?' He gestures around his studio. 'Anyway, it was much too dangerous. We'd never have been able to come back.'

What? Why not? What's so scary? What's going on? I set the shot glass down on the table. The glass shakes and rattles against the wood. Salvatore's half naked, leaning against the edge of the table. His forehead's creased like he's thinking too hard.

'So what happened to your sister? Where is she?' he asks.

I swallow.

'She's gone. She left. Don't know where.'

'Right, makes sense. She was desperate to go,' says Salvatore. 'What about the kid? Kid was the reason she wanted to run . . .'

'The kid's still here. In the villa with his nanny.'

He frowns, shakes his head. Stubs out his fag inside a glass.

'She left the kid here? Are you sure?'

'Yeah, I'm sure.' What kind of a stupid fucking question is that?

'No, that's not right. Shit, you'd better be careful. She'll be back. She'll come back for you and the boy . . .'

All the muscles in my body tense. I hold his gaze. 'What? Why do I need to be careful?'

He doesn't reply.

'Why the fuck do I need to be careful?' My voice is uneven. My lips curve down. A sick feeling spreads from my gut and up my throat. 'Salvatore?'

'Hey . . . I saved your life; you should be grateful,' he says, grabbing my wrists, looking into my eyes.

'You *saved my life*?' I pull my arms free.

'Look, it wasn't my idea, OK?' His voice is raised. 'Your fucking mental sister wanted me to help her kill you. That night, she went mad! Said a dead body was the only way she could get away, away from that *stronzo*, Ambrogio. That they wouldn't come after her. She was probably right.'

I step away from Salvatore, support myself on the wooden stool. What the fuck is he saying? My fucking sister fucking *what*?

'I don't understand.' I shake my head. That doesn't sound at all like my twin. Beth is the good one. Beth is the angel. 'You're lying!' I say.

'I'm not! I'm telling you. I think you should know. She was desperate. *Pazzo*. She said you were her only chance to escape, to get away from her husband, from Sicily, everything.'

It doesn't make sense. Unless . . . she *was* desperate. Unless she was frightened. Unless she really did go nuts.

'When? When was she going to *kill* me?'

'At first she thought it was enough to swap places, to give her the time she needed to run, but then I guess she wanted more.'

'More?'

'She wanted you dead. She was hysterical, crying, begging me to help her. I managed to persuade her to change her mind. She wasn't going to do it. I think –'

'Is that . . . is that what the argument was about?' I remember them fighting that night by the car.

'Yeah . . . yeah, we argued,' he says. He holds my gaze, his eyes searching, strained.

'How? How was she going to do it?' Did she know about Ambrogio's gun?

'It doesn't matter now . . .' He folds his arms and looks down at the floorboards, traces a knot in the wood with a big toe, round and round and spiralling, spiralling, down, down, down.

We stare at the floor.

I'm glad I killed her; I got there first (for once). But it still fucking hurts – even my sister? My very own sister? It feels like I've been stabbed in the heart. My head flops down into my hands; the ground spins round beneath my feet. I guess I was wrong about Beth being good. Perhaps I was wrong about everything? What does this mean? I'm completely lost. Does this mean I'm the good one? Surely not?

'I said I wouldn't do it. You should be grateful,' he says.

'I am grateful,' I say to the floor. I'm speaking on autopilot. I don't know what I'm saying. For some reason, I laugh, but it's empty, hollow.

I want to get out of here.

I look around for the rest of my clothes. Salvatore watches me pull on my bra and do it back up, but at first I can't do the hooks.

'Why? Why did she want to run? It doesn't make any sense. Her life seems so perfect.'

'You mean you don't know?'

I shake my head; my eyes cloud with tears. Oh my God, not crying *again*.

'Your sister never told you?'

'Told me what? As far as I knew she was living the dream.'

'Shit,' says Salvatore. 'You really don't know?'

I wish he'd stop saying that.

'Are you going to tell me?' I turn around and look into his eyes. He frowns, looks away. Annoyed.

He crosses his arms against his chest; his biceps press against his pecs. I hold my breath. I have no idea what he's going to say, but suddenly I feel it: it's going to be bad. It's going to change everything.

'You'd better sit down.'

I pull up the stool, its wooden legs scrape against the floor-boards. I sink down hard, suddenly dizzy. Weak as a child. My whole body is cold now. I want to drink some more vodka. I stretch the dress out over my lap. I wish I had my old jumper.

'There's a fucking war going on out there,' says Salvatore, gesturing to the window with an open hand.

'A war? Where? Here in Taormina?'

'Fighting. Everywhere. All over Sicily. On the streets. In broad daylight. They'll shoot a guy walking down the street. And it's only going to get worse.'

'What are you talking about? What *war*?'

I'm sure I'd have seen something on the news, in the *Metro* in London. I wouldn't have come.

'A turf war.' Salvatore sighs. 'Ambrogio was in deep with Cosa Nostra, which means Beth's in deep and the kid's in deep . . . It's a family affair.'

I look up at him like he's speaking Greek.

'What's that? Like the *Mafia* or something?'

He nods; his mouth turns down at the corners. 'They're animals. *Vermini*.'

I can't believe it. Not the *Mafia*. That stuff only happens in films. Doesn't it? Oh. Now I get it. That's where all the money comes from, why Ambrogio had a gun. I *thought* Nino looked dodgy. It all makes sense now. My sister would have *hated* that. I take a deep breath.

'And this *war*?' I ask.

'It's all about territory. Palermo, Catania, Agrigento . . . everywhere. It's over for Cosa Nostra, but they will fight to their death. Criminal gangs from the south have moved in, from Africa and the Middle East. They're fighting for control: the drugs trade, heroin, prostitution, everything. Cocaine . . .'

'Oh. I see,' I say. It's bad.

'The kid's in the middle of it . . .' says Salvatore. 'Ambrogio's *nonno*, Ambrogio's dad: all Cosa Nostra. Ernie's bloodline is Sicilian . . .'

'Elizabeth didn't know.' I suddenly get it. 'When she met him in Oxford, she had no idea. They got married in Milan, where Ambrogio's mother came from.'

'Yeah, that's right,' says Salvatore.

'And Ernesto . . . he is only a baby. She didn't want to bring him up just for him to get shot in the head.'

Salvatore nods.

'Something like that. Ambrogio bought Ernesto a gun and Beth went crazy. Kid's not even one year old. She wanted out. They'd kill her if they knew she tried to run. Once you're in, you're in. There's no turning back.'

'Even when you're dead, there's a special place in hell . . .' I interrupt.

Salvatore looks at me with his cool, blue eyes. 'Beth was scared, scared for the kid.'

I think I get it. I understand. Ambrogio and Beth were going to run. But that wasn't enough. Beth wanted more. She wanted to get away from Ambrogio. That's why I'm here. I was the body double. I was the *body*. I stand up from the stool, unsteady on my feet, and pull the dress back over my head. I walk over to Salvatore and reach my arms around his neck.

'So, you really don't mind, about me not being Beth?' I'm the lesser of two evils: I bet he's relieved. I rest my head on Salvatore's broad chest. I can feel his heartbeat under his ribs. His skin is sticky. He smells musky, like sweat.

'No way, baby, I just wish I was fucking you both at the same time.'

I let myself out of his villa and walk back round to Beth's. I think I believe him. There's no way Beth fell in love with this guy. For him it was just sex — fucking fantastic sex, so I can't really *blame* him. (I'm sure it was better with me than with Beth.) And for her he was useful. He was just a way out. Poor Salvatore. I guess he's just a typical guy. But now he's a guy who knows too much. Now he's a problem.

Chapter Thirty-one

I storm into the lounge and sink into Beth's soft plush sofa. How dare she? How could she? My very own sister, plotting to *kill* me? I hear Salvo's voice ring loud in my head: *She wanted me to help her kill you.* I can't believe it. *Said a dead body was the only way she could get away . . . that they wouldn't come after her.* BITCH! BITCH! BITCH! There was *nothing* good about my sister. She was a witch. I grab Beth's iPhone. I need to google 'Cosa Nostra' so I know what I'm dealing with here. 'Cosa Nostra, also known as the Italian Mob. Criminal activities include: racketeering, drug trafficking, murder, corruption, fraud, illegal waste management, extortion, assault, smuggling, gambling, loan sharking, money laundering, fencing and robbery.' Are you kidding me? They sound *awesome*!

There's a knock at the door. Urgh, what now? Emilia's out at the park with Ernesto. I guess I'll just have to get it myself. No rest for the wicked, I suppose. I really need to hire a butler. I hope it's not Salvatore or Nino. I pull back the curtain to see who it is. Shit, the police. Am I fucked? Two male officers stand on the doormat. This is terrible news. I look down at my legs, look down at my arms. The bruises look suspect. I don't want them to see; they'll start asking questions. I have to get changed.

'Just a second!' I call through the villa.

I run upstairs and into Beth's bedroom. Search through her wardrobe for something to wear. Something long. Something modest. Innocent. Feminine. Not too bling. I pull on a tracksuit by Juicy Couture – bright-pink velour as soft as kittens – and sprint back downstairs.

'Elisabetta Caruso?'

'Yes?' I say. '*Sì?*'

'*Posso entrare, per favore?*'

'English, please? I don't speak Italian.'

'Please, may we come in?'

Oh God, it's all over. They're going to arrest me!

I step aside and let the two officers in through the door: two men in uniform with sullen expressions on world-weary faces.

'I am Commissario Edillio Grasso and this is Commissario Savastano,' one says.

Savastano? He's got to be kidding me. I've seen *Gomorrah*. This is insane. I know Savastano's a Mafia name. They've hired a cop from a Camorra family? I know it's a fictional TV series, but all the same, that seems very unwise. I wouldn't trust him as far as I could throw him. They need to have a word with HR.

'Please, sit down,' I say, gesturing to a sofa covered with cushions.

'Thank you, *signora*. You have a beautiful home.' We look around the living room, at the crystal chandeliers twinkling in the sunlight, at the porcelain ornaments arranged on the mantelpiece, at the bouquets of roses in antique vases. I *do* have nice stuff.

'Thank you,' I say. Hurry up and tell me. Whatever it is, tell me now and then fuck off.

'Signora Caruso, I'm afraid we have some upsetting news.' My whole body tenses; *this is it*.

'It's about your husband.'

Phew.

'I don't know where he is and he's not answering his phone,' I say quickly.

I do my best acting, give them a *Please God, not my husband!* expression. Strangely, it works. I've come a long way since that donkey. The one that speaks English gives me a sympathetic look.

'You are Ambrogio Caruso's wife, that is correct?'

'Yes?'

'I'm sorry, *signora*,' he says. He's the larger of the two men, the one with hair sticking out in tufts from under his police hat, with dandruff in his eyebrows and yellowing teeth. 'Your husband's body was found at the bottom of the cliffs near the Continental Hotel. It appears he committed suicide.'

I look from the eyes of one police officer to the next, searching for reassurance, searching for hope; they look back with apologetic faces. They're pretty convincing. I guess they do this kind of acting all the time. I wouldn't like to be a policeman in Sicily. I don't get the impression that they like it much either. I guess it's Mob rule and these guys are just puppets, like in the Opera dei Pupi onstage in Palermo. I read about that on Trip-Advisor. I'd quite like to see it, once this has blown over. *If* this *does* blow over. I always loved Punch and Judy as a child. Mainly Punch.

'Suicide?' I ask at last; my voice is breathless, almost a whisper. I really think I ought to cry.

'Yes, *signora*. My colleague here saw the body this morning and recognized him immediately. Commissario Savastano is certain it's Signor Caruso. And he was identified by his signet ring; it has the initials AC?'

Oops, we should have taken that off; it might have bought us some time.

The smaller of the two police officers, the one with the little piece of toilet paper still stuck to his cheek from where he cut himself shaving, rifles through a battered black rucksack and pulls out a clear plastic bag. It contains a gold signet ring. He passes it to me.

'This belonged to your husband, did it not?' asks the other officer.

I take a cursory glance, then notice an inscription engraved inside the yellow-gold band: '*With all my heart, Beth*'. That must have been a gift from when she still liked him. I could pretend I don't recognize it. But it's definitely his; I'd just make them suspicious. I shove it back into the officer's palm, fling my head into my hands and sob: noisy, wet, hysterical sobs. He puts an arm around my shoulder and I slobber on his starched white shirt.

'Would you like to come to the morgue to formally identify the body?' he asks when I've calmed down a bit.

'No! No! I don't want to see it!'

I leap up from the armchair, pace up and down the room along the edge of the luxurious carpet, trampling on all the embroidered lilies. I've got to get rid of these cops. I don't want them here in my villa, cramping my style, wasting my time, making me nervous . . .

'As I said, it *appears* to have been suicide. *Signora*, what was your husband's state of mind like yesterday?'

I look at the police officer. He wants to know if my husband was depressed.

'He seemed upset. He'd had a row with somebody, one of his friends. I don't know who. I don't know what about.'

The larger policeman nods. He has a big head. He reminds me a bit of a llama.

'*Signora*, did your husband have any enemies? Anyone who wanted him dead?'

I pause for a moment, as if to consider this.

'Ambrogio? No. He had only friends. Everyone loved him.'

'We only ask, *signora*, because we want to be sure it was suicide.'

I cock my head to one side. My innocent brain cannot conceive an alternative.

'You mean . . . ?' My woolly woman's thinking cannot quite comprehend.

'We think he might have been murdered.'

'*Murdered?*'

'We can't rule it out at this stage.'

Shit.

'Is there any *evidence* he was murdered?'

'Not yet, no. At the moment it does look like he jumped, but it could have been staged.'

'*Staged?*'

What does he know about the stage? The stage at the amphitheatre? I hope we cleaned up all the blood, but it was very dark.

I flop down on the sofa. I steady myself on its arm and sink down into the plump pillows. Why does this place have so many cushions? My sister was obsessed with soft furnishings.

'Yes. He could have been killed . . . and then someone could have thrown him over the cliff . . . when he was already dead.'

'I see,' I say. Genius. I should have faked a suicide note. 'Well, as far as I know, he didn't have any enemies. Last night, as I say, he seemed upset. *Depressed.*' I pause. They're both listening attentively, even the one who doesn't speak English. 'I was worried this morning when I couldn't find him that he might have done something stupid. Something like this! My husband has a tendency to . . . overreact.'

'Overreact?'

I sigh and sink further back into the sofa, hug a cushion up close to my chest.

'Yes, you know . . . you lovely Italians. You're all so passionate. *Romantic.*' I smile at the police officers. They know what I mean. 'Always flying off the handle about some little thing that's upset you, making a mountain out of a molehill . . .'

'A molehill, *signora*?'

They stare back with blank faces. That must be a new idiom. Perhaps they don't have moles in Sicily?

'He's threatened suicide before, when he's been upset about something. I never really paid much attention. I just thought it was just a figure of speech, you know?'

They glance at each other and then the larger one writes something down on a well-thumbed notepad. Perhaps I'll shut up now. Perhaps I've already said too much?

'*Signora*, where were you last night?' he asks.

My shoulders tense. I don't like this question.

'Me? Why? I was right here in the villa.'

'Did anyone see you?'

What's all this? Are they looking for alibis? Am I being cross-examined? The walls of the living room get closer and closer. The ceiling gets lower. There's not enough air.

'Please answer the question.'

'I was alone with my son. He's ten months old.' I think. Something like that. Or five months? Or seven? Is he already *one*?

I need some fresh air. I'm getting stressed out. First I discover my sister was plotting to kill me and now these cops are sniffing around. My blood pressure's gone batshit fucking crazy. I leap up from the sofa, push open a window and stick my head outside. Take a deep breath: frangipani. I glance back inside at the two police officers; the llama writes something down. Again. What is he writing? A crime novel? A police show? Is he writing an episode of *Montalbano*? I wonder if they suspect me.

'The body's in the morgue in Catania.'

I stick my head back inside the room.

'Here is the card with the contact details, so you can organize the funeral,' says the police officer. He presses a small, black card into the palm of my hand.

'Oh. Right. Thanks,' I say. 'When can I have the car back?' I really liked that Lamborghini.

'We will bring back the car when forensics have finished their examination, later this afternoon, I hope.' He looks at me and frowns. 'We must warn you, *signora*, the news of your husband's death will appear in today's newspapers. *Arrivederci, signora*. We are sorry for your loss.'

'Will you let me know if you discover anything else? Any clues?' I ask, my eyes brimming with crocodile tears.

'*Certo, signora. Arrivederci*,' he says. The other man gives me an awkward wave. They don't smile. I don't wave back. They stand up and let themselves out.

Great. Now I've got to organize a funeral. That's going to be a royal pain in the ass. We should have taken that signet ring off and smashed up his face. Pulled out his teeth. Otherwise, I think, that went quite well. Or else I'm destined to end my days in an Italian prison, watching daytime TV I don't understand. Canteen food. Card games. Mice. Drugs smuggled in up somebody's ass. I cannot abide communal showers. But no, it's fine. I'll get Amanda Knox's lawyer, turn my experience into a bestselling book. And anyway, what are they going to say? That I'm not really Beth? Where's the proof? Nowhere. There isn't any. Without a *body*, Beth's not even *dead*. So then it's all about Ambrogio's corpse. But the papers will cover it this afternoon: suicide. Case closed. There was nothing suspicious at all about that. It was the perfect murder, and only my second! What can I say, I'm a quick learner. I'm taking it all rather in my stride: cool, calm, professional, expert . . . To be perfectly honest, I don't even feel guilty; it was either going to be *me* or *them*. Beth and Ambrogio started it all. I only came here to have a nice holiday. I'm Cyndi Lauper; I'm just a girl and I want to have fun.

I stretch out on the sofa, kick off my shoes and rest my feet up on the arm. The only glitch is that everyone here knew Ambrogio was fine. He was in good spirits, laughing and joking, just the day before. Can't happy people kill themselves? Of course they can. People put on a brave face when they're dying inside. That's what Ambrogio was doing, smiling on the outside, crying himself to sleep every night. Poor baby, it really was too much for him . . . the stress of his black-market business transactions, dealing with those *animals* in the Cosa Nostra. You can understand why a man like that might want to end his sea of troubles by jumping off a cliff into a troubled sea. Perhaps someone overheard him arguing with that priest? Yes! Of course! There were people in that church milling around after Mass. They might tell the cops that the priest is a suspect. That would take any heat off *his wife*.

Do they have the death penalty in Italy? I'd better google it. I grab Beth's iPhone. Nope. They abolished it after the Nazis on 1 January 1948. Thank goodness for that! What did people do before we had Google? Google is the new God, Twitter is Christ and Instagram is the Holy Spirit. Amen.

Chapter Thirty-two

I look in the mirror, deep into my eyes. They're a dark sea-green: rock pools filled with algae and glistening moss. I smile at my reflection. I'm prettier now that I'm Beth. My eyes crinkle a little at the corners, laughter lines extend at each side. I stretch out my skin so it's smooth and taut. Perhaps I'll get Botox? Stay forever young? Like Alphaville or Cher or some kind of android. I lick sun-chapped lips. I miss my signature bright-purple lipstick. My lime-green nail polish. My beanie hat. I can't wear those things. They're not very 'Beth'. I can't eat kebabs. Can't bully Ed. I'm almost beginning to miss the slobs . . .

What shall I do about Salvatore? He knows too much. He knows *everything*. He knows it was me who killed Ambrogio. He knows that I'm not Beth. He said he preferred Elizabeth's ass. I don't know why Beth seemed to trust him. I guess she just used him because she had no choice. She was using him just like she used me. She didn't love *him* and she didn't love *Alvie*. Anyway, he needs to go. Salvatore might talk to the police. He could blow my cover. Break it all. Everything I've worked so hard for. My well-earned prize. My golden reward. No, there's no question: he has to die. But how?

I've been lucky so far. Beginner's luck. Perhaps it's just a winning streak? I should hit the casinos in Palermo while I'm on a roll. Get back online and ace blackjack. But I don't want to push it, don't want to get caught. I don't want to have to go on the run. I'm not scared of a little Cosa Nostra in my life. It all sounds like fun.

A door slams. Footsteps thud along the corridor: heavy,

metallic – Nino! Of course. His boots sound like that. And he said he'd be back. I rub my eyes so it looks like I've been crying, mess up my hair so it's all dishevelled, force my mouth into a pout. Men are pussies for crying women; I'll bet Nino is too, heartless as he is, heartless and soulless and dead inside.

'Betta?'

'Yes?'

I turn away from the mirror.

He stomps towards me across the room. I keep my eyes low, fixed on the tassels that frame the Persian carpet. I see his steel-capped boots before I see him.

'Betta?'

I look up at Nino with eyes full of terror. I shake my head. *No. No.* My hands are trembling – not too much, but just enough.

'Betta,' he says again, sitting down on the couch next to me. I can smell the leather of his jacket, the Marlboro he smoked before coming in.

'Your husband?'

I nod.

'I just heard the news. *Minchia*,' says Nino.

'Yeah,' I say.

He continues to swear in Italian under his breath: *porco* something. I think that means 'pig'.

Nino doesn't like emotion, I can tell. He does his best to pat my back and look concerned, but it's a little stiff. He'd rather be anywhere else but here. Comforting the grieving widows of ex-associates is not part of his job description. I'd better move this on to business or he'll get bored and leave.

'Oh, Nino,' I cry, grasping his hands: cold metal rings dig into my skin.

He pulls away.

'You want a line, Betta? Cheer yourself up? Come on, let's do a line.'

He takes a bag out of his jacket pocket, pulls the coffee table across the carpet and racks up a couple of lines on the glass. They're long and thin and white as teeth. Sure. What the hell. Why not? Let's celebrate!

He takes a €50 note from his black leather wallet and rolls it up. We snort the lines. Wow, that's good shit. I'm already feeling better. This coke's way stronger than the stuff I used to steal from the slobs back in Archway. That was eighty per cent baking powder, at least.

'You gonna talk now? Huh? You gonna tell me what you know?'

I sniff back the tears that are not falling and wipe my nose with the back of my hand.

'OK,' I say.

'Let's start with the bruises. Who beat you up?'

Whoop! Whoop! This coke's got a kick to it. I'm alive. I'm invincible. I'm magic. I can fly. I'm so high I don't care if the whole house burns down with me sitting in it. Now, what were we talking about?

'Salvatore,' I say.

Well, he *kind of* beat me up. It's just a tiny little white lie. I'm not a liar, I'm just creative. Everything I say is true, like the witches in *Macbeth*.

I turn towards Nino, let my thigh press up against his own. I'm wearing Beth's Wonderbra and a hell of a lot of Miss Dior Chérie. I bite my lip.

'He did it,' I say.

'Salvatore? Yeah, I heard that name. The neighbour, right? He a friend of your husband's?' Nino asks.

I pause, long enough to create some suspicion. 'They weren't exactly *friends* . . .' I say.

I widen my eyes and keep eye contact, willing Nino to read between the lines. *Salvatore killed Ambrogio and attacked his wife.*

'Why did he hit you? Was he jealous?' says Nino. 'Were Salvatore and Ambrogio fighting over you?'

Sure, why not. I hadn't thought of that.

'Yes,' I sob, then let my tears do the talking, sink my head down into my hands. My shoulders heave. My breathing becomes irregular.

'*Stronzo!*' says Nino, leaping up from the couch. 'That *figlio di puttana* kill your husband, Betta? *Vaffanculo. Stronzo!*'

I look up at Nino, pacing the carpet, his steel-capped boots thumping and clunking, his knuckles dripping with silver and gold. I don't say anything, just watch.

'I'm gonna teach that cocksucking son of a bitch a lesson. Il Professore was like a brother to me.'

I nod my head like I understand.

'A brother!'

'So what are you going to do?' I ask. I really hope he's going to kill him.

'I'll take care of it,' he growls.

Nino slams the door. The engine of his people carrier purrs as it crawls down the drive and off down the road.

Well, that was easy. Just like that. I fucking love it. Nino's elegant and understated. A black mamba or black widow: subtle, sombre, lethal as fuck. I light myself a celebratory fag, blow smoke up to the chandeliers. Beth would have a fit if she saw me smoking in here. She used to make Ambrogio go out on the terrace. But Beth is gone. And so is Ambrogio. Ha ha! Guess what? Salvo's next. I let my neck sink into the cushions, roll my head from side to side. As my coke high numbs my brain, a growing smile spreads across my lips.

I've been here for *hours*, watching, waiting. I'm sitting on the terrace and staring at the road. This is my eighth cigarette. My mouth tastes like a funeral pyre, but the nicotine's helping. A bit. At least I'm not shaking any more. I'm glugging down a bottle of Nero d'Avola (wine's so much nicer when it's not out of a box) and comfort-eating *torta della Nonna*. I shove fistful after fistful into my face. I eat and eat until I can't eat any more, then I eat some more until it's all gone. I pick up the crumbs between my fingers and lick the plate until it's clean. It's sweet, creamy, decadent, delicious. I want some more, but there's nothing left; I light another cig instead.

It's starting to get dark, but I'll wait all night if I have to. I need to see it. I need to be sure. I won't sleep if I don't know, so there's just no point in going to bed. Who'd be able to sleep on a night like this? Who in their right mind? You'd have to be a sociopath. A textbook psycho: Thomas Ripley or Patrick Bateman. Or maybe Amy Dunne. Given the choice, I'd be Amy, or one of those *glamorous* psychopaths you read about in books. But I'm not. I care. I want to know.

I check Beth's watch: 8.30 p.m. I've already been here three hours *at least*. My ass feels numb. I've got pins and needles like Elizabeth's doll. I told Emilia no supper. She's been hanging around a lot lately. Watching me. Staring. Acting like there's something she can't bring herself to tell me. It's driving me crazy. Twitching the curtains. Listening. Worrying. Anyway, she wasn't surprised about dinner. I don't think Beth ate actual food: a pistachio for breakfast, a lettuce leaf for lunch, half a cherry tomato for supper, a lick of granita for desert. I've got no appetite. Not with all this weight on my mind. Not now I've eaten all that cake. He might not even do it tonight. But he has to. He's a professional. He won't like leaving a loose end like this. Nino will want to finish things up. Right now. Tonight. I know I would.

Shit, I'm feeling kind of queasy. It's not the wine. It's not the cake. It's not the constant chain-smoking, I'm used to that. Nino's *killing* Salvatore. This time tomorrow, he'll be *dead*. And it's all my fault, my crazy idea. I've never actually *murdered* someone. I mean, I haven't killed them 'with intent'. Isn't that the term they use in court? Isn't that what Judge Judy says? That's the difference between manslaughter and murder. That's the fucking crucial point. Beth and Ambrogio, they were different. I mean, Beth was an accident – at least, I think. And as for Ambrogio, I had no choice! That was clearly self-defence. It really was Ambrogio or me. But this is different. Premeditated. I feel sick, in a good way. Like butterflies before a gig. I kinda like it . . . Man, I'm fucking high!

I need to go to the toilet. I've needed to pee for the best part of an hour, but I'm scared I'll miss him if I leave. My eyes are glued to the road. But I can't hold it in. It's the physical pain of a too-full bladder and the mental pain of denying release. I glance at the villa; the lights are off. Ernie's asleep. I think Emilia's gone home. I jump off the sunbed and run on to the lawn, still watching the road like a hawk. Like a drone. I pull down my knickers and squat. The hiss of piss on grass. Just like that Joni Mitchell album, *The Hissing of Summer Lawns*. I'm in mid flow when suddenly I hear it: the purr of a vehicle down there on the road. I look up and see it: a big, black car with its headlights off, driving slowly, slow as a hearse. It's Nino's people carrier. It glides past the villa and stops at the end of Salvatore's drive. I pull on my pants and stand up.

YES!!!

'You did it?' I breathe.

'I did it,' comes a voice in the darkness.

I wasn't asleep; I was staring up at the infinite blackness that is the ceiling. I sit up in bed and reach for the light on the bedside table. I flick it on and it almost blinds me. Nino leans over me, his eyes like fire.

'You did it,' I whisper.

I look into his eyes for a split second longer; I feel hot, like I'm burning from the inside out.

'Nino,' I gasp, 'no one's ever killed for me before. It's . . . so . . . fucking . . . hot.'

Nino is my superhero.

'You like it?'

'Uh-huh.'

'Yeah, me too. I'm in the right job.'

And I can't help it; I need to know. My curiosity's going to kill me, like some kind of idiot cat: 'What is it you do exactly, you know, for a living?'

Nino laughs. 'You don't know?'

'Not *exactly*.' I shake my head.

He laughs again: his shoulders shake and the mattress shudders, a sound like dirty water going down a drain.

'I kill people,' he says. 'For cash.'

And I'm not sure if he's joking or if he's telling the truth, but then he laughs and laughs and laughs some more, like it's the very last time before somebody puts a bullet between his eyeballs, and I know it's the truth. Fuck, he's sexy: Italian accent, hair slick and shiny as oil. And oh my God, I really want him. I never wanted anyone so much in my life. Nino is hotter than Christian Grey.

'Awesome,' I say.

He wipes a tear from the corner of a dead black eye. 'I thought you were a good girl,' Nino says, leaning towards me. 'Hated violence. Hated killing.' He raises an eyebrow. 'Ambrogio said you were a *pacifist*?'

I want to reach out and grab him. 'Well, I guess you were both wrong. I'm full of surprises.'

A gravitational pull seems to draw us together, like he is the sun and I am Mars. Or is it the other way around? I tear back the sheets so Nino can get in. He jumps on top of me, still wearing his jacket and steel-capped boots. Metal studs dig into my flesh. Nino's tongue darts into my mouth and I taste blood; is his lip bleeding? Or is it Salvatore's?

Nino rips off my nightie and pulls it over my head. He tugs at my knickers and kicks them down my thighs. I am completely naked. He stops and looks me up and down, licking his lips: a dog about to devour a bone. I watch with wide eyes and breathe in his scent: sweat mixed with blood. My pussy is aching.

He leans in towards me: his hot, wet breath, his lips an inch from my lips. 'Betta, Madonna, I never knew you were so *bad*.'

He throws off his jacket and kicks his boots to the floor. He pulls his gun from his belt and slams it down on the bedside table.

'No,' I say, 'keep it.'

'What?' says Nino.

'The gun. I like it. Give it to me.'

I reach over to the table, looking into his eyes. I take the gun; it's loaded, heavy. Nino's pupils are dark and wide. I lie down on the bed with the barrel between my legs. I wonder if there's a safety catch. I wonder if it's on. I rub the gun against my clit. What would happen if it went off?

'Oh yeah,' says Nino.

I play with the gun and Nino watches. It feels cold and hard inside me. I moan. The barrel vanishes and reappears, in and out, in and out. It twists and slides, its edges rough, cold, hard, metallic. A shiver runs down my spine.

'Oh yeah.'

Nino takes the gun and puts it back on the table, kneels down in front of me on the bed; I know what he wants. I open his flies and pull down his jeans. Holy fuck; he's enormous, the biggest I've seen. Even bigger than Salvatore's. Just like Mark Wahlberg's. Just like Mr Dick. It doesn't look real. A purple vein protrudes from the skin. He smells fleshy, corporeal. I open my mouth. Nino is trembling; his eyes flicker and blaze.

'Come here, *puttana*,' he says, grabbing my shoulders and forcing me down and over the bed. My pussy aches so much it hurts. His fingernails dig into my waist, pulling me, squeezing. I'm so wet I'm dripping.

'Are you sure he's dead?' I say into the headboard.

'His brains are on his kitchen floor. Domenico's cleaning him up.'

I kind of wish I'd killed him myself now . . . but it's too late for that. Nino enters me all in one go, so deep and hard I can't help but scream. He grabs my hair and forces my face down into the pillow. I can't breathe. I can't move. He pounds me and pounds me on my G-spot. Mean. Rough. I turn my face to the side and groan.

'Don't stop! Don't stop!'

His hands slide up across my back, up my neck and over my shoulders. He puts his finger in my mouth and I bite hard. I'm panting, breathing, begging him, pleading: 'Don't stop. Do not fucking stop.'

He slaps my ass; it smarts, like a snakebite.

'Hey,' I say, pulling away. I pretend to be cross, but I actually liked it.

He flips me around and lies flat on the bed. I move up his body and lower myself down. I slide on to his cock, slowly, slowly. I ride him now and he pulls my waist closer. He feels amazing, so full and fat. It builds and it builds and it builds and it builds and I'm coming, I'm coming, I'm coming and *fuck*!

He flips me back over. I'm dizzy. I'm high. His fingers feel for my ass and, suddenly, he pushes one inside. Oh my God! I wasn't expecting *that*. He thrusts his cock inside my ass. It burns. Is that normal? I haven't done this before. My hand slips and I bang my head. Nino pulls me back up. He breathes into my hair, his breath hot and wet at the back of my neck. His fingers rub my clit and he's fucking my ass. Fuck *normal*, this is fucking spectacular! They say the ass is the new vagina. He comes inside and my insides clench; something liquid squirts from my cunt: violent, strange. And I'm coming again like never before.

He killed for me!

Nino killed Salvatore!

I can't breathe.

I can't see.

Oh my God.

Nino's my happily ever after.

I think Nino might be my soulmate.

DAY SIX:
Greed

The love of money is the root of all financial success,
so why am I so broke?
@AlvinaKnightly69

Chapter Thirty-three

It was Beth's fault I got kicked out of the Girl Guides in 2001. All through that year, Beth and I organized countless charity bake sales, fun runs, swimathons, sleepathons, galas, discos and sponsored bike rides. I read twelve Enid Blyton novels back to back for the Easter readathon (you can never recover from that kind of thing). I dressed up as a hot dog for the fancy-dress picnic. I knitted three kilos of scarves. We were the most benevolent Guides in our unit. We were doing our good turns, keeping the law as decreed by the late, great Baron Baden-Powell. We met the Girl Guides' President, Her Royal Highness Sophie, Countess of Wessex, collected the badges for 'Fire Safety', 'First Aid' and 'Survival', and worked our way up to the dizzying heights of 'Patrol Leader'.

To say I was *crushed* is an understatement; *crucified* more like.

I'd been an example, a role model. The Rainbows, the Brownies and the other Girl Guides had all looked up to me. I can still hear the applause echoing off the walls in the old church hall, the catch in Beaver's voice as she announced the record amount that I'd raised for good causes that year. Brown Owl's eyes filled with pride as I collected my badge for 'Community Action'. Squirrel cried tears of joy.

At its height, our mania for fundraising saw us organize one event per week; it was pretty full on. The pressure finally got to me just before our fourteenth birthday. We did a firework display for Save the Children, a sponsored silence for the NSPCC and a gala dinner for UNICEF. The stress was immense. I didn't sleep for a month.

It was worth it though: in 2001, I earned £5,487.56; that's not bad for a kid in full-time education. I was running out of places to hide the cash; it was mostly pound coins, coppers, silvers, fivers, a few tens, a few twenties, some cheques and a couple of postal orders. I got up one morning and couldn't find any pants because my drawers were all stuffed full of banknotes. I decided I needed a savings account. I went to my local Lloyds that Saturday morning and explained my predicament. Needless to say, the clerk was impressed by all the babysitting I'd been doing and my natural flair for saving. He tried to talk me into getting an ISA, but I had other plans. I needed an Internet bank account.

I'd recently watched the film *Rain Man*, starring Dustin Hoffman and Tom Cruise. I bought a self-help book about counting cards; it didn't look that difficult when Raymond did it, and if an autistic guy could do it, then I figured so could I. I lost five grand in online casinos in twenty-four hours. Add to that blow an angry phone call from a lawyer representing Save the Children and my shock exclusion from the Girl Guides: it was a bad October.

But I would have been a terrible Girl Guide if I hadn't been ready for any eventuality; the Guiding motto is '*Be prepared*' after all. I prepared an empty Pepsi bottle with petrol from my mum's old Volvo and acquired a box full of matches. One Tuesday night, when everyone was sleeping, I tiptoed downstairs in my pyjamas, threw on my duffel coat and sneaked out of the front door. It was only a few minutes' walk to the old church hall. I was tucked up back in bed before the fire engines came flashing. The howl of the sirens. The roar of the flames. The faint smell of smoke creeping into our bedroom, seeping in through the single glazing. Acrid. Sour. Eyes stinging. Throat tickling. Beth slept through the whole damn thing. I would have burnt down Save the Children too, but their headquarters was in London and that was too far away.

No one ever guessed it was me. Apart from Beth, but she

didn't say anything. I'm not sure why she kept it a secret. She didn't even tell Mum.

'*B*uongiorno.'

It's Emilia. She has *caffè*, a croissant and freshly squeezed orange juice balanced on a tray. What did I do before I had staff? Nescafé granules? PG Tips? I don't remember. It's another life.

It's a beautiful day. Emilia pulls the blind cord to reveal a blinding rectangle of azure sky. A jungle of palm leaves throws black shadows across the crazy paving. I sit up. Nino? I look over at the crumpled-up pillow on the far side of the bed. He's gone. Of course. Even in my dreams I can't make them stay; I know that's what my sister would say. Fuck my sister: *Elizabeth, the murderer.* Or at least *attempted.* Ha. She's not even a proper killer. She tried and failed; *I'm on body number three.*

'Is Ernie up?'

'Not yet, *signora.*'

'Let him sleep. I'll go see him when I'm dressed.' Perhaps I'll take him to the beach today. That could be fun. Kids like sandcastles, right?

'*Certo,*' she says with a tilt of the head. She makes her way to the door, but then pauses. '*Signora?*'

I look up, a face full of pastry. 'Uh-huh?'

Oh God, what now? What's she going to say? Can't I have my breakfast in peace?

'*Sono preoccupata.* Worried. I hear you screaming this morning.'

'Screaming?'

'*Sì.*'

What the hell is she talking about? What screaming? Did she hear me having sex with Nino last night? (Fuck, that was good. I'm almost in love. Almost.) Perhaps she heard me shrieking with pleasure, but screaming? No.

'I wasn't screaming.'

'Perhaps you had an *incubo* . . . a nightmare?'

'I just lost my husband. My whole life's a nightmare.' I give Emilia a pointed look. 'Can I have another croissant?'

'*Certo.*'

'Perhaps another cappuccino?'

She turns to leave the room. But then stops.

'*Signora,*' she says.

'Yes, Emilia?'

'I am very sorry about Signor Caruso. When my husband was murdered, I didn't speak to another man for more than ten years. I wear only black.'

'My husband wasn't murdered. It was suicide.'

'*Sì, signora.*'

'So off you pop.'

'*Signora?*'

'What?'

'I want to say you, you and Ernesto, you are family for me. For you I do anything. I die for you!'

'Wow, Emilia. That's a little over the top, but I appreciate the sentiment. Now, how about that cappuccino?'

She *finally* leaves the room.

Hmm . . . I wonder what that was about. Maybe Emilia's concerned about me? Perhaps she's just a *nice person*? Weird. I'll have to keep an eye on her. It's all getting rather personal, too close for comfort. But I need Emilia. She's good with the baby. She washes my clothes. She cooks my dinner. She's like some kind of saint. I still haven't worked out how to make my own coffee; it's like alchemy. I need to keep her onside.

I stand in the window and look out at the street. A policeman is walking down the road to the villa. Is that Commissario Savastano? I can't see his face. Is he coming here? I freeze, my coffee cup suspended in mid-air. He disappears somewhere near Salvatore's villa. What's he doing over there? Have they found Salvatore's body already? Did they see his brains spilled out on the floor? His blood splattered all over the fridge like a mural by Jackson Pollock? I take a deep breath. Ah, Salvatore. It's such a waste. He was fantastic in bed. Really quite talented; he could have been a pro, like that Italian porn star, Rocco. Still, he wasn't a patch on Nino . . .

I don't like these coppers snooping around.

So what if they link me to Salvatore's death? Ha! Good luck to them. That wasn't even me. So what if I set Nino up to kill him? There's no proof of that. No evidence. It's Nino's word against mine. Salvo's blood's not on *my* hands. Anyway, it's the same old story, someone change the fucking record. Seriously, I'm bored to tears: no body, no murder. And there won't be a body; Nino's a professional and Domenico is too. Nino knows what he is doing, I'm sure of that. They'll have cleaned up the mess: no brains. No blood. They'll have dealt with the corpse. Nino's smarter and sexier than those lazy fucking cops – corrupt, most of them, anyway – taking hand-outs from the Mafia to look the other way. I'm sure we could bribe them, if it came to it.

No, it's fine. As far as anyone knows, Salvatore decided to take a long, lonely vacation to Italy's most secluded beach. He's an artist, isn't he? He has an artist's temperament. Perhaps he felt like being a recluse and immersing himself in his sculptures. Yes, I'm pretty sure he mentioned something like that just before he left. The pressures of modern-day living in Taormina were getting to him. He wanted to return to the purity of nature, to be inspired by the sea and the sound of the waves . . . some bullshit like that. In fact, he definitely told me he was going away. I'm willing to put my hand on a Bible and swear it in court.

I check Beth's iPhone charging by the bed to see if there's anything urgent I need to respond to. There are 325 'Likes' for my selfie with Ernie. Another tweet from Taylor Swift. And three missed calls; they're all from my mum. Oh God, what now? She's left a voicemail, but I can't be bothered to listen to it. I'm definitely not calling her back.

I get dressed in a little number that's too cute to be true: a pink, silk, pussy-bow blouse with a matching knee-length frou-frou skirt. I look simply *adorable*. Just like Miss Universe, when they're doing the bit where she has to talk and wear clothes. This outfit's going straight on to Instagram. I twirl in the mirror and the nightmare comes back in a lightning flash! I was dreaming about Beth! She was chasing me, calling me. She was coming for me like some kind of zombie; I was running for my life! Now I remember! It was a bad dream. Why can't Beth leave me the fuck alone? Even now when she's supposed to be dead! This is getting really annoying. Why can't I have nice, normal nightmares like everyone else? Falling down lift shafts or being pursued by giant spiders. Teeth falling out. The end of the world or Armageddon. But no, I've got to dream about Beth.

You know what I need? I need a plan. If you fail to plan, you plan to fail. I need to move on. Live my life (Beth's life). Enough of this crap. Enough dicking around. Enough of my sister. I'll contact Beth's lawyer. Sort out the inheritance from Ambrogio's will. I'll get another beautician. Hire a new nanny, just in case. Wham bam. Job done. In your face.

Chapter Thirty-four

'So where is it?' says Nino, pushing through the door and into the living room.

Whoa, where did *he* come from? He's as quiet as a Prius. Does he have his own house keys? I put down the copy of *The Female Eunuch* that I'd started to read (one of the few books that I brought with me; I'd forgotten all about it at the bottom of my bag, tucked away with my Swiss army knife). I wonder what Germaine would think of Nino.

'Where's what?'

'The fucking painting?'

Painting? Yes, there had been something about a painting. Something about a Caravaggio. 'The Caravaggio?' I ask. What is that anyway? A picture of an Italian caravan? A watercolour of the RV from *Breaking Bad*?

'Yes, of course the Caravaggio. What do you think?' He paces the carpet, restless, anxious, like he's had too much coke. He's probably had too much coke.

'Ooh,' I say, 'shall we do some coke? I don't know where the painting is.'

'*You don't know where it is?*'

'No.'

Nino takes off his hat and slams it down on the coffee table, runs his fingers through ebony hair. I like that hat. I think I might steal it. 'You're his fucking wife, of course you know where it is.' He takes out the bag of cocaine and racks up.

'So anyway,' I say, changing the subject, 'how come you didn't sleep over last night? I wanted you to stay.'

He looks up and frowns.

'I do not sleep.'

'What do you mean, *you don't sleep*? Everyone sleeps.'

Nino snorts his line and wipes his nose with the back of his hand.

'Where is the painting, Betta?'

'What are you, like a vampire or something? Are you Edward from *Twilight*? Are you one of the Volturi?'

'What the fuck are you talking about? Who is Edward?'

'You *have* to sleep. I need at least ten hours a night. It's good for your skin.'

'I have a siesta in the afternoons.'

'A siesta? Like a nap?'

'I work at night.'

'What are you, a *baby*?'

'In Sicily, everyone has a siesta. It's too hot to work in the day.'

Only mad dogs and English girls go out in the midday sun . . .

Nino hands me the rolled-up €50.

'So you're nocturnal? Like a bat? Like a bushbaby?' I say.

Nino nods. I thought he'd looked a bit like a bat that first time I saw him, gliding down the driveway in his long, black coat.

'Still, it would have been nice if you'd stayed, instead of just taking off. We could have spooned,' I say. I do my line.

Nino sighs. 'Betta. I know you know where the painting is, so just fucking tell me.'

Shit, he's right. Beth would know this. Where would Ambrogio hide a painting? A *Caravaggio*?

'Ambrogio didn't want to tell me. He said it was better if I didn't know. Safer,' I say.

Nino shrugs.

'Well, it's gotta be somewhere in the villa and we gotta find it,' he says.

I snort another line. Fuck, that's good: a brain orgasm. Or something. The back of my brain is fizzy, like Coca-Cola. Is this what happiness feels like?

'OK, so we'll look.'

I give Nino a million-megawatt smile. A real one. Like I mean it. God bless cocaine. I'm going to be so helpful this time. Useful. Super-proactive Alvie! Obviously, I mean Beth.

Nino snorts another line. He paces the room. 'So who was the client? Who was Ambrogio gonna sell it to?'

'Sorry, come again?' I'm supposed to know *this*? 'I . . . I . . . I . . .'

'And don't tell me that you don't know, cos he wouldn't fucking tell me. Wanted to handle this one by himself.'

I pause, look down at his waistband where the handle of the gun is sticking out. I've got to keep this bad boy sweet. 'I'm sorry, baby, I don't know.'

Nino kicks the leg of the coffee table and the ceramic lamp wobbles precariously. I catch it before it falls and smashes. The label on the bottom says '*Wedgwood*'.

'Betta, you can stop with the innocent-wife act. I know you two were in this together. He told me, the client, he likes my wife. So who the fuck is he?'

It's a good question. I wish I knew . . . but Nino's reminded me of something: Ambrogio took me with him to visit that priest. He liked me, I mean the priest liked Beth. Caravaggio . . . Caravaggio . . . I knew I'd heard that word before. I look up at Nino and grin.

'The priest!' I say. 'The priest is the client.' Thank God for that. I'm catching on.

Nino smiles an unpleasant smile. 'Now we're getting somewhere. *Bene*. Which priest is that? There are hundreds of thousands in Sicily.'

'At the church on the square.' Shit, what was it called? 'The . . . the . . . the Chiesa di San Giuseppe?' I twist Beth's ring around on my finger. I hope I said that right.

'Right here? In Taormina?'

'That's right, in Taormina.'

Nino lets out a long, slow whistle, leans back in the sofa and smooths his moustache with a finger and thumb. His moustache looks a bit like a slug. But sexy. 'You've got to be kidding me. The church on Piazza I X Aprile?'

I think so . . . 'Yes. Yes, that was it.'

'What's his name, this priest?' He laughs, sitting up. He reaches into his jacket and pulls out his smokes. He offers one to me, but I shake my head. He seems to have cheered up . . . is that the painting or the coke?

'I don't know. He was really, really old. He had a big nose . . . he reminded me of Belial in *Paradise Lost*?'

If he was Belial, then Nino's got to be Moloch. I'll be Satan; he was the hero.

'A big nose? Whatever. We'll find him. How much did you agree?' Nino blows out a lungful of smoke. It stings my eyes.

'It wasn't me. I didn't agree anything.'

'Your husband, Il Professore. What was the price?'

'I have no idea. Actually, Nino, last time they met they had an argument. I think the deal might be off . . .'

Nino freezes, looks at me. If looks could kill . . . I guess that was the wrong thing to say. I eye his gun.

'Oh no, it's not off. No fucking way. When was this?'

'A couple of days ago . . . I guess.' I have no idea. I've lost track of time. I don't even know what day it is today. Tuesday? Saturday? Christmas morning?

'We're selling this piece-of-shit painting if it's the last thing we do. That priest wants to buy it. We're not leaving it sitting up here in this villa when it's worth twenty million dollars.'

'Twenty million dollars?' I can't have heard right. That cocaine's tricking and tickling my brain.

'At least. At auction, perhaps more. But on the black market we'll get a tenth, if we're lucky.'

'A tenth, so two million?' Oh my God.

'Bravo, baby. Great fucking maths. I bet Ambrogio wanted

more. That's what the argument was about. Greedy bastard. His papà had been sitting on that thing since the '90s.'

'Really? That long?'

'Fucking pain in the ass to sell something that hot. Do you know how long it took to find that buyer?'

'Erm . . . no.'

'Your husband told you none of this, Betta? You two even speak?' He looks at me sideways. 'This was a big fucking deal for Ambrogio, the biggest fucking deal of his life. All those other paintings he was selling? Nothing, *merda* on toilet paper compared to this . . .'

'I see,' I say. I don't really get it. I'm concerned that my head might be about to explode. Nino seems to be talking far too fast, like a New York car salesman or Jimmy Carr.

'This painting, that we still need to fucking find by the way, isn't just any old Caravaggio. Not that there are any regular paintings by this guy. It's *The Nativity*. You understand?'

'I understand.' I don't understand.

I grab Beth's phone and google 'Caravaggio Nativity' while Nino isn't looking. The Internet says there are only about fifty paintings by this guy in the entire world. But this one of the nativity? According to Wikipedia, this is the big one, the fucking star of the show. This is his masterpiece.

'Shit,' I say.

'Yeah, shit. You didn't know? You're married to *Ambrogio Caruso* and you don't know this? Fuck . . .'

Nino's stroking his moustache. My heart is beating at a million miles an hour. I didn't really know what Ambrogio did for a living. If I were Beth, I would know. My skin is burning. I'm far too hot. I know about Waterhouse, Hogarth and Gainsborough, Turner and all the pre-Raphaelites. I know about Freud and Bacon and Banksy, but not about this. I haven't read up on Italian art; I would never pick this as my subject on *Mastermind*. I bet Beth knew all about this stuff. She was the one who went on the trip to the National Gallery when we were thirteen.

'Art's never really been my thing; that was all Ambrogio,' I say. 'Shall we do one more line?'

Nino racks up a couple more lines with his shiny silver credit card. Where would Ambrogio have hidden this painting? I kind of wish I hadn't killed him now; I could have asked him. So annoying. Why aren't I clairvoyant? Or what's the one where you can speak with the dead? Clairaudient? Psychic? I wish I was a shaman. If only I'd known about this painting before he died, but Ambrogio was so shady when I asked about his job: *I'm just the middle man. It's really not that interesting.* Twenty million dollars? THIS IS THE MOST INTERESTING THING I'VE EVER HEARD IN MY LIFE.

Could be a nice little earner. If we can find it.

I do some more googling while Nino racks up. *The Nativity* was stolen in 1969 from the Chiesa di San Lorenzo in Palermo. Apparently, a couple of chancers with razor blades had seen it on TV a few weeks before, on a show about Italy's hidden treasures. They weren't even Mafia, they were amateurs. They weren't in the Mob. They knew the church. They recognized the painting. Of course, in those days security was useless, nothing like it is today; the painting was protected by some old geezer who probably slept through the whole fucking thing. One night, they cut it down from above the altar and drove off with the painting in a three-wheeled van. A three-wheeled van! Just like Del Boy: 'Trotter's Independent Trading: New York, Paris, Peckham. Palermo'!

We clearly need to find this painting. It sounds pretty fucking special. I snort my line.

'So how come Ambrogio's dad had this painting?'

Nino looks restless. He picks up the corner of the Persian carpet and looks underneath. He moves the sofa and looks down the back by the wall. *Niente. Nada. Zilch.*

'It changed hands a few times; Rosario Riccobono had it before he was got in 1982. Ambrogio's papa bought it from U Paccarè, you know, Gerlando Alberti, the cigarettes and heroin guy? That was back in 1991.'

I have no idea who these people are.

'So, how come he never sold it before?' My lips have gone numb. Am I speaking funny? I can't feel my face, like in that song. I hope I'm not dribbling. Nino looks under the dining table, pulls back the chairs and checks underneath.

'You think it's easy to sell something like this? This painting is hot. The FBI are all over it. It's on all the world's most-wanted lists . . . No, Ambrogio was lucky. He finally got the painting when his parents died. He wasn't stupid, Ambrogio's papa, he needed to let the heat cool off. He even got this *stronzo*, Gaspare Spatuzza – a former guy turned police rat – got him to make up some story about it.'

'What story?'

'The *rat* told the cops that the painting had been eaten by rats – by rats! – while being stored in some shed at a farm. Can you imagine anyone being so stupid? It's worth twenty million dollars and some joker feeds it to rats? He said it was so fucked up that they burnt the remains. The police ate it up. Ate it up.' He takes an angry drag on the stub of his fag. 'Just goes to show they have no respect for us wise guys. That's why they'll never beat us. They think we're retarded, so they underestimate us . . . It's *wise* guys. *Wise.*'

I'm listening in a kind of trance, my little grey cells working in overdrive, gradually placing the pieces of the puzzle, putting it all together. Now I see. It all makes sense. The metaphorical lightbulb flicks on. Ambrogio had finally found a buyer. He was going to sell his stolen painting and then he and Beth planned to disappear. My dead body was a decoy for Beth: I was just bait, a red fucking herring, like a carrot or a duck. The funeral, the police and the international press were going to create one royal mess. Everyone would think that *Princess* Beth was dead, so she would have been safe. She could have run and no one would have chased her. What's the point if she's in the ground? Ambrogio was going to play the part of the mourning widower. Then he'd scram, sneak out of Taormina in the middle of the night when the whole world and its dog thought he was grieving his wife. He'd probably arranged to meet my twin in Hawaii, Tahiti or Bora Bora. They planned to take their kid and their millions and get away from this bloodthirsty mob, run away from this *Mafia war*. They'd planned to elope and start over. Nice.

But something went wrong – namely, my sister. Something turned her off her husband. She didn't just want to get out of Sicily, she wanted to get away from *him*. It can't have just been the sex situation; that's just ridiculous, even for Beth. Even for me. There must have been something else. He wasn't a wife beater, wasn't a thug. So what? What was it? Was she really in love with Salvatore? I'll figure it out. But first I'm going to make some cash.

'I'll help you find it,' I say, standing up.

Chapter Thirty-five

We've looked everywhere, inside the villa and out. In the garage. In the shed. In what felt like a hundred bedrooms and bathrooms. I found some interesting things – a room full of brand-new copies of Beth's book, Ambrogio's secret collection of porn (apparently he was into 'college', 'babysitters' and 'teens', all pretty vanilla) and a vintage ostrich handbag that I'm definitely going to keep – but the painting is nowhere. I am seriously starting to freak the fuck out. We've been searching for hours, fuelled by cocaine and strong, black coffee, thick with sugar (the sugar's for me, Nino seems to prefer it bitter and black. I have no idea how he drinks it like that). I thought about asking Emilia if she's seen it, even asking Ernesto. But it's probably not a good idea. Where would Ambrogio keep a painting? A painting worth twenty million dollars? He'd keep it close, right? He'd need to keep it safe. I walk back into the bedroom he'd shared with Beth and stand in the doorway, leaning my forehead against the cool of the wood. This is hopeless; it's gone.

'Betta? Where are you?' A voice booms from the hall, making me jump. It's Nino. He sounds cross.

'Over here,' I say. 'Come and help me look in the bedroom.'

I walk into the room and stand in the middle of the thick, cream carpet. I scan the ceiling for a door to an attic, but there's nothing. Nino walks in and stands just behind me.

'Betta, come on, we've searched in here.' He speaks in a hiss, whispers like an adder. We have to be quiet. Ernie might wake up. He puts his hand on my shoulder. His signet ring is a blood-red ruby, the size of an eyeball, set in gold.

'I don't know,' I say. 'I've just got a feeling. Something that valuable, something that special, you'd want to keep it close . . .'

'In the room where you sleep,' Nino says, pacing the carpet in his heavy black boots. This is killing him, I can tell. *Patience* clearly isn't his thing. I doubt he listens to Take That. I walk around my sister's bedroom, my fingers trailing over mahogany: the wardrobe, the dressing table, the chest of drawers. There isn't a speck of dust; it's incredible. Emilia's worth her weight in gold.

I look under the bed. Nino looks stressed.

'For fuck's sake. We've looked everywhere. We're just going to have to search again, the whole fucking house, properly this time.'

We're just about to leave the room when Nino says, 'Have you checked inside that wardrobe? There could be a false back.'

We look at each other, then rush for the wardrobe. I yank open the door and pull aside the clothes, Ambrogio's trousers, jackets, shirts, ties. My fingers feel for the corners of a panel at the back, but the wood is stuck firm.

'No,' I say, stepping away.

'Let me try,' Nino says.

He dives into the wardrobe like he's looking for Aslan. I hear him cursing under his breath. *'Niente. Merda.'*

He pulls himself out and thumps the door! THUMP! Shit. He's losing his cool. Any minute now, he'll pull out his gun!

'Betta, come on! Where the hell is it? I know you know, so quit fucking around.'

I'm starting to sweat. My chest feels tight. I sit down on the bed, rub my face with my hands. Come on, Alvie, where? Where? I'm burning up. Is it the coke or the climate? It's Death Valley, Nevada, in the middle of a heatwave. My breathing is shallow; I can't get enough air. I stand up and walk over to the window, yank it open and take a deep breath. I squeeze my eyes shut. Something valuable. Something important. Something special that you want to protect. An image of Ernie pops up in my head.

I run out to the hall and Nino follows after.

'Hey, Betta! Where are you going?'

'Shh, come with me. We've got to be quiet.'

Ernie's asleep in his cot; I can hear him snoring in the darkness – softly, softly, in and out. I tiptoe in and flick on the night light: baby blue in the shape of a moon. There's a rug on the floor by the baby's bed. I lift it up; it's a hunch, but it's right! Underneath the carpet is a small trapdoor. It's got to be in there, surely? I lift the rug with trembling fingers and pull up the door: the hinge creaks open. I glance over at Ernie, but he's still fast asleep; he didn't hear a thing. I pull the trapdoor open wide and rest it against the folded rug. I reach down low beneath the floorboards; I feel a heavy canvas bag. I grab the handles and pull it up. I don't think there's a painting in here. It's way too small. I look up at Nino, and he shakes his head. I unzip the bag anyway; I'll take a quick peek, just in case. Oh my God! Hidden inside are hundreds of bags of fine white powder. I've never seen so much coke in my life. This must be Ambrogio's private stash. It looks stunning, white like an Arctic landscape. As fresh and pure as snow. I smooth the plastic with my palms. Mmm, drugs! I wonder if Beth knew about all this stored in baby Ernie's room. She would have freaked out.

'Keep looking,' says Nino. 'Down there.'

I'm about to zip the bag back up when Nino reaches down and grabs a baggie. I look up and he shrugs. Fair enough. Ambrogio's dead. What's he going to do? He shoves the coke in his jacket pocket. I grab myself another baggie and pop it down my bra. I close the bag and haul it to one side. I peer back through the trapdoor. There, beneath the floorboards and wrapped in brown paper, is a long, slim, dusty canvas. I can't believe it. That's got to be it! It has to be *The Nativity*. I can't breathe. I can't move. I can only stare. Twenty million dollars right here? I can't believe all this stuff's in the nursery. Isn't that dangerous? Beth can't have known where Ambrogio hid it. She'd never have allowed it. Or perhaps she did and that was the problem? I bet that really pissed her off. Class As and a gun for her precious baby? The hottest piece of art on the planet? Beth was mad at her husband, guaranteed. I bet that was why she hated Ambrogio. She probably wanted him dead.

Nino pushes me out of the way and reaches down through the trapdoor. Very carefully, as though he were delivering a newborn baby, as though he were holding the infant Christ, he scoops out the painting. It smells musty, old. It looks really fragile. It's longer than I thought. It's a huge picture. Nino places it on to the floor. His eyes seem to blaze in the shadows. We found it!

'Close it,' he hisses, and points to the trapdoor.

He stands up with the canvas in his arms. The painting's enormous, really massive. I lower the trapdoor down with a creak. The dust makes me sneeze: ATCHOO! ATCHOO! I cover my nose with both my hands. This time Ernie wakes and stirs and starts to complain. He lets out a high-pitched cat-like mewl as I pull the rug back over the trapdoor. Please don't wake up, please don't cry. Nino and I stand motionless, listening, waiting for Ernie to scream the house down. He doesn't move. He gurgles a bit and then falls back to sleep. Lucky.

I stand up slowly. A floorboard creaks.

Ernie wakes up and screams. Oh God, here we go. I walk over to the crib. I look over at Nino; he looks even more terrified than I do, a look of pure panic on his hardened face: *Don't you dare give that thing to me.* Where is Emilia when you need her? I pick up Ernie and shh, shh, shh. What does he want? Why is he crying? Food? Drink? Sleep? Poo? I rock him and pat him and shush him and kiss him. I shrug at Nino, who's staring, fuming. Hey, what can I do?

'What do you want?' I say to the baby.

He looks at me with his big, tear-filled eyes, his lower lip wobbling. He sniffs. He cries. A little bubble of snot blows out from his nose. I grab a tissue from the bedside table and dab at his face. I kiss him and rock him and hug him and squeeze him. At last, he stops. I lower him back down in his cot. As soon as his little head touches the pillow, he starts crying again. It's a sound far worse than anything I've heard in my whole life: *the screaming of summer lambs*. Goosebumps all over my skin. The hairs on the back of my neck stand on end.

'What? What now? You don't like your cot?'

I pick him back up and Ernie stops crying.

I put him back down and he starts crying again.

Up.

Down.

Up.

Down.

'*Ma che cazzo?*' shouts Nino. He's cross.

'I think he just wants me to hold him,' I say. 'Do you want me to hold you?' I whisper to Ernie. The baby leans his hot red cheek against my chest and sucks his thumb. 'I'm just going to hold him, for a bit. Just until he falls asleep.' Hopefully soon. Poor lamb.

Nino carries the canvas back down the corridor and into Beth and Ambrogio's room. I follow him with the baby. We lay the painting on the bed, then I close the bedroom door behind us. I take a chair and push it up against the handle, just in case anyone should come in. Emilia perhaps. Or the fucking police. I haven't told Nino about that policeman, the one I saw going next door. I don't want to annoy him any more than I already have (in other words, a lot).

Nino has the painting rolled up at one end of the bed. I head over and join him. I run the palm of my hand along the canvas; it's ancient, rough. Dust and cobwebs. He unsticks the dull, brown paper and unfurls the painting across the bed. It's lucky it's a superking, although even this surface is far too small. The painting is three metres long at least. We can only unroll part of it, or it will fall off the edge of the bed and on to the floor. The picture is brownish with torn, jagged edges from where the wannabe mobsters hacked it from its frame with a razor.

I have no idea what this painting's supposed to look like, but I know that it's the Caravaggio as soon as I see it. I can feel it in my bones. Out of the corner of my eye, I see Nino make the sign of the cross across his chest; he's gone all religious in the presence of something so valuable. Money does funny things to people. Or perhaps it's the religious theme that's touched him; he had that picture of Jesus in his car after all. He might be genuinely moved.

I guess we can only see about a third of the picture like this, but here is the newborn Christ: tiny, naked, pink. He's lying on a white cloth on a hay-covered floor. He looks fragile and kind of beautiful, a bit like baby Ernie (who's still not sleeping, by the way. He's pulling on fistfuls of my hair and slobbering all over my shoulder. Bless). Jesus gazes up into the adoring eyes of his mother, a dishevelled-looking Virgin Mary. She slumps, exhausted, her hair and clothes completely undone. She's clearly just given birth; she looks totally knackered. Must have been a difficult labour. I wonder if Jesus got stuck like me. They didn't have gas or morphine back then. You can't do a caesarean in a shed.

On the right-hand side of the painting, a man sits with his back to us, wearing white tights on his crossed legs and a flowing, grass-green shirt: a Robin Hood type. He's touching the baby Jesus with his toe. I don't know who he is. He looks too young to be Joseph, too well dressed to be a shepherd. Perhaps he's early paparazzi? He didn't want to miss this shot. On the left are the long, golden-yellow robes of someone I presume to be a king or a saint.

'*Mamma mia*,' says Nino.

'Thank fuck we found it,' I say.

'Ma, ma, ma,' says Ernie.

Beth's iPhone bleeps: a sound like a bird. Tweet. Tweet. Tweet. God, is that Taylor *again*? I pick it up and take a look. There's a message from 'Mummy'; how old was Beth, five? I click into the message and take a sharp breath.

'Tried to call. Boarding a flight to Catania. I'll take a cab from the airport. Will be with you in 24 hours. I love you, Mum.'

Shit.

'What? What's the matter?' says Nino.

'Oh, nothing. It's just my mum. I'll call her back. Here,' I say, shoving the baby into Nino's arms. 'I'll just be a minute.'

I don't know who looks more terrified, the baby or him. Ernie starts crying. Again.

I grab the phone and storm out of the room, run downstairs and into the kitchen. My hands are shaking. My fingers miss the tiny buttons. The last thing I need is my mum turning up. I jab at the icon to make the call. I've got to talk her out of it. She can't come here to the villa. But my mother's phone is off or, more likely, in airplane mode; she's already boarded the plane.

Chapter Thirty-six

I've made a real effort. I've dressed up for the occasion: short black minidress, long black veil, black lace gloves and classic patent Louboutins. I've even got an antique lace handkerchief to mop the mascara from my eyes. Blood-red lipstick. Lots and lots of kohl. I look the part: the hot young widow on day one of mourning. I really ought to take a picture. Instagram would go nuts for this shit. Never mind Tinder.

The church is empty. The air is cool and damp. I push through heavy wooden doors and step into darkness: the smell of incense, the flicker of candles. I can see the priest standing behind the altar, his grey head bowed. He's dressed in white vestments embellished with gold. I found him; he's here. The priest is muttering something under his breath. Is he praying? He hears me coming and looks up. It takes a moment for him to recognize me, but when he does, his wrinkled face cracks into a smile.

'Betta, you came.'

He opens his arms wide to embrace me. He looks like a saint in those flowing white robes. But I know he's not. He's fucking corrupt. It's just a clever disguise. I climb the steps to the altar and we stand for a moment in total silence. I study the priest's calm demeanour: steady eyes, benevolent smile. Back at the villa, I was convinced he was the client, but now I'm here, I'm not so sure. *Is he corrupt? How do I ask him? If he isn't the buyer, I'm screwed.*

'Betta, I'm so sorry about your husband,' says the priest. He places a hand on my left shoulder: a father comforting a daughter. His hand looks gnarled and old. 'I just heard this afternoon. I'm so sorry for your loss. May *Cristo* comfort you at this difficult time.'

'Thank you,' I say, looking down at the floor: worn-out flagstones, chiselled inscriptions. What does that say? Are we standing on a grave?

'I'm glad you came. I was going to pay you a visit.' He gives me a look: loaded, imploring.

'Is it safe to talk?' I ask, looking up. The priest's eyes flicker left, then right.

'We are alone.'

He leads me by the hand towards a polished wooden pew. We sit beneath a life-size statue of Jesus, the one that had been staring right at me before. He has the same pained expression on his face, beneath a crown of nasty-looking thorns. On the walls hang Renaissance scenes from the New Testament; I recognize Mary and Jesus, of course. That guy with a beard could be St Peter? He's holding golden keys by the gates of Heaven. I doubt he'd let me in. The priest takes my gloved hands in his blue-veined hands. His liver-spotted skin is as transparent as tracing paper and as cold as the skin of a corpse.

'I read the newspaper. Suicide?' he says.

I draw a sharp breath. 'Yes, it certainly seems like that. He was found on the rocks at the bottom of a cliff.'

The priest nods, a grave and knowing look on his face. 'Cosa Nostra.' He whispers this, as though he were swearing, uttering a curse word in the house of God.

We sit without speaking. I study the long, black, iron nails that protrude from Jesus's hands and feet. It reminds me of Beth's doll, all those pins I stuck in. The Cosa Nostra. OK. Sure. This will be the priest's version of the truth. The truth is just what we choose to believe. There's no objective reality.

'You still have the painting?' he asks suddenly. He looks at me with rheumy eyes.

'I do,' I say. My shoulders ease back. I can relax. He's definitely the buyer.

'You still want to sell?'

I nod. 'Uh-huh.'

I can see he really wants it. I wonder how much. He runs his hands along his thighs, smooths the creases in his robes, sits up a little straighter.

'We have to be careful, Betta,' he says softly. 'There are people out there who know: the people who killed your husband. It's not safe for you here any more. Whoever it is that killed your husband will stop at nothing to steal that picture.'

Yeah. Whatever. 'I understand.'

'You should leave,' he says.

I shoot him a glance. 'Don't worry about me.'

The priest turns away. He's looking up at Jesus. Jesus looks back. They seem to be having some secret conversation. I think of Tallulah: it reminds me of Beth and her imaginary friend. He hesitates before proceeding.

'I agreed three million with your husband, but he wanted more.' He sighs. '"The love of money is the root of all evil." Timothy 6:10.'

'That's what you were arguing about last time we came?' I say. Where does a priest get three million euros? They pay the clergy way too much in this country.

'Not arguing, not arguing. Business negotiations.'

I shake my head, tuck a stray lock of hair behind my ear. 'It's worth twenty million dollars at least,' I say, trying to sound authoritative. I know what I'm talking about, Nino and Google have filled me in.

The priest turns to me. 'Betta, you have to understand, this painting is wanted all over the world. Now that your husband is dead, it's even more dangerous. I can offer you two million. That's my final offer.'

'Your *final* offer?'

'Yes.'

I give the priest my sweetest smile. Just because I'm a woman, he thinks I'm naive. Two million euros? That's daylight robbery.

I want more than that. I study the priest for signs of weakness, listen to his raspy breath. He stares straight back at me, steadfast, firm. This guy is confident; he has God on his side. If I don't sell it to him, I have no other buyer and no means of finding one. I could push for three million, but no doubt he'd tell me to get lost. I don't want to lose him. He knows I am compromised by the death of my husband. Lowering his offer by one million euros is a mean trick to play, especially for a priest. At least the poor will inherit the earth.

'Two million euros,' I agree, gritting my teeth. I don't want the hassle and I am crap at negotiating. But two million euros is better than nothing, and Nino will be pleased that I've got us a deal. I offer my hand and the priest shakes it. His face lights up with a youthful radiance; he's gone from ninety to nineteen in an instant.

'I'll collect it tonight,' he says with a smile. 'I'll come to your house with the money. Then you should go. Ambrogio wanted to take you to safety; now you must go alone.'

'Of course,' I say.

There's no chance I'm leaving. Leave that villa? Leave that view? Has he seen that pool? *Leave Taormina?* He must think I'm mad.

'Who's this?' asks the priest, pointing at Nino.

The weather's disgusting; the sky's split open and raindrops fall like silver bullets. It's my coldest night so far in Sicily. I've had to find a pair of Beth's socks. I've even put on a jumper. We're in the living room with the curtains drawn against the thunder and lightning. I'm thinking of lighting a fire. Nino's draped across the sofa, his bare feet resting on the coffee table, a glass of *sangue di Sicilia* in his hand.

'This is Nino,' I say, closing the door behind the priest. He wipes his feet on the doormat, brushes the raindrops from the front of his jacket. He turns towards me and frowns.

'Don Franco,' says Nino, with a slight nod of the head. Is that his name? I thought Nino didn't know him. I guess Taormina's a small place.

'Nino,' growls the priest.

He turns to me, his voice a whisper. 'I told your husband, I only deal with him and you.' His eyes flash; he suddenly looks cross.

'My husband is dead. Nino's a friend,' I say.

'I know his kind,' says the priest in my ear. I smell alcohol on his breath: holy wine?

I look down at the old-fashioned suitcase he's clutching: golden buckles of interlocking Gs. The leather is mottled with dark-brown rain spots. It looks pretty heavy. It's bursting at the seams.

'I'll go and wait in the kitchen,' Nino says, standing up. He stretches his arms up over his head, then downs his drink. He slams the glass back down on the coffee table and does a half bow. '*Buonasera.*'

Nino gives me a strange look as he turns to leave. He widens his eyes as if trying to say something; I have no idea what. It's probably not important. He turns his back and walks out of the room. It's just me and the priest. I hug my arms close to my body. A chill runs down my spine. I really wish I'd lit that fire.

'Where is it?' asks the priest.

No small talk, then. No '*How are you, Elizabeth? How was your afternoon? Coming down in stair-rods, isn't it?*' Straight down to business. Fine.

He looks even older in everyday clothes, standing here beside me. He's swapped his priest's robes for a pale-grey suit, camel cashmere sweater and burgundy cravat. He could be my grand-dad. He looks as weak as a child. I reckon I could take him down with my bare hands, and I fight like a girl.

'Show me the money,' I say with a smile.

He sets his suitcase down on the carpet and bends down to open it, one arm on the back of the sofa, the other at the small of his back. It hurts him to bend. Arthritis? His fingers fumble with the buckles.

'I'll do it,' I say.

He moves aside and I lower the suitcase flat on the floor. The buckles click and I lift the lid: stacks of freshly pressed €500 notes. It's a hell of a lot of money, more than I've ever seen in my life. Why does a priest have all this cash? And why is he buying a stolen painting? I'm sure there was something about 'Thou shalt not steal' in the Ten Commandments.

'Two million?' I ask.

'Two million,' he says.

I pick up a wad of €500s and weigh it in my hand. It feels like sex. I consider tipping it all out on the floor and counting it, but it would take for ever. I think I believe him. He's a priest after all, albeit a corrupt one. Nino and I can count it later. And I'm *definitely* counting it. Not like in movies when they just take their word. What if it's Monopoly money on the inside? I gesture for the priest to follow me across the room. We walk through an arch framed by marble columns into an adjoining dining room. We've moved the furniture out of the way and spread out the painting over a large Persian rug. The priest stops and stares. I stand by a column and watch him.

'*Dio santo! Che bellissima!*' he says under his breath. He claps his hands together and touches his lips with his fingers. I watch as he lowers himself to his knees, as if in prayer, at the foot of the painting, a few inches from the edge. He's afraid to touch it. He moves carefully on hands and knees around the picture, studying it, taking in the detail.

'I was worried that the thieves and the centuries might have destroyed it, that it might have been damaged, but – it's perfect,' he says at last, standing up. He comes over to me, his eyes brimming with tears. '*Grazie*, Betta.'

He holds my hands, again, but I pull them away. If he likes it that much, he could have paid me three million.

'Shall we roll it up, so that you can take it home?' I ask. I just want the money. The priest and the picture can go.

He hesitates. He doesn't want to move it. If we roll it up, he won't be able to see it. It's like he's waited so long he's reluctant to let it out of his sight.

'Of course,' he says with a smile. Are those dentures or his real teeth? They look too shiny and new.

We stand side by side at the foot of the painting, the priest on the right and me on the left. He bends over slowly to take hold of the edge. He lifts the painting a little, but then stops. There's a small, black stamp in the corner of the canvas. He looks up at me with a funny look on his wrinkled face and then bends down lower, kneeling, studying the stamp close up.

'What's wrong?' I say.

Chapter Thirty-seven

'*Non capito*,' says the priest.

Oh God, what now? 'Come again?'

'This painting . . . it's forged.'

Someone drops a cannonball in my stomach. The priest scratches his balding head.

'I don't understand.'

He leaps to his feet with a younger man's vigour. The painting flops back down flat on the floor. He points.

'*Sì, sì*, I see it now. The technique . . . *come si dice*? It's not Caravaggio's.'

'What are you talking about? Of course it's Caravaggio's.'

There's a tremor in my voice. I'm shaking, unsteady. I feel my jaw begin to clench. I take a step backwards. I'm standing behind him, still facing the painting.

'This pigment, the red in the Madonna's dress; it's modern. It's not Caravaggio's palette; he used iron oxide. And the *oscuro*; it's far too light. No . . . no . . .' He shakes his head. 'And her hands . . . they're clumsy, manly. They don't look right. Caravaggio's hands are graceful. Elegant.'

'No, no! If Ambrogio were here, Ambrogio would tell you. Ambrogio knew!'

'And here, look, *il bambino*, the Christ. The foreshortening of the body is wrong, his form . . .'

My shoulders are tight. My neck is tense. This is all bullshit. I'm going to blow.

'Oh, Elisabetta, it is so disappointing. After all this time! A forgery! A fake! A pale imitation of the original. Of course, it is completely worthless.'

Oh my God, is he talking about *me*?

'A copy is never, ever as good. It loses the magic of the original, the intangible beauty, the *je ne sais quoi*. It has no soul, no integrity, no . . .'

I take Ambrogio's gun from the top of my trousers and shoot the priest in the back of the head. He falls backwards on to the Persian rug, crashes down like a lemon tree. THUD! Dead. That'll show him. I am JUST as good as Beth. His feet rest on the edge of the painting, so I lift up his ankles and swing them around. A little circle spreads from his head, getting wider and wider: a two-pence piece, a Sicilian blood orange, a saucer, a football. I don't want the blood to go on the painting. The priest is lying at an awkward angle, bent like a boomerang. I grab him around the waist and haul him back around so that he's parallel with the edge of the canvas. He's heavy, like he's filled with wet concrete, but I just about manage. I get a head rush when I stand back up. I forgot to eat dinner. That's not like me.

I study the growing circle of blood spreading out from his head. It's as shiny and red as Ambrogio's Lambo. It looks pretty cool. I grab Beth's phone and take a selfie, smile with my face right next to the priest's. The flash goes off like a lightning bolt. I check the picture, but I'm a mess. I run my fingers through my hair and try again. Pout. Click. The photo's great. Now that would be perfect for Instagram. It's a shame I can't share it.

Nino bursts into the room. He must have heard the gunshot . . . but even if he missed it, when the priest fell down, the whole house shook.

'What happened? You OK?'

I look up and smile, licking my lips. 'Yes, I'm very well, thank you,' I say. I've never felt better. I feel powerful. Invincible. My whole body tingles. That rush: I'm alive.

'Where'd the priest go?'

I step aside so he can get a good view. 'There!' I nod towards the body lying flat on the floor.

Nino freezes. 'You fucking shot him?'

'I did.' I smile. 'I did.'

I'm magic. I'm special. Who wants to be *good* when you can be *great*! *This is fucking fantastic!* That tingle up and down my spine. That rush through my brain. I love that feeling! I know what I'm doing. This is what I was born to do! This! This is it! I fucking love it. It's like riding too fast on a scooter. I'm high!

The priest lies face down on the carpet; something oozes from the hole in his head. The gun is lying on the carpet by the priest. We both look at it. Then Nino looks at me: a mixture of horror and admiration.

'Are you fucking crazy? Are you fucking out of your fucking mind?' he says. I shrug. 'What happened? Why'd you do it?'

I stand with my legs spread out and my hands on my hips. I don't like the way Nino's shouting at me. 'I had no choice. He said the painting was forged. That it wasn't a real Caravaggio. He would have left with the money.' That's not strictly true. I didn't *have* to kill him. I killed him for the rush. The money was secondary. The fact that he was a stingy bastard third.

Nino's mouth hangs open. He doesn't speak. The baby starts crying. Oh God, not again. I run out the door and up the stairs.

'Mamma's coming, baby, don't cry.'

I run into the nursery and pick the baby up out of his cot. He is soft and warm. He smells sweet like rice pudding. I think of Ambrosia. I think of Ambrogio. I give him a cuddle and kiss his head. His nappy feels full, so I pick up a fresh one and some wet wipes from his nursery, then run back downstairs. The baby wriggles and hollers in my arms.

'The money's over there in the suitcase. I think we should count it,' I say to Nino as I enter the room; he's standing with his hands in his pockets, leaning his forehead against the wall. Weird. He doesn't reply. A '*Thank you, Elizabeth*' would be nice. 'It's better this way. I didn't trust that priest.'

I lay the baby down on the sofa, bend over and grab the gun from the carpet. I blow imaginary dust off the barrel and wipe it with my shirt. I tuck it back into my waistband. 'He was really old anyway.'

I look over at Nino. He isn't moving. He's still standing with his back to me, his face turned to the wall.

'*Madonna mia,*' he says at last. Then he turns to face me. His voice is raised. 'Do you know who this guy is?'

'This guy?' I poke the priest with my good toe. 'He *was* a priest.'

'A priest. A priest. Yes, he was a priest, but he was also a *guy* : Franco Motisi, the right-hand man of a *consigliere* from Palermo, from a rival clan. I recognized him when he came in.'

'Rival what? Franco who?' I take off Ernie's dirty nappy. Ernie kicks me in the face. The poor thing's still crying. I really wish Emilia were here . . . I'm not good at multitasking. Eating Pringles and watching Netflix, maybe, but not this shit. This is fifty shades of gross.

'He's Cosa Nostra. A big fucking deal.' Nino headbutts the wall. Again. I think he's pissed off.

'*He's* Cosa Nostra? I don't understand.' I sit back in the sofa, suddenly light-headed. My blood sugar's too low. I need to eat some carbs.

'He wasn't buying the painting to hang on his bedroom wall. He was the fucking middle man. You do not mess with his boss.'

'I do not what? Who is his boss?'

'We have to leave Sicily. Right now. It's over.' He kicks over a table; its leg breaks off. The table looked priceless. I'm pretty sure it was an antique. Probably a Chippendale.

'We have to *leave*?' I clean Ernie's bottom with one of the wet wipes. A little jet of pee just misses my eye. I slam on a nappy and do it up tight. Oh God, where is Emilia? No one told me motherhood would be so damn hard. I can't take much more of this! Help!

'You think he came here unprotected? Go look outside. His guys will be waiting in the van with their guns.'

'What?' I say. 'No.' I'm filling with panic. 'He came here alone. He trusted me. He –'

'Betta, I recognized him. I'm telling you. You think I'm dreaming?'

The baby's about to roll off the sofa. I grab Ernie and hold him against my chest, his little face leans on my shoulder. He looks at me and yawns, then finally stops crying. Closes his eyes. Yes, please fall asleep.

'Shh, shh.' I rub his back.

I run over to the window and open up a crack in the curtains. Rain streams down. It's dark and wet. There are three cars parked outside on the driveway: Ambrogio's Lambo, Nino's people carrier and the priest's white van. The lights are off inside the van, but I can still see the outlines of what looks like two men standing in front of it. Two men with guns. Oh shit.

I turn and see Nino sitting on the sofa, his head in his hands. He looks up towards me; his face is pale. Is Nino *scared*? I don't believe it. Nino pulls his gun from the band of his trousers. I take Ambrogio's gun and weigh it in my hands. I'm not sure what to do with it, but I'll give it a go. I fiddle around with the different bits and a chamber opens. I look inside: there's only one bullet. It's not ideal. Nino stands and makes his way to the door. I begin to follow.

'No,' he says. 'You stay here; you've caused enough trouble . . .'

'No fucking way. I'm coming too.'

He looks into my eyes and shakes his head. 'Lose the kid.'

The baby's fallen asleep now, on my shoulder. His eyes are closed, but his eyeballs flicker around under his eyelids; I wonder what he's dreaming about. Me or Beth? His face looks peaceful. If I put him down now, I might wake him up. I don't want him to start crying again. But Nino's right, it's no place for a baby, even if I was enjoying my cuddle. My mother never hugged me: I didn't know I missed it. I creep back upstairs, tip-toeing quietly, and lay him gently in his cot.

'Go to sleep, little Ernie. I'll come back and see you . . . Mummy loves you.'

I blow him a kiss. There's a musical mobile hanging over his bed; I wind it up and it plays him a song: 'Twinkle, Twinkle'. I lean in and kiss him on his forehead. It's a miracle that he hasn't woken up. Perhaps I'm getting the hang of this parent thing? I am a good mother after all. I run back downstairs to see Nino.

'We shoot to kill,' Nino says, cocking his gun. 'They see this dead guy here, we're fucked. They see this painting and we're fucked. So no fucking around.'

'All right. OK.'

'This way; follow me.'

Nino runs along the corridor, into the kitchen and through the French doors at the back of the villa. He runs around the edge of the house and I follow after him through howling wind and stinging rain. It's torrential, black, a fucking monsoon; I can barely see a metre ahead. We creep out on to the driveway and tiptoe towards the rear of the van. They've left the music on, techno is blaring. Oh, is that Underworld? 'Born Slippy'? I fuck-ing love that song . . . The two men are standing outside the front door, guns at the ready. I take one side and Nino takes the other. Nino's gun goes off, so I shoot too. KA-POW! KA-POW! This is ace!

Someone screams; who was that? My guy has flopped down on the ground, but Nino's guy is still alive. His legs are twitching. He's getting up! Nino shot him in the side of the neck, but he's far from dead. He has a sawn-off shotgun in his hand and, before I know it, he's shot Nino back! Nino yells, then shoots again.

KA-POW! KA-POW! KA-POW!

This is *such* a thrill. I'm having the time of my life!

Nino's guy collapses, dead. This time Nino shot him in the head.

'Are you OK?' I run over to Nino, my heartbeat thumping in time to the music. I really want to turn it up. I feel like dancing with Nino.

'*Stronzo* shot me in the arm,' Nino says.

He's leaning up against the van, his forehead pressed against the metal. He's clutching the top of his arm with his hand, blood seeping through his fingers. His gun's dropped to the ground.

'Aaargh!' he says.

Ouch. That looks nasty. A tourniquet. That's what he needs. I remember that from Girl Guides: First Aid badge. Comes in handy. Something tight to stop the bleeding. I pull off my shirt, wet from the rain and stand here, shivering, in my bra: it's one of the Louis Vuitton-lover's, delicate black lace with a little white bow. I twist the shirt into a bandage.

'Come here,' I say, taking Nino's shoulders.

'*Non mi rompere la minchia,*' says Nino.

I pull off Nino's leather jacket and throw it on to the bonnet of the van. There's a hole in his arm and it's gushing with blood. I rip off his shirt. He's shaking. It's pouring; water streaks down his chest, his skin glistening in the rain.

'Oh wow! What is that?'

There's something there on Nino's back. I haven't noticed it before; he had his top on when we fucked. I hold his shoulders and turn him around. There on his back is a life-size tattoo of the Virgin Mary. Her face is beautiful; her hair is covered with a delicate veil. A single tear slides down her cheek towards rosebud lips. Her hands are held in prayer. It looks striking in the moon-light, the raindrops adding to her tears. She looks a bit like Beth.

'What the fuck are you doing?' says Nino.

I'm standing and staring.

'Your tattoo – it's amazing.'

'Is now the time?'

'I've always wanted a tattoo. Maybe not that one . . . But something cool.'

303

He doesn't look impressed.

'Did you get it done around here?'

He doesn't answer.

I pull my shirt underneath his arm, loop it around and tie it in a knot.

'Aaargh,' says Nino. '*Puttanacci.*'

'Hey!' I say. You do a guy a favour . . .

He takes a deep breath and then nods at the men. 'They fucking dead?'

I turn towards them. 'I'm out of bullets.'

'Get my gun.'

I pick up Nino's gun from the ground. It's wet from the rain. Will it still work? I'm not sure gunpowder's supposed to get soggy. Oh well, I don't exactly have much choice. I creep through the pouring rain over to the men lying by the front door. They both have gunshot wounds to the head and are bleeding all over the doormat. I wish I had my mobile. I want to take a picture. The bodies look awesome lying there in the rain. I'll take one later when Nino's not here . . .

'They look pretty dead.' I laugh.

'We gotta look in the back of the van,' Nino says, weakly.

Nino slumps on the roof of the van and I stand next to him by the back door. I aim his gun at the door.

'Open it!' he says.

I pull the handle and throw the door open. It's dark, but I can see that the van is empty. There's no one inside. Nino runs his fingers through wet hair. He looks stressed out. Rain pelts his face and his cheeks glisten white in the light from the moon.

'Betta,' he says. 'We leave tonight.'

Chapter Thirty-eight

'Let's take the Lambo; there'll be room for the suitcase in the boot.'

'Oh, great idea: a red Lamborghini. No one will notice us in that.'

'The Lambo's fast.' I shrug. 'Plus I like it. I don't want to leave it here. It's a waste.' I wonder how much you'd get for a classic Miura. Ambrogio said 1972; that's *old school*.

'We take my car,' Nino says, clasping kitchen roll to the top of his arm to stop the bleeding. It's the pricey kind with absorbent pockets that they advertise all the time on TV. The paper's good for mopping up wine, coffee, gin and spilt milk. Apparently it's not so great with blood. I look at the mess all over his arm: black and shiny and wet. I sigh; he's not going to be much use like that.

'Where're we even going?' I ask.

'Don't know. Naples?' Nino says.

I'm racking up a couple of lines. One for Nino to help with the *pain* (it's a very effective anaesthetic) and one for me. Just because. I use Nino's credit card to neaten them up on the low glass coffee table. I roll up a banknote and give it to Nino.

He snorts his line with his good hand.

'You're welcome,' I say.

'I need a saw,' he says.

'Naples is too close. They'll find us. It's easy. Let's drive to London instead.'

He wipes his nose with the back of his hand; there's a little bit of blood running down from his nostril, drip, drip, drip, drip . . . He doesn't even seem to notice. I hope his nose doesn't fall off like Daniella Westbrook. That would make his moustache look odd.

'Can you get me a saw?' he says.

I snort my line, throw my head back and close my eyes. Mmm, cocaine. It feels safe, warm and cosy, like being hugged, like being in the womb. But better, because Beth isn't there. I light up two cigarettes, one for me and one for Nino. I stick one in his mouth. Oh my God, it's like being a carer. I'm not sure I have the patience to be a full-time nurse. I don't think I have the aptitude.

Beth, Beth, Beth. Life's so much better without her . . . now that I *am* her. I wonder how Beth would have dealt with all this. She'd probably have run screaming or cried in the corner. Hidden under the table. Behind the sofa. She wasn't cut out for this world, not like I am. She wanted to kill me! Ha! I'm still here! And where is she? *Long* gone. No, my sister wasn't a killer. That's why she was leaving; she'd never have coped. I, on the other hand, am a duck to water. I was made for this shit. I'm a *natural*. I was *born* for this life. If I hadn't killed Beth, hadn't murdered Ambrogio, then they'd have killed me. I got in first. I had no choice. Betrayed by my very own flesh and blood. Now I am the one with all the power. I am the one in control. I am the one with the suitcase full of cash. *I am the one with the gun.*

I grab the case and fling it open. Stare at the money and catch my breath. It looks so fucking beautiful; it almost doesn't look real. Stack upon stack upon stack of perfect banknotes. They're all magenta and pastel mauve with tiny stars in yellow and white. They look magic. They look special. I pull out a €500 note and study it carefully, check in the light for the watermark. It certainly feels real as I rub it between my fingers: smooth, crisp, legit! I take a stack of notes and start to count them.

'Five hundred, a thousand, one thousand five hundred, two thousand –'

'Betta!'

'Shh, Nino! I'm trying to count. Now I'll have to start again. Five hundred, a thousand –'

'Will you get me a fucking saw?'

I look at Nino and roll my eyes.

'Fine,' I say. 'I'm going. I'm going.'

I dump the cash back in the suitcase, crush the life out of my cigarette inside a vase. A speck of tobacco's still burning, glowing; a plume of white smoke curls, fades, disappears.

'Hurry up. We need to leave.' He wipes sweat from his forehead with the back of a bloodied hand, leaving a streak of red across his face. It looks hot, like Rambo or something. He looks like he's fresh out of 'Nam.

'Salvatore had a chainsaw; I'll run next door and get it,' I say.

I jump up from the sofa and head for the door.

Wait. Why does he need a saw?

Bile rises in my throat; rancid, acid, raw. I swallow it back down. I can't let Nino see me puke. I hold my breath and count to ten. One, two, three, four, five, six, seven, eight, nine, ten . . . It doesn't work. I still feel ill. I help him hold the leg in place, vibrating with the blade. The thigh is slippery with blood; the skin is cold and flabby. The chainsaw whirs and hacks through bone: nails scraping down a blackboard, the shrieking of a dentist's drill. My eyeballs water from the stench of charring flesh and burning bone: pork chops on a barbeque. A cough, a splutter from the saw; the femur's sliced in two.

We've dragged the men from the van inside and laid them on the carpet with the priest. Nino's making a hell of a mess; flesh and fragments of bone splinter and splatter all over his clothes. The carpet's drenched with blood. It smells like a slaughterhouse: iron and fear. The petrol from the chainsaw. There are three large cases and a roll of bin bags. We'd have folded them up, but they wouldn't have fit. Nino's done this before. He's pretty quick with the chainsaw with only one arm; it's slicing through flesh like butter. We pile the body parts into the cases: the heads, the arms and the torsos at the bottom, the legs folded up on the top: it's human Tetris. The smell of mince before you cook it. I can taste the blood in the air.

'Help me saw up the carpet,' says Nino.

We saw up the carpet and tuck the squares into the cases with the bodies. We shove more bin bags on top of that and zip the cases shut. I turn to Nino and study his red-flecked face; there's blood in his moustache. Then I look down at my clothes: soggy and wet. I've completely ruined this bra.

'I'm going to get changed,' I say.

I climb the stairs on tiptoe – Ernie's still sleeping; I don't want to wake him – then creep along the corridor into Beth's bedroom. I take off my clothes in the bathroom and wash off the blood in the sink. Little pink droplets splatter up the mirror. I rinse them off with clean water and shove the dirty clothes in a bag; we'll dump them somewhere later on. I grab a shirt from Beth's walk-in wardrobe, a red one so that the blood won't show. It's a crimson silk blouse with fluted sleeves; it's feminine, floaty and soft. I think I saw this on The Outnet last week. I pull it on. It fits me perfectly. I pull on the gold Prada sandals and Balenciaga hot pants as well. I know, I know, the cellulite. But you know what? Fuck it. I'm just going to wear them. They're nice. They suit me. I like them.

I find another suitcase and throw in a few more skirts, shirts and dresses: that Dolce & Gabbana outfit I like. A pair of Jimmy Choos. A belt by Dior. And, of course, Beth's Roberto Cavalli dress. Then I run back into the bedroom and pull all the jewellery boxes off Beth's dressing table. I throw them into the case. I put the diamond necklace back into its box and throw that in too. Do I need Mr Dick? Not now I've got Nino. I leave him tucked at the bottom of a drawer. So long, lover. I check

I've got the passports: mine and Beth's, then I'm ready to go. Almost.

We need to run and we can't take that picture. I drag the painting out of the house and on to the patio. I'm not as careful this time; we don't need to sell it. There's a stainless-steel barbecue that should do the job. I need to cut the painting up so that it will burn, but there's no more petrol in the chainsaw after all those bodies. I leave the painting on the patio, then run into the kitchen. I rifle through the cutlery drawer and grab the sharpest knife I can find. The metal clinks; I hope it doesn't wake Ernie. But if he can sleep through a shoot-out, he can sleep through this.

I run back out on to the patio and squat down on the floor by the painting. I saw through the baby Jesus, the Virgin Mary's face and an angel's wings. It's hard work: the canvas is pretty tough. The blade screeches and squeals. I turn the painting horizontally and slice through the man in the golden robes. I decapitate the Virgin Mary, cut the head off a cow. I saw the man in the green shirt and the shepherd with the beard in half. By the time I've finished, I'm sweating, my arm is aching. I throw the knife down to the ground, sit back and study the painting. It's cut into manageable chunks so it will fit in the barbecue. I hope the priest was right, or I've just sawn through twenty million dollars' worth of canvas. Fuck it. It's too late now. At least I've got the money.

I pile the pieces of painting on to the barbecue, then grab my cigarettes and lighter. I light a fag with my Zippo and take a drag: ahh, that's better. I empty the fuel from the lighter all over the canvas, throw my fag on the painting and watch it burn. Slowly, slowly, the cigarette glows orange, then red and crumbles to ash. A black hole burns in the fabric; its edges glowing white, then gold, then flame. The fire spreads slowly as the different-coloured oil paints burn. I watch the flames change hue: bluish-white, then blue and light red, then bluish-green. It must be the elements in the paints: the copper, the lead, the tin.

The fumes are pungent, toxic. There's a stench of burnt cloth. Heat hits my cheeks and my eyes sting. Thick smoke curls and disappears. When the canvas is burning, nice and hot, I turn my back on the fire.

Nino's mopping the floor with his good hand. Luckily, the floor is laid with tiles, not floorboards; Nino says it's impossible to get bloodstains out of wood. The blood's almost gone. Emilia will notice that the carpet is missing, but she won't know why. There's something really sexy about a man mopping a floor. The intense concentration. The regular rhythm back and forth. I watch him scrubbing the tiles with blood on his hands, his arms, his face and his shirt; he's drenched. He shoves the mop back into the bucket.

'I need some clothes,' he says. 'I'm taking a shower, then we're out of here.' The floor is spotless. The suitcases are lined up ready by the door. He's done a pretty good job, considering he's only using one arm. At least he's stopped whining about the pain – I guess the cocaine worked.

I fetch Nino some of Ambrogio's clothes: a pair of blue jeans, a black polo shirt and a butter-soft leather jacket. I breathe in deep and close my eyes: Ambrogio's wardrobe smells of Ambrogio: Armani Code Black. I remember the very first moment I met him, when he walked into Beth's college bar. I remember us dancing that night in Oxford; he had the moves like Jagger. I shake my head and pull the doors shut. Don't think about Ambrogio, Alvie. Ambrogio is gone. Dead as a doornail. Dodo-esque. He wasn't who you thought he was. He wasn't very nice.

Nino takes the clothes into the shower room and I hear a low hum as the water turns on. I sit at the desk in Elizabeth's bedroom, my head in my hands. My skin feels dry. My forehead's peeling. It's all this hot weather; it's all this stress. I slather on more of Beth's Crème de la Mer. I steal a blob of her eye cream.

I should book that facial with Cristina Hair and Beauty, but not right now. We've got to get out of here.

I walk down the corridor to Ernie's nursery. His night light is on: the little moon. It casts a blue light over his sleeping face. He looks serene, like an angel. Like the infant Christ. Cuddly toys surround the baby. There's a gorgeous mobile with fluffy white clouds. Ernie's cute when he's not crying. I stroke his soft cheek with the tip of my finger, brush a lock of hair from his face. I like watching him sleep; he's so innocent, pure. We'll start a new life: me, Ernie and Nino. We'll set up home somewhere nice in London. We'll be fine once we get off this mad island. We'll be safe and sound.

I scoop him up and set him down in his carrier. How is this carrier going to fit in the Lambo? It's just a two-seater. I don't think there's enough room. Ernie's not going to fit in the car! I know Nino wants to take his wheels, but there's no way I'm leaving a classic Miura to rot on the fucking drive!

The front door slams shut. Shit. Who is that? Nino's still in the shower. Is it my mother? The Mob? The fucking police? I peer over the bannister: Emilia is standing in the entrance hall, looking lost and wet from the rain. Emilia. Great. Still inconvenient, but at least she's not lethal. I run downstairs with Ernie in his carrier. He seems heavier than I remember. The plastic carrier knocks into my ankles, cuts into my calves, bangs against bone. I struggle downstairs. Emilia turns and watches me run, a worried look on her wrinkled face. She's standing there in a floral nightdress; a pale-blue dressing gown hangs at her sides. She's clutching a brown leather handbag. Her hair is loose around her shoulders. She has varicose veins on her legs.

'Emilia, um, is everything all right? You're a bit . . .'

'*Signora*, I hear the guns! And now . . . I am . . . *preoccupata*!'

She looks around as though searching for gunmen, wringing her hands, biting her lip; her eyes flick left and right down the hallway. She watches me carry the baby towards her and set him down on the floor between us. I shake my arm and rub my ankle. There's a scratch on my leg; it's even drawn blood. My palm is sore from the weight of the handle. That thing's fucking heavy. Emilia's staring at my hand. Oh shit, I'm Beth. I'm supposed to be right-handed; I used the wrong one. How could I forget? I'm not sure if she's noticed. Not this. Not now. We're supposed to be *leaving*. Seriously, I do not have the time. I'm just going to risk it . . .

'Emilia,' I say, grabbing her forearm and squeezing it tight. 'We are in danger. I need your help.'

Emilia gasps. She takes a couple of baby steps back and steadies herself on the handle of the door.

'*Ma perché?*' she asks. 'Why?'

'You heard the gunshots?'

'*Sì!* What happened? Is Ernesto OK?'

She leans over the carrier and peers in at the baby. He's staring back up at us, sucking his dummy. He looks pretty happy to me.

'Ernie's fine, but we need to get out of here . . .'

'You need me to keep him?'

'Is that OK?'

'Of course, of course, but where do you go?' She leans over the carrier and covers the baby up with his blanket, tucks pale-blue wool up beneath his chin. He hugs his cuddly sheep.

'Oh, just out of town. I won't be gone long. But listen, Emilia, it's very important, you can't stay at this villa. It's far too dangerous. My husband's friends –'

'*Mamma mia* . . . I call the police!' She covers her mouth with her hands.

'No! No, don't do that. Just stay at home. Do you understand? Go home with Ernesto. Keep him safe.'

She wraps her dressing gown around her waist and hugs herself tight, rubbing her arms. Now I feel kind of bad that I've scared her. Kind of, but not really.

'Don't worry, Emilia. It's going to be OK, but just . . . please . . . don't call the police.'

She shakes her head.

'And don't tell anyone about this.'

'*Sì, signora.*'

'*No one,* OK? I'll call you later.'

'*Va bene.* OK.'

We look down at the baby tucked up in his blanket and Emilia sighs.

'*Mamma mia, che bello,*' she says. 'He look just like his mamma.'

Emilia tries a reassuring smile. Bless her. She's like the loving mother I never had. She's like that Supernanny on TV.

'Thank you, Emilia. I'm really sorry. I've got to go.'

I give her a hug and she hugs me back. I like Emilia. Beth was right: she is *amazing.* She's saved my ass a hundred times. I actually wish we could take her with us. But she needs to stay here with the baby. I lean over the carrier and give Ernie a kiss on his tiny forehead. My heart breaks. He's so soft and milky. I think he smiles, but it could just be wind. My stomach twinges, my eyes fill with tears: I may never see my baby again! I turn to go. But Emilia stops me.

'Wait, *signora*!'

She reaches down inside her bag and pulls out a sealed brown envelope.

'You ask me to keep this safe for you? Perhaps you forget?'

She hands me the envelope.

'Oh yes, of course. Thank you, Emilia.'

What's inside? I rip it open: two plane tickets to London, dated Thursday, 27 August, 9 a.m. That's the morning after Beth died. One ticket is for Alvina Knightly, the other one's for Ernesto. I check in the envelope, but that was everything. There's no ticket for poor old Salvatore. No ticket for me, as Elizabeth Caruso (no wonder she insisted that we switch passports). No ticket for Ambrogio. Well, I guess that explains that.

I tuck the tickets back into the envelope. My sister had it all figured out. Though I don't know how she thought she'd get away with it. My corpse would have given her a head start, but it wouldn't have bought her that much time. Still, desperate times call for desperate measures; even I know that by now.

'Thank you, Emilia. That's very helpful.'

I look down at the baby for one last time. A lump in my throat. I don't want to leave him. I never did take him to the beach. Perhaps we could keep him . . . But then I remember the Lamborghini: I really fucking love that car.

Emilia picks up the baby in his carrier and I walk with them down the drive to the road. The rain has stopped, but there's still a fine drizzle. The cold mist chills my sunburnt skin.

'It's OK, *signora*, I don't say anything.' She puts her finger to her lips and says, 'Shh.'

I watch Emilia's back disappear as she and the baby walk off down the road. I get the feeling Emilia knows everything. She knows who I am. She knows Salvo is dead. I suppose I should kill her, but do you know what? I really don't want to. She's good with the kid. I feel I can trust her. I think she'll keep quiet. It's quicker and easier just to get out of town. I'll come back for Ernie when this is all over. I'll come back for him when it's safe.

I close the front door of the villa behind me. It's suddenly silent. Far too quiet. I miss my little son already. His chubby cheeks, his cheeky smile . . . I check Beth's iPhone. No new messages. What about my mother? Isn't she coming? She's on the plane now on her way here from Oz. Oh God, this could be fucking disastrous. She could always tell me and Beth apart. Perhaps I should warn her? This is a war zone. But what would I say? It's just like in *GoodFellas*. It's just like in *The Sopranos*. She'd have no idea; all she watches is fucking *Bake Off*. She wouldn't know what I was talking about. I don't want to speak to her, never mind see her. But if I don't stop her, she'll show up at the villa and it'll all be my fault if she's shot in the head . . .

I pace the hallway, up and down. Up and down. Down and up again. This is a very important decision. She could be here in a minute, an hour. It might be useful to have her out of the way. I have to warn her. Shall I? Shan't I? Perhaps I should just flip a coin?

Give me one good reason why *I* shouldn't kill her?

Because she's my mum?

I have to warn her; it's the right thing to do.

On second thoughts, perhaps not.

I push through the doors, back into the living room. Nino's frantic, looking for something, behind sofas, under tables, behind curtains . . .

'Where is it?' he says.

'What? The painting . . . ?'

Oh my God, not this again. I can't take much more. He stops and stands with his hand on his hip. Panting. Waiting. Angry frown. He does not look amused, like Queen Victoria.

'Betta. What the fuck? What have you done with it?'

'It was fake so I burnt it. We can't take it with us. We can't leave it here . . .'

I watch Nino's face turn murder-red.

'You fucking *what*?'

He grabs me by the throat and slams me up against the wall. The back of my head knocks against plaster. I feel his breath hot and wet on my face. He's squeezing my neck, his body pressing into me. Then he grabs his gun and shoves it against the soft part of my throat, by my jaw.

'Say it again, what the fuck did you do?'

'I-I-I don't know, Nino, please! Let me go.'

'The painting?' he says.

'No . . . no!' I shake my head. My skin begins to prickle with sweat. My legs begin to quiver. *Shit.*

Cold metal digs into my throat. My head pounds, my temples throb.

'Nino! Nino! Don't shoot! Don't shoot!'

'Where is it?' he says. I screw up my eyes.

'It's a fake . . . the priest said . . .'

'Is it fucking *on fire*?'

'It's . . . in the garden.'

'Twenty million dollars and it's fucking on fire?'

Nino jabs his gun further into my throat, forcing the metal against my jaw. Then he suddenly releases me. He turns and runs towards the garden.

'It's a fucking fake!' I call after him.

I drop down to the floor and catch my breath. Rub my throat. Nino is hot when he's angry.

'Shit! What's that?' I say, slamming on the brakes. I don't like this car. If I write it off, we can go get the Lambo.

The people carrier skids, swerves and crashes into a tree. Nino and I fly towards the windscreen, but then our seat belts throw us back. Something shatters: the sound of smashed glass. I've bust the headlight, at least. The cases with the bodies thud in the boot and the suitcase with the money, Beth's diamonds and our clothes flies off the back seat.

'What the fuck?' says Nino, holding his arm with his good hand.

I rub my neck. I think I have whiplash. I must have been driving pretty fast.

'There, on the road; I saw something moving.'

'That black thing?'

'That black thing.'

'It's a fucking snake.'

'I thought so! Gross!' I say.

Nino looks at me. If looks could kill . . .

'You crashed my car because of a snake?'

'A snake *in the road*. I didn't *crash*. It was a bump. That's what bumpers are for.'

'You realize we're in a hurry?'

'Is it *poisonous*?'

'There are men with guns who want to find us and kill us.'

'What kind of snake is it?'

'Are you listening to me?'

'What kind of snake is it?'

'Are you out of your mind?'

'OK, fine! I'm just curious. I've never seen a snake in the wild before. *Is it* poisonous?'

'Why the fuck do you care? You're in a car.'

'All right. OK.'

'*I'm* fucking poisonous.'

'Fine.'

'Just drive.'

'OK.'

'You're gonna drive? Really?'

'Yes.'

'You don't want to get out and make friends with the snake?'

'No. I'll just run it over. Let's go.'

I reverse back from the tree trunk and drive down the road and over the snake. I can't move my head to the left or the right. (I might have crashed a little too convincingly.) Nino's knuckles whiten as he grips on to his seat with his good hand.

'And watch where you're going. *Cristo!*,' he says. 'In this country, we drive on the right.'

DAY SEVEN:
Pride

Sex, drugs and murder: what's not to like?
@AlvinaKnightly69

Chapter Thirty-nine

It was Beth's fault about the accident.

When I was little, I changed my name to Matilda. You know, Matilda, the girl in that book by Roald Dahl? She has magic powers. I didn't change it officially, not by deed poll or anything like that, just at school, in the playground; I got some of the kids to call me Matilda.

It all started on our seventh birthday.

Beth had left her new scooter on the pavement outside our house and I hadn't been able to resist. I didn't have one of my own, you see. It was a birthday present to Beth, from Mum, and drop-dead gorgeous, shiny and red, just sitting there, waiting, begging me to take it for a spin.

I jumped on the scooter and raced down the road. Beth was standing on the pavement with a group of some kids from our school. Her friends. The popular crew. 'Faster, faster!' they all shouted. So faster I went: gravel spitting, wheels shrieking, cheeks flapping and warping in the wind. It was the first time in my life that I'd ever felt free, whizzing, flying maybe thirty miles an hour? I'm good at this, I thought, I'm truly spectacular. I must be a natural . . . 'Stop!' shouted Beth. 'Come back, Alvie! Mum's going to kill you! There are cars!' She was just jealous because it was *her* scooter. She didn't want me to have a go. I almost made it to the end of our road, but then what?

The kerb?

I don't know.

I flipped right over the handlebars and smacked my head on the pavement, split it open at the top on the right.

WHACK!

And then nothing.

I awoke to the taste of iron and the sound of my own screams. I was only a child; I didn't understand when the doctors talked. I didn't know what the 'prefrontal cortex' was. It didn't make sense. All I wanted was to rip off my head and fling it somewhere far, far away so I could get some sleep.

The pain was incredible. Unbearable: a drill bearing down in my brain, day and night, night and day, day and night again. I was in hospital for weeks, vomiting, crying, tearing my hair out, hooked up to something that must have been morphine, glaring at the glow-in-the-dark stars some schmuck had stuck up on the ceiling. Mum went *crazy*, of course she did. Said it wasn't my scooter, I was going too fast, it was all my own fault, blah, blah, blah. Elizabeth would *never* have been so stupid. Then she bought my sister a helmet.

When I got back to school, over a month later, I told all the kids I was magic. They asked where I'd been and what had happened, so I made something up. I didn't want to tell them I'd been lying in bed, staring at stars with tubes coming out of me. So bite me; I lied. The scar on my skull was where they'd put in the potion, where they'd done the spells. I had magic powers, like Matilda in that book; I was *special*. I could make pencils stand on end on the desk just by looking at them, get chalk to fly and write on the board. I didn't have to prove it; I just said it and it was true.

Everyone forgot about it after a while, but the scar's still there somewhere under my hair. It's my Harry Potter lightning bolt. My own Superman 'S'. I'm just like Samson before Delilah. It's the source of my powers: my unique strength. Fred West had one just like it! Perhaps that's the reason why I am how I am? Why things have never worked out. Is that why I am the *bad* one? What if it's that and not the hearts? Perhaps if Beth had banged her head, she'd have woken up and been me? She'd have had my miserable life? And I would have had hers?

But I *do* have hers!

And *she was* bad!

It wasn't as black and white as I thought, more *Fifty Shades of Grey*. Beth wasn't an angel and I'm not the devil. I'm actually quite sweet once you get to know me. Not that anyone bothers. My fingers feel beneath my hair and find the scar. Yup, it's still there. There's a dent in the cranium and a funny, lumpy, raised bit of skin.

You can touch it if you like, if you call me Matilda.

Sunday, 30 August 2015, 5 a.m.
Taormina, Sicily

'We'll need more than that or they won't sink.'

'For fuck's sake, the sun's almost up; someone will see.'

'We can't throw them in like that. *They will float.*'

'We can't stand here in broad daylight with a bag of dead priest. Why did we come here?'

Nino and I are standing on a beach, filling the suitcases with pebbles. There aren't any big rocks, so we're flinging in fistfuls of stones. There isn't much room, but Nino says we need to weigh down the cases. When bodies get old, they get kind of gassy and then they float. Apparently. The stones are cool and damp from the night before. It's taking for ever. I grab a handful of smooth, round pebbles and throw them into a bag. They make a loud CLUNK! as they land. I scan the beach in case someone has heard us, but there's nobody here. Nino zips up the second case and then helps me fill the last. I stand with my hands on my hips and catch my breath. Looking out to sea, I notice a tiny island attached to the land by a narrow path.

'What's that?' I ask, pointing at the black mass looming up from the water.

'Isola Bella. What am I, a fucking tour guide? Betta, how do you not know that by now? Did you never leave that villa? Did Il Professore keep you locked up?' He nods at the case. I think he wants me to help. He still thinks I'm Beth. Come on, Alvie: be more Beth.

The island is probably beautiful in daylight, but at this hour, the hour before dawn, it looks like an enormous sea monster, rising up from the depths. The sun is beginning to edge over the horizon, casting a long, black shadow from the island towards where we're standing on the beach. I light a cigarette and breathe smoke out towards the sea, studying the view.

'Betta! COME ON.'

I think he wants me to hurry up.

I bend over and grab more stones, chuck them in the suitcase so he can see that I'm helping, making myself useful.

I look up over Nino's shoulder and draw a sharp breath. I can see the silhouette of a man running along the shore where the beach meets the sea. He's getting closer and closer. Shit. I grab the lid of the suitcase and zip it closed.

'Nino,' I say, gesturing behind him, 'we've got company.'

A dog runs up to us barking and wagging its tail. It's a grubby-looking mongrel with straggly grey hair; it's been for a swim in the sea. The dog is very interested in what's in our suitcase. It's going crazy, barking and sniffing and scratching at the lid. Its master runs closer.

'Silvio! No! *Scusa mi*,' says the jogger. The dog whimpers, hesitates with one paw in the air, then runs in a circle chasing its tail. 'Silvio!' It scurries off. '*Scusa mi. Buongiorno.*'

'*Buongiorno*,' says Nino, with a half-hearted wave.

I stand and glare, smoking my fag. The man and the mongrel jog off along the beach. They get smaller and smaller. I look at Nino.

'Give me your gun.'

'What? No.'

'Give it to me. My gun's out of bullets.'

'No way,' Nino says.

'We should kill him. Quick! He's getting away!'

'He didn't see anything,' says Nino.

'It looks fucking dodgy . . .'

'We're not killing any more people today.'

'Shame.'

'Unless they're about to kill us.'

'OK. Fine. Whatever.'

I flick my cigarette butt out towards the sea. Nino grabs another armful of rocks and throws them in the suitcase.

'We're geologists collecting samples,' he says.

'At five o'clock in the morning?'

I should have just grabbed it and shot him myself. He saw us. He saw *me*. He got a good look at my face.

When the suitcase is packed full of pebbles, I zip it back up and together we lug the priest along the beach towards the people carrier. He's fucking heavy. Even heavier than Ambrogio. We keep having to put the case down on the sand to catch our breath. Nino's no help with only one arm. Useless. Really, it would be quicker to do it myself. Then, with a superhuman effort, we load the suitcase into the boot and run back down the beach for the other two. I'm exhausted. This definitely counts as exercise. It's like Olympic weightlifting. I'm burning more calories than running or swimming, or fucking Pilates. We haul the cases on top of the priest and then Nino notices the car.

'What the fuck did you do?'

The front of the car hangs off at an angle. The licence plate has cracked. The headlights are all smashed up. It looks pretty bad. Result!

'Oh. It was just a little bump . . .'

'It's totally fucked; we can't drive it like that. The police will stop us.' He pulls what's left of the broken bumper off the car and throws it on to the back seat. Awesome.

325

'Oh, what a shame. We'll have to go get the Lambo . . .'

'Betta. *Madonna!* You're driving me crazy!'

We get back in the car. I try not to look smug.

'I know a place where we can dump them,' Nino says. 'Take a left.'

I swerve around a sharp corner; we're thrown by the force. Nino crashes into the door. He clutches his arm where he's been shot and shoots me a dirty look. My driving's like a ride at Alton Towers: Nemesis, Oblivion or the Runaway Mine Train. People pay good money to be scared on those roller coasters. Really, what is his problem? My Yves Saint Laurent tourniquet is drenched. Blood's seeping through and dripping down his side. The car smells like a butcher's.

'Argh!' Nino says. He pulls the shirt off his arm.

'What are you taking that thing off for? You're going to bleed everywhere,' I say. 'I don't want that on me. I've only just got changed. This is Versace. Now where?'

'Straight ahead. Pass me that top,' Nino says, pointing to a scrunched-up T-shirt with his good hand. He'd pulled it off one of the guys before chopping them up. I'm impressed by his foresight.

'Nino, I'm driving. Get it yourself,' I say.

'Call that driving? If my arm wasn't fucked, I'd show you driving. You drive like a girl.'

'I am a girl.'

'Right.'

Nino grunts. I floor the accelerator. The engine roars. My head slams back against the headrest. I'll see how fast I can go.

'Argh!' says Nino *again*.

He's the girl: scared of my driving, whining about his arm. It's not even that bad. The bullet barely grazed it.

'When we've dumped these bodies, we're getting the Lambo,' I say. 'Your car is shit.'

'It's a Mercedes!' he says. 'It was a good car until you crashed it.' He leans over and grabs the T-shirt himself, wraps it around the top of his arm. He grips one end of the T-shirt in his teeth and ties the ends tight. He wipes sweat from his forehead with his good hand.

'Pull over,' says Nino. 'We're here.'

I slam on the brakes.

We've stopped on a bridge, fifteen metres up, at least. It's windy, cool. I open the car door and step out. Waves crash against the rocks below us, sending white foam spraying. I can taste the salt, the iodine. I look down through the railings at deep, black water; I wonder how many bodies are down there. It's the perfect place to dump them. I get the feeling Nino's been here before. We struggle with the cases, but somehow, eventually, hurl them over the railing, one by one. They plop and splash and bubble as they sink down, down, down. I turn, expecting to see Nino, but he's already back in the car. How does he move so silently? He's like a sexy ghost, Patrick Swayze in that film; I forget what it was called.

I back up the people carrier. I'm excited about driving the Lambo again. I wonder how fast it can go. Ambrogio clocked 180, but I want to do more. I'll show Nino how *girls* can drive. We'll be in London by nightfall.

We pull out of the villa and crawl down the drive: a plume of smoke from the burning painting. Goodbye, *La Perla Nera*. So long. Farewell. *Arrivederci*. I wonder when I'll see you again. I steer the Lambo out on to the road, but then screech to a halt.

'Shit! I forgot! I'll just be a minute.'

I reverse the car back into the drive.

'Forgot what? We don't have a minute!'

'I know, I know, I won't be long. It's just . . . hang on.'

I jump out of the car and shut the door on Nino's stunned face. Nino watches through the windscreen, shaking his head.

I sprint across the gravel and push through the door of Elizabeth's villa. My feet pound the stairs at lightning speed. I burst into Beth's bedroom. Now where did I put it? This place is a train wreck from when I just packed. Clothes everywhere. Jewellery. Shoes. It reminds me of my old place back in Archway, apart from the jewellery, obvs. I sit on the bed, my head in my hands. Think, Alvie, think. This is important. Where did you put him?

He's still in the pram!

I run back downstairs, along the hallway. The pram is parked underneath the stairs. I reach inside and find the picture of Channing Tatum, rolled up tight, below Ernie's chair.

'I'm sorry,' I say, smoothing the paper. 'I'll never leave you again.'

I floor the pedal and we whizz past the amphitheatre, race through gardens and gorgeous citrus orchards. The scent of fresh lemons cuts through the metallic stench of blood. The roof is down and the sky is pink with the first signs of a gorgeous dawn. We turn the corner.

'There!' says Nino.

'What?'

'In the rear-view. Don't you see it?' he shouts.

'See what? That car? Who gives a shit?'

'They're following us! *Merda!* We shouldn't have come here. We should have left before.' He slams his good fist down on the dashboard. I think he's upset about the picture.

'How do you know they're following us?'

'They're getting closer. Go! Go!'

OK, Nino, whatever you say. You want a car chase? This is going to be fun. I hit the accelerator. The Lambo lurches forwards. My stomach flips. My eyes flick up to the rear-view mirror: a sinister black Land Rover speeds towards us. Shit. Maybe Nino's right?

'It's them, the priest's clan!' Nino says, clutching his chair. We swerve around a bend and despite his efforts his arm still slams against the inside of the door. He makes a strange, small sound, like a whimper, like a kitten in a bin bag. I think he's scared of my driving. So am I. The Land Rover tailing us picks up speed.

'That's Don Rizzo! Oh *Madonna*, we're dead!'

I see two mean-looking men in the rear-view mirror.

'What do I do?' I say.

'Just move. Fuck. You said you could drive.'

Do bumper cars count? I might have been lying about that . . .

KA-POW! KA-POW!

Gunfire cracks as tyres squeal. 'Shit!' I say. I think they scraped the paintwork! Now we'll have to get that fixed. So annoying. It's a beautiful car.

'Drive!' shouts Nino. *'Cazzo!'*

I floor the accelerator. The wind whips my face. I wish I wasn't wearing these stupid high heels; they're digging in. I can hardly walk in them, never mind drive, but they just go so well with this outfit.

'I can't go any faster!'

KA-POW! KA-POW!

I'm doing a hundred miles an hour. The road is winding, pot-holed, steep.

I see a turning up ahead and slam on the brakes.

'What are you doing?'

'Going down there.'

I spin the steering wheel and swerve around the corner on to a narrow tree-lined street. My foot slips off the pedal and I stall. Stupid shoes! The Lambo stutters. The tyres screech. The acrid stench of burning rubber. We grind to a halt.

'Move!' roars Nino.

'It's not my fault! It's the shoes!' I say. 'Have you ever tried driving in six-inch heels?'

I fire it up and hit the gas; we speed down the road. Holy fuck. This is insane. In the rear-view mirror I see the Land Rover approaching, getting closer, closer, closer. Shit.

'Take a left,' says Nino. 'That road leads to Taormina.'

'Into town? Are you sure?'

'Trust me. Go left.'

I flick my hair up out of my eyes and do what he says. We speed through the streets and into Taormina. The engine roars. The Land Rover is gaining on us.

'Now right,' shouts Nino.

It's a fucking sharp bend. The tyres scream. There's an old brick arch over the road ahead. The road is too narrow. We're not going to make it. I close my eyes and accelerate. The Lambo scrapes through a tiny alley, cobblestones rumble beneath. Oh my God, the paint! The car! We'll never find this exact shade of red. I open my eyes and we're through, into a small square. When I turn to look, I see the Land Rover enter the alley: a shower of sparks, a screech of steel on stone and it's motionless. Stopped dead. I see the men struggle to open their doors, but they're stuck.

'Yes!'

'*Sì!*'

Nino and I do a high five.

'Yay! Go, me! Go, Alvie!' I say.

That was pretty easy, actually. What can I say? I'm a pro.

'Who's Alvie?' says Nino.

'Oh, no one,' I say. Whoops.

I grab Nino's gun and shoot out the back. The Land Rover's windscreen shatters and smashes. I pop a bullet into each of their heads. Two perfect shots!

'Awesome!' I say.

Police sirens sound in the distance: a high-pitched, skin-pimpling NEENAW, NEENAW. Nino glares at me. He's not smiling.

330

'Fucking move!'

He throws the guns out of the window of the car and into the sea as we drive back over the bridge. I'm about to complain, but then I see his face: he looks heart-broken. I guess he really liked that gun. And it's not a good idea to drive around with a murder weapon; we might get pulled over. It's not worth the risk. I kick off my shoes and floor the accelerator. It's easier barefoot. I love driving this car.

Chapter Forty

Let's talk a little bit about self-realization. A week ago, my life was *shit*. I hated my job. I was clinically depressed. I got kicked out of my flat by a couple of slobs. I fucking wanted to fucking die. Now? Hello, sunshine! There are rainbows and butterflies and big pots of gold. I have found my sweet spot. I am in my element. And do you know what? It's actually great to be alive.

Alvie. Is. ALIVE.

Finally, *finally*, I've found something I'm good at. Something I'm better at than Beth.

Alvina Knightly: murderess.

> *Killing: I was born*
> *To do it. It suits me like*
> *A favourite dress.*

Not that fucking fuchsia-pink thing; that was so tight I couldn't breathe. Not that violet chiffon church-girl dress. Perhaps the little black Louis Vuitton? That suited me . . .

I'll shout it out loud: I LOVE TO KILL. What can I say? That's my *thing*. Killing is an art like everything else; I do it exceptionally well. I told you, didn't I? I'm a great artist: Caravaggio, Shakespeare, Mozart, Knightly.

I've blossomed into a murderous butterfly; I'm a gorgeous death's-head hawkmoth. There is a certain beauty in death, a certain style to killing well. It feels good to realize your potential. Feels fucking great to *let it go*. And you know what else? This business *pays*. I'd have worked a century at that magazine to earn two million euros . . . and even then, do you think I'd have saved it? Not a fucking chance in hell. The money . . . the car . . . the villa . . . the diamonds . . . I feel richer than the Queen. Richer than J. K. Rowling or President Putin. Richer than Taylor Swift or Miley Cyrus, or Adele.

This is better than winning the lottery because I've *earned* it. I've worked hard for it. I've discovered my talent, found my true calling. But you can't go killing willy-nilly. You've got to be clever. Got to be smart. The trick is not to get caught.

If only Mum and Beth could see me now. If only the whole world could! But perhaps they will? You know what, I almost want to get caught! I want to be infamous! Everyone would know my name. Everyone would fear me! *'Alvie? Oh yes, I've heard of her,'* they'd say. And then they'd run the other way.

Thank you, Beth, for this opportunity. Thank you, darling Ambrogio. I think they call it synchronicity. When you're in flow, your whole damn life falls into place. The universe or God supports you. Everything just seems to work out. Everything is *great*.

Messina Ferry Port, Sicily

'*P*assaporto? Carta d'identità?'
I hesitate. I have both Beth's and my passport in my bag.
'*Passaporto?*' he repeats.

Who am I again? I could be Beth or Alvina. It's too hot to think and I'm starting to sweat. The sun has come up and is boring a hole in the top of my head. I'm dehydrated. My lips feel cracked and my tongue is stuck to the roof of my mouth. I'd kill for a vodka and iced limonata. Who the hell am I? I think the police might start looking for Beth. Alvie could have been travelling around Sicily these past few days, doing some sightseeing before heading home to London. Yes, that's what I've been doing, if anyone asks. Palermo? Magnificent. Catania? Divine. Of course I climbed Mount Etna; you can't beat that sea view at sunrise. The temples of Agrigento? Stunning examples of Magna Graecia architecture. But who's going to ask me? No one.

'*Passaporto!*'

Oh man . . . now he's cross. They're very short-tempered, these Italian men.

I hand over my passport to the guy standing in the little plastic booth. He's wearing a dark-blue hat with a visor, an official-looking uniform. I hope he's not police.

'*Grazie,*' he says, peering into the car. He's been up all night too, by the looks of him. It's been a busy night for us all. He examines Nino's passport. Then he studies my face, looks at my passport. I hold my breath . . . what am I worried about? It looks like me. It *is* me. There's no way he'll question it. '*Grazie, signora.*' He slams it shut.

I take my passport quickly, so Nino doesn't see, and steal a glance at Nino's passport as the man hands it back through the wound-down window. It says his name is *Giannino Maria Brusca*. I laugh out loud.

'Your middle name's Maria?'

Nino looks at me. 'So?'

'Maria is a girl's name!'

He frowns. 'Not in Italy.'

'I can't believe you have a girl's name.'

'Betta, shut up. Just drive the car.'

'And your name's not even Nino!'

'Nino is short for Giannino. Drive; there's a space over there.'

'I'm going to call you Nicola,' I say, still laughing. 'That's a pretty girl's name.' I drive the car up the ramp to the ferry.

'In Italy, Nicola is a name for a boy.'

'Maria's a boy's name and Nicola's a boy's name? You guys are nuts.'

'I told you, shut up. You're going to get yourself shot.'

'Nancy! Is Nancy a girl's name?'

'Yes.'

'I'm going to call you Nancy,' I say.

Nino is sitting there, quietly seething. But I can't help it; I'm laughing hysterically, weeping, bent double and crying with laughter.

'I mean it, Betta, you better shut up. I killed a guy for less than that.'

'Oh really?' I say, wiping a tear from my eye. He's cracking me up.

'Yeah. Really. I killed a guy for looking at me funny. I'd kill a girl for laughing at my name . . .' Nino glares.

I stop laughing. I think I believe him. He may actually kill me. Not good.

I park the Lambo between a Maserati and a Fiat. I hate ferries, especially ferry car decks. They always stink of petrol and make me feel sick. I miss Ambrogio's yacht. I only got to try it once. It's a shame we wrote it off.

The cars are packed so tightly together I can barely open the door. I inch sideways out of the Lambo and pull the suitcase with the money out after me; I'm not leaving two million euros in a car park. I'm not taking any risks; there are murderers, thieves and rapists everywhere. You're never, ever safe. Then I follow Nino up some steep little steps to the deck. When Beth's Ladymatic reads 6.30 a.m., the ferry sets sail on the Tyrrhenian Sea. Nino and I lean up against the railings and stare out at the water. This morning it's cloudy; the water's a gunmetal grey.

The ferry starts swaying, left and right, up and down on the choppy water. It's windy today. I'm already nauseous. Nino pulls a pack of Marlboros from his jacket pocket with his good hand, offers me a smoke. I take one and light our cigarettes. Nino shelters the flame with a scuffed-up hand. His knuckles are busted. There's blood under his fingernails, a dark red-brown. A couple of non-smokers standing beside us scowl and then move away down the deck. We are alone.

'I've been thinking,' I say, exhaling a lungful towards the horizon. I turn to face Nino, give him a winning smile. 'I want to work with you.'

'Want to what?'

'I want to work with you. I want to be your partner.'

Nino looks up at me, squinting; the sun's breaking through some dirty white clouds. He puts on his sunglasses. He doesn't seem to like daylight very much.

'My partner?'

'Your *partner*. I think we'd be great. What do you say?'

I lean in towards him and look into his eyes. I can't really see through his blackout glasses, but I look where I expect them to be. I'm wearing Beth's Wonderbra, my cleavage positioned strategically.

'You're *pazzo*,' says Nino.

'What's up?' I say, raising an eyebrow.

Nino stubs his cigarette out on the metal rail and then throws it out to sea. I take a drag and then throw mine out after. Nino lets the heavy metal door slam in my face as he storms inside the ferry. I push through and run after him towards the first bar we see.

'*Un caffè*,' he says to the barista, his voice like gravel.

'*Due caffè*,' I say. 'And a water.'

His hand shakes as he takes his cup. Nino doesn't drink water. He's like a cactus. Or a camel. I really don't know how he's still alive. We sit down on some nasty plastic chairs at a sticky plastic table. I fucking hate ferry 'restaurants'. They seem to be designed to put you off your food. The coffee tastes burnt. The boat tosses and turns on the angry sea. The horizon undulates through porthole windows like it's made out of wobbly blue-and-green jelly. Now I really feel sick. We sit in silence and sip.

'So,' says Nino at last, his forehead folded in deep ravines.

'You're unbelievable. You got *me* to kill Salvatore, but now you want to be a . . . a . . . an *assassina*?'

He crumples his plastic coffee cup inside his fist. It makes a cracking sound, like a skull.

'Yeah. Sorry about that. I wish I'd done it now. I kinda liked it . . .'

'Liked what?'

'Killing . . . the priest . . . and those guys.'

He holds my gaze.

'Betta, you're killing me. What are you talking about? You kinda liked it?'

I think about his question for a moment, then smile, lick my lips. 'No, I fucking loved it. It's the most fun I've ever had in my life.'

Nino stands up from the table; his chair scrapes the floor. I get up, grab the suitcase and run after him.

'Nino! Wait. How much do you get for a job? Huh?' I ask.

'It depends . . .' he says, walking away, his pace brisk, his back to me.

'How much?' I ask.

'In Sicily?'

'In Sicily.'

We walk down a corridor towards a door marked '*Uomini*': the men's. Nino pushes through. Its hinges squeal like a dying pig. I look both ways down the corridor. Fuck it. I follow after him. The toilets are empty. It stinks of vomit: someone's thrown up and they haven't cleaned up. There's no ventilation or windows. I stand with my back up against the door. Cold plastic presses against the thin material of Beth's shirt. Nino stands at the urinal and unzips his flies. I watch him pee.

'Anywhere from two thousand euros if I'm doing a guy a favour to −'

'Two thousand euros? You'd kill a guy for two thousand euros?' He's got to be kidding me. Although, having said that, I'd do it for free. I'd do it for the rush.

'To ten thousand. Twenty thousand if it's a difficult job.'

The hiss of piss on ceramic. The stench of urine. There's a puddle on the ground in the corner; thick, black mould spreads up along the wall. I cover my mouth with my hand.

'But that's in Sicily; it's hardly Monte Carlo. London will be different. Lucrative,' I say.

A flushing sound comes from a cubicle. I guess the toilets weren't empty after all. We aren't alone. We lower our voices so that no one will hear.

'Twenty thousand is the most I ever made. That was high profile: a government official.' Nino's whisper sounds just like a snake.

'Good for your CV,' I say. 'Imagine if I'm working; that's double the money, half the time. Imagine what we'd make somewhere like London.' Somewhere glamorous, somewhere with style; I long to be rich somewhere obscene. 'Anyway, it's over in Sicily. I know about the war. The Mafia are fucked.'

Nino's finished peeing. He zips up his flies and walks over to the sink, glares at me in the mirror as he washes his hands.

'I'm fucked, thanks to you. I can never come back to Sicily.'

A man pushes open a cubicle door. He is short and skinny with a baseball cap: 'ROMA'. Must be a tourist. The man looks at me and frowns, then looks over at Nino and does a double take. Nino stares back, entirely still. He reminds me of a mantis, poised and ready to attack at a split second's notice. The man bows his head and scurries out through the door like a frightened cricket. He didn't even wash his hands. That's disgusting. I guess Nino freaked him out. Perhaps it was the blood. His arm looks fucked. I suppose, objectively, Nino looks kind of scary. But I still think he's hot.

'You heard of Giovanni Falcone?' he says into the mirror. 'He was one of mine. Well, it wasn't just me . . . there were some other guys . . . they all went to jail.'

'We'd make a killing,' I say.

'You ever heard of him?'

'Heard of who?'

'It doesn't matter.'

It's hot. Sticky. Humid. It's fucking uncomfortable. I want to go back out on deck. Get some fresh air. I come up behind him and put my hand around his waist, pull him towards me.

'Baby, baby . . . the two of us together? We'd be legendary,' I say.

I watch him splash water over his hands and reach for the soap dispenser. He pushes the nozzle, but nothing comes out. He pushes it again, harder and harder, but it's empty. He rips it off the wall with his good hand and throws it across the room. It smashes against the wall: the crack of hard plastic.

'You kill one guy and you think you're Al Capone.'

'It's quality, not quantity . . .' He doesn't know about the others . . . I wish I could tell him. I wish I could come clean, no secrets between us. I want to tell him that I'm not Beth.

'You're a talented amateur, Betta. I've got twenty years' experience . . . a reputation . . .' Nino says.

'So what? It doesn't mean anything now. You said we could never go back.'

Nino swears in Italian under his breath.

'Name one female hitman,' I say.

'A *hitwoman*?' he says. Nino looks up, searching my eyes. It does not compute; I've short-circuited his brain.

'Uh-huh. You can't.'

'There's a reason,' he says. He pushes me away and walks over to the hand dryer, but it doesn't work. He pulls a lever on the towel dispenser to get a paper towel to dry his hands, but there aren't any left.

'You know I'm good. Those were perfect shots just now in the car.'

'Who said I was hiring?' He yanks the lever up and down, up and down. Nothing. He rips the paper-towel dispenser off the wall with his good hand. 'Just because you're Ambrogio's wife, you think you got a job? You got no training, no experience. And where did all of this bloodlust come from? A week ago you didn't even like guns!'

Nino throws the paper-towel dispenser down a toilet. My head's spinning. I need some air. The ground's swelling, the ferry's swaying, back and forth, to and fro. I sprint across the room, push past Nino and just miss the toilet. I throw up all over the floor.

'It's a bad idea.'

Chapter Forty-one

Arona, Italy

'Are we nearly there yet?' I ask. After hours and hours of Metallica, I'd kill for something sunnier. No one could say I have a sunny disposition or a penchant for upbeat country, but Nino's killing me with the heavy metal. I can't take much more thrash. Perhaps a song by Taylor Swift? 'I Knew You Were Trouble' — that's a good one.

'Nearly where?' he replies.

'I dunno. France?'

He looks at me sideways. 'We haven't even passed the Swiss border.'

'So . . . that's a no, then?'

'And there's still the whole of Switzerland to drive through, after we leave Italy.'

'Oh,' I say. I should have looked at a map. Beth would have looked at a map and googled for loo stops and scenic spots for a picnic.

'And your driving is giving me neck ache.'

'Neck ache? How? I'm the one with *whiplash*.' Whatever.

'You are making me tense.'

Turns out it's quite a long drive to London. The sky's a tedious shade of blue. There's the same old cliffs, the same old sea. The roads are so hot they're starting to melt: the scent of scorched tarmac. The grass is so dry it could spontaneously combust. The landscape hasn't changed in forever. Mountains on the right, sea on the left. We finally stop for a break somewhere near the Italian border: a little town called Arona. There's an enormous lake – Lago Maggiore. If I wasn't so knackered, I'd get out and explore. The lake stretches out as far as the eye can see in both directions: a deep, inky blue. Tree-covered hills roll all around us, smart white houses with terracotta roofs. It looks pretty awesome, but there are too many tourists. And my legs have seized up from sitting in one position; I'll probably fall over if I try to walk.

We pull into a quiet little side street and wind up the roof on the Lambo, lock the doors. I push back the driver's seat and try to sleep. I can't. The seat is uncomfortable. I've got a numb bum. I can feel the leather sticking to my skin from where my thighs are sweating.

I look around for something to do. Nino's asleep with his mouth hanging open. It's not a good look. I'm so bored, I have a flick through the Bible; I think Nino packed it so we'd have somewhere to rack up. Bibles always remind me of Adam and Eve, of how Eve was made from one of Adam's spare ribs, like Frankenstein's monster.

> The idols of nations are silver and gold,
> Made by the hands of men.
> They have mouths, but they cannot speak,
> Eyes, but they cannot see,
> They have ears, but cannot hear,
> Nor is there breath in their mouths.
> Those who make them will be like them,
> And so will all who trust them.

What's wrong with gold? I'm still bored.

> There are six things the Lord hates, seven that are detestable to him: haughty eyes, a lying tongue, hands that shed innocent blood, a heart that devises wicked schemes, feet that are quick to rush into evil, a false witness who pours out lies, and a man who stirs up dissension among brothers.

Sounds like the Lord is pretty intolerant; he can't have many friends. I guess he has a point though: most people are fuckers.

And now I'm thinking about *Him*, I can't get that fucking ridiculous song out of my head: the one Beth and I used to sing at Girl Guides. It plays over and over again in my mind on an incessant loop. I want to shoot myself in the head to get rid of it, pull the trigger in my mouth so I die properly, not like Ed Norton at the end of *Fight Club*, who can still talk with half his head blown off and gallons of blood clogging up his throat.

Oh, you'll never get to heaven
(Oh, you'll never get to heaven)
In a baked-bean tin
(In a baked-bean tin)
Cos a baked-bean tin
(Cos a baked-bean tin)
'S got baked beans in
('S got baked beans in),
Oh, you'll never get to heaven in a baked-bean
tin cos a baked-bean tin's got baked beans in.
I ain't gonna grieve my Lord no more, no more,
I ain't gonna grieve my Lord,
I ain't gonna grieve my Lord,
I ain't gonna grieve my Lord no more.

Oh, you'll never get to heaven
(Oh, you'll never get to heaven)
On a Boy Scout's knee
(On a Boy Scout's knee)
Cos a Boy Scout's knee
(Cos a Boy Scout's knee)
'S too wobbly

('S too wobbly),
Oh, you'll never get to heaven on a Boy Scout's knee cos a Boy
Scout's knee's too wobbly.
I ain't gonna grieve my Lord no more, no more,
I ain't gonna grieve my Lord,
I ain't gonna grieve my Lord,
I ain't gonna grieve my Lord no more.

Oh, you'll never get to heaven . . .

'Shut the fuck up, Betta,' says Nino.
Oh. I must have been singing out loud.

When we wake up, it's well into the afternoon. We'd intended
to have just a little nap; it's not ideal. We need to get out of the
country. Nino wakes up, stretches and yawns.
    'Sleep all right?'
    'Hm,' he grunts. 'What time is it?'
    'Four.'
    He turns on the car radio. Fiddles with the stations. Please, no
more Metallica.
    'It's your turn to drive. I've had enough.'
    He raises his eyebrows. 'My arm?'
    'So? Isn't that better yet?'
    'Do you really think I'd let you drive if I could do it myself?'
    'Hey, I'm not that bad. I got us this far . . .'
    'You crashed my car.'
    I'd forgotten about that. Nino's twizzling the knob on the
radio. The static is making a horrible noise.
    'Urgh, turn that off.'
    'Shut up, I want to hear something.'
    The voice on the radio is shouting in Italian. I'd rather put
some music on. I wonder if Nino likes Justin Bieber. Or something depressing by Adele?

'Blah, blah, blah, blah Elizabeth Caruso . . .' says the voice on the radio.

'What the fuck?' I say.

'Shh,' says Nino, turning up the volume. The radio blabbers for another twenty to thirty seconds. I study Nino's face trying to gauge his reaction.

'What? What? Tell me!' I say.

'They interviewed a security guard. Do you know a security guard? At the amphitheatre? Francesco something.'

Shit. 'Yeah. Why?' So his name was Francesco? Funny, he didn't look like a Francesco. More like a Carlo, or maybe a Claudio.

'He said he was worried about you. About your safety. Said you hadn't seemed yourself recently, whatever that means. And he said you are *bellissima*. Beautiful. Anyway, it's OK,' says Nino. 'The police are looking for you. They don't know about me.'

'They're looking for me? How is that OK?' I search his eyes for understanding.

'Because they're not looking for me.'

Such a dick. 'What else did it say?'

Nino pulls out the coke and racks up a line on the Bible. He offers me a €50 note. I suck it up.

'They know about the shootings. Someone reported hearing gunshots. They found the two bodies in the Land Rover. The police know you're missing and they're worried about you.'

'So what does it mean, if they're looking for me? Can I still leave the country?' Oh God, please, just let us get out of Italy. We'll be OK once we're in Switzerland. The Swiss are chilled out; just look at Roger Federer.

'I don't know,' says Nino, opening the car door, standing up and stretching his legs.

'What do you mean, *you don't know*?' I jump out of the car. 'Where are you going?'

'I'm going to buy breakfast. You want something?'

What's he on about, breakfast? It's 4 p.m.

'No. What about the border? The Italian police?'

'I'm gonna find a pizzeria. You like pepperoni? Stay with the car. Do not fucking move.' He grabs the car keys from the ignition and shoves them in his pocket.

'Hey!'

He walks down the street.

'I'm thirsty,' I shout.

'I'll buy some beers,' he calls over his shoulder. He disappears around a corner.

'I don't like beer! And buy me some tampons and some paracetamol. I think I'm getting my period.'

I'm feeling all crampy. It's that or I've been sitting too long in this seat. Great, that's the last thing I need, to bleed for five days. Don't get me wrong, I do like blood; I just prefer other people's. I flop back in my seat.

Fucking hell, this whole thing's a nightmare. I grab my handbag, open it up. I look at the passports, mine and Beth's. I put mine on the dashboard ready to use and throw Beth's passport back into the bottom of the bag. I'll have to be Alvie if they're looking for Beth. My instincts were right in the ferry port. I suddenly feel sick. I wind down the window to get some air, let the breeze blow over my face. What if Nino notices the passport? This had better fucking work.

I look around the car. It's a mess: polystyrene cups, greasy panini wrappers, empty packs of Marlboros. Nino's drugs are on the dashboard. My cocaine is in the back. If we're going to cross the border, we don't want any trouble. We'll have to get rid of this shit. I find my coke and then grab Nino's; I sneak out of the car. It's a crazy-hot day now. The cooling breeze has gone. The sun burns my shoulders, my forehead, my nose, and the skin at the back of my neck feels raw. There's a bin down the road; I'll chuck the drugs in there. Nino's going to kill me, but I'm not taking the risk. I have one final dab with a licked little finger, then dump the coke in the bottom of the bin. I cover it up with a copy of *Corriere della Sera*. Then, on second thoughts, I fish out the newspaper. I have a quick flick through the headlines and pictures on the cover and the first few pages, just in case there's something about me. About Beth. But there's nothing. Not yet.

Switzerland is bumpy and makes me feel carsick. France is boring and flat. It's a relief when we reach the Channel Tunnel, although that does mean driving through Calais, which is a *merde*-hole. I've never understood why people like France. Beth and I went to Paris once for a weekend with Mum. Two whole days was two days too long. People think Paris is the '*city of love*', but the streets just smell of piss and are chock-full of homeless people. Japanese folk go there and need therapy for the culture shock. Seriously. They fly there, expecting Disney castles and Coco Chanel. They queue for five hours for the Eiffel Tower, sit in a madman's taxi honk-honk-honking around a gridlocked Arc de Triomphe, then catch gonorrhoea from a man named Marcel. Someone feeds them some garlic purée, some raw cow and a cheese with some maggots living in it, they passively smoke about twenty packs of Gauloises and they're homesick for Harajuku. Honest-to-God truth, that happens to every single one of them. Less Woody Allen's *Midnight in Paris*, more *Bridge Over the River Kwai/Seine*.

Nino's sleeping in the passenger seat, snoring like a walrus. He's tired and grumpy now that I've chucked all his drugs. We pass Dijon (where the mustard comes from. I fucking hate mustard. I'm not going to eat any) and a place called Arras (isn't that a rug in *Hamlet*?). These towns are nothing more than signs on the *autoroute*. As far as I can tell, the whole of France is just dark-grey tarmac and empty brown fields. No wonder they're all insane. It's so boring. All they do is fuck and eat. Actually, that's not a bad life. Perhaps I will move here?

If I do move to France, it definitely won't be to Calais. Calais is an ugly industrial no-man's-land of metal cooling pipes, giant turbines and steam. I don't know why anyone would ever want to live here. It's pissing down with rain and all the frogs have come out. Its only redeeming feature is a supermarket selling booze for €1.99. I consider driving in and stocking up, but then I remember: I'm not poor any more. I can pay for the overpriced alcohol in London, and then some. I have money to burn. I no longer need to have a heart attack every time somebody charges me £15 for a gin and tonic. It was worth all the killing.

'Shall we get something to eat? I fancy a frog burger.'

Nino's still snoring, so I wake him up.

'Hungry?' I ask.

'Let's find a McDonald's,' he says, rubbing his eyes.

We drive around the city through drizzle until we see the golden arches.

'I'll order,' I say. 'I know how to speak McDonald's French from watching *Pulp Fiction*.'

Nino looks at me blankly. Perhaps he's not into Tarantino. Weird.

'But you've got to have a quarter-pounder with cheese. I don't know the other things,' I say.

'Whatever,' he says. He's still half asleep.

We pull into the drive-through and I wind down the window.

The girl in the window says, '*Bonjour.*'

'*Bonjour,*' I say, holding up two fingers. 'Two Royales with cheese.'

'Royales with cheese, *c'est deux Royales avec du fromage?*' she says with a frown. She has long blonde hair and long, blonde eyelashes. She looks far too young to be working.

I say it again, louder and slower.

'Two Royales with cheeeeeeeeese.'

She types something into her touchscreen computer. I think she gets it.

'*Cinq euros, s'il vous plaît, madame,*' she says.

'Huh?' I say.

'*Cinq euros,*' she says, holding up five fingers.

'Oh. OK. Five . . . Nino,' I say, 'have you got any cash?'

He nods towards the priest's suitcase. I grab the case from the back shelf and haul it on to my lap. I undo the buckles and open it up. The money looks so pretty I don't want to touch it. It smells like fresh paint. I peel a €500 note from the top of a pile. It is clean and crisp, as though just off the press. I stick my arm out through the car window and give it to the girl. She's staring at the suitcase. Oh, the money. She takes the note between her fingertips and rustles around for some change. It takes ages.

'*Quatre cent quatre-vingt-quinze euros. Merci,*' she says, holding out the notes for me to take. The notes look dirty and crumpled, like someone's wiped their ass with them. 'No, it's OK, you can keep the change,' I say, wrinkling my nose. 'Just give me the burgers.'

She doesn't understand. I shake my head.

'*Non.*'

Nino leans over and grabs the money through the window, shoves it into the glove compartment. The girl hands me the burgers and we drive off.

'What did you do that for? I was just trying to *be nice,*' I say.

'Well, don't. It doesn't suit you,' Nino says.

Chapter Forty-two

I look out of the window, but I can't see any fish. Just black. We're sitting in the Lamborghini, squeezed into a carriage with dozens of cars. They actually load the cars into a train and then drive the train through the Channel Tunnel. It all seems rather pointless. Why not just let the cars drive through the tunnel? The French . . . they're nuts. I didn't want to get on another ferry after the last time. I don't think Nino did either. So I suppose the train thing is better than being seasick. Except that the carriage stinks of car fumes and there's nothing to do. I can taste petrol. This would be a really cool place to start a fire.

'Shall we get out and go for a walk?' I say.

'Where are we gonna go? We're seventy metres below the sea in a metal tube,' says Nino. Nino's still cross because I trashed his drugs.

I look over at Nino slumped in the passenger seat, the collar of Ambrogio's black leather jacket pulled up under his ears, his eyes as dead and bleak as black holes and the fading scar on his cratered face as long and thin as a line of coke.

'I don't know, just up and down the train?'

'What's the fucking point in that?'

'We could stretch our legs.'

'I don't need to stretch my legs.'

'We could look at some of the cars.'

Nino glares and shakes his head. 'We've been driving on endless motorways, looking at nothing but cars. And you want to go look at more cars? This is the best-looking car on the whole fucking train. Look at this.'

He's right. I'm bored of cars. I'm bored of driving. I can't drive, so I've been making up for lack of technique with increased speed. If you started a fire in the Channel Tunnel, I guess the whole train would explode. All these cars are filled with petrol. There are hundreds of cars all packed together. You'd only have to light one match and leave it underneath one car and the whole fucking thing would blow like dynamite. There'd be fire at Folkstone and fire at Calais, roaring out like the mouths of dragons. It would be fucking spectacular. I really want to do it, but there's no way out. We'd both burn to death.

Would it be worth it for the rush?

'Nino?' I ask, resting my hand on his shoulder. I can feel the heat from his body rise through the leather. 'Do you want to die?'

'What? Right now?'

'Yeah. Right now.'

He thinks about this for a second. I can hear the cogs in his brain go *whir*. 'We've got two million euros in a suitcase, a bag full of diamonds and a classic Lamborghini. No, Betta, I want to fucking live.'

Fair point.

'OK. Just checking.' He forgot about the villa. When all this is over, I'm going to sell it. It's got to be worth a ton and a half. 'Shall we buy a mansion in Beverly Hills?'

'No. I want a villa near Naples, by the sea.'

Nino's still scowling. I like it when he's angry. I like the way his eyes burn a hole in your head like bullets or a drill or the edge of the kerb and his gold tooth flashes like gunfire. I like the guttural growl of his voice. I wonder if he'll propose when we get to London. If he does, I'll say yes.

When we get to England, I'll make a plan: a cunning plan for me, Ernie and Nino. That's just what we need, a magnificent plan! A genius strategy. We can travel the world, just the three of us, killing and fucking and sailing and speeding and shopping and tanning and building sky-high sandcastles on cocaine-white beaches with vodka-clear waters and stars in our eyes. We can forget about Beth and Ambrogio. And Salvatore. And those other guys. Oh, and that priest, I forgot about him.

St James's, London

'Yeah, but why has it got to be the Ritz?' says Nino. I'm stuck in first gear in bottleneck traffic, bumper to bumper on Pall Mall.

'It's fucking expensive,' he says.

'I know it is. I've always wanted to go there.'

'What do you do? Bathe in champagne?'

'If you want to . . .'

'Do they feed you gold?'

'Probably, actually . . .'

'Unless Kate Moss and Naomi Campbell are going to suck my dick, then I don't think it's worth it.'

'You probably don't get sexual favours from supermodels included in the price of the room, no. But what do you need them for? You've already got me.'

Nino snorts. I think it was a laugh.

We turn on to Piccadilly and stop the car outside the hotel. It says 'THE RITZ' in big, flashy letters. There's a colonnade. A Union Jack.

I toss the car keys to the valet and step out of the Lambo.

'Don't crash it.'

'No, ma'am.'

'Or lose it.'

'Ma'am.'

The doorman bows low – black bowler hat with golden trim, long black overcoat, big gold buttons; you can see your face in his shiny shoes. He opens the heavy, glass-pannelled door. We step inside the Ritz: a bright, light-filled atrium. Buckingham

Palace or Versailles. The air is filled with the scent of roses; there's an enormous bouquet in the centre of the room. Beth liked roses. She would've loved those. I guess this place is Beth's kind of scene. Nino and I walk through the entrance towards the reception.

'How's your arm?'

Nino looks up and grimaces. 'It still fucking hurts, but it's a little bit better.'

'Cool,' I say.

The men at reception stop talking and look up as we approach. They're wearing three-piece suits in a light shade of grey with matching ties. They probably think we're underdressed.

'Good evening, madam, sir,' says a man.

'Hi,' I say.

There's an enormous, floor-to-ceiling mirror behind reception, an ornate, antique, golden clock. Roman numerals read 11.30. Wall lamps cast a warm, gold glow. I catch a glimpse of myself in the mirror: eyelashes extended, eyebrows waxed, long blonde hair a honeyed hue. I look like Beth.

'Madam? Madam? How can I help you?'

'Hmm?' I say. I must have got distracted looking at Beth.

'We need a room,' Nino says. I look over at him, standing there in Ambrogio's baby-soft leather jacket. There's a little fleck of red on his neck by his jaw. It looks like he's cut himself shaving.

'The Royal Suite's the only room we have available,' says the man, studying his computer screen, clicking a mouse.

'Oh, that sounds lovely,' I say. My voice sounds funny: breathy, husky. I sound like Beth.

'That particular suite is £4,500 per night, plus VAT.'

'*Ma quanto?*' says Nino. I think that's Italian for '*I'm not paying that*'.

I grab the suitcase from Nino and slam it down on the desk. The man jumps. 'Do you take euros?' I say.

'Oh, you don't need to pay now. You can pay in the morning,' says the man. He smiles with relief. 'There's a bureau de change in the hotel. Could we please swipe a card for confirmation?'

I'm not giving him my debit card, there's no money on the account. And I'm not giving him Beth's either; the cops might be tracking it. I take a stack of €500 notes and thrust them into the man's hands.

'We paid,' I say.

The man nods and takes the money.

'That's perfect,' I say. It's strange: I could have sworn that was Beth talking. I shake my head and look at Nino. He hasn't noticed. Perhaps I'm going nuts?

'Would you please be so kind as to show us some identification so we can sign you in? A passport or a driving licence?'

'Of course,' I say with a smile.

I hand the man a passport. Then I realize that it's Beth's.

'Very good,' says the man. 'Sign here please.' I hope the cops aren't searching for Beth in London. That would be just my luck. I sign the paper: Elizabeth Caruso. I even use my right hand; I'm getting pretty good. I glance over at Nino, but I don't think he's noticed. He's examining his messed-up arm. 'Here is the key card for the Royal Suite. My colleague Matthew will be your butler for the duration of your stay. If you need anything at all please don't hesitate –'

'That won't be necessary,' says Nino, his voice a growl.

'Please allow Matthew to take your cases up to your room.'

'I'll take them,' says Nino, intercepting. He grabs the cases, one in each hand. I see him wince in pain.

'Very good, sir,' says the man.

Shame, I would have liked a butler. That would've been fun. We follow Matthew along a corridor – red carpets, cut-crystal chandeliers, curtains embroidered with golden thread – towards our suite. Matthew presses a button and we wait for the lift. It's an old-fashioned one with polished wooden panels, a portrait of a lady in Victorian dress and a shiny brass handrail. I study Matthew's youthful features: floppy blond hair, clean shaven, pale-blue eyes. His starched white collar digs into his chin. He looks like every member of every boy band you've ever seen. There's even a dimple in his chin. He doesn't look a day over twelve. He sees me looking and smiles; I look away, study the floor: white marble tiles, a golden 'R'. The lift pings and we're there.

'This way, sir, madam,' he says.

Nino and I follow Matthew down yet another corridor, until we come to our door: Room 1012. He slips the key card into the handle and the door clicks open. He pushes through into a vast, palatial sitting room, with period furniture and an enormous painting in a wrought bronze frame. There's a marble fireplace with miniature statues of Grecian women on either side, a mantelpiece with what look like urns and shining, twisting candelabras. Nino gives Matthew a wedge of €500 notes as a tip. His blue eyes widen. He hesitates, then takes it.

'Don't let anyone up here,' says Nino, grabbing Matthew's forearm with a vice-like grip.

'No, sir. Of course, sir.'

'No one,' says Nino.

'Sir.'

Matthew bows again and turns to leave. I guess we're not killing him then. Nino places the suitcase with the euros on the bed next to the suitcase with our clothes and the diamonds. I walk through the suite, as though in a dream, float through the sitting room, dining room, bedroom, bathroom, dressing room, study. The suite is even bigger and better than the villa in Taormina. Perhaps we could just live here?

'Oh wow! We did it! We really did it!'

I grab the suitcase and flip it open. 'Look at all this money. And it's ours, all ours! No mobsters, no priests, no Salvatore!' I grab fistfuls of banknotes and fling them up high, way up high into the sky. I spread them out all over the bed. They feel smooth and sleek, almost silky. The banknotes flutter and fall through the sky like purple snowflakes. I tip the suitcase upside down and empty the money out on to the bed. It looks like a swimming pool at sunset: the banknotes are ripples on the water, violent purple and fuchsia pink. I want to dive in, splash around like a hot girl in a porno, get soaking wet. I can almost feel it, the cool of the water, the warm rays of the sun caressing my back.

'Just look at it, Nino! Fuck!' I turn to face Nino and see the fire spark in his eyes.

'I'm looking,' he says, his eyes fixed on mine.

'We did it,' I breathe. I can't believe it.

'We did it,' he says. '*Minchia.*'

I grab Nino and throw him back on to the bed. I sit on top of him, pulling off his shirt. The buttons pop and fall on to the floor. The fabric tears, rips. I pull off my top and unfasten my bra, move down his legs to unfasten his flies. I kiss his chest from the little dip at the base of his neck all the way down to his hip bones. I unbuckle his belt and yank down the zip. Oh my God . . . he's already erect.

'The car, the money, the diamonds: we're rich! We can do whatever the hell we like!'

I straddle Nino, looking into his eyes, and ease on top. He feels amazing. I can feel him up hard against my G-spot, full and wide and deep inside. Nino reaches and grabs my breasts, teasing my nipples, pinching, hurting. I ride him slowly, then faster and faster. My palms press down into his palms, hot and slippery with sweat. Our fingers slide and intertwine. I push his hands above his head.

He feels so good as I sit down deeper, filling me up, making me whole. He grabs my hips to pull me in closer, his fingernails digging into my flesh.

'Say my name.'

'*Betta.*'

And I ride him and ride him and ride him and ride, sweat dripping down my back, sweat sliding down my chest. Breathless. Panting. Weightless. Hot. I feel the heat rising up in my body, and I'm burning, floating like ashes and flame. I am the smoke and Nino's the fire. My head feels light; my shoulders float. I feel free. I feel fucking invincible.

'You're a bad boy, Nino. A bad, bad boy. A bad, bad, bad, bad, bad, bad boy.' And I feel him coming in waves inside me, over and over and over again. I lean back on his cock, breathing hard. And I'm coming and coming for what feels like for ever, my mind expanding, my body floating, my heartbeat exploding like gunfire.

Chapter Forty-three

I step out of the shower and wrap myself up in a fluffy white bathrobe, towel-dry my hair and leave it over one shoulder. Mmm, I smell good. That complimentary shower gel's delicious. Citrus and grapefruit; I'm good enough to eat. It's the Ritz's own brand, just like at Tesco. I'm going to steal a few of the miniature bottles. And the bathrobe. And the slippers.

When I get back in the bedroom, I see Nino is sleeping, sprawled out on the bed in exactly the same position I left him. He looks serene. He looks peaceful. He reminds me of my baby Ernie, or Ambrogio perhaps, when he was dead.

There's an antique bureau up against the wall; I walk over and take a look. There's a writing desk with an old inkwell and headed paper. The paper looks expensive, creamy and thick. There are 'Ritz London' pens and some 'Ritz London' post-cards: a photo of its magnificent facade, its columns and flowers bathed in sunlight. I pull open a little wooden drawer to find a beautiful letter opener: ivory handle, shiny silver blade. It's not a knife, but it looks nice and sharp. I wonder how sharp it is exactly. I left that Swiss army knife in Sicily.

'Nino?'

Nothing.

'NINO!'

'MERDA!'

Nino jumps. I think I scared him. At least he woke up. He opens his eyes, but when he sees it's just me and not some kind of monster, he closes them again. Rolls over. Snores. I sit down next to him on the bed. I grab his wrist and slice open his finger in a deep, clean line with the letter opener. The blood pours out and spills over his hand, drips down heavily on to the sheets.

'ARGH!' says Nino. 'What the fuck?' He clutches his hand to his chest. That definitely woke him . . .

'Hold still,' I say. 'Give me your finger.' He shakes his head. He looks freaked out.

'Give me your finger or your balls are next.' We look down at his cock. He's still stark naked. Nino decides it's not worth the risk.

'What are you doing?'

'You'll see.' I grab hold of his finger and reach for a little glass vial tucked away in the pocket of my bathrobe. I bought it a long time ago at a flea market in London, I just never had the chance to use it.

'You don't think I've bled enough from this arm?' His eyes are glued to his bleeding finger, to the blood gushing out and snaking down his wrist to his elbow, running fast along his forearm, in long red lines the colour of wine.

'Look, it's a necklace!' I say, clutching the vial and filling the small bottle up with his blood. 'I'm going to wear it around my neck for ever and ever. Angelina Jolie and Billy Bob Thornton had ones just like it!' The vial fills to overflowing with Nino's blood. I screw on its tiny lid.

'You didn't need to slice my finger open! *Sei pazza*,' he says.

Nino nurses his bleeding hand. It's on the same side as his bleeding arm. He looks wounded, hurt. Pitiful, like a rabbit at the side of the road. Like a puppy that someone's just kicked. *How could you?*

'Stop it,' I say.

'*Me* stop it?'

'Yes.'

'Stop what exactly?'

I roll my eyes.

'Can't you just . . .'

'What? Just what?'

'Be more *Nino*.'

He sighs.

'It can't have hurt *that* much. Not really. And anyway, don't you think it's kinda romantic?' He doesn't say anything. 'I got one for you too, look! They come as a pair.' I pull out the other necklace with its little glass vial. I'm really quite pleased with them. They're vintage, antique, but it doesn't look like they've ever been used.

'No, not for me,' Nino says, eyeing the vial. 'I don't wear necklaces.'

'Oh. OK.' Fair enough, I suppose. It isn't really his style.

I lean in and kiss him, a long, deep, lingering kiss on the mouth. He kisses me back. He can't be that cross.

'You *be more Betta*,' he says with a laugh. 'I never knew you were half this crazy.'

I think that's the first time that I've seen him smiling. I thought I'd like it, but I don't want to be *Betta*: the second choice, the number two, the fucking plan B. I want to be *Alpha*. I want to be me: Alvina Knightly. I'd almost forgotten. It's only been a few short days, but it feels like for ever. I get the feeling that Nino would like Alvie. I need to tell someone; it's driving me nuts. And I'm sure that he would understand. Nino and Alvie for ever and ever, killing and fucking and fucking and killing! I'll tell him tonight in the bar.

'I'll call reception and get you a plaster,' I say.

When Matthew has gone and Nino has got his plaster wrapped tightly around his red finger, we stand at the foot of the bed.

'Let's get dressed and get something to eat,' I say. 'I think there's a restaurant in the hotel?' Nino looks like he could do with some food. He's a little bit pale. He takes my bathrobe and pulls it down off my shoulders; it falls down my body and into a pool on the floor at my feet. I am completely naked.

'Oh!' I say. What's all this? Does he want to have sex? Not again? Oh my God, he's worse than *me*.

'Wait,' he says.

'What?' I stand and watch him search through our suitcase, the one with Beth's jewellery and Ambrogio's clothes.

'Wear this,' he says. He holds up Beth's diamond necklace, the one that I tried on before. It looks even more beautiful here in the lamplight: the diamonds sparkle like trillions of stars. I catch my breath. Beth caught me last time. But Beth's not here. Now they're all mine.

'I want you to wear it.'

Oh my God. He fastens the diamonds around my neck; the stones burn as cold as ice on my skin. I catch a glimpse of myself in the mirror, nude apart from the dazzling jewels that seem to blaze upon my chest, so bright they hurt my retinas.

I look down at the diamonds and stroke the largest, at the centre of my chest between my breasts. He's so romantic. I'm actually speechless.

Nino kisses me on the forehead. 'Why don't you go downstairs and get us a drink? I'll meet you in the bar once I've taken a shower.'

'OK,' I say. 'See you later.'

I'm waiting for Nino in the Rivoli Bar. I run my finger around the rim of my Martini and smile at the barman. Beth's diamond necklace sparkles in the lamplight, the rocks the size of a baby's head. Her rings are flashing, effervescent. I can't see them, but I'm sure Beth's diamond earrings are equally dazzling (I put those on to go with the necklace). Everything about me is scintillating, sparkling. I look a million dollars. I breathe in deeply – synthetic magnolia – and begin to relax. A swig of vodka Martini, shaken, not stirred: like Ambrogio used to order, like in James Bond. It tastes of freedom and clear blue skies. There's a spiral of orange peel and a single olive in a tiny silver chest for me to add, should I care to do so. I dump them both in and stir.

I fucking love being a millionaire.

I run my palms along the cool, smooth bar. The Rivoli is silent, empty except for me. It's a quarter to one in the morning. I can't remember what day it is. It's probably Monday, but it doesn't make any difference. I spin on my bar stool: mahogany, leopard print, golden cherubs, Louis XVI armchairs and tables so polished they're dark, shining mirrors. There's a trolley stacked high with different-sized tumblers, champagne flutes, shot glasses, fifty different types of spirit. A silver cocktail shaker has 'Ritz London' engraved in letters so tiny I can hardly read them.

I'm still waiting for Nino.

I'm starving, so I order beluga caviar from the bar menu: fifty quid. It arrives on a silver plate in a doll-sized portion: glossy black eggs like tiny eyes. There are three miniature blinis, a quarter of a lemon in a net, a cup of chopped shallots, a cup of chopped parsley and some strange yellow powder. I'm not sure what I'm supposed to do, so I just look at it: abstract art by somebody famous I'm supposed to appreciate. I eat the free peanuts instead.

A man enters the room. It's not Nino. He sits at the opposite end of the bar and orders a whisky straight up. Spins on his stool. Plays with his phone. Behind the man, hanging up on the wall, is a gorgeous, gilt scene: a woman reclining with a swan against a radiant sunset. The sun's rays are spread out across a brilliant sky, a golden-orange glow. Scalloped clouds swirl. The woman is naked, bare-breasted, beautiful, with free-flowing hair and an open mouth. The swan lies on top of her, majestic, regal, his wings wide open. It's only once I've finished my Martini that I realize the woman is being raped by the swan. I remember that from the History Channel: the woman is Leda and Zeus is the swan. It's fucking disgusting. I suddenly feel sick.

I look at the empty doorway. Scan the room: it's quiet, empty. I watch the second hand on Beth's Ladymatic. *Tick-tock, tick-tock.* Time is passing oh so slowly. It slows and stops like a melting clock by Salvador Dalí. I look around at the room and everything's frozen still, like a painting. The colours are oil paints. The windows, the furniture, tables and chairs, they're all painted on. It's all two-dimensional. Nothing is moving. And I know Nino isn't coming. That's why I've been waiting. He's not going to come.

I snap out of it.

Shit.

'Can I use your phone?' I say to the barman. 'I want to call the room.'

'Of course, madam,' he says. He hands me the receiver. I snatch it away and punch in the numbers: 1012. I listen to it ring out and then dial again. Nothing. Perhaps he's already on his way down? But somehow I know he isn't. I sign for the drink and run out of the bar, along the corridor, up the stairs. What if he's taken the lift and I've missed him? I take out the key card and open the door.

'Nino?' I say.

I can't see any of Nino's things: his clothes, his shoes, our bag. The suite is empty. I scour the rooms for the suitcase, fling open the wardrobes, look under the bed. I yank open drawers and search for the money. I check all the tables for the Lambo's valet ticket. Search on the floor. Nothing. Everything's gone.

Shit.

Nino's hat is on the bedside table: the black fedora with the ribbed grey band. I pick it up. It smells of him. It's the only sign he was ever in here. I grab the phone and collapse on the bed, call the concierge.

'Valet, please.' Someone connects me. 'Hello, this is Room 1012. Is our car still there?'

A pause . . .

'I'm sorry, madam, but your husband's just taken the car . . .'

'I see,' I say and hang up. 'Fuck.'

I run to the window and push it out wide, look down at the street. It's cold and it's raining. There's the red Lambo; the valet is just getting out. Nino's there with the cases, the money.

'Nino!' I shout. He opens the car door. He doesn't look up.

I kick off my heels and sprint out of the room, race down the hall. I can't let that asshole get away. The lift is too slow. I'm taking the stairs. I race down the steps, stumbling, tripping. I pass reception without making eye contact. The men at reception look up and stare. Matthew smiles when I rush past. Fucking Nino. Fucking fuck. I really thought we had a future. I thought we had something special. The doorman bows low as he opens the door.

I burst out into the street. The rain pounds down. I'm two seconds too late. My fingertips graze the back of the Lambo as Nino floors the accelerator. I run and run as fast as I can, the raindrops hitting me hard in the face, sliding down my neck, chilling my back. The car speeds away down Piccadilly. I can see the back of his head. His slick black hair. He doesn't even turn around. I'm still holding his stupid fedora. I throw it after him, then sit down in a puddle on the pavement and cry. That's it! He's gone. I can forget the proposal. I can forget the plan. It's just me, on my own, lonely and alone once again. Not even Beth to hate. And I've killed everyone else.

Shit shit fuck fuck shit
Fuck fuck shit shit fuck fuck shit
Shit fuck shit fuck shit.

My fingers trail the wallpaper, cool and smooth, as I glide down the endless corridor. My feet seem to be moving all by themselves. Finally, I see the door to the suite. I steady myself against the door frame, fumble with the lock. The key card clicks and the little green light flashes on. I push into the suite. Everything's the same, except slightly different. Pixelated, like being inside a video game. My vision is blurry with tears. It's suddenly quiet. It feels way too big. All this space, just for me? I flop down on the sofa. Dazed. Numb. Now what am I going to do? I can't stay here after tonight; I don't have the money. I can't go back to the slobs' place now. The slobs would never let me, even if I begged them. I think of my old room in Archway . . . I wonder what it's like now, all cleared out. A space on the wall where my Channing poster once hung; a grimy rectangle marking its edges, Blu-Tack remnants in the corners. I wonder what became of him? I bet the slobs threw him out with the sex toys. (I should never have left Mr Dick in Taormina.) There'll be a new bucket on the floor, to catch the rain. My stuff will be gone, but otherwise, I guess, my room will be exactly the same – same old futon, same old carpets – as though I never left, as though nothing has changed. Perhaps nothing has and it's all in my head?

Sicily's already beginning to fade, to evanesce, like a bad dream . . . I grab my phone and scroll through the photos. Me and Ernie. My selfie with the priest. The mobsters' bodies in the rain. It really did happen! I'm not going mad. I hug a red velvet cushion into my chest and rest my head on its side.

Nino's left the TV on. It's some twenty-four-hour news channel: BBC World. The story is about the refugee crisis: Syria, Calais, Lampedusa. The sound's turned down but at the bottom of the screen a bright-red banner reads: 'BREAKING NEWS: Experts confirm that the missing Caravaggio painting *The Nativity with St Francis and St Lawrence* has been found damaged in a house fire in Taormina, Sicily. The FBI have been searching for Caravaggio's masterpiece, worth $30 million, since 1969, when it was stolen from the Oratory of San Lorenzo in Palermo.'

I burnt thirty million dollars?

I scream.

I run and jump at the screen, pull the television off the wall. It crashes on to the carpet. The power cuts out. I jump and jump and jump on the screen: CRACK, CRACK, CRACK. I lean, bent double with my hands on my knees, and catch my breath. *Thirty million dollars? Thirty fucking million?* I yank open the minibar and grab a bottle of gin: Bombay Sapphire. Is the bottle blue or is it the gin? I down it in one. It's not very nice. I feel a bit better.

Beth's phone makes a noise: Tweet, tweet, tweet. Who's that now? Not Taylor *again*. I reach into my handbag and grab the phone: six missed calls and two texts from my mum: 'Beth, where are you? I'm outside your villa. It's burnt to the ground! The firemen are here, but it's completely destroyed. CALL ME BACK. ARE YOU OK?' 'Beth, darling, I've got your son. Don't worry, he was safe with Emilia, but I'm going to take him back to the hotel and give him some mashed-up bananas.'

And I scream.

And scream.

And scream.

I grab a golden candelabra and swipe it across the table: a lamp, a bowl of fruit and a crystal figurine fly across the floor. I tip over the armchair and sofa. I run and jump at the curtains, yanking them down. There's a rip and they're in a red pile on the floor. I wrap myself in the curtains, curl into a ball. No money. No villa. No car. No Nino. No yacht. No baby Ernesto. I want to disappear.

A rap at the door sounds like gunfire. Shit. What now? Fuck off. Go away. Who could that be at this time of night? My mind races: could it be my mum? Oh God, no, please, please not my mum! But how would she know where I am? Nino? But no, he's long gone. Elizabeth? No, don't be stupid, Alvina; it couldn't be Beth. Those guys from Sicily who were following us? No, didn't I kill them? The fucking police? Calm down, Alvie. You're paranoid. Another loud knock, a drill to the brain. I take a deep breath.

'Coming,' I say.

I climb out of the curtains, fluff up my hair, rub my palms up and down my face. I slide the door open, inch by inch. It's

Matthew. Thank fuck. Maybe I'll kill him? It might cheer me up. He stumbles backwards when he sees me.

'Everything OK, madam? I thought I . . . er . . . er . . . heard a noise?'

'A noise? No.'

'Like a scream?'

'No, no.'

'Are you sure you're OK?'

'I'm absolutely fine.'

'Cos you look pretty f–'

'What?' I glare, willing him to say it; go on, say it.

'Freaked out.' His eyes are wide. His hands are trembling by his sides.

'Well, so do you.'

I shut the door, make sure that it's locked. I look freaked out? I walk over to the mirror and do a double take. Elizabeth's face stares back at me. Elizabeth's face. Elizabeth's eyes. My heart beats faster. I shake my head. Don't be ridiculous, Alvie. Don't be a dick. That's insane. But I step a bit closer, my nose an inch from the mirror . . . I'm wearing Beth's jewellery, her diamond necklace. Why did Nino give me that? I look into my eyes; they're filled with tears. And it's true.

I am Elizabeth. I am Beth.

A sick feeling spreads from my gut. What the hell? My heart beats faster. The reflection in the mirror screams a silent scream.

'Elizabeth?'

Oh my God.

I AM ELIZABETH.

I AM BETH.

My face, my eyes, my smile; it's her!

I shake my head and look around in a panic, grab an urn from the mantelpiece and hurl it at the mirror. It shatters into a thousand pieces; shards of glass smash into the fireplace, falling like rain. My heart beats faster. Where is my heart? I feel for my chest, underneath my bra. My pulse thumps: BU-BUMP! BU-BUMP! and it's all right. It's OK. My heart is on the right. It's on the right side, not the left. Quit fucking around. You're losing it, Alvina. Mad, mad, mad. You're fucking out of your fucking mind. Too much coke. Not enough sleep. Too much blood. I need some fresh air.

I run over to the window, lean out and look down at the pavement. Take a deep breath. The raindrops fall: heavy, fat. A leaden sky. A thick, black night. Nino. Nino. He did this to me. How could he leave? It's all his fault. Of course he's run; it's exactly what I would have done, if I'd thought of it first. In a funny kind of way, I'm impressed. You see, we're the same, me and Nino, two peas in a pod. We're made for each other. He's Mr Right. I'm Cinderella. Nino's my Prince fucking Charming. He has *so* picked the wrong girl to fuck with. I refuse to lose. He will not win. I'm finding Nino, if it's the last thing I do.

'It's not over, Giannino Maria!' I shout out of the window.

I'm finding that *stronzo* and, leisurely, painfully, taking my time, I will find him and I will kill him.

Or marry him.

Nino needs to meet Alvie.

Epilogue

Alvina Knightly
Ritz Hotel,
150 Piccadilly,
London W1J 9BR

Mr Channing Tatum
c/o CAA
2000 Avenue of the Stars
Los Angeles CA 90067

Monday, 31 August 2015, 3.56 a.m.

RE: ~~Marriage~~

Dear Mr Tatum,
My name is Alvina Knightly, but you can call me Alvie, or Al (though that sounds a bit like a man's name), and I am not only your biggest fan, but also potentially your future wife. I have admired you from afar for some time (since the first Magic Mike movie came out in the UK), but it's not just your chiselled abs and toned torso that I appreciate, I also really like your dick. I also think you are a better actor than Ryan Gosling, though not quite as good as Matthew McConaughey; he's really talented.

Let me tell you a bit about myself, so you can decide whether or not you want to marry me (you should, by the way). Like I said, my name is Alvina and I am ~~twenty-six~~ twenty-one years old. At the moment, I live in London, England, at the Ritz Hotel (as you can see from this headed notepaper), but this is not my permanent address. I hope to find somewhere to live after I pawn my sister's diamond necklace, which should be worth in the region of £70–80 grand and which she gave to me for my birthday. That should be enough for a deposit on a studio flat in Archway. There might also be some insurance money to claim for the villa I burnt down in Sicily, but I'm not sure right now.

I am an amicable, friendly and fun-loving people person. I get on with everybody and love animals, kids and tourists. I like opera, poetry, Lamborghinis, travelling, alcohol, ~~killing~~ and sex. Especially sex. I am very experienced in the bedroom department and have been told I give good head. To date, I have slept with 303 men, though this was over an eight-year period – I don't want you to go thinking I'm a slut.

I have had several long-term (longer than one night) relationships, the most recent of which ended recently (tonight) and amicably (he is still alive), and while there is still a chance that the two of us might get back together, I wanted to alert you to my current availability. I am going to try and track him down (using the GPS tracing app I downloaded on to his phone while he was in the shower), but I'd guesstimate there is only about a fifty per cent chance of that resulting in a marriage proposal.

In the meantime, I am sending you this c/o your agent in LA; I don't know your home address, but you can rest assured that I _will_ find out. You can call me back on 00 44 7766 9 75 6330 at your convenience (within twenty-four hours of receipt of this letter) and let me know when and where you want to meet.

Yours ~~sincerely~~ wetly,
Alvina

PS I forgot to mention, I look like a younger, sexier version of Angelina Jolie, only a lot skinnier and blonder and better-looking. I would include a photograph with this letter, but I don't have one.

PPS I've changed my mind about you calling me Al; it might make you think about Al Gore, which is sure to result in erectile dysfunction.

Acknowledgements

Firstly, I would like to thank my parents for creating me. Without them, I wouldn't be here today and I would never have been able to write *Mad*. Thanks for your support throughout my education and beyond. Mum, Dad, *do not* read the trilogy. Just wait for the movies to come out and close your eyes for the naughty bits. Deal?

Secondly, I would like to thank my seriously sexy Italian husband, Paolo (who is in no way the inspiration for any of the seriously hot Italian men in the novels). Thank you for all your support when I said I was going to quit my job and write a novel; it was very nice of you to pay all the bills. *Ti amo.*

Thirdly, I would like to thank my amazing tutor at the Faber Academy, Richard Skinner. Richard, thanks for telling me not to censor myself, for giving me the confidence to write a character as delightfully deranged as Alvina Knightly and for all your wisdom and friendship ever since. Go Team Skinner! (Guy's a *legend*.)

Thanks too to all my colleagues on the Faber Academy course for the fun and fantastic feedback. I couldn't have asked for a more talented or committed group of writers with whom to share the journey. Lydia Rose Ruffles, Felicia Yap, Michael Dias, Ilana Lindsey, Sam Osman, Helen Allen, Sarah Edghill, Paola Lopez, Gina North, Margaret Watts, Kate Vick and Ally, you mad, gorgeous bunch! I love you.

Thanks to all my lovely friends who read and commented on the manuscript: Clare, Chris, Sophie, Alex, Ezzat, Alessandra and others. Special thanks goes to Lisa Taleb; your kindness and encouragement really meant the world to me. You are more like a sister than a friend and I couldn't have done this without you.

Thanks to my agents, Simon Trewin, Erin Malone, Alicia Gordon, Annemarie Blumenhagen and Tracey Fisher at WME. Wow, what an incredible team! I have been consistently delighted by your insight, wisdom and professionalism, and working with you has been a joy. I am eternally grateful.

Thank you so much to my wonderful and indefatigable editors, Jessica Leeke and Maya Ziv at PRH. Working with you on this trilogy has been an absolute dream. Your dedication and belief in this project has been overwhelming. If these novels are any good, it's thanks to you!